AF498876

Tom Godwin

The Barbarians from a Far Planet: Tom Godwin Boxed Set
(Illustrated Edition)

e-artnow 2020

Tom Godwin

The Barbarians from a Far Planet: Tom Godwin Boxed Set (Illustrated Edition)

For The Cold Equations, Space Prison, The Nothing Equation, The Barbarians, Cry from a Far Planet

Illustrator: George Schelling, Juan Carlos Barberis, Martinez

e-artnow, 2020
Contact: info@e-artnow.org

ISBN 978-80-273-0924-5

Contents

For The Cold Equations

> The Frontier is a strange place-and a frontier is not always easy to recognize. It may lie on the other side of a simple door marked "No Admittance" —but it is always deadly dangerous.

He was not alone.

There was nothing to indicate the fact but the white hand of the tiny gauge on the board before him.

The control room was empty but for himself; there was no sound other than the murmur of the drives-but the white hand had moved. It had been on zero when the little ship was launched from the Stardust; now, an hour later, it had crept up. There was something in the supplies closet across the room, it was saying, some kind of a body that radiated heat.

It could be but one kind of a body —a living, human body.

He leaned back in the pilot's chair and drew a deep, slow breath, considering what he would have to do. He was an EDS pilot, inured to the sight of death, long since accustomed to it and to viewing the dying of another man with an objective lack of emotion, and he had no choice in what he must do. There could be no alternative-but it required a few moments of conditioning for even an EDS pilot to prepare himself to walk across the room and coldly, deliberately, take the life of a man he had yet to meet.

He would, of course, do it. It was the law, stated very bluntly and definitely in grim Paragraph L, Section 8, of Interstellar Regulations: Any stowaway discovered in an EDS shall be jettisoned immediately following discovery.

It was the law, and there could be no appeal.

It was a law not of men's choosing but made imperative by the circumstances of the space frontier. Galactic expansion had followed the development of the hyperspace drive and as men scattered wide across the frontier there had come the problem of contact with the isolated first-colonies and exploration parties. The huge hyperspace cruisers were the product of the combined genius and effort of Earth and were long and expensive in the building. They were not available in such numbers that small colonies could possess them. The cruisers carried the colonists to their new worlds and made periodic visits, running on tight schedules, but they could not stop and turn aside to visit colonies scheduled to be visited at another time; such a delay would destroy their schedule and produce a confusion and uncertainty that would wreck the complex interdependence between old Earth and the new worlds of the frontier.

Some method of delivering supplies or assistance when an emergency occurred on a world not scheduled for a visit had been needed and the Emergency Dispatch Ships had been the answer. Small and collapsible, they occupied little room in the hold of the cruiser; made of light metal and plastics, they were driven by a small rocket drive that consumed relatively little fuel. Each cruiser carried four EDS's and when a call for aid was received the nearest cruiser would drop into normal space long enough to launch an EDS with the needed supplies or personnel, then vanish again as it continued on its course.

The cruisers, powered by nuclear converters, did not use the liquid rocket fuel but nuclear converters were far too large and complex to permit their installation in the EDS. The cruisers were forced by necessity to carry a limited amount of the bulky rocket fuel and the fuel was rationed with care; the cruiser's computers determining the exact amount of fuel each EDS would require for its mission. The computers considered the course coordinates, the mass of the EDS, the mass of pilot and cargo; they were very precise and accurate and omitted nothing from their calculations. They could not, however, foresee, and allow for, the added mass of a stowaway.

The Stardust had received the request from one of the exploration parties stationed on Woden; the six men of the party already being stricken with the fever carried by the green kala midges and their own supply of serum destroyed by the tornado that had torn through their camp. The Stardust had gone through the usual procedure; dropping into normal space to launch the EDS with the fever serum, then vanishing again in hyperspace. Now, an hour later, the gauge was saying there was something more than the small carton of serum in the supplies closet.

He let his eyes rest on the narrow white door of the closet. There, just inside, another man lived and breathed and was beginning to feel assured that discovery of his presence would now be too late for the pilot to alter the situation. It was too late-for the man behind the door it was far later than he thought and in a way he would find terrible to believe.

There could be no alternative. Additional fuel would be used during the hours of deceleration to compensate for the added mass of the stowaway; infinitesimal increments of fuel that would not be missed until the ship had almost reached its destination. Then, at some distance above the ground that might be as near as a thousand feet or as far as tens of thousands of feet, depending upon the mass of ship and cargo and the preceding period of deceleration, the unmissed increments of fuel would make their absence known; the EDS would expend its last drops of fuel with a sputter and go into whistling free fall. Ship and pilot and stowaway would merge together upon impact as a wreckage of metal and plastic, flesh and blood, driven deep into the soil. The stowaway had signed his own death warrant when he concealed himself on the ship; he could not be permitted to take seven others with him.

He looked again at the telltale white hand, then rose to his feet. What he must do would be unpleasant for both of them; the sooner it was over, the better. He stepped across the control room, to stand by the white door.

"Come out!" His command was harsh and abrupt above the murmur of the drive.

It seemed he could hear the whisper of a furtive movement inside the closet, then nothing. He visualized the stowaway cowering closer into one corner, suddenly worried by the possible consequences of his act and his self-assurance evaporating.

"I said out!"

He heard the stowaway move to obey and he waited with his eyes alert on the door and his hand near the blaster at his side.

The door opened and the stowaway stepped through it, smiling. "All right —I give up. Now what?"

It was a girl.

He stared without speaking, his hand dropping away from the blaster and acceptance of what he saw coming like a heavy and unexpected physical blow. The stowaway was not a man-she was a girl in her teens, standing before him in little white gypsy sandals with the top of her brown, curly head hardly higher than his shoulder, with a faint, sweet scent of perfume coming from her and her smiling face tilted up so her eyes could look unknowing and unafraid into his as she waited for his answer.

Now what? Had it been asked in the deep, defiant voice of a man he would have answered it with action, quick and efficient. He would have taken the stowaway's identification disk and ordered him into the air lock. Had the stowaway refused to obey, he would have used the blaster. It would not have taken long; within a minute the body would have been ejected into space-had the stowaway been a man.

He returned to the pilot's chair and motioned her to seat herself on the boxlike bulk of the drive-control units that set against the wall beside him. She obeyed, his silence making the smile fade into the meek and guilty expression of a pup that has been caught in mischief and knows it must be punished.

"You still haven't told me," she said. "I'm guilty, so what happens to me now? Do I pay a fine, or what?"

"What are you doing here?" he asked. "Why did you stow away on this EDS?"

"I wanted to see my brother. He's with the government survey crew on Woden and I haven't seen him for ten years, not since he left Earth to go into government survey work."

"What was your destination on the Stardust?"

"Mimir. I have a position waiting for me there. My brother has been sending money home all the time to us-my father and mother and I —and he paid for a special course in linguistics I was taking. I graduated sooner than expected and I was offered this job on Mimir. I knew it would be almost a year before Gerry's job was done on Woden so he could come on to Mimir and that's why I hid in the closet, there. There was plenty of room for me and I was willing to pay the fine. There were only the two of us kids-Gerry and I —and I haven't seen him for so long, and I didn't want to wait another year when I could see him now, even though I knew I would be breaking some kind of a regulation when I did it."

I knew I would be breaking some kind of a regulation-In a way, she could not be blamed for her ignorance of the law; she was of Earth and had not realized that the laws of the space frontier must, of necessity, be as hard and relentless as the environment that gave them birth. Yet, to protect such as her from the results of their own ignorance of the frontier, there had been a sign over the door that led to the section of the Stardust that housed the EDS; a sign that was plain for all to see and heed:

UNAUTHORIZED PERSONNEL
KEEP OUT!

"Does your brother know that you took passage on the Stardust for Mimir?"

"Oh, yes. I sent him a spacegram telling him about my graduation and about going to Mimir on the Stardust a month before I left Earth. I already knew Mimir was where he would be stationed in a little over a year. He gets a promotion then, and he'll be based on Mimir and not have to stay out a year at a time on field trips, like he does now."

There were two different survey groups on Woden, and he asked, "What is his name?"

"Cross-Gerry Cross. He's in Group Two-that was the way his address read. Do you know him?"

Group One had requested the serum; Group Two was eight thousand miles away, across the Western Sea.

"No, I've never met him," he said, then turned to the control board and cut the deceleration to a fraction of a gravity; knowing as he did so that it could not avert the ultimate end, yet doing the only thing he could do to prolong that ultimate end. The sensation was like that of the ship suddenly dropping and the girl's involuntary movement of surprise half lifted her from the seat.

"We're going faster now, aren't we?" she asked. "Why are we doing that?"

He told her the truth. "To save fuel for a little while."

"You mean, we don't have very much?"

He delayed the answer he must give her so soon to ask: "How did you manage to stow away?"

"I just sort of walked in when no one was looking my way," she said. "I was practicing my Gelanese on the native girl who does the cleaning in the Ship's Supply office when someone came in with an order for supplies for the survey crew on Woden. I slipped into the closet there after the ship was ready to go and just before you came in. It was an impulse of the moment to stow away, so I could get to see Gerry-and from the way you keep looking at me so grim, I'm not sure it was a very wise impulse.

"But I'll be a model criminal-or do I mean prisoner?" She smiled at him again. "I intended to pay for my keep on top of paying the fine. I can cook and I can patch clothes for everyone and I know how to do all kinds of useful things, even a little bit about nursing."

There was one more question to ask:

"Did you know what the supplies were that the survey crew ordered?"

"Why, no. Equipment they needed in their work, I supposed."

Why couldn't she have been a man with some ulterior motive? A fugitive from justice, hoping to lose himself on a raw new world; an opportunist, seeking transportation to the new colonies where he might find golden fleece for the taking; a crackpot, with a mission —

Perhaps once in his lifetime an EDS pilot would find such a stowaway on his ship; warped men, mean and selfish men, brutal and dangerous men-but never, before, a smiling, blue-eyed girl who was willing to pay her fine and work for her keep that she might see her brother.

He turned to the board and turned the switch that would signal the Stardust. The call would be futile but he could not, until he had exhausted that one vain hope, seize her and thrust her into the air lock as he would an animal-or a man. The delay, in the meantime, would not be dangerous with the EDS decelerating at fractional gravity.

A voice spoke from the communicator. "Stardust. Identify yourself and proceed."

"Barton, EDS 34G11. Emergency. Give me Commander Delhart."

There was a faint confusion of noises as the request went through the proper channels. The girl was watching him, no longer smiling.

"Are you going to order them to come back after me?" she asked.

The communicator clicked and there was the sound of a distant voice saying, "Commander, the EDS requests —"

"Are they coming back after me?" she asked again. "Won't I get to see my brother, after all?"

"Barton?" The blunt, gruff voice of Commander Delhart came from the communicator. "What's this about an emergency?"

"A stowaway," he answered.

"A stowaway?" There was a slight surprise to the question. "That's rather unusual-but why the 'emergency' call? You discovered him in time so there should be no appreciable danger and I presume you've informed Ship's Records so his nearest relatives can be notified."

"That's why I had to call you, first. The stowaway is still aboard and the circumstances are so different —"

"Different?" the commander interrupted, impatience in his voice. "How can they be different? You know you have a limited supply of fuel; you also know the law, as well as I do: 'Any stowaway discovered in an EDS shall be jettisoned immediately following discovery.' "

There was the sound of a sharply indrawn breath from the girl. "What does he mean?"

"The stowaway is a girl."

"What?"

"She wanted to see her brother. She's only a kid and she didn't know what she was really doing."

"I see." All the curtness was gone from the commander's voice. "So you called me in the hope I could do something?" Without waiting for an answer he went on. "I'm sorry —I can do nothing. This cruiser must maintain its schedule; the life of not one person but the lives of many depend on it. I know how you feel but I'm powerless to help you. I'll have you connected with Ship's Records."

The communicator faded to a faint rustle of sound and he turned back to the girl. She was leaning forward on the bench, almost rigid, her eyes fixed wide and frightened.

"What did he mean, to go through with it? To jettison me … to go through with it-what did he mean? Not the way it sounded … he couldn't have. What did he mean … what did he really mean?"

Her time was too short for the comfort of a lie to be more than a cruelly fleeting delusion.

"He meant it the way it sounded."

"No!" She recoiled from him as though he had struck her, one hand half upraised as though to fend him off and stark unwillingness to believe in her eyes.

"It will have to be."

"No! You're joking-you're insane! You can't mean it!"

"I'm sorry." He spoke slowly to her, gently. "I should have told you before —I should have, but I had to do what I could first; I had to call the Stardust. You heard what the commander said."

"But you can't —if you make me leave the ship, I'll die."

"I know."

She searched his face and the unwillingness to believe left her eyes, giving way slowly to a look of dazed terror.

"You-know?" She spoke the words far apart, numb and wonderingly.

"I know. It has to be like that."

"You mean it-you really mean it." She sagged back against the wall, small and limp like a little rag doll and all the protesting and disbelief gone. "You're going to do it-you're going to make me die?"

"I'm sorry," he said again. "You'll never know how sorry I am. It has to be that way and no human in the universe can change it."

"You're going to make me die and I didn't do anything to die for —I didn't do anything —"

He sighed, deep and weary. "I know you didn't, child. I know you didn't —"

"EDS." The communicator rapped brisk and metallic. "This is Ship's Records. Give us all information on subject's identification disk."

He got out of his chair to stand over her. She clutched the edge of the seat, her upturned face white under the brown hair and the lipstick standing out like a blood-red cupid's bow.

"Now?"

"I want your identification disk," he said.

She released the edge of the seat and fumbled at the chain that suspended the plastic disk from her neck with fingers that were trembling and awkward. He reached down and unfastened the clasp for her, then returned with the disk to his chair.

"Here's your data, Records: Identification Number T837 —"

"One moment," Records interrupted. "This is to be filed on the gray card, of course?"

"Yes."

"And the time of the execution?"

"I'll tell you later."

"Later? This is highly irregular; the time of the subject's death is required before —"

He kept the thickness out of his voice with an effort. "Then we'll do it in a highly irregular manner-you'll hear the disk read, first. The subject is a girl and she's listening to everything that's said. Are you capable of understanding that?"

There was a brief, almost shocked, silence, then Records said meekly: "Sorry. Go ahead."

He began to read the disk, reading it slowly to delay the inevitable for as long as possible, trying to help her by giving her what little time he could to recover from her first terror and let it resolve into the calm of acceptance and resignation.

"Number T8374 dash Y54. Name: Marilyn Lee Cross. Sex: Female. Born: July 7, 2160. She was only eighteen. Height: 5-3. Weight: 110. Such a slight weight, yet enough to add fatally to the mass of the shell-thin bubble that was an EDS. Hair: Brown. Eyes: Blue. Complexion: Light. Blood Type: O. Irrelevant data. Destination: Port City, Mimir. Invalid data —"

He finished and said, "I'll call you later," then turned once again to the girl. She was huddled back against the wall, watching him with a look of numb and wondering fascination.

"They're waiting for you to kill me, aren't they? They want me dead, don't they? You and everybody on the cruiser wants me dead, don't you?" Then the numbness broke and her voice was that of a frightened and bewildered child. "Everybody wants me dead and I didn't do anything. I didn't hurt anyone —I only wanted to see my brother."

"It's not the way you think-it isn't that way, at all," he said. "Nobody wants it this way; nobody would ever let it be this way if it was humanly possible to change it."

"Then why is it! I don't understand. Why is it?"

"This ship is carrying kala fever serum to Group One on Woden. Their own supply was destroyed by a tornado. Group Two-the crew your brother is in-is eight thousand miles away across the Western Sea and their helicopters can't cross it to help Group One. The fever is invariably fatal unless the serum can be had in time, and the six men in Group One will die unless this ship reaches them on schedule. These little ships are always given barely enough fuel to reach their destination and if you stay aboard your added weight will cause it to use up all its fuel before it reaches the ground. It will crash, then, and you and I will die and so will the six men waiting for the fever serum."

It was a full minute before she spoke, and as she considered his words the expression of numbness left her eyes.

"Is that it?" she asked at last. "Just that the ship doesn't have enough fuel?"

"Yes."

"I can go alone or I can take seven others with me-is that the way it is?"

"That's the way it is."

"And nobody wants me to have to die?"

"Nobody."

"Then maybe-Are you sure nothing can be done about it? Wouldn't people help me if they could?"

"Everyone would like to help you but there is nothing anyone can do. I did the only thing I could do when I called the Stardust."

"And it won't come back-but there might be other cruisers, mightn't there? Isn't there any hope at all that there might be someone, somewhere, who could do something to help me?"

She was leaning forward a little in her eagerness as she waited for his answer.

"No."

The word was like the drop of a cold stone and she again leaned back against the wall, the hope and eagerness leaving her face. "You're sure-you know you're sure?"

"I'm sure. There are no other cruisers within forty light-years; there is nothing and no one to change things."

She dropped her gaze to her lap and began twisting a pleat of her skirt between her fingers, saying no more as her mind began to adapt itself to the grim knowledge.

It was better so; with the going of all hope would go the fear; with the going of all hope would come resignation. She needed time and she could have so little of it. How much?

The EDS's were not equipped with hull-cooling units; their speed had to be reduced to a moderate level before entering the atmosphere. They were decelerating at .10 gravity; approaching their destination at a far higher speed than the computers had calculated on. The Stardust had been quite near Woden when she launched the EDS; their present velocity was putting them nearer by the second. There would be a critical point, soon to be reached, when he would have to resume deceleration. When he did so the girl's weight would be multiplied by the gravities of deceleration, would become, suddenly, a factor of paramount importance; the factor the computers had been ignorant of when they determined the amount of fuel the EDS should have. She would have to go when deceleration began; it could be no other way. When would that be-how long could he let her stay?

"How long can I stay?"

He winced involuntarily from the words that were so like an echo of his own thoughts. How long? He didn't know; he would have to ask the ship's computers. Each EDS was given a meager surplus of fuel to compensate for unfavorable conditions within the atmosphere and relatively little fuel was being consumed for the time being. The memory banks of the computers would still contain all data pertaining to the course set for the EDS; such data would not be erased until the EDS reached its destination. He had only to give the computers the new data; the girl's weight and the exact time at which he had reduced the deceleration to .10.

"Barton." Commander Delhart's voice came abruptly from the communicator, as he opened his mouth to call the Stardust. "A check with Records shows me you haven't completed your report. Did you reduce the deceleration?"

So the commander knew what he was trying to do.

"I'm decelerating at point ten," he answered. "I cut the deceleration at seventeen fifty and the weight is a hundred and ten. I would like to stay at point ten as long as the computers say I can. Will you give them the question?"

It was contrary to regulations for an EDS pilot to make any changes in the course or degree of deceleration the computers had set for him but the commander made no mention of the violation, neither did he ask the reason for it. It was not necessary for him to ask; he had not become commander of an interstellar cruiser without both intelligence and an understanding of human nature. He said only: "I'll have that given the computers."

The communicator fell silent and he and the girl waited, neither of them speaking. They would not have to wait long; the computers would give the answer within moments of the asking. The new factors would be fed into the steel maw of the first bank and the electrical impulses would go through the complex circuits. Here and there a relay might click, a tiny cog turn over, but it would be essentially the electrical impulses that found the answer; formless, mindless, invisible, determining with utter precision how long the pale girl beside him might live. Then a second steel maw would spit out the answer.

The chronometer on the instrument board read 18:10 when the commander spoke again.

"You will resume deceleration at nineteen ten."

She looked toward the chronometer, then quickly away from it. "Is that when ... when I go?" she asked. He nodded and she dropped her eyes to her lap again.

"I'll have the course corrections given you," the commander said. "Ordinarily I would never permit anything like this but I understand your position. There is nothing I can do, other than what I've just done, and you will not deviate from these new instructions. You will complete your report at nineteen ten. Now-here are the course corrections."

The voice of some unknown technician read them to him and he wrote them down on the pad clipped to the edge of the control board. There would, he saw, be periods of deceleration when he neared the atmosphere when the deceleration would be five gravities-and at five gravities, one hundred and ten pounds would become five hundred fifty pounds.

The technician finished and he terminated the contact with a brief acknowledgment. Then, hesitating a moment, he reached out and shut off the communicator. It was 18:13 and he would have nothing to report until 19:10. In the meantime, it somehow seemed indecent to permit others to hear what she might say in her last hour.

He began to check the instrument readings, going over them with unnecessary slowness. She would have to accept the circumstances and there was nothing he could do to help her into acceptance; words of sympathy would only delay it.

It was 18:20 when she stirred from her motionlessness and spoke.

"So that's the way it has to be with me?"

He swung around to face her. "You understand now, don't you? No one would ever let it be like this if it could be changed."

"I understand," she said. Some of the color had returned to her face and the lipstick no longer stood out so vividly red. "There isn't enough fuel for me to stay; when I hid on this ship I got into something I didn't know anything about and now I have to pay for it."

She had violated a man-made law that said KEEP OUT but the penalty was not of men's making or desire and it was a penalty men could not revoke. A physical law had decreed: h amount of fuel will power an EDS with a mass of m safely to its destination; and a second physical law had decreed: h amount of fuel will not power an EDS with a mass of m plus x safely to its destination.

EDS's obeyed only physical laws and no amount of human sympathy for her could alter the second law.

"But I'm afraid. I don't want to die-not now. I want to live and nobody is doing anything to help me; everybody is letting me go ahead and acting just like nothing was going to happen to me. I'm going to die and nobody cares."

"We all do," he said. "I do and the commander does and the clerk in Ship's Records; we all care and each of us did what little he could to help you. It wasn't enough-it was almost nothing-but it was all we could do."

"Not enough fuel—I can understand that," she said, as though she had not heard his own words. "But to have to die for it. Me, alone—"

How hard it must be for her to accept the fact. She had never known danger of death; had never known the environments where the lives of men could be as fragile and fleeting as sea foam tossed against a rocky shore. She belonged on gentle Earth, in that secure and peaceful society where she could be young and gay and laughing with the others of her kind; where life was precious and well-guarded and there was always the assurance that tomorrow would come. She belonged in that world of soft winds and warm suns, music and moonlight and gracious manners and not on the hard, bleak frontier.

"How did it happen to me, so terribly quickly? An hour ago I was on the Stardust, going to Mimir. Now the Stardust is going on without me and I'm going to die and I'll never see Gerry and Mama and Daddy again—I'll never see anything again."

He hesitated, wondering how he could explain it to her so she would really understand and not feel she had, somehow, been the victim of a reasonlessly cruel injustice. She did not know what the frontier was like; she thought in terms of safe-and-secure Earth. Pretty girls were not jettisoned on Earth; there was a law against it. On Earth her plight would have filled the newscasts and a fast black Patrol ship would have been racing to her rescue. Everyone, everywhere, would have known of Marilyn Lee Cross and no effort would have been spared to save her life. But this was not Earth and there were no Patrol ships; only the Stardust, leaving them behind at many times the speed of light. There was no one to help her, there would be no Marilyn Lee Cross smiling from the newscasts tomorrow. Marilyn Lee Cross would be but a poignant memory for an EDS pilot and a name on a gray card in Ship's Records.

"It's different here; it's not like back on Earth," he said. "It isn't that no one cares; it's that no one can do anything to help. The frontier is big and here along its rim the colonies and exploration parties are scattered so thin and far between. On Woden, for example, there are only sixteen men-sixteen men on an entire world. The exploration parties, the survey crews, the little first-colonies—they're all fighting alien environments, trying to make a way for those who will follow after. The environments fight back and those who go first usually make mistakes only once. There is no margin of safety along the rim of the frontier; there can't be until the way is made for the others who will come later, until the new worlds are tamed and settled. Until then men will have to pay the penalty for making mistakes with no one to help them because there is no one to help them."

"I was going to Mimir," she said. "I didn't know about the frontier; I was only going to Mimir and it's safe."

"Mimir is safe but you left the cruiser that was taking you there."

She was silent for a little while. "It was all so wonderful at first; there was plenty of room for me on this ship and I would be seeing Gerry so soon ...I didn't know about the fuel, didn't know what would happen to me—"

Her words trailed away and he turned his attention to the viewscreen, not wanting to stare at her as she fought her way through the black horror of fear toward the calm gray of acceptance.

Woden was a ball, enshrouded in the blue haze of its atmosphere, swimming in space against the background of star-sprinkled dead blackness. The great mass of Manning's Continent sprawled like a gigantic hourglass in the Eastern Sea with the western half of the Eastern Continent still visible. There was a thin line of shadow along the right-hand edge of the globe and the Eastern Continent was disappearing into it as the planet turned on its axis. An hour before the entire continent had been in view, now a thousand miles of it had gone into the thin edge of shadow and around to the night that lay on the other side of the world. The dark blue spot that was Lotus Lake was approaching the shadow. It was somewhere near the southern edge of the lake that Group Two had their camp. It would be night there, soon, and quick behind the coming of night the rotation of Woden on its axis would put Group Two beyond the reach of the ship's radio.

He would have to tell her before it was too late for her to talk to her brother. In a way, it would be better for both of them should they not do so but it was not for him to decide. To each of them the last words would be something to hold and cherish, something that would cut like the blade of a knife yet would be infinitely precious to remember, she for her own brief moments to live and he for the rest of his life.

He held down the button that would flash the grid lines on the viewscreen and used the known diameter of the planet to estimate the distance the southern tip of Lotus Lake had yet to go until it passed beyond radio range. It was approximately five hundred miles. Five hundred miles; thirty minutes-and the chronometer read 18:30. Allowing for error in estimating, it could not be later than 19:05 that the turning of Woden would cut off her brother's voice.

The first border of the Western Continent was already in sight along the left side of the world. Four thousand miles across it lay the shore of the Western Sea and the Camp of Group One. It had been in the Western Sea that the tornado had originated, to strike with such fury at the camp and destroy half their prefabricated buildings, including the one that housed the medical supplies. Two days before the tornado had not existed; it had been no more than great gentle masses of air out over the calm Western Sea. Group One had gone about their routine survey work, unaware of the meeting of the air masses out at sea, unaware of the force the union was spawning. It had struck their camp without warning; a thundering, roaring destruction that sought to annihilate all that lay before it. It had passed on, leaving the wreckage in its wake. It had destroyed the labor of months and had doomed six men to die and then, as though its task was accomplished, it once more began to resolve into gentle masses of air. But for all its deadliness, it had destroyed with neither malice nor intent. It had been a blind and mindless force, obeying the laws of nature, and it would have followed the same course with the same fury had men never existed.

Existence required Order and there was order; the laws of nature, irrevocable and immutable. Men could learn to use them but men could not change them. The circumference of a circle was always pi times the diameter and no science of Man would ever make it otherwise. The combination of chemical A with chemical B under condition C invariably produced reaction D. The law of gravitation was a rigid equation and it made no distinction between the fall of a leaf and the ponderous circling of a binary star system. The nuclear conversion process powered the cruisers that carried men to the stars; the same process in the form of a nova would destroy a world with equal efficiency. The laws were, and the universe moved in obedience to them. Along the frontier were arrayed all the forces of nature and sometimes they destroyed those who were fighting their way outward from Earth. The men of the frontier had long ago learned the bitter futility of cursing the forces that would destroy them for the forces were blind and deaf; the futility of looking to the heavens for mercy, for the stars of the galaxy swung in their long, long sweep of two hundred million years, as inexorably controlled as they by the laws that knew neither hatred nor compassion.

The men of the frontier knew-but how was a girl from Earth to fully understand? H amount of fuel will not power an EDS with a mass of m plus x safely to its destination. To himself and her brother and parents she was a sweet-faced girl in her teens; to the laws of nature she was x, the unwanted factor in a cold equation.

She stirred again on the seat. "Could I write a letter? I want to write to Mama and Daddy and I'd like to talk to Gerry. Could you let me talk to him over your radio there?"

"I'll try to get him," he said.

He switched on the normal-space transmitter and pressed the signal button. Someone answered the buzzer almost immediately.

"Hello. How's it going with you fellows now-is the EDS on its way?"

"This isn't Group One; this is the EDS," he said. "Is Gerry Cross there?"

"Gerry? He and two others went out in the helicopter this morning and aren't back yet. It's almost sundown, though, and he ought to be back right away-in less than an hour at the most."

"Can you connect me through to the radio in his 'copter?"

"Huh-uh. It's been out of commission for two months-some printed circuits went haywire and we can't get any more until the next cruiser stops by. Is it something important-bad news for him, or something?"

"Yes-it's very important. When he comes in get him to the transmitter as soon as you possibly can."

"I'll do that; I'll have one of the boys waiting at the field with a truck. Is there anything else I can do?"

"No, I guess that's all. Get him there as soon as you can and signal me."

He turned the volume to an inaudible minimum, an act that would not affect the functioning of the signal buzzer, and unclipped the pad of paper from the control board. He tore off the sheet containing his flight instructions and handed the pad to her, together with pencil.

"I'd better write to Gerry, too," she said as she took them. "He might not get back to camp in time."

She began to write, her fingers still clumsy and uncertain in the way they handled the pencil and the top of it trembling a little as she poised it between words. He turned back to the viewscreen, to stare at it without seeing it.

She was a lonely little child, trying to say her last good-by, and she would lay out her heart to them. She would tell them how much she loved them and she would tell them to not feel badly about it, that it was only something that must happen eventually to everyone and she was not afraid. The last would be a lie and it would be there to read between the sprawling, uneven lines; a valiant little lie that would make the hurt all the greater for them.

Her brother was of the frontier and he would understand. He would not hate the EDS pilot for doing nothing to prevent her going; he would know there had been nothing the pilot could do. He would understand, though the understanding would not soften the shock and pain when he learned his sister was gone. But the others, her father and mother-they would not understand. They were of Earth and they would think in the manner of those who had never lived where the safety margin of life was a thin, thin line-and sometimes not at all. What would they think of the faceless, unknown pilot who had sent her to her death?

They would hate him with cold and terrible intensity but it really didn't matter. He would never see them, never know them. He would have only the memories to remind him; only the nights to fear, when a blue-eyed girl in gypsy sandals would come in his dreams to die again —

He scowled at the viewscreen and tried to force his thoughts into less emotional channels. There was nothing he could do to help her. She had unknowingly subjected herself to the penalty of a law that recognized neither innocence nor youth nor beauty, that was incapable of sympathy or leniency. Regret was illogical-and yet, could knowing it to be illogical ever keep it away?

She stopped occasionally, as though trying to find the right words to tell them what she wanted them to know, then the pencil would resume its whispering to the paper. It was 18:37 when she folded the letter in a square and wrote a name on it. She began writing another, twice looking up at the chronometer as though she feared the black hand might reach its rendezvous before she had finished. It was 18:45 when she folded it as she had done the first letter and wrote a name and address on it.

She held the letters out to him. "Will you take care of these and see that they're enveloped and mailed?"

"Of course." He took them from her hand and placed them in a pocket of his gray uniform shirt.

"These can't be sent off until the next cruiser stops by and the Stardust will have long since told them about me, won't it?" she asked. He nodded and she went on, "That makes the letters not important in one way but in another way they're very important-to me, and to them."

"I know. I understand, and I'll take care of them."

She glanced at the chronometer, then back at him. "It seems to move faster all the time, doesn't it?"

He said nothing, unable to think of anything to say, and she asked, "Do you think Gerry will come back to camp in time?"

"I think so. They said he should be in right away."

She began to roll the pencil back and forth between her palms. "I hope he does. I feel sick and scared and I want to hear his voice again and maybe I won't feel so alone. I'm a coward and I can't help it."

"No," he said, "you're not a coward. You're afraid, but you're not a coward."

"Is there a difference?"

He nodded. "A lot of difference."

"I feel so alone. I never did feel like this before; like I was all by myself and there was nobody to care what happened to me. Always, before, there was Mama and Daddy there and my friends around me. I had lots of friends, and they had a going-away party for me the night before I left."

Friends and music and laughter for her to remember-and on the viewscreen Lotus Lake was going into the shadow.

"Is it the same with Gerry?" she asked. "I mean, if he should make a mistake, would he have to die for it, all alone and with no one to help him?"

"It's the same with all along the frontier; it will always be like that so long as there is a frontier."

"Gerry didn't tell us. He said the pay was good and he sent money home all the time because Daddy's little shop just brought in a bare living but he didn't tell us it was like this."

"He didn't tell you his work was dangerous?"

"Well-yes. He mentioned that, but we didn't understand. I always thought danger along the frontier was something that was a lot of fun; an exciting adventure, like in the three-D shows." A wan smile touched her face for a moment. "Only it's not, is it? It's not the same at all, because when it's real you can't go home after the show is over."

"No," he said. "No, you can't."

Her glance flicked from the chronometer to the door of the air lock then down to the pad and pencil she still held. She shifted her position slightly to lay them on the bench beside her, moving one foot out a little. For the first time he saw that she was not wearing Vegan gypsy sandals but only cheap imitations; the expensive Vegan leather was some kind of grained plastic, the silver buckle was gilded iron, the jewels were colored glass. Daddy's little shop just brought in a bare living-She must have left college in her second year, to take the course in linguistics that would enable her to make her own way and help her brother provide for her parents, earning what she could by part-time work after classes were over. Her personal possessions on the Stardust would be taken back to her parents-they would neither be of much value nor occupy much storage space on the return voyage.

"Isn't it —" She stopped, and he looked at her questioningly. "Isn't it cold in here?" she asked, almost apologetically. "Doesn't it seem cold to you?"

"Why, yes," he said. He saw by the main temperature gauge that the room was at precisely normal temperature. "Yes, it's colder than it should be."

"I wish Gerry would get back before it's too late. Do you really think he will, and you didn't just say so to make me feel better?"

"I think he will-they said he would be in pretty soon." On the viewscreen Lotus Lake had gone into the shadow but for the thin blue line of its western edge and it was apparent he had overestimated the time she would have in which to talk to her brother. Reluctantly, he said to her, "His camp will be out of radio range in a few minutes; he's on that part of Woden that's in the shadow" —he indicated the viewscreen —"and the turning of Woden will put him beyond contact. There may not be much time left when he comes in-not much time to talk to him before he fades out. I wish I could do something about it —I would call him right now if I could."

"Not even as much time as I will have to stay?"

"I'm afraid not."

"Then —" She straightened and looked toward the air lock with pale resolution. "Then I'll go when Gerry passes beyond range. I won't wait any longer after that —I won't have anything to wait for."

Again there was nothing he could say.

"Maybe I shouldn't wait at all. Maybe I'm selfish-maybe it would be better for Gerry if you just told him about it afterward."

There was an unconscious pleading for denial in the way she spoke and he said, "He wouldn't want you to do that, to not wait for him."

"It's already coming dark where he is, isn't it? There will be all the long night before him, and Mama and Daddy don't know yet that I won't ever be coming back like I promised them I would. I've caused everyone I love to be hurt, haven't I? I didn't want to —I didn't intend to."

"It wasn't your fault," he said. "It wasn't your fault. They'll know that. They'll understand."

"At first I was so afraid to die that I was a coward and thought only of myself. Now, I see how selfish I was. The terrible thing about dying like this is not that I'll be gone but that I'll never see them again; never be able to tell them that I didn't take them for granted; never be able to tell them I knew of the sacrifices they made to make my life happier, and I knew all the things they did for me and that I loved them so much more than I ever told them. I've never told them any of those things. You don't tell them such things when you're young and your life is all before you-you're afraid of sounding sentimental and silly.

"But it's so different when you have to die-you wish you had told them while you could and you wish you could tell them you're sorry for all the little mean things you ever did or said to them. You wish you could tell them that you didn't really mean to ever hurt their feelings and for them to only remember that you always loved them far more than you ever let them know."

"You don't have to tell them that," he said. "They will know-they've always known it."

"Are you sure?" she asked. "How can you be sure? My people are strangers to you."

"Wherever you go, human nature and human hearts are the same."

"And they will know what I want them to know-that I love them?"

"They've always known it, in a way far better than you could ever put in words for them."

"I keep remembering the things they did for me, and it's the little things they did that seem to be the most important to me, now. Like Gerry-he sent me a bracelet of fire-rubies on my sixteenth birthday. It was beautiful-it must have cost him a month's pay. Yet, I remember him more for what he did the night my kitten got run over in the street. I was only six years old and he held me in his arms and wiped away my tears and told me not to cry, that Flossy was gone for just a little while, for just long enough to get herself a new fur coat and she would be on the foot of my bed the very next morning. I believed him and quit crying and went to sleep dreaming about my kitten coming back. When I woke up the next morning, there was Flossy on the foot of my bed in a brand-new white fur coat, just like he had said she would be.

"It wasn't until a long time later that Mama told me Gerry had got the pet-shop owner out of bed at four in the morning and, when the man got mad about it, Gerry told him he was either going to go down and sell him the white kitten right then or he'd break his neck."

"It's always the little things you remember people by; all the little things they did because they wanted to do them for you. You've done the same for Gerry and your father and mother; all kinds of things that you've forgotten about but that they will never forget."

"I hope I have. I would like for them to remember me like that."

"They will."

"I wish —" She swallowed. "The way I'll die —I wish they wouldn't ever think of that. I've read how people look who die in space-their insides all ruptured and exploded and their lungs out between their teeth and then, a few seconds later, they're all dry and shapeless and horribly ugly. I don't want them to ever think of me as something dead and horrible, like that."

"You're their own, their child and their sister. They could never think of you other than the way you would want them to; the way you looked the last time they saw you."

"I'm still afraid," she said. "I can't help it, but I don't want Gerry to know it. If he gets back in time, I'm going to act like I'm not afraid at all and —"

The signal buzzer interrupted her, quick and imperative.

"Gerry!" She came to her feet. "It's Gerry, now!"

He spun the volume control knob and asked: "Gerry Cross?"

"Yes," her brother answered, an undertone of tenseness to his reply. "The bad news-what is it?"

She answered for him, standing close behind him and leaning down a little toward the communicator, her hand resting small and cold on his shoulder.

"Hello, Gerry." There was only a faint quaver to betray the careful casualness of her voice. "I wanted to see you —"

"Marilyn!" There was sudden and terrible apprehension in the way he spoke her name. "What are you doing on that EDS?"

"I wanted to see you," she said again. "I wanted to see you, so I hid on this ship —"

"You hid on it?"

"I'm a stowaway ... I didn't know what it would mean —"

"Marilyn!" It was the cry of a man who calls hopeless and desperate to someone already and forever gone from him. "What have you done?"

"I ... it's not —" Then her own composure broke and the cold little hand gripped his shoulder convulsively. "Don't, Gerry —I only wanted to see you; I didn't intend to hurt you. Please, Gerry, don't feel like that —"

Something warm and wet splashed on his wrist and he slid out of the chair, to help her into it and swing the microphone down to her own level.

"Don't feel like that-Don't let me go knowing you feel like that —"

The sob she had tried to hold back choked in her throat and her brother spoke to her. "Don't cry, Marilyn." His voice was suddenly deep and infinitely gentle, with all the pain held out of it. "Don't cry, sis-you mustn't do that. It's all right, honey-everything is all right."

"I —" Her lower lip quivered and she bit into it. "I didn't want you to feel that way —I just wanted us to say good-by because I have to go in a minute."

"Sure-sure. That's the way it will be, sis. I didn't mean to sound the way I did." Then his voice changed to a tone of quick and urgent demand. "EDS-have you called the Stardust? Did you check with the computers?"

"I called the Stardust almost an hour ago. It can't turn back, there are no other cruisers within forty light-years, and there isn't enough fuel."

"Are you sure that the computers had the correct data-sure of everything?"

"Yes-do you think I could ever let it happen if I wasn't sure? I did everything I could do. If there was anything at all I could do now, I would do it."

"He tried to help me, Gerry." Her lower lip was no longer trembling and the short sleeves of her blouse were wet where she had dried her tears. "No one can help me and I'm not going to cry any more and everything will be all right with you and Daddy and Mama, won't it?"

"Sure-sure it will. We'll make out fine."

Her brother's words were beginning to come in more faintly and he turned the volume control to maximum. "He's going out of range," he said to her. "He'll be gone within another minute."

"You're fading out, Gerry," she said. "You're going out of range. I wanted to tell you-but I can't, now. We must say good-by so soon-but maybe I'll see you again. Maybe I'll come to you in your dreams with my hair in braids and crying because the kitten in my arms is dead; maybe I'll be the touch of a breeze that whispers to you as it goes by; maybe I'll be one of those gold-winged larks you told me about, singing my silly head off to you; maybe, at times, I'll be nothing you can see but you will know I'm there beside you. Think of me like that, Gerry; always like that and not-the other way."

Dimmed to a whisper by the turning of Woden, the answer came back:

"Always like that, Marilyn-always like that and never any other way."

"Our time is up, Gerry—I have to go, now. Good—" Her voice broke in mid-word and her mouth tried to twist into crying. She pressed her hand hard against it and when she spoke again the words came clear and true:

"Good-by, Gerry."

Faint and ineffably poignant and tender, the last words came from the cold metal of the communicator:

"Good-by, little sister—"

She sat motionless in the hush that followed, as though listening to the shadow-echoes of the words as they died away, then she turned away from the communicator, toward the air lock, and he pulled down the black lever beside him. The inner door of the air lock slid swiftly open, to reveal the bare little cell that was waiting for her, and she walked to it.

She walked with her head up and the brown curls brushing her shoulders, with the white sandals stepping as sure and steady as the fractional gravity would permit and the gilded buckles twinkling with little lights of blue and red and crystal. He let her walk alone and made no move to help her, knowing she would not want it that way. She stepped into the air lock and turned to face him, only the pulse in her throat to betray the wild beating of her heart.

"I'm ready," she said.

He pushed the lever up and the door slid its quick barrier between them, enclosing her in black and utter darkness for her last moments of life. It clicked as it locked in place and he jerked down the red lever. There was a slight waver to the ship as the air gushed from the lock, a vibration to the wall as though something had bumped the outer door in passing, then there was nothing and the ship was dropping true and steady again. He shoved the red lever back to close the door on the empty air lock and turned away, to walk to the pilot's chair with the slow steps of a man old and weary.

Back in the pilot's chair he pressed the signal button of the normal-space transmitter. There was no response; he had expected none. Her brother would have to wait through the night until the turning of Woden permitted contact through Group One.

It was not yet time to resume deceleration and he waited while the ship dropped endlessly downward with him and the drives purred softly. He saw that the white hand of the supplies closet temperature gauge was on zero. A cold equation had been balanced and he was alone on the ship. Something shapeless and ugly was hurrying ahead of him, going to Woden where its brother was waiting through the night, but the empty ship still lived for a little while with the presence of the girl who had not known about the forces that killed with neither hatred nor malice. It seemed, almost, that she still sat small and bewildered and frightened on the metal box beside him, her words echoing hauntingly clear in the void she had left behind her:

I didn't do anything to die for—I didn't do anything—

Space Prison

The sound came swiftly nearer, rising in pitch and swelling in volume. Then it broke through the clouds, tall and black and beautifully deadly-the Gern battle cruiser, come to seek them out and destroy them.

Humbolt dropped inside the stockade, exulting. For two hundred years his people had been waiting for the chance to fight the mighty Gern Empire...

...with bows and arrows against blasters and bombs!

PART 1

For seven weeks the *Constellation* had been plunging through hyperspace with her eight thousand colonists; fleeing like a hunted thing with her communicators silenced and her drives moaning and thundering. Up in the control room, Irene had been told, the needles of the dials danced against the red danger lines day and night.

She lay in bed and listened to the muffled, ceaseless roar of the drives and felt the singing vibration of the hull. *We should be almost safe by now*, she thought. *Athena is only forty days away.*

Thinking of the new life awaiting them all made her too restless to lie still any longer. She got up, to sit on the edge of the bed and switch on the light. Dale was gone-he had been summoned to adjust one of the machines in the ship's X-ray room-and Billy was asleep, nothing showing of him above the covers but a crop of brown hair and the furry nose of his ragged teddy bear.

She reached out to straighten the covers, gently, so as not to awaken him. It happened then, the thing they had all feared.

From the stern of the ship came a jarring, deafening explosion. The ship lurched violently, girders screamed, and the light flicked out.

In the darkness she heard a rapid-fire *thunk-thunk-thunk* as the automatic guard system slid inter-compartment doors shut against sections of the ship suddenly airless. The doors were still thudding shut when another explosion came, from toward the bow. Then there was silence; a feeling of utter quiet and motionlessness.

The fingers of fear enclosed her and her mind said to her, like the cold, unpassionate voice of a stranger: *The Gerns have found us.*

The light came on again, a feeble glow, and there was the soft, muffled sound of questioning voices in the other compartments. She dressed, her fingers shaking and clumsy, wishing that Dale would come to reassure her; to tell her that nothing really serious had happened, that it had not been the Gerns.

It was very still in the little compartment-strangely so. She had finished dressing when she realized the reason: the air circulation system had stopped working.

That meant the power failure was so great that the air regenerators, themselves, were dead. And there were eight thousand people on the *Constellation* who would have to have air to live....

The *Attention* buzzer sounded shrilly from the public address system speakers that were scattered down the ship's corridors. A voice she recognized as that of Lieutenant Commander Lake spoke:

"War was declared upon Earth by the Gern Empire ten days ago. Two Gern cruisers have attacked us and their blasters have destroyed the stern and bow of the ship. We are without a drive and without power but for a few emergency batteries. I am the *Constellation*'s only surviving officer and the Gern commander is boarding us to give me the surrender terms.

"None of you will leave your compartments until ordered to do so. Wherever you may be, remain there. This is necessary to avoid confusion and to have as many as possible in known locations for future instructions. I repeat: you will not leave your compartments."

The speaker cut off. She stood without moving and heard again the words: *I am the* Constellation's *only surviving officer....*

The Gerns had killed her father.

He had been second-in-command of the Dunbar expedition that had discovered the world of Athena and his knowledge of Athena was valuable to the colonization plans. He had been quartered among the ship's officers-and the Gern blast had destroyed that section of the ship.

She sat down on the edge of the bed again and tried to reorient herself; to accept the fact that her life and the lives of all the others had abruptly, irrevocably, been changed.

The Athena Colonization Plan was ended. They had known such a thing might happen-that was why the *Constellation* had been made ready for the voyage in secret and had waited for months for the chance to slip through the ring of Gern spy ships; that was why she had raced at full speed, with her communicators silenced so there would be no radiations for the Gerns to find her by. Only forty days more would have brought them to the green and virgin world of Athena, four hundred light-years beyond the outermost boundary of the Gern Empire. There they should have been safe from Gern detection for many years to come; for long enough to build planetary defenses against attack. And there they would have used Athena's rich resources to make ships and weapons to defend mineral-depleted Earth against the inexorably increasing inclosure of the mighty, coldly calculating colossus that was the Gern Empire.

Success or failure of the Athena Plan had meant ultimate life or death for Earth. They had taken every precaution possible but the Gern spy system had somehow learned of Athena and the *Constellation*. Now, the cold war was no longer cold and the Plan was dust....

* * * * *

Billy sighed and stirred in the little-boy sleep that had not been broken by the blasts that had altered the lives of eight thousand people and the fate of a world.

She shook his shoulder and said, "Billy."

He raised up, so small and young to her eyes that the question in her mind was like an anguished prayer: *Dear God-what do Gerns do to five-year-old boys?*

He saw her face, and the dim light, and the sleepiness was suddenly gone from him. "What's wrong, Mama? And why are you scared?"

There was no reason to lie to him.

"The Gerns found us and stopped us."

"Oh," he said. In his manner was the grave thoughtfulness of a boy twice his age, as there always was. "Will they-will they kill us?"

"Get dressed, honey," she said. "Hurry, so we'll be ready when they let Daddy come back to tell us what to do."

* * * * *

They were both ready when the *Attention* buzzer sounded again in the corridors. Lake spoke, his tone grim and bitter:

"There is no power for the air regenerators and within twenty hours we will start smothering to death. Under these circumstances I could not do other than accept the survival terms the Gern commander offered us.

"He will speak to you now and you will obey his orders without protest. Death is the only alternative."

Then the voice of the Gern commander came, quick and harsh and brittle:

"This section of space, together with planet Athena, is an extension of the Gern Empire. This ship has deliberately invaded Gern territory in time of war with intent to seize and exploit a Gern world. We are willing, however, to offer a leniency not required by the circumstances. Terran technicians and skilled workers in certain fields can be used in the factories we shall build on Athena. The others will not be needed and there is not room on the cruisers to take them.

"Your occupation records will be used to divide you into two groups: the Acceptables and the Rejects. The Rejects will be taken by the cruisers to an Earth-type planet near here and left, together with the personal possessions in their compartments and additional, and ample, supplies. The Acceptables will then be taken on to Athena and at a later date the cruisers will return the Rejects to Earth.

"This division will split families but there will be no resistance to it. Gern guards will be sent immediately to make this division and you will wait in your compartments for them. You will obey their orders promptly and without annoying them with questions. At the first instance of resistance or rebellion this offer will be withdrawn and the cruisers will go their way again."

* * * * *

In the silence following the ultimatum she could hear the soft, wordless murmur from the other compartments, the undertone of anxiety like a dark thread through it. In every compartment parents and children, brothers and sisters, were seeing one another for the last time....

The corridor outside rang to the tramp of feet; the sound of a dozen Gerns walking with swift military precision. She held her breath, her heart racing, but they went past her door and on to the corridor's end.

There she could faintly hear them entering compartments, demanding names, and saying, *"Out-out!"* Once she heard a Gern say, "Acceptables will remain inside until further notice. Do not open your doors after the Rejects have been taken out."

Billy touched her on the hand. "Isn't Daddy going to come?"

"He-he can't right now. We'll see him pretty soon."

She remembered what the Gern commander had said about the Rejects being permitted to take their personal possessions. She had very little time in which to get together what she could carry....

There were two small bags in the compartment and she hurried to pack them with things she and Dale and Billy might need, not able to know which of them, if any, would be Rejects. Nor could she know whether she should put in clothes for a cold world or a hot one. The Gern commander had said the Rejects would be left on an Earth-type planet but where could it be? The Dunbar Expedition had explored across five hundred light-years of space and had found only one Earth-type world: Athena.

The Gerns were almost to her door when she had finished and she heard them enter the compartments across from her own. There came the hard, curt questions and the command: "Outside-hurry!" A woman said something in pleading question and there was the soft thud of a blow and the words: "Outside-do not ask questions!" A moment later she heard the woman going down the corridor, trying to hold back her crying.

Then the Gerns were at her own door.

She held Billy's hand and waited for them with her heart hammering. She held her head high and composed herself with all the determination she could muster so that the arrogant Gerns would not see that she was afraid. Billy stood beside her as tall as his five years would permit, his teddy bear under his arm, and only the way his hand held to hers showed that he, too, was scared.

The door was flung open and two Gerns strode in.

The were big, dark men, with powerful, bulging muscles. They surveyed her and the room with a quick sweep of eyes that were like glittering obsidian, their mouths thin, cruel slashes in the flat, brutal planes of their faces.

"Your name?" snapped the one who carried a sheaf of occupation records.

"It's" —she tried to swallow the quaver in her voice and make it cool and unfrightened — "Irene Lois Humbolt-Mrs. Dale Humbolt."

The Gern glanced at the papers. "Where is your husband?"

"He was in the X-ray room at —"

"You are a Reject. Out-down the corridor with the others."

"My husband-will he be a —"

"Outside!"

It was the tone of voice that had preceded the blow in the other compartment and the Gern took a quick step toward her. She seized the two bags in one hand, not wanting to release Billy, and swung back to hurry out into the corridor. The other Gern jerked one of the bags from her hand and flung it to the floor. "Only one bag per person," he said, and gave her an impatient shove that sent her and Billy stumbling through the doorway.

She became part of the Rejects who were being herded like sheep down the corridors and into the port airlock. There were many children among them, the young ones frightened and crying, and often with only one parent or an older brother or sister to take care of them. And there were many young ones who had no one at all and were dependent upon strangers to take their hands and tell them what they must do.

When she was passing the corridor that led to the X-ray room she saw a group of Rejects being herded up it. Dale was not among them and she knew, then, that she and Billy would never see him again.

* * * * *

"Out from the ship-faster-faster — —"

The commands of the Gern guards snapped like whips around them as she and the other Rejects crowded and stumbled down the boarding ramp and out onto the rocky ground. There was the pull of a terrible gravity such as she had never experienced and they were in a bleak, barren valley, a cold wind moaning down it and whipping the alkali dust in bitter clouds. Around the valley stood ragged hills, their white tops laying out streamers of wind-driven snow, and the sky was dark with sunset.

"Out from the ship-faster — —"

It was hard to walk fast in the high gravity, carrying the bag in one hand and holding up all of Billy's weight she could with the other.

"They lied to us!" a man beside her said to someone. "Let's turn and fight. Let's take — —"

A Gern blaster cracked with a vivid blue flash and the man plunged lifelessly to the ground. She flinched instinctively and fell over an unseen rock, the bag of precious clothes flying from her hand. She scrambled up again, her left knee half numb, and turned to retrieve it.

The Gern guard was already upon her, his blaster still in his hand. "Out from the ship-faster."

The barrel of his blaster lashed across the side of her head. "Move on-move on!"

She staggered in a blinding blaze of pain and then hurried on, holding tight to Billy's hand, the wind cutting like knives of ice through her thin clothes and blood running in a trickle down her cheek.

"He hit you," Billy said. "He hurt you." Then he called the Gern a name that five-year-old boys were not supposed to know, with a savagery that five-year-old boys were not supposed to possess.

When she stopped at the outer fringe of Rejects she saw that all of them were out of the cruiser and the guards were going back into it. A half mile down the valley the other cruiser stood, the Rejects out from it and its boarding ramps already withdrawn.

When she had buttoned Billy's blouse tighter and wiped the blood from her face the first blast of the drives came from the farther cruiser. The nearer one blasted a moment later and they lifted together, their roaring filling the valley. They climbed faster and faster, dwindling as they went. Then they disappeared in the black sky, their roaring faded away, and there was left only the moaning of the wind around her and somewhere a child crying.

And somewhere a voice asking, "Where are we? In the name of God-what have they done to us?"

She looked at the snow streaming from the ragged hills, felt the hard pull of the gravity, and knew where they were. They were on Ragnarok, the hell-world of 1.5 gravity and fierce beasts and raging fevers where men could not survive. The name came from an old Teutonic myth and meant: *The last day for gods and men.* The Dunbar Expedition had discovered Ragnarok and her father had told her of it, of how it had killed six of the eight men who had left the ship and would have killed all of them if they had remained any longer.

She knew where they were and she knew the Gerns had lied to them and would never send a ship to take them to Earth. Their abandonment there had been intended as a death sentence for all of them.

And Dale was gone and she and Billy would die helpless and alone....

"It will be dark-so soon." Billy's voice shook with the cold. "If Daddy can't find us in the dark, what will we do?"

"I don't know," she said. "There's no one to help us and how can I know-what we should do — —"

She was from the city. How could she know what to do on an alien, hostile world where armed explorers had died? She had tried to be brave before the Gerns but now-now night was at hand and out of it would come terror and death for herself and Billy. They would never see Dale again, never see Athena or Earth or even the dawn on the world that had killed them....

She tried not to cry, and failed. Billy's cold little hand touched her own, trying to reassure her.

"Don't cry, Mama. I guess —I guess everybody else is scared, too."

Everyone else....

She was not alone. How could she have thought she was alone? All around her were others, as helpless and uncertain as she. Her story was only one out of four thousand.

"I guess they are, Billy," she said. "I never thought of that, before."

She knelt to put her arms around him, thinking: *Tears and fear are futile weapons; they can never bring us any tomorrows. We'll have to fight whatever comes to kill us no matter how scared we are. For ourselves and for our children. Above all else, for our children....*

"I'm going back to find our clothes," she said. "You wait here for me, in the shelter of that rock, and I won't be gone long."

Then she told him what he would be too young to really understand.

"I'm not going to cry any more and I know, now, what I must do. I'm going to make sure that there is a tomorrow for you, always, to the last breath of my life."

* * * * *

The bright blue star dimmed and the others faded away. Dawn touched the sky, bringing with it a coldness that frosted the steel of the rifle in John Prentiss's hands and formed beads of ice on his gray mustache. There was a stirring in the area behind him as the weary Rejects prepared to face the new day and the sound of a child whimpering from the cold. There had been no time the evening before to gather wood for fires — —

"Prowlers!"

The warning cry came from an outer guard and black shadows were suddenly sweeping out of the dark dawn.

They were things that might have been half wolf, half tiger; each of them three hundred pounds of incredible ferocity with eyes blazing like yellow fire in their white-fanged tiger-wolf faces. They came like the wind, in a flowing black wave, and ripped through the outer guard line as though it had not existed. The inner guards fired in a chattering roll of gunshots, trying to turn them, and Prentiss's rifle licked out pale tongues of flame as he added his own fire. The prowlers came on, breaking through, but part of them went down and the others were swerved by the fire so that they struck only the outer edge of the area where the Rejects were grouped.

At that distance they blended into the dark ground so that he could not find them in the sights of his rifle. He could only watch helplessly and see a dark-haired woman caught in their path, trying to run with a child in her arms and already knowing it was too late. A man was running toward her, slow in the high gravity, an axe in his hands and his cursing a raging, savage snarl. For a moment her white face was turned in helpless appeal to him and the others; then the prowlers were upon her and she fell, deliberately, going to the ground with her child hugged in her arms beneath her so that her body would protect it.

The prowlers passed over her, pausing for an instant to slash the life from her, and raced on again. They vanished back into the outer darkness, the farther guards firing futilely, and there was a silence but for the distant, hysterical sobbing of a woman.

It had happened within seconds; the fifth prowler attack that night and the mildest.

* * * * *

Full dawn had come by the time he replaced the guards killed by the last attack and made the rounds of the other guard lines. He came back by the place where the prowlers had killed the woman, walking wearily against the pull of gravity. She lay with her dark hair tumbled and stained with blood, her white face turned up to the reddening sky, and he saw her clearly for the first time.

It was Irene.

He stopped, gripping the cold steel of the rifle and not feeling the rear sight as it cut into his hand.

Irene....He had not known she was on Ragnarok. He had not seen her in the darkness of the night and he had hoped she and Billy were safe among the Acceptables with Dale.

There was the sound of footsteps and a bold-faced girl in a red skirt stopped beside him, her glance going over him curiously.

"The little boy," he asked, "do you know if he's all right?"

"The prowlers cut up his face but he'll be all right," she said. "I came back after his clothes."

"Are you going to look after him?"

"Someone has to and" —she shrugged her shoulders —"I guess I was soft enough to elect myself for the job. Why-was his mother a friend of yours?"

"She was my daughter," he said.

"Oh." For a moment the bold, brassy look was gone from her face, like a mask that had slipped. "I'm sorry. And I'll take care of Billy."

* * * * *

The first objection to his assumption of leadership occurred an hour later. The prowlers had withdrawn with the coming of full daylight and wood had been carried from the trees to build fires. Mary, one of the volunteer cooks, was asking two men to carry her some water when he approached. The smaller man picked up one of the clumsy containers, hastily improvised from canvas, and started toward the creek. The other, a big, thick-chested man, did not move.

"We'll have to have water," Mary said. "People are hungry and cold and sick."

The man continued to squat by the fire, his hands extended to its warmth. "Name someone else," he said.

"But — —"

She looked at Prentiss in uncertainty. He went to the thick-chested man, knowing there would be violence and welcoming it as something to help drive away the vision of Irene's pale, cold face under the red sky.

"She asked you to get her some water," he said. "Get it."

The man looked up at him, studying him with deliberate insolence, then he got to his feet, his heavy shoulders hunched challengingly.

"I'll have to set you straight, old timer," he said. "No one has appointed you the head cheese around here. Now, there's the container you want filled and over there" —he made a small motion with one hand —"is the creek. Do you know what to do?"

"Yes," he said. "I know what to do."

He brought the butt of the rifle smashing up. It struck the man under the chin and there was a sharp cracking sound as his jawbone snapped. For a fraction of a second there was an expression of stupefied amazement on his face then his eyes glazed and he slumped to the ground with his broken jaw setting askew.

"All right," he said to Mary. "Now you go ahead and name somebody else."

* * * * *

He found that the prowlers had killed seventy during the night. One hundred more had died from the Hell Fever that often followed exposure and killed within an hour.

He went the half mile to the group that had arrived on the second cruiser as soon as he had eaten a delayed breakfast. He saw, before he had quite reached the other group, that the *Constellation*'s Lieutenant Commander, Vincent Lake, was in charge of it.

Lake, a tall, hard-jawed man with pale blue eyes under pale brows, walked forth to meet him as soon as he recognized him.

"Glad to see you're still alive," Lake greeted him. "I thought that second Gern blast got you along with the others."

"I was visiting midship and wasn't home when it happened," he said.

He looked at Lake's group of Rejects, in their misery and uncertainty so much like his own, and asked, "How was it last night?"

"Bad-damned bad," Lake said. "Prowlers and Hell Fever, and no wood for fires. Two hundred died last night."

"I came down to see if anyone was in charge here and to tell them that we'll have to move into the woods at once-today. We'll have plenty of wood for the fires there, some protection from the wind, and by combining our defenses we can stand off the prowlers better."

Lake agreed. When the brief discussion of plans was finished he asked, "How much do you know about Ragnarok?"

"Not much," Prentiss answered. "We didn't stay to study it very long. There are no heavy metals on Ragnarok's other sun. Its position in the advance of the resources of any value. We gave Ragnarok a quick survey and when the sixth man died we marked it on the chart as un-inhabitable and went on our way.

"As you probably know, that bright blue star is Ragnarok's other sun. It's position in the advance of the yellow sun shows the season to be early spring. When summer comes Ragnarok will swing between the two suns and the heat will be something no human has ever endured. Nor the cold, when winter comes.

"I know of no edible plants, although there might be some. There are a few species of rodent-like animals-they're scavengers-and a herbivore we called the woods goat. The prowlers are the dominant form of life on Ragnarok and I suspect their intelligence is a good deal higher than we would like it to be. There will be a constant battle for survival with them.

"There's another animal, not as intelligent as the prowlers but just as dangerous-the unicorn. The unicorns are big and fast and they travel in herds. I haven't seen any here so far —I hope we don't. At the lower elevations are the swamp crawlers. They're unadulterated nightmares. I hope they don't go to these higher elevations in the summer. The prowlers and the Hell Fever, the gravity and heat and cold and starvation, will be enough for us to have to fight."

"I see," Lake said. He smiled, a smile that was as bleak as moonlight on an arctic glacier. "Earth-type —remember the promise the Gerns made the Rejects?" He looked out across the camp, at the snow whipping from the frosty hills, at the dead and the dying, and a little girl trying vainly to awaken her brother.

"They were condemned, without reason, without a chance to live," he said. "So many of them are so young ...and when you're young it's too soon to have to die."

* * * * *

Prentiss returned to his own group. The dead were buried in shallow graves and inventory was taken of the promised "ample supplies." These were only the few personal possessions the Rejects had been permitted to take plus a small amount of food the Gerns had taken from the *Constellation*'s stores. The Gerns had been forced to provide the Rejects with at least a little food-had they openly left them to starve, the Acceptables, whose families were among the Rejects, might have rebelled.

Inventory of the firearms and ammunition showed the total to be discouragingly small. They would have to learn how to make and use bows and arrows as soon as possible.

With the first party of guards and workmen following him, Prentiss went to the tributary valley that emptied into the central valley a mile to the north. It was as good a camp site as could be hoped for; wide and thickly spotted with groves of trees, a creek running down its center.

The workmen began the construction of shelters and he climbed up the side of the nearer hill. He reached its top, his breath coming fast in the gravity that was the equivalent of a burden half his own weight, and saw what the surrounding terrain was like.

To the south, beyond the barren valley, the land could be seen dropping in its long sweep to the southern lowlands where the unicorns and swamp crawlers lived. To the north the hills climbed gently for miles, then ended under the steeply sloping face of an immense plateau. The plateau reached from western to eastern horizon, still white with the snows of winter and looming so high above the world below that the clouds brushed it and half obscured it.

He went back down the hill as Lake's men appeared. They started work on what would be a continuation of his own camp and he told Lake what he had seen from the hill.

"We're between the lowlands and the highlands," he said. "This will be as near to a temperate altitude as Ragnarok has. We survive here-or else. There's no other place for us to go."

An overcast darkened the sky at noon and the wind died down to almost nothing. There was a feeling of waiting tension in the air and he went back to the Rejects, to speed their move into the woods. They were already going in scattered groups, accompanied by prowler guards, but there was no organization and it would be too long before the last of them were safely in the new camp.

He could not be two places at once-he needed a subleader to oversee the move of the Rejects and their possessions into the woods and their placement after they got there.

He found the man he wanted already helping the Rejects get started: a thin, quiet man named Henry Anders who had fought well against the prowlers the night before, even though his determination had been greater than his marksmanship. He was the type people instinctively liked and trusted; a good choice for the subleader whose job it would be to handle the multitude of details in camp while he, Prentiss, and a second subleader he would select, handled the defense of the camp and the hunting.

"I don't like this overcast," he told Anders. "Something's brewing. Get everyone moved and at work helping build shelters as soon as you can."

"I can have most of them there within an hour or two," Anders said. "Some of the older people, though, will have to take it slow. This gravity-it's already getting the hearts of some of them."

"How are the children taking the gravity?" he asked.

"The babies and the very young-it's hard to tell about them yet. But the children from about four on up get tired quickly, go to sleep, and when they wake up they've sort of bounced back out of it."

"Maybe they can adapt to some extent to this gravity." He thought of what Lake had said that morning: *So many of them are so young ... and when you're young it's too soon to have to die.* "Maybe the Gerns made a mistake-maybe Terran children aren't as easy to kill as they thought. It's your job and mine and others to give the children the chance to prove the Gerns wrong."

He went his way again to pass by the place where Julia, the girl who had become Billy's foster-mother, was preparing to go to the new camp.

It was the second time for him to see Billy that morning. The first time Billy had still been stunned with grief, and at the sight of his grandfather he had been unable to keep from breaking.

"The Gern hit her," he had sobbed, his torn face bleeding anew as it twisted in crying. "He hurt her, and Daddy was gone and then-and then the other things killed her — —"

But now he had had a little time to accept what had happened and he was changed. He was someone much older, almost a man, trapped for a while in the body of a five-year-old boy.

"I guess this is all, Billy," Julia was saying as she gathered up her scanty possessions and Irene's bag. "Get your teddy bear and we'll go."

Billy went to his teddy bear and knelt down to pick it up. Then he stopped and said something that sounded like *"No."* He laid the teddy bear back down, wiping a little dust from its face as in a last gesture of farewell, and stood up to face Julia empty-handed.

"I don't think I'll want to play with my teddy bear any more," he said. "I don't think I'll ever want to play at all anymore."

Then he went to walk beside her, leaving his teddy bear lying on the ground behind him and with it leaving forever the tears and laughter of childhood.

* * * * *

The overcast deepened, and at midafternoon dark storm clouds came driving in from the west. Efforts were intensified to complete the move before the storm broke, both in his section of the camp and in Lake's. The shelters would be of critical importance and they were being built of the materials most quickly available; dead limbs, brush, and the limited amount of canvas and blankets the Rejects had. They would be inadequate protection but there was no time to build anything better.

It seemed only a few minutes until the black clouds were overhead, rolling and racing at an incredible velocity. With them came the deep roar of the high wind that drove them and the wind on the ground began to stir restlessly in response, like some monster awakening to the call of its kind.

Prentiss knew already who he wanted as his other subleader. He found him hard at work helping build shelters; Howard Craig, a powerfully muscled man with a face as hard and grim as a cliff of granite. It had been Craig who had tried to save Irene from the prowlers that morning with only an axe as a weapon.

Prentiss knew him slightly-and Craig still did not know Irene had been his daughter. Craig had been one of the field engineers for what would have been the Athena Geological Survey. He had had a wife, a frail, blonde girl who had been the first of all to die of Hell Fever the night before, and he still had their three small children.

"We'll stop with the shelters we already have built," he told Craig. "It will take all the time left to us to reinforce them against the wind. I need someone to help me, in addition to Anders. You're the one I want.

"Send some young and fast-moving men back to last night's camp to cut all the strips of prowler skins they can get. Everything about the shelters will have to be lashed down to something solid. See if you can find some experienced outdoorsmen to help you check the jobs.

"And tell Anders that women and children only will be placed in the shelters. There will be no room for anyone else and if any man, no matter what the excuse, crowds out a woman or child I'll personally kill him."

"You needn't bother," Craig said. He smiled with savage mirthlessness. "I'll be glad to take care of any such incidents."

Prentiss saw to it that the piles of wood for the guard fires were ready to be lighted when the time came. He ordered all guards to their stations, there to get what rest they could. They would have no rest at all after darkness came.

He met Lake at the north end of his own group's camp, where it merged with Lake's group and no guard line was needed. Lake told him that his camp would be as well prepared as possible under the circumstances within another hour. By then the wind in the trees was growing swiftly stronger, slapping harder and harder at the shelters, and it seemed doubtful that the storm would hold off for an hour.

But Lake was given his hour, plus half of another. Then deep dusk came, although it was not quite sundown. Prentiss ordered all the guard fires lighted and all the women and children into the shelters. Fifteen minutes later the storm finally broke.

It came as a roaring downpour of cold rain. Complete darkness came with it and the wind rose to a velocity that made the trees lean. An hour went by and the wind increased, smashing at the shelters with a violence they had not been built to withstand. The prowler skin lashings held but the canvas and blankets were ripped into streamers that cracked like rifle shots in the wind before they were torn completely loose and flung into the night.

One by one the guard fires went out and the rain continued, growing colder and driven in almost horizontal sheets by the wind. The women and children huddled in chilled misery in what meager protection the torn shelters still gave and there was nothing that could be done to help them.

The rain turned to snow at midnight, a howling blizzard through which Prentiss's light could penetrate but a few feet as he made his rounds. He walked with slogging weariness, forcing himself on. He was no longer young-he was fifty-and he had had little rest.

He had known, of course, that successful leadership would involve more sacrifice on his part than on the part of those he led. He could have shunned responsibility and his personal welfare would have benefited. He had lived on alien worlds almost half his life; with a rifle and a knife he could have lived, until Ragnarok finally killed him, with much less effort than that required of him as leader. But such an action had been repugnant to him, unthinkable. What he knew of survival on hostile worlds might help the others to survive.

So he had assumed command, tolerating no objections and disregarding the fact that he would be shortening his already short time to live on Ragnarok. It was, he supposed, some old instinct that forbade the individual to stand aside and let the group die.

The snow stopped an hour later and the wind died to a frigid moaning. The clouds thinned, broke apart, and the giant star looked down upon the land with its cold, blue light.

The prowlers came then.

They feinted against the east and west guard lines, then hit the south line in massed, ferocious attack. Twenty got through, past the slaughtered south guards, and charged into the interior of the camp. As they did so the call, prearranged by him in case of such an event, went up the guard lines:

"Emergency guards, east and west —*close in!*"

In the camp, above the triumphant, demoniac yammering of the prowlers, came the screams of women, the thinner cries of children, and the shouting and cursing of men as they tried to fight the prowlers with knives and clubs. Then the emergency guards-every third man from the east and west lines-came plunging through the snow, firing as they came.

The prowlers launched themselves away from their victims and toward the guards, leaving a woman to stagger aimlessly with blood spurting from a severed artery and splashing dark in the starlight on the blue-white snow. The air was filled with the cracking of gunfire and the deep, savage snarling of the prowlers. Half of the prowlers broke through, leaving seven dead guards behind them. The others lay in the snow where they had fallen and the surviving emergency guards turned to hurry back to their stations, reloading as they went.

The wounded woman had crumpled down in the snow and a first aid man knelt over her. He straightened, shaking his head, and joined the others as they searched for injured among the prowlers' victims.

They found no injured; only the dead. The prowlers killed with grim efficiency.

* * * * *

"John ——"

John Chiara, the young doctor, hurried toward him. His dark eyes were worried behind his frosted glasses and his eyebrows were coated with ice.

"The wood is soaked," he said. "It's going to be some time before we can get fires going. There are babies that will freeze to death before then."

Prentiss looked at the prowlers lying in the snow and motioned toward them. "They're warm. Have their guts and lungs taken out."

"What ——"

Then Chiara's eyes lighted with comprehension and he hurried away without further questions.

Prentiss went on, to make the rounds of the guards. When he returned he saw that his order had been obeyed.

The prowlers lay in the snow as before, their savage faces still twisted in their dying snarls, but snug and warm inside them babies slept.

* * * * *

The prowlers attacked again and again and when the wan sun lifted to shine down on the white, frozen land there were five hundred dead in Prentiss's camp: three hundred by Hell Fever and two hundred by prowler attacks.

Five hundred—and that had been only one night on Ragnarok.

Lake reported over six hundred dead. "I hope," he said with bitter hatred, "that the Gerns slept comfortably last night."

"We'll have to build a wall around the camp to hold out the prowlers," Prentiss said. "We don't dare keep using up what little ammunition we have at the rate we've used it the last two nights."

"That will be a big job in this gravity," Lake said. "We'll have to crowd both groups in together to let its circumference be as small as possible."

It was the way Prentiss had planned to do it. One thing would have to be settled with Lake: there could not be two independent leaders over the merged groups.

Lake, watching him, said, "I think we can get along. Alien worlds are your specialty rather than mine. And according to the Ragnarok law of averages, there will be only one of us pretty soon, anyway."

All were moved to the center of the camp area that day and when the prowlers came that night they found a ring of guards and fires through which they could penetrate only with heavy sacrifices.

There was warmth to the sun the next morning and the snow began to melt. Work was commenced on the stockade wall. It would have to be twelve feet high so the prowlers could not jump over it and, since the prowlers had the sharp claws and climbing ability of cats, its top would have to be surmounted with a row of sharp outward-and-downward projecting stakes. These would be set in sockets in the top rail and tied down with strips of prowler skin.

The trees east of camp were festooned for a great distance with the remnants of canvas and cloth the wind had left there. A party of boys, protected by the usual prowler guards, was sent out to climb the trees and recover it. All of it, down to the smallest fragment, was turned over to the women who were physically incapable of helping work on the stockade wall. They began patiently sewing the rags and tatters back into usable form again.

The first hunting party went out and returned with six of the tawny-yellow sharp-horned woods goats, each as large as an Earth deer. The hunters reported the woods goats to be hard to stalk and dangerous when cornered. One hunter was killed and another injured because of not knowing that.

They also brought in a few of the rabbit-sized scavenger animals. They were all legs and teeth and bristly fur, the meat almost inedible. It would be a waste of the limited ammunition to shoot any more of them.

There was a black barked tree which the Dunbar Expedition had called the lance tree because of its slender, straightly outthrust limbs. Its wood was as hard as hickory and as springy as cedar. Prentiss found two amateur archers who were sure they could make efficient bows and arrows out of the lance tree limbs. He gave them the job, together with helpers.

The days turned suddenly hot, with nights that still went below freezing. The Hell Fever took a constant, relentless toll. They needed adequate shelters-but the dwindling supply of ammunition and the nightly prowler attacks made the need for a stockade wall even more imperative. The shelters would have to wait.

He went looking for Dr. Chiara one evening and found him just leaving one of the makeshift shelters.

A boy lay inside it, his face flushed with Hell Fever and his eyes too bright and too dark as he looked up into the face of his mother who sat beside him. She was dry-eyed and silent as she looked down at him but she was holding his hand in hers, tightly, desperately, as though she might that way somehow keep him from leaving her.

Prentiss walked beside Chiara and when the shelter was behind them he asked, "There's no hope?"

"None," Chiara said. "There never is with Hell Fever."

Chiara had changed. He was no longer the stocky, cheerful man he had been on the *Constellation*, whose brown eyes had smiled at the world through thick glasses and who had laughed and joked as he assured his patients that all would soon be well with them. He was thin and his face was haggard with worry. He had, in his quiet way, been fully as valiant as any of those who had fought the prowlers. He had worked day and night to fight a form of death he could not see and against which he had no weapon.

"The boy is dying," Chiara said. "He knows it and his mother knows it. I told them the medicine I gave him might help. It was a lie, to try to make it a little easier for both of them before the end comes. The medicine I gave him was a salt tablet-that's all I have."

And then, with the first bitterness Prentiss had ever seen him display, Chiara said, "You call me 'Doctor.' Everyone does. I'm not —I'm only a first-year intern. I do the best I know how to do but it isn't enough-it will never be enough."

"What you have to learn here is something no Earth doctor knows or could teach you," he said. "You have to have time to learn-and you need equipment and drugs."

"If I could have antibiotics and other drugs ... I wanted to get a supply from the dispensary but the Gerns wouldn't let me go."

"Some of the Ragnarok plants might be of value if a person could find the right ones. I just came from a talk with Anders about that. He'll provide you with anything possible in the way of equipment and supplies for research-anything in the camp you need to try to save lives. He'll be at your shelter tonight to see what you want. Do you want to try it?"

"Yes-of course." Chiara's eyes lighted with new hope. "It might take a long time to find a cure-maybe we never would-but I'd like to have help so I could try. I'd like to be able, some day once again, to say to a scared kid, 'Take this medicine and in the morning you'll be better,' and know I told the truth."

The nightly prowler attacks continued and the supply of ammunition diminished. It would be some time before men were skilled in the use of the bows and arrows that were being made; and work on the wall was pushed ahead with all speed possible. No one was exempt from labor on it who could as much as carry the pointed stakes. Children down to the youngest worked alongside the men and women.

The work was made many times more exhausting by the 1.5 gravity. People moved heavily at their jobs and even at night there was no surcease from the gravity. They could only go into a coma-like sleep in which there was no real rest and from which they awoke tired and aching. Each morning there would be some who did not awaken at all, though their hearts had been sound enough for working on Earth or Athena.

The killing labor was recognized as necessary, however, and there were no complaints until the morning he was accosted by Peter Bemmon.

He had seen Bemmon several times on the *Constellation*; a big, soft-faced man who had attached much importance to his role as a minor member of the Athena Planning Board. But even on the *Constellation* Bemmon had felt he merited a still higher position, and his ingratiating attitude when before his superiors had become one of fault-finding insinuations concerning their ability as compared with his when their backs were turned.

This resentment had taken new form on Ragnarok, where his former position was of utterly no importance to anyone and his lack of any skills or outdoor experience made him only one worker among others.

The sun was shining mercilessly hot the day Bemmon chose to challenge Prentiss's wisdom as leader. Bemmon was cutting and sharpening stakes, a job the sometimes-too-lenient Anders had given him when Bemmon had insisted his heart was on the verge of failure from doing heavier work. Prentiss was in a hurry and would have gone on past him but Bemmon halted him with a sharp command:

"You-wait a minute!"

Bemmon had a hatchet in his hand, but only one stake lay on the ground; and his face was red with anger, not exertion. Prentiss stopped, wondering if Bemmon was going to ask for a broken jaw, and Bemmon came to him.

"How long," Bemmon asked, anger making his voice a little thick, "do you think I'll tolerate this absurd situation?"

"What situation?" Prentiss asked.

"This stupid insistence upon confining me to manual labor. I'm the single member on Ragnarok of the Athena Planning Board and surely you can see that this bumbling confusion of these people"—Bemmon indicated the hurrying, laboring men, women and children around them—"can be transformed into efficient, organized effort only through proper supervision. Yet my abilities along such lines are ignored and I've been forced to work as a common laborer—a wood chopper!"

He flung the hatchet down viciously, into the rocks at his feet, breathing heavily with resentment and challenge. "I demand the respect to which I'm entitled."

"Look," Prentiss said.

He pointed to the group just then going past them. A sixteen-year-old girl was bent almost double under the weight of the pole she was carrying, her once pretty face flushed and sweating. Behind her two twelve-year-old boys were dragging a still larger pole. Behind them came several small children, each of them carrying as many of the pointed stakes as he or she could walk under, no matter if it was only one. All of them were trying to hurry, to accomplish as much as possible, and no one was complaining even though they were already staggering with weariness.

"So you think you're entitled to more respect?" Prentiss asked. "Those kids would work harder if you were giving them orders from under the shade of a tree-is that what you want?"

Bemmon's lips thinned and hatred was like a sheen on his face. Prentiss looked from the single stake Bemmon had cut that morning to Bemmon's white, unblistered hands. He looked at the hatchet that Bemmon had thrown down in the rocks and at the V notch broken in its keen-edged blade. It had been the best of the very few hatchets they had....

"The next time you even nick that hatchet I'm going to split your skull with it," he said. "Pick it up and get back to work. I mean *work*. You'll have broken blisters on every finger tonight or you'll go on the log-carrying force tomorrow. Now, move!"

What Bemmon had thought to be his wrath deserted him before Prentiss's fury. He stooped to obey the order but the hatred remained on his face and when the hatchet was in his hands he made a last attempt to bluster:

"The day may come when we'll refuse to tolerate any longer your sadistic displays of authority."

"Good," Prentiss said. "Anyone who doesn't like my style is welcome to try to change it-or to try to replace me. With knives or clubs, rifles or broken hatchets, Bemmon-any way you want it and any time you want it."

"I——" Bemmon's eyes went from the hatchet in his half raised hand to the long knife in Prentiss's belt. He swallowed with a convulsive jerk of his Adam's apple and his hatchet-bearing arm suddenly wilted. "I don't want to fight-to replace you——"

He swallowed again and his face forced itself into a sickly attempt at an ingratiating smile. "I didn't mean to imply any disrespect for you or the good job you're doing. I'm very sorry."

Then he hurried away, like a man glad to escape, and began to chop stakes with amazing speed.

But the sullen hatred had not been concealed by the ingratiating smile; and Prentiss knew Bemmon was a man who would always be his enemy.

* * * * *

The days dragged by in the weary routine, but overworked muscles slowly strengthened and people moved with a little less laborious effort. On the twentieth day the wall was finally completed and the camp was prowler proof.

But the spring weather was a mad succession of heat and cold and storm that caused the Hell Fever to take its toll each day and there was no relaxation from the grueling labor. Weatherproof shelters had to be built as rapidly as possible.

So the work of constructing them began; wearily, sometimes almost hopelessly, but without complaint other than to hate and curse the Gerns more than ever.

There was no more trouble from Bemmon; Prentiss had almost forgotten him when he was publicly challenged one night by a burly, threatening man named Haggar.

"You've bragged that you'll fight any man who dares disagree with you," Haggar said loudly. "Well, here I am. We'll use knives and before they even have time to bury you tonight I'm goin' to have your stooges kicked out and replaced with men who'll give us competent leadership instead of blunderin' authoritarianism."

Prentiss noticed that Haggar seemed to have a little difficulty pronouncing the last word, as though he had learned it only recently.

"I'll be glad to accommodate you," Prentiss said mildly. "Go get yourself a knife."

Haggar already had one, a long-bladed butcher knife, and the duel began. Haggar was surprisingly adept with his knife but he had never had the training and experience in combat that interstellar explorers such as Prentiss had. Haggar was good, but considerably far from good enough.

Prentiss did not kill him. He had no compunctions about doing such a thing, but it would have been an unnecessary waste of needed manpower. He gave Haggar a carefully painful and bloody lesson that thoroughly banished all his lust for conflict without seriously injuring him. The duel was over within a minute after it began.

Bemmon, who had witnessed the challenge with keen interest and then watched Haggar's defeat with agitation, became excessively friendly and flattering toward Prentiss afterward. Prentiss felt sure, although he had no proof, that it had been Bemmon who had spurred the simple-minded Haggar into challenging him to a duel.

If so, the sight of what had happened to Haggar must have effectively dampened Bemmon's desire for revenge because he became almost a model worker.

* * * * *

As Lake had predicted, he and Prentiss worked together well. Lake calmly took a secondary role, not at all interested in possession of authority but only in the survival of the Rejects. He spoke of the surrender of the *Constellation* only once, to say:

"I knew there could be only Ragnarok in this section of space. I had to order four thousand people to go like sheep to what was to be their place of execution so that four thousand more could live as slaves. That was my last act as an officer."

Prentiss suspected that Lake found it impossible not to blame himself subconsciously for what circumstances had forced him to do. It was irrational-but conscientious men were quite often a little irrational in their sense of responsibility.

Lake had two subleaders: a genial, red-haired man named Ben Barber, who would have been a farmer on Athena but who made a good subleader on Ragnarok; and a lithe, cat-like man named Karl Schroeder.

Schroeder claimed to be twenty-four but not even the scars on his face could make him look more than twenty-one. He smiled often, a little too often. Prentiss had seen smiles like that before. Schroeder was the type who could smile while he killed a man-and he probably had.

40

But, if Schroeder was a born fighter and perhaps killer, they were characteristics that he expended entirely upon the prowlers. He was Lake's right hand man; a deadly marksman and utterly without fear.

One evening, when Lake had given Schroeder some instructions concerning the next day's activities, Schroeder answered him with the half-mocking smile and the words, "I'll see that it's done, Commander."

"Not 'Commander,'" Lake said. "I —all of us-left our ranks, titles and honors on the *Constellation*. The past is dead for us."

"I see," Schroeder said. The smile faded away and he looked into Lake's eyes as he asked, "And what about our past dishonors, disgraces and such?"

"They were left on the *Constellation*, too," Lake said. "If anyone wants dishonor he'll have to earn it all over again."

"That sounds fair," Schroeder said. "That sounds as fair as anyone could ever ask for."

He turned away and Prentiss saw what he had noticed before: Schroeder's black hair was coming out light brown at the roots. It was a color that would better match his light complexion and it was the color of hair that a man named Schrader, wanted by the police on Venus, had had.

Hair could be dyed, identification cards could be forged-but it was all something Prentiss did not care to pry into until and if Schroeder gave him reason to. Schroeder was a hard and dangerous man, despite his youth, and sometimes men of that type, when the chips were down, exhibited a higher sense of duty than the soft men who spoke piously of respect for Society-and then were afraid to face danger to protect the society and the people they claimed to respect.

* * * * *

A lone prowler came on the eleventh night following the wall's completion. It came silently, in the dead of night, and it learned how to reach in and tear apart the leather lashings that held the pointed stakes in place and then jerk the stakes out of their sockets. It was seen as it was removing the third stake-which would have made a large enough opening for it to come through-and shot. It fell back and managed to escape into the woods, although staggering and bleeding.

The next night the stockade was attacked by dozens of prowlers who simultaneously began removing the pointed stakes in the same manner employed by the prowler of the night before. Their attack was turned back with heavy losses on both sides and with a dismayingly large expenditure of precious ammunition.

There could be no doubt about how the band of prowlers had learned to remove the stakes: the prowler of the night before had told them before it died. It was doubtful that the prowlers had a spoken language, but they had some means of communication. They worked together and they were highly intelligent, probably about halfway between dog and man.

The prowlers were going to be an enemy even more formidable than Prentiss had thought.

The missing stakes were replaced the next day and the others were tied down more securely. Once again the camp was prowler proof-but only for so long as armed guards patrolled inside the walls to kill attacking prowlers during the short time it would take them to remove the stakes.

The hunting parties suffered unusually heavy losses from prowler attacks that day and that evening, as the guards patrolled inside the walls, Lake said to Prentiss:

"The prowlers are so damnably persistent. It isn't that they're hungry-they don't kill us to eat us. They don't have any reason to kill us-they just hate us."

"They have a reason," Prentiss said. "They're doing the same thing we're doing: fighting for survival."

Lake's pale brows lifted in question.

"The prowlers are the rulers of Ragnarok," Prentiss said. "They fought their way up here, as men did on Earth, until they're master of every creature on their world. Even of the unicorns and swamp crawlers. But now we've come and they're intelligent enough to know that we're accustomed to being the dominant species, ourselves.

"There can't be two dominant species on the same world-and they know it. Men or prowlers-in the end one is going to have to go down before the other."

"I suppose you're right," Lake said. He looked at the guards, a fourth of them already reduced to bows and arrows that they had not yet had time to learn how to use. "If we win the battle for supremacy it will be a long fight, maybe over a period of centuries. And if the prowlers win-it may all be over within a year or two."

* * * * *

The giant blue star that was the other component of Ragnarok's binary grew swiftly in size as it preceded the yellow sun farther each morning. When summer came the blue star would be a sun as hot as the yellow sun and Ragnarok would be between them. The yellow sun would burn the land by day and the blue sun would sear it by the night that would not be night. Then would come the brief fall, followed by the long, frozen winter when the yellow sun would shine pale and cold, far to the south, and the blue sun would be a star again, two hundred and fifty million miles away and invisible behind the cold yellow sun.

The Hell Fever lessened with the completion of the shelters but it still killed each day. Chiara and his helpers worked with unfaltering determination to find a cure for it but the cure, if there was one, eluded them. The graves in the cemetery were forty long by forty wide and more were added each day. To all the fact became grimly obvious: they were swiftly dying out and they had yet to face Ragnarok at its worst.

The old survival instincts asserted themselves and there were marriages among the younger ones. One of the first to marry was Julia.

She stopped to talk to Prentiss one evening. She still wore the red skirt, now faded and patched, but her face was tired and thoughtful and no longer bold.

"Is it true, John," she asked, "that only a few of us might be able to have children here and that most of us who tried to have children in this gravity would die for it?"

"It's true," he said. "But you already knew that when you married."

"Yes ...I knew it." There was a little silence. "All my life I've had fun and done as I pleased. The human race didn't need me and we both knew it. But now-none of us can be apart from the others or be afraid of anything. If we're selfish and afraid there will come a time when the last of us will die and there will be nothing on Ragnarok to show we were ever here.

"I don't want it to end like that. I want there to be children, to live after we're gone. So I'm going to try to have a child. I'm not afraid and I won't be."

When he did not reply at once she said, almost self-consciously, "Coming from me that all sounds a little silly, I suppose."

"It sounds wise and splendid, Julia," he said, "and it's what I thought you were going to say."

* * * * *

Full spring came and the vegetation burst into leaf and bud and bloom, quickly, for its growth instincts knew in their mindless way how short was the time to grow and reproduce before the brown death of summer came. The prowlers were suddenly gone one day, to follow the spring north, and for a week men could walk and work outside the stockade without the protection of armed guards.

Then the new peril appeared, the one they had not expected: the unicorns.

The stockade wall was a blue-black rectangle behind them and the blue star burned with the brilliance of a dozen moons, lighting the woods in blue shadow and azure light. Prentiss and the hunter walked a little in front of the two riflemen, winding to keep in the starlit glades.

"It was on the other side of the next grove of trees," the hunter said in a low voice. "Fred was getting ready to bring in the rest of the woods goat. He shouldn't have been more than ten minutes behind me-and it's been over an hour."

42

They rounded the grove of trees. At first it seemed there was nothing before them but the empty, grassy glade. Then they saw it lying on the ground no more than twenty feet in front of them.

It was-it had been—a man. He was broken and stamped into hideous shapelessness and something had torn off his arms.

For a moment there was dead silence, then the hunter whispered, *What did that?*

The answer came in a savage, squealing scream and the pound of cloven hooves. A formless shadow beside the trees materialized into a monstrous charging bulk; a thing like a gigantic gray bull, eight feet tall at the shoulders, with the tusked, snarling head of a boar and the starlight glinting along the curving, vicious length of its single horn.

"Unicorn!" Prentiss said, and jerked up his rifle.

The rifles cracked in a ragged volley. The unicorn squealed in fury and struck the hunter, catching him on its horn and hurling him thirty feet. One of the riflemen went down under the unicorn's hooves, his cry ending almost as soon as it began.

The unicorn ripped the sod in deep furrows as it whirled back to Prentiss and the remaining rifleman; not turning in the manner of four-footed beasts of Earth but rearing and spinning on its hind feet. It towered above them as it whirled, the tip of its horn fifteen feet above the ground and its hooves swinging around like great clubs.

Prentiss shot again, his sights on what he hoped would be a vital area, and the rifleman shot an instant later.

The shots went true. The unicorn's swing brought it on around but it collapsed, falling to the ground with jarring heaviness.

"We got it!" the rifleman said. "We — —"

It half scrambled to its feet and made a noise; a call that went out through the night like the blast of a mighty trumpet. Then it dropped back to the ground, to die while its call was still echoing from the nearer hills.

From the east came an answering trumpet blast; a trumpeting that was sounded again from the south and from the north. Then there came a low and muffled drumming, like the pounding of thousands of hooves.

The rifleman's face was blue-white in the starlight. "The others are coming-we'll have to run for it!"

He turned, and began to run toward the distant bulk of the stockade.

"No!" Prentiss commanded, quick and harsh. "Not the stockade!"

The rifleman kept running, seeming not to hear him in his panic. Prentiss called to him once more:

"Not the stockade —*you'll lead the unicorns into it!*"

Again the rifleman seemed not to hear him.

The unicorns were coming in sight, converging in from the north and east and south, the rumble of their hooves swelling to a thunder that filled the night. The rifleman would reach the stockade only a little ahead of them and they would go through the wall as though it had been made of paper.

For a little while the area inside the stockade would be filled with dust, with the squealing of the swirling, charging unicorns and the screams of the dying. Those inside the stockade would have no chance whatever of escaping. Within two minutes it would be over, the last child would have been found among the shattered shelters and trampled into lifeless shapelessness in the bloody ground.

Within two minutes all human life on Ragnarok would be gone.

There was only one thing for him to do.

He dropped to one knee so his aim would be steady and the sights of his rifle caught the running man's back. He pressed the trigger and the rifle cracked viciously as it bucked against his shoulder.

The man spun and fell hard to the ground. He twisted, to raise himself up a little and look back, his face white and accusing and unbelieving.

"You shot me!"

Then he fell forward and lay without moving.

Prentiss turned back to face the unicorns and to look at the trees in the nearby grove. He saw what he already knew, they were young trees and too small to offer any escape for him. There was no place to run, no place to hide.

There was nothing he could do but wait; nothing he could do but stand in the blue starlight and watch the devil's herd pound toward him and think, in the last moments of his life, how swiftly and unexpectedly death could come to man on Ragnarok.

* * * * *

The unicorns held the Rejects prisoners in their stockade the rest of the night and all the next day. Lake had seen the shooting of the rifleman and had watched the unicorn herd kill John Prentiss and then trample the dead rifleman.

He had already given the order to build a quick series of fires around the inside of the stockade walls when the unicorns paused to tear their victims to pieces; grunting and squealing in triumph as bones crushed between their teeth and they flung the pieces to one side.

The fires were started and green wood was thrown on them, to make them smoulder and smoke for as long as possible. Then the unicorns were coming on to the stockade and every person inside it went into the concealment of the shelters.

Lake had already given his last order: There would be absolute quiet until and if the unicorns left; a quiet that would be enforced with fist or club wherever necessary.

The unicorns were still outside when morning came. The fires could not be refueled; the sight of a man moving inside the stockade would bring the entire herd charging through. The hours dragged by, the smoke from the dying fires dwindled to thin streamers. The unicorns grew increasingly bolder and suspicious, crowding closer to the walls and peering through the openings between the rails.

The sun was setting when one of the unicorns trumpeted; a sound different from that of the call to battle. The others threw up their heads to listen, then they turned and drifted away. Within minutes the entire herd was gone out of sight through the woods, toward the north.

Lake waited and watched until he was sure the unicorns were gone for good. Then he ordered the All Clear given and hurried to the south wall, to look down across the barren valley and hope he would not see what he expected to see.

Barber came up behind him, to sigh with relief. "That was close. It's hard to make so many people stay absolutely quiet for hour after hour. Especially the children-they don't understand."

"We'll have to leave," Lake said.

"Leave?" Barber asked. "We can make this stockade strong enough to hold out unicorns."

"Look to the south," Lake told him.

Barber did so and saw what Lake had already seen; a broad, low cloud of dust moving slowly toward them.

"Another herd of unicorns," Lake said. "John didn't know they migrated-the Dunbar Expedition wasn't here long enough to learn that. There'll be herd after herd coming through and no time for us to strengthen the walls. We'll have to leave tonight."

* * * * *

Preparations were made for the departure; preparations that consisted mainly of providing each person with as much in the way of food or supplies as he or she could carry. In the 1.5 gravity, that was not much.

They left when the blue star rose. They filed out through the northern gate and the rear guard closed it behind them. There was almost no conversation among them. Some of them turned to take a last look at what had been the only home they had ever known on Ragnarok, then they all faced forward again, to the northwest, where the foothills of the plateau might offer them sanctuary.

They found their sanctuary on the second day; a limestone ridge honey-combed with caves. Men were sent back at once to carry the food and supplies left in the stockade to the new home.

They returned, to report that the second herd of unicorns had broken down the walls and ripped the interior of the stockade into wreckage. Much of the food and supplies had been totally destroyed.

Lake sent them back twice more to bring everything, down to the last piece of bent metal or torn cloth. They would find uses for all of it in the future.

* * * * *

The cave system was extensive, containing room for several times their number. The deeper portions of the caves could not be lived in until ventilation ducts were made, but the outer caves were more than sufficient in number. Work was begun to clear them of fallen rubble, to pry down all loose material overhead and to level the floors. A spring came out of the ridge not far from the caves and the approach to the caves was so narrow and steep that unicorns could scramble up it only with difficulty and one at a time. And should they ever reach the natural terrace in front of the caves they would be too large to enter and could do no more than stand outside and make targets of themselves for the bowmen within.

Anders was in charge of making the caves livable, his working force restricted almost entirely to women and children. Lake sent Barber out, with a small detachment of men, to observe the woods goats and learn what plants they ate. And then learn, by experimenting, if such plants could be safely eaten by humans.

The need for salt would be tremendously increased when summer came. Having once experienced a saltless two weeks in the desert Lake doubted that any of them could survive without it. All hunting parties, as well as Barber's party, were ordered to investigate all deposits that might contain salt as well as any stream or pond that was white along the banks.

The hunting parties were of paramount importance and they were kept out to the limits of their endurance. Every man physically able to do so accompanied them. Those who could not kill game could carry it back to the caves. There was no time to spare; already the unicorns were decreasing in numbers and the woods goats were ranging farther and farther north.

At the end of twenty days Lake went in search of Barber and his party, worried about them. Their mission was one that could be as dangerous as any hunting trip. There was no proof that humans and Ragnarok creatures were so similar as to guarantee that food for one might not be poison for the other. It was a very necessary mission, however; dried meat, alone, would bring grave deficiency diseases during the summer which dried herbs and fruits would help prevent.

When he located Barber's party he found Barber lying under a tree, pale and weak from his latest experiment but recovering.

"I was the guinea pig yesterday," Barber said. "Some little purple berries that the woods goats nibble at sometimes, maybe to get a touch of some certain vitamin or something. I ate too many, I guess, because they hit my heart like the kick of a mule."

"Did you find anything at all encouraging?" Lake asked.

"We found four different herbs that are the most violent cathartics you ever dreamed of. And a little silvery fern that tastes like vanilla flavored candy and paralyzes you stiff as a board on the third swallow. It's an hour before you come back out of it.

"But on the good side we found three different kinds of herbs that seem to be all right. We've been digging them up and hanging them in the trees to dry."

Lake tried the edible herbs and found them to be something like spinach in taste. There was a chance they might contain the vitamins and minerals needed. Since the hunting parties were living exclusively on meat he would have to point out the edible herbs to all of them so they would know what to eat should any of them feel the effects of diet deficiency.

He traveled alone as he visited the various hunting parties, finding such travel to be safer each day as the dwindling of the unicorns neared the vanishing point. It was a safety he did not welcome; it meant the last of the game would be gone north long before sufficient meat was taken.

None of the hunting parties could report good luck. The woods goats, swift and elusive at best, were vanishing with the unicorns. The last cartridge had been fired and the bowmen, while improving all the time, were far from expert. The unicorns, which should have been their major source of meat, were invulnerable to arrows unless shot at short range in the side of the neck just behind the head. And at short range the unicorns invariably charged and presented no such target.

He made the long, hard climb up the plateau's southern face, to stand at last on top. It was treeless, a flat, green table that stretched to the north for as far as he could see. A mountain range, still capped with snow, lay perhaps a hundred miles to the northwest; in the distance it looked like a white, low-lying cloud on the horizon. No other mountains or hills marred the endless sweep of the high plain.

The grass was thick and here and there were little streams of water produced by the recently melted snow. It was a paradise land for the herbivores of Ragnarok but for men it was a harsh, forbidding place. At that elevation the air was so thin that only a moderate amount of exertion made the heart and lungs labor painfully. Hard and prolonged exertion would be impossible.

It seemed unlikely that men could hunt and dare unicorn attacks at such an elevation but two hunting parties were ahead of him; one under the grim Craig and one under the reckless Schroeder, both parties stripped down to the youngest, strongest men among all the Rejects.

He found Schroeder early one morning, leading his hunters toward a small band of woods goats. Two unicorns were grazing in between and the hunters were swinging downwind from them. Schroeder saw him coming and walked back a little way to meet him.

"Welcome to our breathtaking land," Schroeder greeted him. "How are things going with the rest of the hunting parties?"

Schroeder was gaunt and there was weariness beneath his still lithe movements. His whiskers were an untamed sorrel bristling and across his cheekbone was the ugly scar of a half healed wound. Another gash was ripped in his arm and something had battered one ear. He reminded Lake of a battle-scarred, indomitable tomcat who would never, for as long as he lived, want to relinquish the joy of conflict and danger.

"So far," he answered, "you and Craig are the only parties to manage to tackle the plateau."

He asked about Schroeder's luck and learned it had been much better than that of the others due to killing three unicorns by a method Schroeder had thought of.

"Since the bowmen have to be to one side of the unicorns to kill them," Schroeder said, "it only calls for a man to be the decoy and let the unicorns chase him between the hidden bowmen. If there's no more than one or two unicorns and if the decoy doesn't have to run very far and if the bowmen don't miss it works well."

"Judging from your beat-up condition," Lake said, "you must have been the decoy every time."

"Well — —" Schroeder shrugged his shoulders. "It was my idea."

"I've been wondering about another way to get in shots at close range," Lake said. "Take the skin of a woods goat, give it the original shape as near as possible, and a bowman inside it might be able to fake a grazing woods goat until he got the shot he wanted.

"The unicorns might never suspect where the arrows came from," he concluded. "And then, of course, they might."

"I'll try it before the day is over, on those two unicorns over there," Schroeder said. "At this elevation and in this gravity my own method is just a little bit rough on a man."

* * * * *

Lake found Craig and his men several miles to the west, all of them gaunt and bearded as Schroeder had been.

"We've had hell," Craig said. "It seems that every time we spot a few woods goats there will be a dozen unicorns in between. If only we had rifles for the unicorns...."

Lake told him of the plan to hide under woods goats' skins and of the decoy system used by Schroeder.

"Maybe we won't have to use Schroeder's method," he said. "We'll see if the other works —I'll give it the first try."

This he was not to do. Less than an hour later one of the men who helped dry the meat and carry it to the caves returned to report the camp stricken by a strange, sudden malady that was killing a hundred a day. Dr. Chiara, who had collapsed while driving himself on to care for the sick, was sure it was a deficiency disease. Anders was down with it, helpless, and Bemmon had assumed command; setting up daily work quotas for those still on their feet and refusing to heed Chiara's requests concerning treatment of the disease.

Lake made the trip back to the caves in a fraction of the length of time it had taken him to reach the plateau, walking until he was ready to drop and then pausing only for an hour or two of rest. He spotted Barber's camp when coming down off the plateau and he swung to one side, to tell Barber to have a supply of the herbs sent to the caves at once.

He reached the caves, to find half the camp in bed and the other half dragging about listlessly at the tasks given them by Bemmon. Anders was in grave condition, too weak to rise, and Dr. Chiara was dying.

He squatted down beside Chiara's pallet and knew there could be no hope for him. On Chiara's pale face and in his eyes was the shadow of his own foreknowledge.

"I finally saw what it was" —Chiara's words were very low, hard to hear —"and I told Bemmon what to do. It's a deficiency disease, complicated by the gravity into some form not known on Earth."

He stopped to rest and Lake waited.

"Beri-beri —pellagra-we had deficiency diseases on Earth. But none so fatal-so quickly. I told Bemmon-ration out fruits and vegetables to everybody. Hurry-or it will be too late."

Again he stopped to rest, the last vestige of color gone from his face.

"And you?" Lake asked, already knowing the answer.

"For me-too late. I kept thinking of viruses-should have seen the obvious sooner. Just like — —"

His lips turned up a little at the corners and the Chiara of the dead past smiled for the last time at Lake.

"Just like a damned fool intern...."

That was all, then, and the chamber was suddenly very quiet. Lake stood up to leave, and to speak the words that Chiara could never hear:

"We're going to need you and miss you-Doctor."

* * * * *

He found Bemmon in the food storage cavern, supervising the work of two teen-age boys with critical officiousness although he was making no move to help them. At sight of Lake he hurried forward, the ingratiating smile sliding across his face.

"I'm glad you're back," he said. "I had to take charge when Anders got sick and he had everything in such a mess. I've been working day and night to undo his mistakes and get the work properly under way again."

Lake looked at the two thin-faced boys who had taken advantage of the opportunity to rest. They leaned wearily against the heavy pole table Bemmon had had them moving, their eyes already dull with the incipient sickness and watching him in mute appeal.

"Have you obeyed Chiara's order?" he asked.

"Ah-no," Bemmon said. "I felt it best to ignore it."

"Why?" Lake asked.

"It would be a senseless waste of our small supply of fruit and vegetable foods to give them to people already dying. I'm afraid" —the ingratiating smile came again —"we've been letting him exercise an authority he isn't entitled to. He's really hardly more than a medical student and his diagnoses are only guesses."

"He's dead," Lake said flatly. "His last order will be carried out."

He looked from the two tired boys to Bemmon, contrasting their thinness and weariness with the way Bemmon's paunch still bulged outward and his jowls still sagged with their load of fat.

"I'll send West down to take over in here," he said to Bemmon. "You come with me. You and I seem to be the only two in good health here and there's plenty of work for us to do."

The fawning expression vanished from Bemmon's face. "I see," he said. "Now that I've turned Anders's muddle into organization, you'll hand my authority over to another of your favorites and demote me back to common labor?"

"Setting up work quotas for sick and dying people isn't organization," Lake said. He spoke to the two boys, "Both of you go lie down. West will find someone else." Then to Bemmon, "Come with me. We're both going to work at common labor."

They passed by the cave where Bemmon slept. Two boys were just going into it, carrying armloads of dried grass to make a mattress under Bemmon's pallet. They moved slowly, heavily. Like the two boys in the food storage cave they were dull-eyed with the beginning of the sickness.

Lake stopped, to look more closely into the cave and verify something else he thought he had seen: Bemmon had discarded the prowler skins on his bed and in their place were soft wool blankets; perhaps the only unpatched blankets the Rejects possessed.

"Go back to your caves," he said to the boys. "Go to bed and rest."

He looked at Bemmon. Bemmon's eyes flickered away, refusing to meet his.

"What few blankets we have are for babies and the very youngest children," he said. His tone was coldly unemotional but he could not keep his fists from clenching at his sides. "You will return them at once and sleep on animal skins, as all the men and women do. And if you want grass for a mattress you will carry it yourself, as even the young children do."

Bemmon made no answer, his face a sullen red and hatred shining in the eyes that still refused to meet Lake's.

"Gather up the blankets and return them," Lake said. "Then come on up to the central cave. We have a lot of work to do."

He could feel Bemmon's gaze burning against his back as he turned away and he thought of what John Prentiss had once said:

"I know he's no good but he never has guts enough to go quite far enough to give me an excuse to whittle him down."

* * * * *

Barber's men arrived the next day, burdened with dried herbs. These were given to the seriously ill as a supplement to the ration of fruit and vegetable foods and were given, alone, to those not yet sick. Then came the period of waiting; of hoping that it was all not too late and too little.

A noticeable change for the better began on the second day. A week went by and the sick were slowly, steadily, improving. The not-quite-sick were already back to normal health. There was no longer any doubt: the Ragnarok herbs would prevent a recurrence of the disease.

It was, Lake thought, all so simple once you knew what to do. Hundreds had died, Chiara among them, because they did not have a common herb that grew at a slightly higher elevation. Not a single life would have been lost if he could have looked a week into the future and had the herbs found and taken to the caves that much sooner.

But the disease had given no warning of its coming. Nothing, on Ragnarok, ever seemed to give warning before it killed.

Another week went by and hunters began to trickle in, gaunt and exhausted, to report all the game going north up the plateau and not a single creature left below. They were the ones who had tried and failed to withstand the high elevation of the plateau. Only two out of three hunters returned among those who had challenged the plateau. They had tried, all of them, to the best of their ability and the limits of their endurance.

The blue star was by then a small sun and the yellow sun blazed hotter each day. Grass began to brown and wither on the hillsides as the days went by and Lake knew summer was very near. The last hunting party, but for Craig's and Schroeder's, returned. They had very little meat but they brought with them a large quantity of something almost as important: salt.

They had found a deposit of it in an almost inaccessible region of cliffs and canyons. "Not even the woods goats can get in there," Stevens, the leader of that party, said. "If the salt was in an accessible place there would have been a salt lick there and goats in plenty."

"If woods goats care for salt the way Earth animals do," Lake said. "When fall comes we'll make a salt lick and find out."

Two more weeks went by and Craig and Schroeder returned with their surviving hunters. They had followed the game to the eastern end of the snow-capped mountain range but there the migration had drawn away from them, traveling farther each day than they could travel. They had almost waited too long before turning back: the grass at the southern end of the plateau was turning brown and the streams were dry. They got enough water, barely, by digging seep holes in the dry stream beds.

Lake's method of stalking unicorns under the concealment of a woods goat skin had worked well only a few times. After that the unicorns learned to swing downwind from any lone woods goats. If they smelled a man inside the goat skin they charged him and killed him.

With the return of the last hunters everything was done that could be done in preparation for summer. Inventory was taken of the total food supply and it was even smaller than Lake had feared. It would be far from enough to last until fall brought the game back from the north and he instituted rationing much stricter than before.

The heat increased as the yellow sun blazed hotter and the blue sun grew larger. Each day the vegetation was browner and a morning came when Lake could see no green wherever he looked.

They numbered eleven hundred and ten that morning, out of what had so recently been four thousand. Eleven hundred and ten thin, hungry scarecrows who, already, could do nothing more than sit listlessly in the shade and wait for the hell that was coming. He thought of the food supply, so pitifully small, and of the months it would have to last. He saw the grim, inescapable future for his charges: famine. There was nothing he could do to prevent it. He could only try to forestall complete starvation for all by cutting rations to the bare existence level.

And that would be bare existence for the stronger of them. The weaker were already doomed.

He had them all gather in front of the caves that evening when the terrace was in the shadow of the ridge. He stood before them and spoke to them:

"All of you know we have only a fraction of the amount of food we need to see us through the summer. Tomorrow the present ration will be cut in half. That will be enough to live on, just barely. If that cut isn't made the food supply will be gone long before fall and all of us will die.

"If anyone has any food of any kind it must be turned in to be added to the total supply. Some of you may have thought of your children and kept a little hidden for them. I can understand why you should do that-but you must turn it in. There may possibly be some who hid food for themselves, personally. If so, I give them the first and last warning: turn it in tonight. If any hidden cache of food is found in the future the one who hid it will be regarded as a traitor and murderer.

"All of you, but for the children, will go into the chamber next to the one where the food is stored. Each of you-and there will be no exceptions regardless of how innocent you are-will carry a bulkily folded cloth or garment. Each of you will go into the chamber alone. There will be no one in there. You will leave the food you have folded in the cloth, if any, and go out the other exit and back to your caves. No one will ever know whether the cloth you carried contained food or not. No one will ever ask.

"Our survival on this world, if we are to survive at all, can be only by working and sacrificing together. There can be no selfishness. What any of you may have done in the past is of no consequence. Tonight we start anew. From now on we trust one another without reserve.

"There will be one punishment for any who betray that trust-death."

* * * * *

Anders set the example by being the first to carry a folded cloth into the cave. Of them all, Lake heard later, only Bemmon voiced any real indignation; warning all those in his section of the line that the order was the first step toward outright dictatorship and a police-and-spy system in which Lake and the other leaders would deprive them all of freedom and dignity. Bemmon insisted upon exhibiting the emptiness of the cloth he carried; an action that, had he succeeded in persuading the others to follow his example, would have mercilessly exposed those who did have food they were returning.

But no one followed Bemmon's example and no harm was done. As for Lake, he had worries on his mind of much greater importance than Bemmon's enmity.

* * * * *

The weeks dragged by, each longer and more terrible to endure than the one before it as the heat steadily increased. Summer solstice arrived and there was no escape from the heat, even in the deepest caves. There was no night; the blue sun rose in the east as the yellow sun set in the west. There was no life of any kind to be seen, not even an insect. Nothing moved across the burned land but the swirling dust devils and shimmering, distorted mirages.

The death rate increased with appalling swiftness. The small supply of canned and dehydrated milk, fruit and vegetables was reserved exclusively for the children but it was far insufficient in quantity. The Ragnarok herbs prevented any recurrence of the fatal deficiency disease but they provided virtually no nourishment to help fight the heat and gravity. The stronger of the children lay wasted and listless on their pallets while the ones not so strong died each day.

Each day thin and hollow-eyed mothers would come to plead with him to save their children. "...it would take so little to save his life....Please-before it's too late...."

But there was so little food left and the time was yet so long until fall would bring relief from the famine that he could only answer each of them with a grim and final "No."

And watch the last hope flicker and die in their eyes and watch them turn away, to go and sit for the last hours beside their children.

Bemmon became increasingly irritable and complaining as the rationing and heat made existence a misery; insisting that Lake and the others were to blame for the food shortage, that their hunting efforts had been bungling and faint-hearted. And he implied, without actually saying so, that Lake and the others had forbidden him to go near the food chamber because they did not want a competent, honest man to check up on what they were doing.

There were six hundred and three of them the blazing afternoon when the girl, Julia, could stand his constant, vindictive, fault-finding no longer. Lake heard about it shortly afterward, the way she had turned on Bemmon in a flare of temper she could control no longer and said:

"Whenever your mouth is still you can hear the children who are dying today-but you don't care. All you can think of is yourself. You claim Lake and the others were cowards-but you didn't dare hunt with them. You keep insinuating that they're cheating us and eating more than we are-but your belly is the only one that has any fat left on it ———"

She never completed the sentence. Bemmon's face turned livid in sudden, wild fury and he struck her, knocking her against the rock wall so hard that she slumped unconscious to the ground.

"She's a liar!" he panted, glaring at the others. "She's a rotten liar and anybody who repeats what she said will get what she got!"

50

When Lake learned of what had happened he did not send for Bemmon at once. He wondered why Bemmon's reaction had been so quick and violent and there seemed to be only one answer:

Bemmon's belly was still a little fat. There could be but one way he could have kept it so.

He summoned Craig, Schroeder, Barber and Anders. They went to the chamber where Bemmon slept and there, almost at once, they found his cache. He had it buried under his pallet and hidden in cavities along the walls; dried meat, dried fruits and milk, canned vegetables. It was an amount amazingly large and many of the items had presumably been exhausted during the deficiency disease attack.

"It looks," Schroeder said, "like he didn't waste any time feathering his nest when he made himself leader."

The others said nothing but stood with grim, frozen faces, waiting for Lake's next action.

"Bring Bemmon," Lake said to Craig.

Craig returned with him two minutes later. Bemmon stiffened at the sight of his unearthed cache and color drained away from his face.

"Well?" Lake asked.

"I didn't" —Bemmon swallowed —"I didn't know it was there." And then quickly, "You can't prove I put it there. You can't prove you didn't just now bring it in yourselves to frame me."

Lake stared at Bemmon, waiting. The others watched Bemmon as Lake was doing and no one spoke. The silence deepened and Bemmon began to sweat as he tried to avoid their eyes. He looked again at the damning evidence and his defiance broke.

"It-if I hadn't taken it it would have been wasted on people who were dying," he said. He wiped at his sweating face. "I won't ever do it again —I swear I won't."

Lake spoke to Craig. "You and Barber take him to the lookout point."

"What — —" Bemmon's protest was cut off as Craig and Barber took him by the arms and walked him swiftly away.

Lake turned to Anders. "Get a rope," he ordered.

Anders paled a little. "A —rope?"

"What else does he deserve?"

"Nothing," Anders said. "Not-not after what he did."

On the way out they passed the place where Julia lay. Bemmon had knocked her against the wall with such force that a sharp projection of rock had cut a deep gash in her forehead. A woman was wiping the blood from her face and she lay limply, still unconscious; a frail shadow of the bold girl she had once been with the new life she would try to give them an almost unnoticeable little bulge in her starved thinness.

* * * * *

The lookout point was an outjutting spur of the ridge, six hundred feet from the caves and in full view of them. A lone tree stood there, its dead limbs thrust like white arms through the brown foliage of the limbs that still lived. Craig and Barber waited under the tree, Bemmon between them. The lowering sun shone hot and bright on Bemmon's face as he squinted back toward the caves at the approach of Lake and the other two.

He twisted to look at Barber. "What is it-why did you bring me here?" There was the tremor of fear in his voice. "What are you going to do to me?"

Barber did not answer and Bemmon turned back toward Lake. He saw the rope in Anders' hand and his face went white with comprehension.

"No!"

He threw himself back with a violence that almost tore him loose. *"No-no!"*

Schroeder stepped forward to help hold him and Lake took the rope from Anders. He fashioned a noose in it while Bemmon struggled and made panting, animal sounds, his eyes fixed in horrified fascination on the rope.

When the noose was finished he threw the free end of the rope over the white limb above Bemmon. He released the noose and Barber caught it, to draw it snug around Bemmon's neck.

Bemmon stopped struggling then and sagged weakly. For a moment it appeared that he would faint. Then he worked his mouth soundlessly until words came:

"You won't—you can't—really hang me?"

Lake spoke to him:

"We're going to hang you. What you stole would have saved the lives of ten children. You've watched the children cry because they were so hungry and you've watched them become too weak to cry or care any more. You've watched them die each day and each night you've secretly eaten the food that was supposed to be theirs.

"We're going to hang you, for the murder of children and the betrayal of our trust in you. If you have anything to say, say it now."

"You can't! I had a right to live-to eat what would have been wasted on dying people!" Bemmon twisted to appeal to the ones who held him, his words quick and ragged with hysteria. "You can't hang me—I don't want to die!"

Craig answered him, with a smile that was like the thin snarl of a wolf:

"Neither did two of my children."

Lake nodded to Craig and Schroeder, not waiting any longer. They stepped back to seize the free end of the rope and Bemmon screamed at what was coming, tearing loose from the grip of Barber.

Then his scream was abruptly cut off as he was jerked into the air. There was a cracking sound and he kicked spasmodically, his head setting grotesquely to one side.

Craig and Schroeder and Barber watched him with hard, expressionless faces but Anders turned quickly away, to be suddenly and violently sick.

"He was the first to betray us," Lake said. "Snub the rope and leave him to swing there. If there are any others like him, they'll know what to expect."

The blue sun rose as they went back to the caves. Behind them Bemmon swung and twirled aimlessly on the end of the rope. Two long, pale shadows swung and twirled with him; a yellow one to the west and a blue one to the east.

Bemmon was buried the next day. Someone cursed his name and someone spit on his grave and then he was part of the dead past as they faced the suffering ahead of them.

Julia recovered, although she would always wear a ragged scar on her forehead. Anders, who had worked closely with Chiara and was trying to take his place, quieted her fears by assuring her that the baby she carried was still too small for there to be much danger of the fall causing her to lose it.

Three times during the next month the wind came roaring down out of the northwest, bringing a gray dust that filled the sky and enveloped the land in a hot, smothering gloom through which the suns could not be seen.

Once black clouds gathered in the distance, to pour out a cloudburst. The 1.5 gravity gave the wall of water that swept down the canyon a far greater force and velocity than it would have had on Earth and boulders the size of small houses were tossed into the air and shattered into fragments. But all the rain fell upon the one small area and not a drop fell at the caves.

One single factor was in their favor and but for it they could not have survived such intense, continual heat: there was no humidity. Water evaporated quickly in the hot, dry air and sweat glands operated at the highest possible degree of efficiency. As a result they drank enormous quantities of water-the average adult needed five gallons a day. All canvas had been converted into water bags and the same principle of cooling-by-evaporation gave them water that was only warm instead of sickeningly hot as it would otherwise have been.

But despite the lack of humidity the heat was still far more intense than any on Earth. It never ceased, day or night, never let them have a moment's relief. There was a limit to how long human flesh could bear up under it, no matter how valiant the will. Each day the toll of those who had reached that limit was greater, like a swiftly rising tide.

There were three hundred and forty of them, when the first rain came; the rain that meant the end of summer. The yellow sun moved southward and the blue sun shrank steadily. Grass grew again and the woods goats returned, with them the young that had been born in the north, already half the size of their mothers.

For a while there was meat, and green herbs. Then the prowlers came, to make hunting dangerous. Females with pups were seen but always at a great distance as though the prowlers, like humans, took no chances with the lives of their children.

The unicorns came close behind the first prowlers, their young amazingly large and already weaned. Hunting became doubly dangerous then but the bowmen, through necessity, were learning how to use their bows with increasing skill and deadliness.

A salt lick for the woods goats was hopefully tried, although Lake felt dubious about it. They learned that salt was something the woods goats could either take or leave alone. And when hunters were in the vicinity they left it alone.

The game was followed for many miles to the south. The hunters returned the day the first blizzard came roaring and screaming down over the edge of the plateau; the blizzard that marked the beginning of the long, frigid winter. By then they were prepared as best they could be. Wood had been carried in great quantities and the caves fitted with crude doors and a ventilation system. And they had meat-not as much as they would need but enough to prevent starvation.

Lake took inventory of the food supply when the last hunters returned and held check-up inventories at irregular and unannounced intervals. He found no shortages. He had expected none-Bemmon's grave had long since been obliterated by drifting snow but the rope still hung from the dead limb, the noose swinging and turning in the wind.

* * * * *

Anders had made a Ragnarok calendar that spring, from data given him by John Prentiss, and he had marked the corresponding Earth dates on it. By a coincidence, Christmas came near the middle of the winter. There would be the same rationing of food on Christmas day but little brown trees had been cut for the children and decorated with such ornaments as could be made from the materials at hand.

There was another blizzard roaring down off the plateau Christmas morning; a white death that thundered and howled outside the caves at a temperature of more than eighty degrees below zero. But inside the caves it was warm by the fires and under the little brown trees were toys that had been patiently whittled from wood or sewn from scraps of cloth and animal skins while the children slept. They were crude and humble toys but the pale, thin faces of the children were bright with delight when they beheld them.

There was the laughter of children at play, a sound that had not been heard for many months, and someone singing the old, old songs. For a few fleeting hours that day, for the first and last time on Ragnarok, there was the magic of an Earth Christmas.

That night a child was born to Julia, on a pallet of dried grass and prowler skins. She asked for her baby before she died and they let her have it.

"I wasn't afraid, was I?" she asked. "But I wish it wasn't so dark —I wish I could see my baby before I go."

They took the baby from her arms when she was gone and removed from it the blanket that had kept her from learning that her child was still-born.

There were two hundred and fifty of them when the first violent storms of spring came. By then eighteen children had been born. Sixteen were still-born, eight of them deformed by the gravity, but two were like any normal babies on Earth. There was only one difference: the 1.5 gravity did not seem to affect them as much as it had the Earth-born babies.

Lake, himself, married that spring; a tall, gray-eyed girl who had fought alongside the men the night of the storm when the prowlers broke into John Prentiss's camp. And Schroeder married, the last of them all to do so.

That spring Lake sent out two classes of bowmen: those who would use the ordinary short bow and those who would use the longbows he had had made that winter. According to history the English longbowmen of medieval times had been without equal in the range and accuracy of their arrows and such extra-powerful weapons should eliminate close range stalking of woods goats and afford better protection from unicorns.

The longbows worked so well that by mid-spring he could detach Craig and three others from the hunting and send them on a prospecting expedition. Prentiss had said Ragnarok was devoid of metals but there was the hope of finding small veins the Dunbar Expedition's instruments had not detected. They would have to find metal or else, in the end, they would go back into a flint axe stage.

Craig and his men returned when the blue star was a sun again and the heat was more than men could walk and work in. They had traveled hundreds of miles in their circuit and found no metals.

"I want to look to the south when fall comes," Craig said. "Maybe it will be different down there."

They did not face famine that summer as they had the first summer. The diet of meat and dried herbs was rough and plain but there was enough of it.

Full summer came and the land was again burned and lifeless. There was nothing to do but sit wearily in the shade and endure the heat, drawing what psychological comfort they could from the fact that summer solstice was past and the suns were creeping south again even though it would be many weeks before there was any lessening of the heat.

It was then, and by accident, that Lake discovered there was something wrong about the southward movement of the suns.

He was returning from the lookout that day and he realized it was exactly a year since he and the others had walked back to the caves while Bemmon swung on the limb behind them.

It was even the same time of day; the blue sun rising in the east behind him and the yellow sun bright in his face as it touched the western horizon before him. He remembered how the yellow sun had been like the front sight of a rifle, set in the deepest V notch of the western hills —

But now, exactly a year later, it was not in the V notch. It was on the north side of the notch.

He looked to the east, at the blue sun. It seemed to him that it, too, was farther north than it had been although with it he had no landmark to check by.

But there was no doubt about the yellow sun: it was going south, as it should at that time of year, but it was lagging behind schedule. The only explanation Lake could think of was one that would mean still another threat to their survival; perhaps greater than all the others combined.

The yellow sun dropped completely behind the north slope of the V notch and he went on to the caves. He found Craig and Anders, the only two who might know anything about Ragnarok's axial tilts, and told them what he had seen.

"I made the calendar from the data John gave me," Anders said. "The Dunbar men made observations and computed the length of Ragnarok's year —I don't think they would have made any mistakes."

"If they didn't," Lake said, "we're in for something."

Craig was watching him, closely, thoughtfully. "Like the Ice Ages of Earth?" he asked.

Lake nodded and Anders said, "I don't understand."

"Each year the north pole tilts toward the sun to give us summer and away from it to give us winter," Lake said. "Which, of course, you know. But there can be still another kind of axial tilt. On Earth it occurs at intervals of thousands of years. The tilting that produces the summers and winters goes on as usual but as the centuries go by the summer tilt toward the sun grows less, the winter tilt away from it greater. The north pole leans farther and farther from the sun and ice sheets come down out of the north-an Ice Age. Then the north pole's progression away from the sun stops and the ice sheets recede as it tilts back toward the sun."

"I see," Anders said. "And if the same thing is happening here, we're going away from an ice age but at a rate thousands of times faster than on Earth."

"I don't know whether it's Ragnarok's tilt, alone, or if the orbits of the suns around each other add effects of their own over a period of years," Lake said. "The Dunbar Expedition wasn't here long enough to check up on anything like that."

"It seemed to me it was hotter this summer than last," Craig said. "Maybe only my imagination-but it won't be imagination in a few years if the tilt toward the sun continues."

"The time would come when we'd have to leave here," Lake said. "We'd have to go north up the plateau each spring. There's no timber there-nothing but grass and wind and thin air. We'd have to migrate south each fall."

"Yes … migrate." Anders's face was old and weary in the harsh reflected light of the blue sun and his hair had turned almost white in the past year. "Only the young ones could ever adapt enough to go up the plateau to its north portion. The rest of us … but we haven't many years, anyway. Ragnarok is for the young-and if they have to migrate back and forth like animals just to stay alive they will never have time to accomplish anything or be more than stone age nomads."

"I wish we could know how long the Big Summer will be that we're going into," Craig said. "And how long and cold the Big Winter, when Ragnarok tilts away from the sun. It wouldn't change anything-but I'd like to know."

"We'll start making and recording daily observations," Lake said. "Maybe the tilt will start back the other way before it's too late."

* * * * *

Fall seemed to come a little later that year. Craig went to the south as soon as the weather permitted but there were no minerals there; only the metal-barren hills dwindling in size until they became a prairie that sloped down and down toward the southern lowlands where all the creatures of Ragnarok spent the winter.

"I'll try again to the north when spring comes," Craig said. "Maybe that mountain on the plateau will have something."

Winter came, and Elaine died in giving him a son. The loss of Elaine was an unexpected blow; hurting more than he would ever have thought possible.

But he had a son … and it was his responsibility to do whatever he could to insure the survival of his son and of the sons and daughters of all the others.

His outlook altered and he began to think of the future, not in terms of years to come but in terms of generations to come. Someday one of the young ones would succeed him as leader but the young ones would have only childhood memories of Earth. He was the last leader who had known Earth and the civilization of Earth as a grown man. What he did while he was leader would incline the destiny of a new race.

He would have to do whatever was possible for him to do and he would have to begin at once. The years left to him could not be many.

He was not alone; others in the caves had the same thoughts he had regarding the future even though none of them had any plan for accomplishing what they spoke of. West, who had held degrees in philosophy on Earth, said to Lake one night as they sat together by the fire:

"Have you noticed the way the children listen when the talk turns to what used to be on Earth, what might have been on Athena, and what would be if only we could find a way to escape from Ragnarok?"

"I've noticed," he said.

"These stories already contain the goal for the future generations," West went on. "Someday, somehow, they will go to Athena, to kill the Gerns there and free the Terran slaves and reclaim Athena as their own."

He had listened to them talk of the interstellar flight to Athena as they sat by their fires and worked at making bows and arrows. It was only a dream they held, yet without that dream there would be nothing before them but the vision of generation after generation living and dying on a world that could never give them more than existence.

The dream was needed. But it, alone, was not enough. How long, on Earth, had it been from the Neolithic age to advanced civilization-how long from the time men were ready to leave their caves until they were ready to go to the stars?

Twelve thousand years.

There were men and women among the Rejects who had been specialists in various fields. There were a few books that had survived the trampling of the unicorns and others could be written with ink made from the black lance tree bark upon parchment made from the thin inner skin of unicorn hides.

The knowledge contained in the books and the learning of the Rejects still living should be preserved for the future generations. With the help of that learning perhaps they really could, someday, somehow, escape from their prison and make Athena their own.

He told West of what he had been thinking. "We'll have to start a school," he said. "This winter-tomorrow."

West nodded in agreement. "And the writings should be commenced as soon as possible. Some of the textbooks will require more time to write than Ragnarok will give the authors."

A school for the children was started the next day and the writing of the books began. The parchment books would serve two purposes. One would be to teach the future generations things that would not only help them survive but would help them create a culture of their own as advanced as the harsh environment and scanty resources of Ragnarok permitted. The other would be to warn them of the danger of a return of the Gerns and to teach them all that was known about Gerns and their weapons.

Lake's main contribution would be a lengthy book: Terran Spaceships; Types and Operation. He postponed its writing, however, to first produce a much smaller book but one that might well be more important: Interior Features of a Gern Cruiser. Terran Intelligence knew a little about Gern cruisers and as second-in-command of the *Constellation* he had seen and studied a copy of that report. He had an excellent memory for such things, almost photographic, and he wrote the text and drew a multitude of sketches.

He shook his head ruefully at the result. The text was good but, for clarity, the accompanying illustrations should be accurate and in perspective. And he was definitely not an artist.

He discovered that Craig could take a pen in his scarred, powerful hand and draw with the neat precision of a professional artist. He turned the sketches over to him, together with the mass of specifications. Since it might someday be of such vital importance, he would make four copies of it. The text was given to a teen-age girl, who would make three more copies of it....

Four days later Schroeder handed Lake a text with some rough sketches. The title was: Operation of Gern Blasters.

Not even Intelligence had ever been able to examine a Gern hand blaster. But a man named Schrader, on Venus, had killed a Gern with his own blaster and then disappeared with both infuriated Gerns and Gern-intimidated Venusian police in pursuit. There had been a high reward for his capture....

He looked it over and said, "I was counting on you giving us this."

Only the barest trace of surprise showed on Schroeder's face but his eyes were intently watching Lake. "So you knew all the time who I was?"

"I knew."

"Did anyone else on the *Constellation* know?"

"You were recognized by one of the ship's officers. You would have been tried in two more days."

"I see," Schroeder said. "And since I was guilty and couldn't be returned to Earth or Venus I'd have been executed on the *Constellation*." He smiled sardonically. "And you, as second-in-command, would have been my execution's master of ceremonies."

Lake put the parchment sheets back together in their proper order. "Sometimes," he said, "a ship's officer has to do things that are contrary to all his own wishes."

Schroeder drew a deep breath, his face sombre with the memories he had kept to himself.

"It was two years ago when the Gerns were still talking friendship to the Earth government while they shoved the colonists around on Venus. This Gern ... there was a girl there and he thought he could do what he wanted to her because he was a mighty Gern and she was nothing. He did. That's why I killed him. I had to kill two Venusian police to get away-that's where I put the rope around my neck."

"It's not what we did but what we do that we'll live or die by on Ragnarok," Lake said. He handed Schroeder the sheets of parchment. "Tell Craig to make at least four copies of this. Someday our knowledge of Gern blasters may be something else we'll live or die by."

* * * * *

The school and writing were interrupted by the spring hunting. Craig made his journey to the Plateau's snow-capped mountain but he was unable to keep his promise to prospect it. The plateau was perhaps ten thousand feet in elevation and the mountain rose another ten thousand feet above the plateau. No human could climb such a mountain in a 1.5 gravity.

"I tried," he told Lake wearily when he came back. "Damn it, I never tried harder at anything in my life. It was just too much for me. Maybe some of the young ones will be better adapted and can do it when they grow up."

Craig brought back several sheets of unusually transparent mica, each sheet a foot in diameter, and a dozen large water-clear quartz crystals.

"Float, from higher up on the mountain," he said. "The mica and crystals are in place up there if we could only reach them. Other minerals, too —I panned traces in the canyon bottoms. But no iron."

Lake examined the sheets of mica. "We could make windows for the outer caves of these," he said. "Have them double thickness with a wide air space between, for insulation. As for the quartz crystals...."

"Optical instruments," Craig said. "Binoculars, microscopes-it would take us a long time to learn how to make glass as clear and flawless as those crystals. But we have no way of cutting and grinding them."

Craig went to the east that fall and to the west the next spring. He returned from the trip to the west with a twisted knee that would never let him go prospecting again.

"It will take years to find the metals we need," he said. "The indications are that we never will but I wanted to keep on trying. Now, my damned knee has me chained to these caves...."

He reconciled himself to his lameness and confinement as best he could and finished his textbook: Geology and Mineral Identification.

He also taught a geology class during the winters. It was in the winter of the year four on Ragnarok that a nine-year-old boy entered his class; the silent, scar-faced Billy Humbolt.

He was by far the youngest of Craig's students, and the most attentive. Lake was present one day when Craig asked, curiously:

"It's not often a boy your age is so interested in mineralogy and geology, Billy. Is there something more than just interest?"

"I have to learn all about minerals," Billy said with matter-of-fact seriousness, "so that when I'm grown I can find the metals for us to make a ship."

"And then?" Craig asked.

"And then we'd go to Athena, to kill the Gerns who caused my mother to die, and my grandfather, and Julia, and all the others. And to free my father and the other slaves if they're still alive."

"I see," Craig said.

He did not smile. His face was shadowed and old as he looked at the boy and beyond him; seeing again, perhaps, the frail blonde girl and the two children that the first quick, violent months had taken from him.

"I hope you succeed," he said. "I wish I was young so I could dream of the same thing. But I'm not … so let's get back to the identification of the ores that will be needed to make a ship to go to Athena and to make blasters to kill Gerns after you get there."

Lake had a corral built early the following spring, with camouflaged wings, to trap some of the woods goats when they came. It would be an immense forward step toward conquering their new environment if they could domesticate the goats and have goat herds near the caves all through the year. Gathering enough grass to last a herd of goats through the winter would be a problem-but first, before they worried about that, they would have to see if the goats could survive the summer and winter extremes of heat and cold.

They trapped ten goats that spring. They built them brush sunshades-before summer was over the winds would have stripped the trees of most of their dry, brown leaves-and a stream of water was diverted through the corral.

It was all work in vain. The goats died from the heat in early summer, together with the young that had been born.

When fall came they trapped six more goats. They built them shelters that would be as warm as possible and carried them a large supply of the tall grass from along the creek banks; enough to last them through the winter. But the cold was too much for the goats and the second blizzard killed them all.

The next spring and fall, and with much more difficulty, they tried the experiment with pairs of unicorns. The results were the same.

Which meant they would remain a race of hunters. Ragnarok would not permit them to be herdsmen.

* * * * *

The years went by, each much like the one before it but for the rapid aging of the Old Ones, as Lake and the others called themselves, and the growing up of the Young Ones. No woman among the Old Ones could any longer have children, but six more normal, healthy children had been born. Like the first two, they were not affected by the gravity as Earth-born babies had been.

Among the Young Ones, Lake saw, was a distinguishable difference. Those who had been very young the day the Gerns left them to die had adapted better than those who had been a few years older.

The environment of Ragnarok had struck at the very young with merciless savagery. It had subjected them to a test of survival that was without precedent on Earth. It had killed them by the hundreds but among them had been those whose young flesh and blood and organs had resisted death by adapting to the greatest extent possible.

The day of the Old Ones was almost done and the future would soon be in the hands of the Young Ones. They were the ninety unconquerables out of what had been four thousand Rejects; the first generation of what would be a new race.

It seemed to Lake that the years came and went ever faster as the Old Ones dwindled in numbers at an accelerating rate. Anders had died in the sixth year, his heart failing him one night as he worked patiently in his crude little laboratory at carrying on the work started by Chiara to find a cure for the Hell Fever. Barber, trying to develop a strain of herbs that would grow in the lower elevation of the caves, was killed by a unicorn as he worked in his test plot below the caves. Craig went limping out one spring day on the eighth year to look at a new mineral a hunter had found a mile from the caves. A sudden cold rain blew up, chilling him before he could return, and he died of Hell Fever the same day.

Schroeder was killed by prowlers the same year, dying with his back to a tree and a bloody knife in his hand. It was the way he would have wanted to go-once he had said to Lake:

"When my times comes I would rather it be against the prowlers. They fight hard and kill quick and then they're through with you. They don't tear you up after you're dead and slobber and gloat over the pieces, the way the unicorns do."

The springs came a little earlier each year, the falls a little later, and the observations showed the suns progressing steadily northward. But the winters, though shorter, were seemingly as cold as ever. The long summers reached such a degree of heat on the ninth year that Lake knew they could endure no more than two or three years more of the increasing heat.

Then, in the summer of the tenth year, the tilting of Ragnarok-the apparent northward progress of the suns-stopped. They were in the middle of what Craig had called Big Summer and they could endure it-just barely. They would not have to leave the caves.

The suns started their drift southward. The observations were continued and carefully recorded. Big Fall was coming and behind it would be Big Winter.

Big Winter ... the threat of it worried Lake. How far to the south would the suns go-how long would they stay? Would the time come when the plateau would be buried under hundreds of feet of snow and the caves enclosed in glacial ice?

There was no way he could ever know or even guess. Only those of the future would ever know.

On the twelfth year only Lake and West were left of the Old Ones. By then there were eighty-three left of the Young Ones, eight Ragnarok-born children of the Old Ones and four Ragnarok-born children of the Young Ones. Not counting himself and West, there were ninety-five of them.

It was not many to be the beginnings of a race that would face an ice age of unknown proportions and have over them, always, the threat of a chance return of the Gerns.

The winter of the fifteenth year came and he was truly alone, the last of the Old Ones. White-haired and aged far beyond his years, he was still leader. But that winter he could do little other than sit by his fire and feel the gravity dragging at his heart. He knew, long before spring, that it was time he chose his successor.

He had hoped to live to see his son take his place-but Jim was only thirteen. Among the others was one he had been watching since the day he told Craig he would find metals to build a ship and kill the Gerns: Bill Humbolt.

Bill Humbolt was not the oldest among those who would make leaders but he was the most versatile of them all, the most thoughtful and stubbornly determined. He reminded Lake of that fierce old man who had been his grandfather and had it not been for the scars that twisted his face into grim ugliness he would have looked much like him.

A violent storm was roaring outside the caves the night he told the others that he wanted Bill Humbolt to be his successor. There were no objections and, without ceremony and with few words, he terminated his fifteen years of leadership.

He left the others, his son among them, and went back to the cave where he slept. His fire was low, down to dying embers, but he was too tired to build it up again. He lay down on his pallet and saw, with neither surprise nor fear, that his time was much nearer than he had thought. It was already at hand.

He lay back and let the lassitude enclose him, not fighting it. He had done the best he could for the others and now the weary journey was over.

His thoughts dissolved into the memory of the day fifteen years before. The roaring of the storm became the thunder of the Gern cruisers as they disappeared into the gray sky. Four thousand Rejects stood in the cold wind and watched them go, the children not yet understanding that they had been condemned to die. Somehow, his own son was among them ——

He tried feebly to rise. There was work to do —a lot of work to do....

PART 2

It was early morning as Bill Humbolt sat by the fire in his cave and studied the map Craig had made of the plateau's mountain. Craig had left the mountain nameless and he dipped his pen in ink to write: *Craig Mountains*.

"Bill ——"

Delmont Anders entered very quietly, what he had to tell already evident on his face.

"He died last night, Bill."

It was something he had been expecting to come at any time but the lack of surprise did not diminish the sense of loss. Lake had been the last of the Old Ones, the last of those who had worked and fought and shortened the years of their lives that the Young Ones might have a chance to live. Now he was gone-now a brief era was ended, a valiant, bloody chapter written and finished.

And he was the new leader who would decree how the next chapter should be written, only four years older than the boy who was looking at him with an unconscious appeal for reassurance on his face....

"You'd better tell Jim," he said. "Then, a little later, I want to talk to everyone about the things we'll start doing as soon as spring comes."

"You mean, the hunting?" Delmont asked.

"No-more than just the hunting."

He sat for a while after Delmont left, looking back down the years that had preceded that day, back to that first morning on Ragnarok.

He had set a goal for himself that morning when he left his toy bear in the dust behind him and walked beside Julia into the new and perilous way of life. He had promised himself that some day he would watch the Gerns die and beg for mercy as they died and he would give them the same mercy they had given his mother.

As he grew older he realized that his hatred, alone, was a futile thing. There would have to be a way of leaving Ragnarok and there would have to be weapons with which to fight the Gerns. These would be things impossible and beyond his reach unless he had the help of all the others in united, coordinated effort.

To make certain of that united effort he would have to be their leader. So for eleven years he had studied and trained until there was no one who could use a bow or spear quite as well as he could, no one who could travel as far in a day or spot a unicorn ambush as quickly. And there was no one, with the exception of George Ord, who had studied as many textbooks as he had.

He had reached his first goal-he was leader. For all of them there existed the second goal: the hope of someday leaving Ragnarok and taking Athena from the Gerns. For many of them, perhaps, it was only wishful dreaming but for him it was the prime driving force of his life.

There was so much for them to do and their lives were so short in which to do it. For so long as he was leader they would not waste a day in idle wishing....

* * * * *

When the others were gathered to hear what he had to say he spoke to them:

"We're going to continue where the Old Ones had to leave off. We're better adapted than they were and we're going to find metals to make a ship if there are any to be found.

"Somewhere on Ragnarok, on the northwest side of a range similar to the Craig Mountains on the plateau, is a deep valley that the Dunbar Expedition called the Chasm. They didn't investigate it closely since their instruments showed no metals there but they saw strata in one place that was red; an iron discoloration. Maybe we can find a vein there that was too small for them to have paid any attention to. So we'll go over the Craigs as soon as the snow melts from them."

"That will be in early summer," George Ord said, his black eyes thoughtful. "Whoever goes will have to time their return for either just before the prowlers and unicorns come back from the north or wait until they've all migrated down off the plateau."

It was something Humbolt had been thinking about and wishing they could remedy. Men could elude unicorn attacks wherever there were trees large enough to offer safety and even prowler attacks could be warded off wherever there were trees for refuge; spears holding back the prowlers who would climb the trees while arrows picked off the ones on the ground. But there were no trees on the plateau, and to be caught by a band of prowlers or unicorns there was certain death for any small party of two or three. For that reason no small parties had ever gone up on the plateau except when the unicorns and prowlers were gone or nearly so. It was an inconvenience and it would continue for as long as their weapons were the slow-to-reload bows.

"You're supposed to be our combination inventor-craftsman," he said to George. "No one else can compare with you in that respect. Besides, you're not exactly enthusiastic about such hard work as mountain climbing. So from now on you'll do the kind of work you're best fitted for. Your first job is to make us a better bow. Make it like a crossbow, with a sliding action to draw and cock the string and with a magazine of arrows mounted on top of it."

George studied the idea thoughtfully. "The general principle is simple," he said. "I'll see what I can do.
"

"How many of us will go over the Craig Mountains, Bill?" Dan Barber asked.

"You and I," Humbolt answered. "A three-man party under Bob Craig will go into the Western Hills and another party under Johnny Stevens will go into the Eastern Hills."

He looked toward the adjoining cave where the guns had been stored for so long, coated with unicorn tallow to protect them from rust.

"We could make gun powder if we could find a deposit of saltpeter. We already know where there's a little sulphur. The guns would have to be converted to flintlocks, though, since we don't have what we need for cartridge priming material. Worse, we'd have to use ceramic bullets. They would be inefficient-too light, and destructive to the bores. But we would need powder for mining if we ever found any iron. And, if we can't have metal bullets to shoot the Gerns, we can have bombs to blast them with."

"Suppose," Johnny Stevens said, "that we never do find the metals to make a ship. How will we ever leave Ragnarok if that happens?"

"There's another way —a possible way-of leaving here without a ship of our own. If there are no metals we'll have to try it."

"Why wait?" Bob Craig demanded. "Why not try it now?"

"Because the odds would be about ten thousand to one in favor of the Gerns. But we'll try it if everything else fails."

* * * * *

George made, altered, and rejected four different types of crossbows before he perfected a reloading bow that met his critical approval. He brought it to where Humbolt stood outside the caves early one spring day when the grass was sending up the first green shoots on the southern hillsides and the long winter was finally dying.

"Here it is," he said, handing Humbolt the bow. "Try it."

He took it, noting the fine balance of it. Projecting down from the center of the bow, at right angles to it, was a stock shaped to fit the grip of the left hand. Under the crossbar was a sliding stock for the right hand, shaped like the butt of a pistol and fitted with a trigger. Mounted slightly above and to one side of the crossbar was a magazine containing ten short arrows.

The pistol grip was in position near the forestock. He pulled it back the length of the crossbar and it brought the string with it, stretching it taut. There was a click as the trigger mechanism locked the bowstring in place and at the same time a concealed spring arrangement shoved an arrow into place against the string.

He took quick aim at a distant tree and pressed the trigger. There was a twang as the arrow was ejected. He jerked the sliding pistol grip forward and back to reload, pressing the trigger an instant later. Another arrow went its way.

By the time he had fired the tenth arrow in the magazine he was shooting at the rate of one arrow per second. On the trunk of the distant tree, like a bristle of stiff whiskers, the ten arrows were driven deep into the wood in an area no larger than the chest of a prowler or head of a unicorn.

"This is better than I hoped for," he said to George. "One man with one of these would equal six men with ordinary bows."

"I'm going to add another feature," George said. "Bundles of arrows, ten to the bundle in special holders, to carry in the quivers. To reload the magazine you'd just slap down a new bundle of arrows, in no more time than it would take to put one arrow in an ordinary bow. I figured that with practice a man should be able to get off forty arrows in not much more than twenty seconds."

George took the bow and went back in the cave to add his new feature. Humbolt stared after him, thinking, *If he can make something like that out of wood and unicorn gut, what would he be able to give us if he could have metal?*

Perhaps George would never have the opportunity to show what he could do with metal. But Humbolt already felt sure that George's genius would, if it ever became necessary, make possible the alternate plan for leaving Ragnarok.

* * * * *

The weeks dragged into months and at last enough snow was gone from the Craigs that Humbolt and Dan Barber could start. They met no opposition. The prowlers had long since disappeared into the north and the unicorns were very scarce. They had no occasion to test the effectiveness of the new automatic crossbows in combat; a lack of opportunity that irked Barber.

"Any other time, if we had ordinary bows," he complained, "the unicorns would be popping up to charge us from all directions."

"Don't fret," Humbolt consoled him. "This fall, when we come back, they will be."

They reached the mountain and stopped near its foot where a creek came down, its water high and muddy with melting snows. There they hunted until they had obtained all the meat they could carry. They would see no more game when they went up the mountain's canyons. A poisonous weed replaced most of the grass in all the canyons and the animals of Ragnarok had learned long before to shun the mountain.

They found the canyon that Craig and his men had tried to explore and started up it. It was there that Craig had discovered the quartz and mica and so far as he had been able to tell the head of that canyon would be the lowest of all the passes over the mountain.

The canyon went up the mountain diagonally so that the climb was not steep although it was constant. They began to see mica and quartz crystals in the creek bed and at noon on the second day they passed the last stunted tree. Nothing grew higher than that point but the thorny poison weeds and they were scarce.

The air was noticeably thinner there and their burdens heavier. A short distance beyond they came to a small rock monument; Craig's turn-back point.

The next day they found the quartz crystals in place. A mile farther was the vein the mica had come from. Of the other minerals Craig had hoped to find, however, there were only traces.

The fourth day was an eternity of struggling up the now-steeper canyon under loads that seemed to weigh hundreds of pounds; forcing their protesting legs to carry them fifty steps at a time, at the end of which they would stop to rest while their lungs labored to suck in the thin air in quick, panting breaths.

It would have been much easier to have gone around the mountain. But the Chasm was supposed to be like a huge cavity scooped out of the plateau beyond the mountain, rimmed with sheer cliffs a mile high. Only on the side next to the mountain was there a slope leading down into it.

They stopped for the night where the creek ended in a small spring. There the snow still clung to the canyon's walls and there the canyon curved, offering them the promise of the summit just around the bend as it had been doing all day.

The sun was hot and bright the next morning as they made their slow way on again. The canyon straightened, the steep walls of it flattening out to make a pair of ragged shoulders with a saddle between them.

They climbed to the summit of the saddle and there, suddenly before them, was the other side of the world-and the Chasm.

Far below them was a plateau, stretching endlessly like the one they had left behind them. But the chasm dominated all else. It was a gigantic, sheer-walled valley, a hundred miles long by forty miles wide, sunk deep in the plateau with the tops of its mile-high walls level with the floor of the plateau. The mountain under them dropped swiftly away, sloping down and down to the level of the plateau and then on, down and down again, to the bottom of the chasm that was so deep its floor was half hidden by the morning shadows.

"My God!" Barber said. "It must be over three miles under us to the bottom, on the vertical. Ten miles of thirty-three per cent grade-if we go down we'll never get out again."

"You can turn back here if you want to," Humbolt said.

"Turn back?" Barber's red whiskers seemed to bristle. "Who in hell said anything about turning back?"

"Nobody," Humbolt said, smiling a little at Barber's quick flash of anger.

He studied the chasm, wishing that they could have some way of cutting the quartz crystals and making binoculars. It was a long way to look with the naked eye....

Here and there the chasm thrust out arms into the plateau. All the arms were short, however, and even at their heads the cliffs were vertical. The morning shadows prevented a clear view of much of the chasm and he could see no sign of the red-stained strata that they were searching for.

In the southwest corner of the chasm, far away and almost imperceptible, he saw a faint cloud rising up from the chasm's floor. It was impossible to tell what it was and it faded away as he watched.

Barber saw it, too, and said, "It looked like smoke. Do you suppose there could be people-or some kind of intelligent things-living down there?"

"It might have been the vapor from hot springs, condensed by the cool morning air," he said. "Whatever it was, we'll look into it when we get there."

The climb down the steep slope into the chasm was swifter than that up the canyon but no more pleasant. Carrying a heavy pack down such a grade exerted a torturous strain upon the backs of the legs.

The heat increased steadily as they descended. They reached the floor of the valley the next day and the noonday heat was so great that Humbolt wondered if they might not have trapped themselves into what the summer would soon transform into a monstrous oven where no life at all could exist. There could never be any choice, of course-the mountains were passable only when the weather was hot.

The floor of the valley was silt, sand and gravel-they would find nothing there. They set out on a circuit of the chasm's walls, following along close to the base.

In many places the mile-high walls were without a single ledge to break their vertical faces. When they came to the first such place they saw that the ground near the base was riddled with queer little pits, like tiny craters of the moon. As they looked there was a crack like a cannon shot and the ground beside them erupted into an explosion of sand and gravel. When the dust had cleared away there was a new crater where none had been before.

Humbolt wiped the blood from his face where a flying fragment had cut it and said, "The heat of the sun loosens rocks up on the rim. When one falls a mile in a one point five gravity, it's traveling like a meteor."

They went on, through the danger zone. As with the peril of the chasm's heat, there was no choice. Only by observing the material that littered the base of the cliffs could they know what minerals, if any, might be above them.

On the fifteenth day they saw the red-stained stratum. Humbolt quickened his pace, hurrying forward in advance of Barber. The stratum was too high up on the wall to be reached but it was not necessary to examine it in place-the base of the cliff was piled thick with fragments from it.

He felt the first touch of discouragement as he looked at them. They were a sandstone, light in weight. The iron present was only what the Dunbar Expedition had thought it to be; a mere discoloration.

They made their way slowly along the foot of the cliff, examining piece after piece in the hope of finding something more than iron stains. There was no variation, however, and a mile farther on they came to the end of the red stratum. Beyond that point the rocks were gray, without a vestige of iron.

"So that," Barber said, looking back the way they had come, "is what we were going to build a ship out of-iron stains!"

Humbolt did not answer. For him it was more than a disappointment. It was the death of a dream he had held since the year he was nine and had heard that the Dunbar Expedition had seen iron-stained rock in a deep chasm-the only iron-stained rock on the face of Ragnarok. Surely, he had thought, there would be enough iron there to build a small ship. For eleven years he had worked toward the day when he would find it. Now, he had found it-and it was nothing. The ship was as far away as ever....

But discouragement was as useless as iron-stained sandstone. He shook it off and turned to Barber.

"Let's go," he said. "Maybe we'll find something by the time we circle the chasm."

For seven days they risked the danger of death from downward plunging rocks and found nothing. On the eighth day they found the treasure that was not treasure.

They stopped for the evening just within the mouth of one of the chasm's tributaries. Humbolt went out to get a drink where a trickle of water ran through the sand and as he knelt down he saw the flash of something red under him, almost buried in the sand.

He lifted it out. It was a stone half the size of his hand; darkly translucent and glowing in the light of the setting sun like blood.

It was a ruby.

He looked, and saw another gleam a little farther up the stream. It was another ruby, almost as large as the first one. Near it was a flawless blue sapphire. Scattered here and there were smaller rubies and sapphires, down to the size of grains of sand.

He went farther upstream and saw specimens of still another stone. They were colorless but burning with internal fires. He rubbed one of them hard across the ruby he still carried and there was a gritting sound as it cut a deep scratch in the ruby.

"I'll be damned," he said aloud.

There was only one stone hard enough to cut a ruby-the diamond.

* * * * *

It was almost dark when he returned to where Barber was resting beside their packs.

"What did you find to keep you out so late?" Barber asked curiously.

He dropped a double handful of rubies, sapphires and diamonds at Barber's feet.

"Take a look," he said. "On a civilized world what you see there would buy us a ship without our having to lift a finger. Here they're just pretty rocks.

"Except the diamonds," he added "At least we now have something to cut those quartz crystals with."

* * * * *

They took only a few of the rubies and sapphires the next morning but they gathered more of the diamonds, looking in particular for the gray-black and ugly but very hard and tough carbonado variety. Then they resumed their circling of the chasm's walls.

The heat continued its steady increase as the days went by. Only at night was there any relief from it and the nights were growing swiftly shorter as the blue sun rose earlier each morning. When the yellow sun rose the chasm became a blazing furnace around the edge of which they crept like ants in some gigantic oven.

There was no life in any form to be seen; no animal or bush or blade of grass. There was only the barren floor of the chasm, made a harsh green shade by the two suns and writhing and undulating with heat waves like a nightmare sea, while above them the towering cliffs shimmered, too, and sometimes seemed to be leaning far out over their heads and already falling down upon them.

They found no more minerals of any kind and they came at last to the place where they had seen the smoke or vapor.

* * * * *

There the walls of the chasm drew back to form a little valley a mile long by half a mile wide. The walls did not drop vertically to the floor there but sloped out at the base into a fantastic formation of natural roofs and arches that reached almost to the center of the valley from each side. Green things grew in the shade under the arches and sparkling waterfalls cascaded down over many of them. A small creek carried the water out of the valley, going out into the chasm a little way before the hot sands absorbed it.

They stood and watched for some time, but there was no movement in the valley other than the waving of the green plants as a breeze stirred them. Once the breeze shifted to bring them the fresh, sweet scent of growing things and urge them to come closer.

"A place like that doesn't belong here," Barber said in a low voice. "But it's there. I wonder what else is there?"

"Shade and cool water," Humbolt said. "And maybe things that don't like strangers. Let's go find out."

They watched warily as they walked, their crossbows in their hands. At the closer range they saw that the roofs and arches were the outer remains of a system of natural caves that went back into the valley's walls. The green vegetation grew wherever the roofs gave part-time shade, consisting mainly of a holly-leafed bush with purple flowers and a tall plant resembling corn.

Under some of the roofs the corn was mature, the orange colored grains visible. Under others it was no more than half grown. He saw the reason and said to Barber:

"There are both warm and cold springs here. The plants watered by the warm springs would grow almost the year around; the ones watered by the cold springs only in the summer. And what we saw from the mountain top would have been vapor rising from the warm springs."

They passed under arch after arch without seeing any life. When they came to the valley's upper end and still had seen nothing it seemed evident that there was little danger of an encounter with any intelligent-and-hostile creatures. Apparently nothing at all lived in the little valley.

Humbolt stopped under a broad arch where the breeze was made cool and moist by the spray of water it had come through. Barber went on, to look under the adjoining arch.

Caves led into the wall from both arches and as he stood there Humbolt saw something lying in the mouth of the nearest cave. It was a little mound of orange corn; lying in a neat pile as though whatever had left it there had intended to come back after it.

He looked toward the other arch but Barber was somewhere out of sight. He doubted that whatever had left the corn could be much of a menace-dangerous animals were more apt to eat flesh than corn-but he went to the cave with his crossbow ready.

He stopped at the mouth of the cave to let his eyes become accustomed to the darkness inside it. As he did so the things inside came out to meet him.

They emerged into full view; six little animals the size of squirrels, each of them a different color. They walked on short hind legs like miniature bears and the dark eyes in the bear-chipmunk faces were fixed on him with intense interest. They stopped five feet in front of him, there to stand in a neat row and continue the fascinated staring up at him.

The yellow one in the center scratched absently at its stomach with a furry paw and he lowered the bow, feeling a little foolish at having bothered to raise it against animals so small and harmless.

Then he half brought it up again as the yellow one opened its mouth and said in a tone that held distinct anticipation:

"I think we'll eat you for supper."

He darted glances to right and left but there was nothing near him except the six little animals. The yellow one, having spoken, was staring silently at him with only curiosity on its furry face. He wondered if some miasma or some scent from the vegetation in the valley had warped his mind into sudden insanity and asked:

"You think you'll do what?"

It opened its mouth again, to stutter, "I —I — —" Then, with a note of alarm, *"Hey...."*

It said no more and the next sound was that of Barber hurrying toward him and calling, "Hey-Bill-where are you?"

"Here," he answered, and he was already sure that he knew why the little animal had spoken to him.

Barber came up and saw the six chipmunk-bears. "Six of them!" he exclaimed. "There's one in the next cave-the damned thing spoke to me!"

"I thought so," he replied. "You told it we'd have it for supper and then it said, 'You think you'll do what?' didn't it?"

Barber's face showed surprise. "How did you know that?"

"They're telepathic between one another," he said. "The yellow one there repeated what the one you spoke to heard you say and it repeated what the yellow one heard me say. It has to be telepathy between them."

"Telepathy — —" Barber stared at the six little animals, who stared back with their fascinated curiosity undiminished. "But why should they want to repeat aloud what they receive telepathically?"

"I don't know. Maybe at some stage in their evolution only part of them were telepaths and the telepaths broadcasted danger warnings to the others that way. So far as that goes, why does a parrot repeat what it hears?"

There was a scurry of movement behind Barber and another of the little animals, a white one, hurried past them. It went to the yellow one and they stood close together as they stared up. Apparently they were mates....

"That's the other one-those are the two that mocked us," Barber said, and thereby gave them the name by which they would be known: mockers.

* * * * *

The mockers were fresh meat-but they accepted the humans with such friendliness and trust that Barber lost all his desire to have one for supper or for any other time. They had a limited supply of dried meat and there would be plenty of orange corn. They would not go hungry.

They discovered that the mockers had living quarters in both the cool caves and the ones warmed by the hot springs. There was evidence that they hibernated during the winters in the warm caves.

There were no minerals in the mockers' valley and they set out to continue their circuit of the chasm. They did not get far until the heat had become so great that the chasm's tributaries began going dry. They turned back then, to wait in the little valley until the fall rains came.

* * * * *

When the long summer was ended by the first rain they resumed their journey. They took a supply of the orange corn and two of the mockers; the yellow one and its mate. The other mockers watched them leave, standing silent and solemn in front of their caves as though they feared they might never see their two fellows or the humans again.

The two mockers were pleasant company, riding on their shoulders and chattering any nonsense that came to mind. And sometimes saying things that were not at all nonsense, making Humbolt wonder if mockers could partly read human minds and dimly understand the meaning of some of the things they said.

They found a place where saltpeter was very thinly and erratically distributed. They scraped off all the films of it that were visible and procured a small amount. They completed their circuit and reached the foot of the long, steep slope of the Craigs without finding anything more.

It was an awesome climb that lay before them; up a grade so steep and barred with so many low ledges that when their legs refused to carry them farther they crawled. The heat was still very serious and there would be no water until they came to the spring beyond the mountain's summit. A burning wind, born on the blazing floor of the chasm, followed them up the mountain all day. Their leather canteens were almost dry when night came and they were no more than a third of the way to the top.

The mockers had become silent as the elevation increased and when they stopped for the night Humbolt saw that they would never live to cross the mountain. They were breathing fast, their hearts racing, as they tried to extract enough oxygen from the thin air. They drank a few drops of water but they would not touch the corn he offered them.

The white mocker died at midmorning the next day as they stopped for a rest. The yellow one crawled feebly to her side and died a few minutes later.

"So that's that," Humbolt said, looking down at them. "The only things on Ragnarok that ever trusted us and wanted to be our friends-and we killed them."

They drank the last of their water and went on. They made dry camp that night and dreams of cold streams of water tormented their exhausted sleep. The next day was a hellish eternity in which they walked and fell and crawled and walked and fell again.

Barber weakened steadily, his breathing growing to a rattling panting. He spoke once that afternoon, to try to smile with dry, swollen lips and say between his panting gasps, "It would be hell-to have to die-so thirsty like this."

After that he fell with increasing frequency, each time slower and weaker in getting up again. Half a mile short of the summit he fell for the last time. He tried to get up, failed, and tried to crawl. He failed at that, too, and collapsed face down in the rocky soil.

Humbolt went to him and said between his own labored intakes of breath, "Wait, Dan —I'll go on-bring you back water."

Barber raised himself with a great effort and looked up. "No use," he said. "My heart-too much — —"

He fell forward again and that time he was very still, his desperate panting no more.

* * * * *

It seemed to Humbolt that it was half a lifetime later that he finally reached the spring and the cold, clear water. He drank, the most ecstatic pleasure he had ever experienced in his life. Then the pleasure drained away as he seemed to see Dan Barber trying to smile and seemed to hear him say, "It would be hell-to have to die-so thirsty like this."

67

He rested for two days before he was in condition to continue on his way. He reached the plateau and saw that the woods goats had been migrating south for some time. On the second morning he climbed up a gentle roll in the plain and met three unicorns face to face.

They charged at once, squealing with anticipation. Had he been equipped with an ordinary bow he would have been killed within seconds. But the automatic crossbow poured a rain of arrows into the faces of the unicorns that caused them to swing aside in pain and enraged astonishment. The moment they had swung enough to expose the area just behind their heads the arrows became fatal.

One unicorn escaped, three arrows bristling in its face. It watched him from a distance for a little while, squealing and shaking its head in baffled fury. Then it turned and disappeared over a swell in the plain, running like a deer.

He resumed his southward march, hurrying faster than before. The unicorn had headed north and that could be for but one purpose: to bring enough reinforcements to finish the job.

* * * * *

He reached the caves at night. No one was up but George Ord, working late in his combination workshop-laboratory.

George looked up at the sound of his entrance and saw that he was alone. "So Dan didn't make it?" he asked.

"The chasm got him," he answered. And then, wearily, "The chasm-we found the damned thing."

"The red stratum — —"

"It was only iron stains."

"I made a little pilot smelter while you were gone," George said. "I was hoping the red stratum would be ore. The other prospecting parties-none of them found anything."

"We'll try again next spring," he said. "We'll find it somewhere, no matter how long it takes."

"Our time may not be so long. The observations show the sun to be farther south than ever."

"Then we'll make double use of the time we do have. We'll cut the hunting parties to the limit and send out more prospecting parties. We're going to have a ship to meet the Gerns again."

"Sometimes," George said, his black eyes studying him thoughtfully, "I think that's all you live for, Bill: for the day when you can kill Gerns."

George said it as a statement of a fact, without censure, but Humbolt could not keep an edge of harshness out of his voice as he answered:

"For as long as I'm leader that's all we're all going to live for."

He followed the game south that fall, taking with him Bob Craig and young Anders. Hundreds of miles south of the caves they came to the lowlands; a land of much water and vegetation and vast herds of unicorns and woods goats. It was an exceedingly dangerous country, due to the concentration of unicorns and prowlers, and only the automatic crossbows combined with never ceasing vigilance enabled them to survive.

There they saw the crawlers; hideous things that crawled on multiple legs like three-ton centipedes, their mouths set with six mandibles and dripping a stinking saliva. The bite of a crawler was poisonous, instantly paralyzing even to a unicorn, though not instantly killing them. The crawlers ate their victims at once, however, ripping the helpless and still living flesh from its bones.

Although the unicorns feared the crawlers, the prowlers hated them with a fanatical intensity and made use of their superior quickness to kill every crawler they found; ripping at the crawler until the crawler, in an insanity of rage, bit itself and died of its own poison.

They had taken one of the powerful longbows with them, in addition to their crossbows, and they killed a crawler with it one day. As they did so a band of twenty prowlers came suddenly upon them.

Twenty prowlers, with the advantage of surprise at short range, could have slaughtered them. Instead, the prowlers continued on their way without as much as a challenging snarl.

"Now why," Bob Craig wondered, "did they do that?"

"They saw we had just killed a crawler," Humbolt said. "The crawlers are their enemies and I guess letting us live was their way of showing appreciation."

Their further explorations of the lowlands revealed no minerals-nothing but alluvial material of unknown depth-and there was no reason to stay longer except that return to the caves was impossible until spring came. They built attack-proof shelters in the trees and settled down to wait out the winter.

They started north with the first wave of woods goats, nothing but lack of success to show for their months of time and effort.

When they were almost to the caves they came to the barren valley where the Gerns had herded the Rejects out of the cruisers and to the place where the stockade had been. It was a lonely place, the stockade walls fallen and scattered and the graves of Humbolt's mother and all the others long since obliterated by the hooves of the unicorn legions. Bitter memories were reawakened, tinged by the years with nostalgia, and the stockade was far behind them before the dark mood left him.

The orange corn was planted that spring and the number of prospecting parties was doubled.

The corn sprouted, grew feebly, and died before maturity. The prospecting parties returned one by one, each to report no success. He decided, that fall, that time was too precious to waste-they would have to use the alternate plan he had spoken of.

He went to George Ord and asked him if it would be possible to build a hyperspace transmitter with the materials they had.

"It's the one way we could have a chance to leave here without a ship of our own," he said. "By luring a Gern cruiser here and then taking it away from them."

George shook his head. "A hyperspace transmitter *might* be built, given enough years of time. But it would be useless without power. It would take a generator of such size that we'd have to melt down every gun, knife, axe, every piece of steel and iron we have. And then we'd be five hundred pounds short. On top of that, we'd have to have at least three hundred pounds more of copper for additional wire."

"I didn't realize it would take such a large generator," he said after a silence. "I was sure we could have a transmitter."

"Get me the metal and we can," George said. He sighed restlessly and there was almost hatred in his eyes as he looked at the inclosing walls of the cave. "You're not the only one who would like to leave our prison. Get me eight hundred pounds of copper and iron and I'll make the transmitter, some way."

Eight hundred pounds of metal.... On Ragnarok that was like asking for the sun.

The years went by and each year there was the same determined effort, the same lack of success. And each year the suns were farther south, marking the coming of the end of any efforts other than the one to survive.

In the year thirty, when fall came earlier than ever before, he was forced to admit to himself the bleak and bitter fact: he and the others were not of the generation that would escape from Ragnarok. They were Earth-born —they were not adapted to Ragnarok and could not scour a world of 1.5 gravity for metals that might not exist.

And vengeance was a luxury he could not have.

A question grew in his mind where there had been only his hatred for the Gerns before. *What would become of the future generations on Ragnarok?*

With the question a scene from his childhood kept coming back to him; a late summer evening in the first year on Ragnarok and Julia sitting beside him in the warm starlight....

"You're my son, Billy," she had said. "The first I ever had. Now, before so very long, maybe I'll have another one."

Hesitantly, not wanting to believe, he had asked, "What some of them said about how you might die then-it won't really happen, will it, Julia?"

"It ...might." Then her arm had gone around him and she had said, "If I do I'll leave in my place a life that's more important than mine ever was.

"Remember me, Billy, and this evening, and what I said to you, if you should ever be leader. Remember that it's only through the children that we can ever survive and whip this world. Protect them while they're small and helpless and teach them to fight and be afraid of nothing when they're a little older. Never, never let them forget how they came to be on Ragnarok. Someday, even if it's a hundred years from now, the Gerns will come again and they must be ready to fight, for their freedom and for their lives."

He had been too young then to understand how truly she had spoken and when he was old enough his hatred for the Gerns had blinded him to everything but his own desires. Now, he could see....

The children of each generation would be better adapted to Ragnarok and full adaptation would eventually come. But all the generations of the future would be potential slaves of the Gern Empire, free only so long as they remained unnoticed.

It was inconceivable that the Gerns should never pass by Ragnarok through all time to come. And when they finally came the slow, uneventful progression of decades and centuries might have brought a false sense of security to the people of Ragnarok, might have turned the stories of what the Gerns did to the Rejects into legends and then into myths that no one any longer believed.

The Gerns would have to be brought to Ragnarok before that could happen.

* * * * *

He went to George Ord again and said:

"There's one kind of transmitter we could make a generator for —a plain normal-space transmitter, dot-dash, without a receiver."

George laid down the diamond cutting wheel he had been working on.

"It would take two hundred years for the signal to get to Athena at the speed of light," he said. "Then, forty days after it got there, a Gern cruiser would come hell-bent to investigate."

"I want the ones of the future to know that the Gerns will be here no later than two hundred years from now. And with always the chance that a Gern cruiser in space might pick up the signal at any time before then."

"I see," George said. "The sword of Damocles hanging over their heads, to make them remember."

"You know what would happen to them if they ever forgot. You're as old as I am-you know what the Gerns did to us."

"I'm older than you are," George said. "I was nine when the Gerns left us here. They kept my father and mother and my sister was only three. I tried to keep her warm by holding her but the Hell Fever got her that first night. She was too young to understand why I couldn't help her more...."

Hatred burned in his eyes at the memory, like some fire that had been banked but had never died. "Yes, I remember the Gerns and what they did. I wouldn't want it to have to happen to others-the transmitter will be made so that it won't."

* * * * *

The guns were melted down, together with other items of iron and steel, to make the castings for the generator. Ceramic pipes were made to carry water from the spring to a waterwheel. The long, slow job of converting the miscellany of electronic devices, many of them broken, into the components of a transmitter proceeded.

It was five years before the transmitter was ready for testing. It was early fall of the year thirty-five then, and the water that gushed from the pipe splashed in cold drops against Humbolt as the waterwheel was set in motion.

The generator began to hum and George observed the output of it and the transmitter as registered by the various meters he had made.

"Weak, but it will reach the Gern monitor station on Athena," he said, "It's ready to send-what do you want to say?"

"Make it something short," he said. "Make it, *'Ragnarok calling.'*"

George poised his finger over the transmitting key. "This will set forces in motion that can never be recalled. What we do here this morning is going to cause a lot of Gerns-or Ragnarok people-to die."

"It will be the Gerns who die," he said. "Send the signal."

"Like you, I believe the same thing," George said. "I have to believe it because that's the way I want it to be. I hope we're right. It's something we'll never know."

He began depressing the key.

* * * * *

A boy was given the job of operating the key and the signal went out daily until the freezing of winter stopped the waterwheel that powered the generator.

The sending of the signals was resumed when spring came and the prospecting parties continued their vain search for metals.

The suns continued moving south and each year the springs came later, the falls earlier. In the spring of forty-five he saw that he would have to make his final decision.

By then they had dwindled until they numbered only sixty-eight; the Young Ones gray and rapidly growing old. There was no longer any use to continue the prospecting-if any metals were to be found they were at the north end of the plateau where the snow no longer melted during the summer. They were too few to do more than prepare for what the Old Ones had feared they might have to face-Big Winter. That would require the work of all of them.

Sheets of mica were brought down from the Craigs, the summits of which were deeply buried under snow even in midsummer. Stoves were made of fireclay and mica, which would give both heat and light and would be more efficient than the open fireplaces. The innermost caves were prepared for occupation, with multiple doors to hold out the cold and with laboriously excavated ventilation ducts and smoke outlets.

There were sixty of them in the fall of fifty, when all had been done that could be done to prepare for what might come.

* * * * *

"There aren't many of the Earth-born left now," Bob Craig said to him one night as they sat in the flickering light of a stove. "And there hasn't been time for there to be many of the Ragnarok-born. The Gerns wouldn't get many slaves if they should come now."

"They could use however many they found," he answered. "The younger ones, who are the best adapted to this gravity, would be exceptionally strong and quick on a one-gravity world. There are dangerous jobs where a strong, quick slave is a lot more efficient and expendable than complex, expensive machines."

"And they would want some specimens for scientific study," Jim Lake said. "They would want to cut into the young ones and see how they're built that they're adapted to this one and a half gravity world."

He smiled with the cold mirthlessness that always reminded Humbolt of his father-of the Lake who had been the *Constellation's* lieutenant commander. "According to the books the Gerns never did try to make it a secret that when a Gern doctor or biologist cuts into the muscles or organs of a non-Gern to see what makes them tick, he wants them to be still alive and ticking as he does so."

Seventeen-year-old Don Chiara spoke, to say slowly, thoughtfully:

"Slavery and vivisection.... If the Gerns should come now when there are so few of us, and if we should fight the best we could and lose, it would be better for whoever was the last of us left to put a knife in the hearts of the women and children than to let the Gerns have them."

No one made any answer. There was no answer to make, no alternative to suggest.

"In the future there will be more of us and it will be different," he said at last. "On Earth the Gerns were always stronger and faster than humans but when the Gerns come to Ragnarok they're going to find a race that isn't really human any more. They're going to find a race before which they'll be like woods goats before prowlers."

"If only they don't come too soon," Craig said.

"That was the chance that had to be taken," he replied.

He wondered again as he spoke, as he had wondered so often in the past years, if he had given them all their death sentence when he ordered the transmitter built. Yet, the future generations could not be permitted to forget ... and steel could not be tempered without first thrusting it into the fire.

* * * * *

He was the last of the Young Ones when he awoke one night in the fall of fifty-six and found himself burning with the Hell Fever. He did not summon any of the others. They could do nothing for him and he had already done all he could for them.

He had done all he could for them ... and now he would leave forty-nine men, women and children to face the unknown forces of Big Winter while over them hung the sword he had forged; the increasing danger of detection by the Gerns.

The question came again, sharp with the knowledge that it was far too late for him to change any of it. *Did I arrange the execution of my people?*

Then, through the red haze of the fever, Julia spoke to him out of the past; sitting again beside him in the summer twilight and saying:

> *Remember me, Billy, and this evening, and what I said to you ... teach them to fight and be afraid of nothing ... never let them forget how they came to be on Ragnarok....*

She seemed very near and real and the doubt faded and was gone. *Teach them to fight ... never let them forget....* The men of Ragnarok were only fur-clad hunters who crouched in caves but they would grow in numbers as time went by. Each generation would be stronger than the generation before it and he had set forces in motion that would bring the last generation the trial of combat and the opportunity for freedom. How well they fought on that day would determine their destiny but he was certain, once again, what that destiny would be.

It would be to walk as conquerors before beaten and humbled Gerns.

* * * * *

It was winter of the year eighty-five and the temperature was one hundred and six degrees below zero. Walter Humbolt stood in front of the ice tunnel that led back through the glacier to the caves and looked up into the sky.

It was noon but there was no sun in the starlit sky. Many weeks before the sun had slipped below the southern horizon. For a little while a dim halo had marked its passage each day; then that, too, had faded away. But now it was time for the halo to appear again, to herald the sun's returning.

Frost filled the sky, making the stars flicker as it swirled endlessly downward. He blinked against it, his eyelashes trying to freeze to his lower eyelids at the movement, and turned to look at the north.

There the northern lights were a gigantic curtain that filled a third of the sky, rippling and waving in folds that pulsated in red and green, rose and lavender and violet. Their reflection gleamed on the glacier that sloped down from the caves and glowed softly on the other glacier;

the one that covered the transmitter station. The transmitter had long ago been taken into the caves but the generator and waterwheel were still there, frozen in a tomb of ice.

For three years the glacier had been growing before the caves and the plateau's southern face had been buried under snow for ten years. Only a few woods goats ever came as far north as the country south of the caves and they stayed only during the brief period between the last snow of spring and the first snow of fall. Their winter home was somewhere down near the equator. What had been called the Southern Lowlands was a frozen, lifeless waste.

Once they had thought about going to the valley in the chasm where the mockers would be hibernating in their warm caves. But even if they could have gone up the plateau and performed the incredible feat of crossing the glacier-covered, blizzard-ripped Craigs, they would have found no food in the mockers' valley-only a little corn the mockers had stored away, which would soon have been exhausted.

There was no place for them to live but in the caves or as nomads migrating with the animals. And if they migrated to the equator each year they would have to leave behind them all the books and tools and everything that might someday have given them a civilized way of life and might someday have shown them how to escape from their prison.

He looked again to the south where the halo should be, thinking: *They should have made their decision in there by now. I'm their leader-but I can't force them to stay here against their will. I could only ask them to consider what it would mean if we left here.*

Snow creaked underfoot as he moved restlessly. He saw something lying under the blanket of frost and went to it. It was an arrow that someone had dropped. He picked it up, carefully, because the intense cold had made the shaft as brittle as glass. It would regain its normal strength when taken into the caves — —

There was the sound of steps and Fred Schroeder came out of the tunnel, dressed as he was dressed in bulky furs. Schroeder looked to the south and said, "It seems to be starting to get a little lighter there."

He saw that it was; a small, faint paling of the black sky.

"They talked over what you and I told them," Schroeder said. "And about how we've struggled to stay here this long and how, even if the sun should stop drifting south this year, it will be years of ice and cold at the caves before Big Spring comes."

"If we leave here the glacier will cover the caves and fill them with ice," he said. "All we ever had will be buried back in there and all we'll have left will be our bows and arrows and animal skins. We'll be taking a one-way road back into the stone age, for ourselves and our children and their children."

"They know that," Schroeder said. "We both told them."

He paused. They watched the sky to the south turn lighter. The northern lights flamed unnoticed behind them as the pale halo of the invisible sun slowly brightened to its maximum. Their faces were white with near-freezing then and they turned to go back into the caves. "They had made their decision," Schroeder went on. "I guess you and I did them an injustice when we thought they had lost their determination, when we thought they might want to hand their children a flint axe and say, 'Here-take this and let it be the symbol of all you are or all you will ever be.'

"Their decision was unanimous-we'll stay for as long as it's possible for us to survive here."

* * * * *

Howard Lake listened to Teacher Morgan West read from the diary of Walter Humbolt, written during the terrible winter of thirty-five years before:

> *"Each morning the light to the south was brighter. On the seventh morning we saw the sun-and it was not due until the eighth morning!*
>
> *"It will be years before we can stop fighting the enclosure of the glacier but we have reached and passed the dead of Big Winter. We have reached the bottom and the only direction we can go in the future is up.*

"And so," West said, closing the book, "we are here in the caves tonight because of the stubbornness of Humbolt and Schroeder and all the others. Had they thought only of their own welfare, had they conceded defeat and gone into the migratory way of life, we would be sitting beside grass campfires somewhere to the south tonight, our way of life containing no plans or aspirations greater than to follow the game back and forth through the years.

"Now, let's go outside to finish tonight's lesson."

Teacher West led the way into the starlit night just outside the caves, Howard Lake and the other children following him. West pointed to the sky where the star group they called the Athena Constellation blazed like a huge arrowhead high in the east.

"There," he said, "beyond the top of the arrowhead, is where we were going when the Gerns stopped us a hundred and twenty years ago and left us to die on Ragnarok. It's so far that Athena's sun can't be seen from here, so far that it will be another hundred and fifteen years before our first signal gets there. Why is it, then, that you and all the other groups of children have to learn such things as history, physics, the Gern language, and the way to fire a Gern blaster?"

The hand of every child went up. West selected eight-year-old Clifton Humbolt. "Tell us, Clifton," he said.

"Because," Clifton answered, "a Gern cruiser might pass by a few light-years out at any time and pick up our signals. So we have to know all we can about them and how to fight them because there aren't very many of us yet."

"The Gerns will come to kill us," little Marie Chiara said, her dark eyes large and earnest. "They'll come to kill us and to make slaves out of the ones they don't kill, like they did with the others a long time ago. They're awful mean and awful smart and we have to be smarter than they are."

Howard looked again at the Athena constellation, thinking, *I hope they come just as soon as I'm old enough to fight them, or even tonight....*

"Teacher," he asked, "how would a Gern cruiser look if it came tonight? Would it come from the Athena arrowhead?"

"It probably would," West answered. "You would see its rocket blast, like a bright trail of fire — —"

A bright trail of fire burst suddenly into being, coming from the constellation of Athena and lighting up the woods and hills and their startled faces as it arced down toward them.

"It's them!" a treble voice exclaimed and there was a quick flurry of movement as Howard and the other older children shoved the younger children behind them.

Then the light vanished, leaving a dimming glow where it had been.

"Only a meteor," West said. He looked at the line of older children who were standing protectingly in front of the younger ones, rocks in their hands with which to ward off the Gerns, and he smiled in the way he had when he was pleased with them.

Howard watched the meteor trail fade swiftly into invisibility and felt his heartbeats slow from the first wild thrill to gray disappointment. Only a meteor....

But someday he might be leader and by then, surely, the Gerns would come. If not, he would find some way to make them come.

* * * * *

Ten years later Howard Lake was leader. There were three hundred and fifty of them then and Big Spring was on its way to becoming Big Summer. The snow was gone from the southern end of the plateau and once again game migrated up the valleys east of the caves.

There were many things to be done now that Big Winter was past and they could have the chance to do them. They needed a larger pottery kiln, a larger workshop with a wooden lathe, more diamonds to make cutting wheels, more quartz crystals to make binoculars and microscopes. They could again explore the field of inorganic chemistry, even though results in the past had produced nothing of value, and they could, within a few years, resume the metal prospecting up the plateau-the most important project of all.

Their weapons seemed to be as perfect as was possible but when the Gerns came they would need some quick and certain means of communication between the various units that would fight the Gerns. A leader who could not communicate with his forces and coordinate their actions would be helpless. And they had on Ragnarok a form of communication, if trained, that the Gerns could not detect or interfere with electronically: the mockers.

The Craigs were still white and impassable with snow that summer but the snow was receding higher each year. Five years later, in the summer of one hundred and thirty-five, the Craigs were passable for a few weeks.

Lake led a party of eight over them and down into the chasm. They took with them two small cages, constructed of wood and glass and made airtight with the strong medusabush glue. Each cage was equipped with a simple air pump and a pressure gauge.

They brought back two pairs of mockers as interested and trusting captives, together with a supply of the orange corn and a large amount of diamonds. The mockers, in their pressure-maintained cages, were not even aware of the increase in elevation as they were carried over the high summit of the Craigs.

To Lake and the men with him the climb back up the long, steep slope of the mountain was a stiff climb to make in one day but no more than that. It was hard to believe that it had taken Humbolt and Barber almost three days to climb it and that Barber had died in the attempt. It reminded him of the old crossbows that Humbolt and the others had used. They were thin, with a light pull, such as the present generation boys used. It must have required courage for the old ones to dare unicorn attacks with bows so thin that only the small area behind the unicorn's jaws was vulnerable to their arrows....

* * * * *

When the caves were reached, a very gradual reduction of pressure in the mocker cages was started; one that would cover a period of weeks. One pair of mockers survived and had two young ones that fall. The young mockers, like the first generation of Ragnarok-born children of many years before, were more adapted to their environment than their parents were.

The orange corn was planted, using an adaptation method somewhat similar to that used with the mockers. It might have worked had the orange corn not required such a long period of time in which to reach maturity. When winter came only a few grains had formed.

They were saved for next year's seeds, to continue the slow adaptation process.

By the fifth year the youngest generation of mockers was well adapted to the elevation of the caves but for a susceptibility to a quickly fatal form of pneumonia which made it necessary to keep them from exposing themselves to the cold or to any sudden changes of temperature.

Their intelligence was surprising and they seemed to be partially receptive to human thoughts, as Bill Humbolt had written. By the end of the fifteenth year their training had reached such a stage of perfection that a mocker would transmit or not transmit with only the unspoken thought of its master to tell it which it should be. In addition, they would transmit the message to whichever mocker their master's thought directed. Presumably all mockers received the message but only the mocker to whom it was addressed would repeat it aloud.

They had their method of communication. They had their automatic crossbows for quick, close fighting, and their long range longbows. They were fully adapted to the 1.5 gravity and their reflexes were almost like those of prowlers-Ragnarok had long ago separated the quick from the dead.

There were eight hundred and nineteen of them that year, in the early spring of one hundred and fifty, and they were ready and impatient for the coming of the Gerns.

Then the transmitter, which had been in operation again for many years, failed one day.

George Craig had finished checking it when Lake arrived. He looked up from his instruments, remarkably similar in appearance to a sketch of the old George Ord —a resemblance that had been passed down to him by his mother-and said:

"The entire circuit is either gone or ready to go. It's already operated for a lot longer than it should have."

"It doesn't matter," Lake said. "It's served its purpose. We won't rebuild it. "

George watched him questioningly.

"It's served its purpose," he said again. "It didn't let us forget that the Gerns will come again. But that isn't enough, now. The first signal won't reach Athena until the year two thirty-five. It will be the dead of Big Winter again then. They'll have to fight the Gerns with bows and arrows that the cold will make as brittle as glass. They won't have a chance."

"No," George said. "They won't have a chance. But what can we do to change it?"

"It's something I've been thinking about," he said. "We'll build a hyperspace transmitter and bring the Gerns before Big Winter comes."

"We will?" George asked, lifting his dark eyebrows. "And what do we use for the three hundred pounds of copper and five hundred pounds of iron we would have to have to make the generator?"

"Surely we can find five hundred pounds of iron somewhere on Ragnarok. The north end of the plateau might be the best bet. As for the copper —I doubt that we'll ever find it. But there are seams of a bauxite-like clay in the Western hills-they're certain to contain aluminum to at least some extent. So we'll make the wires of aluminum."

"The ore would have to be refined to pure aluminum oxide before it could be smelted," George said. "And you can't smelt aluminum ore in an ordinary furnace-only in an electric furnace with a generator that can supply a high amperage. And we would have to have cryolite ore to serve as the solvent in the smelting process."

"There's a seam of cryolite in the Eastern Hills, according to the old maps," said Lake. "We could make a larger generator by melting down everything we have. It wouldn't be big enough to power the hyperspace transmitter but it should be big enough to smelt aluminum ore."

George considered the idea. "I think we can do it."

"How long until we can send the signal?" he asked.

"Given the extra metal we need, the building of the generator is a simple job. The transmitter is what will take years-maybe as long as fifty."

Fifty years....

"Can't anything be done to make it sooner?" he asked.

"I know," George said. "You would like for the Gerns to come while you're still here. So would every man on Ragnarok. But even on Earth the building of a hyperspace transmitter was a long, slow job, with all the materials they needed and all the special tools and equipment. Here we'll have to do everything by hand and for materials we have only broken and burned-out odds and ends. It will take about fifty years-it can't be helped."

Fifty years ... but that would bring the Gerns before Big Winter came again. And there was the rapidly increasing chance that a Gern cruiser would at any day intercept the first signals. They were already more than halfway to Athena.

"Melt down the generator," he said. "Start making a bigger one. Tomorrow men will go out after bauxite and cryolite and four of us will go up the plateau to look for iron."

* * * * *

Lake selected Gene Taylor, Tony Chiara and Steve Schroeder to go with him. They were well on their way by daylight the next morning, on the shoulder of each of them a mocker which observed the activity and new scenes with bright, interested eyes.

They traveled light, since they would have fresh meat all the way, and carried herbs and corn only for the mockers. Once, generations before, it had been necessary for men to eat herbs to prevent deficiency diseases but now the deficiency diseases, like Hell Fever, were unknown to them.

They carried no compasses since the radiations of the two suns constantly created magnetic storms that caused compass needles to swing as much as twenty degrees within an hour. Each of them carried a pair of powerful binoculars, however; binoculars that had been diamond-carved from the ivory-like black unicorn horn and set with lenses and prisms of diamond-cut quartz.

The foremost bands of woods goats followed the advance of spring up the plateau and they followed the woods goats. They could not go ahead of the goats-the goats were already pressing close behind the melting of the snow. No hills or ridges were seen as the weeks went by and it seemed to Lake that they would walk forever across the endless rolling floor of the plain.

Early summer came and they walked across a land that was green and pleasantly cool at a time when the vegetation around the caves would be burned brown and lifeless. The woods goats grew less in number then as some of them stopped for the rest of the summer in their chosen latitudes.

They continued on and at last they saw, far to the north, what seemed to be an almost infinitesimal bulge on the horizon. They reached it two days later; a land of rolling green hills, scarred here and there with ragged outcroppings of rock, and a land that climbed slowly and steadily higher as it went into the north.

They camped that night in a little vale. The floor of it was white with the bones of woods goats that had tarried too long the fall before and got caught by an early blizzard. There was still flesh on the bones and scavenger rodents scuttled among the carcasses, feasting.

"We'll split up now," he told the others the next morning.

He assigned each of them his position; Steve Schroeder to parallel his course thirty miles to his right, Gene Taylor to go thirty miles to his left, and Tony Chiara to go thirty miles to the left of Taylor.

"We'll try to hold those distances," he said. "We can't look over the country in detail that way but it will give us a good general survey of it. We don't have too much time left by now and we'll make as many miles into the north as we can each day. The woods goats will tell us when it's time for us to turn back."

They parted company with casual farewells but for Steve Schroeder, who smiled sardonically at the bones of the woods goats in the vale and asked:

"Who's supposed to tell the woods goats?"

* * * * *

Tip, the black, white-nosed mocker on Lake's shoulder, kept twisting his neck to watch the departure of the others until he had crossed the next hill and the others were hidden from view.

"All right, Tip," he said then. "You can unwind your neck now."

"Unwind-all right-all right," Tip said. Then, with a sudden burst of energy which was characteristic of mockers, he began to jiggle up and down and chant in time with his movements, "All right all right all right all right ——"

"Shut up!" he commanded. "If you want to talk nonsense I don't care-but don't say 'all right' any more."

"All right," Tip agreed amiably, settling down. "Shut up if you want to talk nonsense. I don't care."

"And don't slaughter the punctuation like that. You change the meaning entirely."

"But don't say all right any more," Tip went on, ignoring him. "You change the meaning entirely."

Then, with another surge of animation, Tip began to fish in his jacket pocket with little hand-like paws. "Tip hungry-Tip hungry."

Lake unbuttoned the pocket and gave Tip a herb leaf. "I notice there's no nonsensical chatter when you want to ask for something to eat."

Tip took the herb leaf but he spoke again before he began to eat; slowly, as though trying seriously to express a thought:

"Tip hungry-no nonsensical."

"Sometimes," he said, turning his head to look at Tip, "you mockers give me the peculiar feeling that you're right on the edge of becoming a new and intelligent race and no fooling."

Tip wiggled his whiskers and bit into the herb leaf. "No fooling," he agreed.

* * * * *

He stopped for the night in a steep-walled hollow and built a small fire of dead moss and grass to ward off the chill that came with dark. He called the others, thinking first of Schroeder so that Tip would transmit to Schroeder's mocker:

"Steve?"

"Here," Tip answered, in a detectable imitation of Schroeder's voice. "No luck."

He thought of Gene Taylor and called, "Gene?"

There was no answer and he called Chiara. "Tony-could you see any of Gene's route today?"

"Part of it," Chiara answered. "I saw a herd of unicorns over that way. Why-doesn't he answer?"

"No."

"Then," Chiara said, "they must have got him."

"Did you find anything today, Tony?" he asked.

"Nothing but pure andesite. Not even an iron stain."

It was the same kind of barren formation that he, himself, had been walking over all day. But he had not expected success so soon....

He tried once again to call Gene Taylor:

"Gene ... Gene ... are you there, Gene?"

There was no answer. He knew there would never be.

* * * * *

The days became weeks with dismaying swiftness as they penetrated farther into the north. The hills became more rugged and there were intrusions of granite and other formations to promise a chance of finding metal; a promise that urged them on faster as their time grew shorter.

Twice he saw something white in the distance. Once it was the bones of another band of woods goats that had huddled together and frozen to death in some early blizzard of the past and once it was the bones of a dozen unicorns.

The nights grew chillier and the suns moved faster and faster to the south. The animals began to migrate, an almost imperceptible movement in the beginning but one that increased each day. The first frost came and the migration began in earnest. By the third day it was a hurrying tide.

Tip was strangely silent that day. He did not speak until the noon sun had cleared the cold, heavy mists of morning. When he spoke it was to give a message from Chiara:

"Howard ... last report ... Goldie is dying ... pneumonia...."

Goldie was Chiara's mocker, his only means of communication-and there would be no way to tell him when they were turning back.

"Turn back today, Tony," he said. "Steve and I will go on for a few days more."

There was no answer and he said quickly, "Turn back-turn back! Acknowledge that, Tony."

"Turning back ..." the acknowledgment came. "... tried to save her...."

The message stopped and there was a silence that Chiara's mocker would never break again. He walked on, with Tip sitting very small and quiet on his shoulder. He had crossed another hill before Tip moved, to press up close to him the way mockers did when they were lonely and to hold tightly to him.

"What is it, Tip?" he asked.

"Goldie is dying," Tip said. And then again, like a soft, sad whisper, "Goldie is dying...."

"She was your mate.... I'm sorry."

78

Tip made a little whimpering sound, and the man reached up to stroke his silky side.
"I'm sorry," he said again. "I'm sorry as hell, little fellow."

* * * * *

For two days Tip sat lonely and silent on his shoulder, no longer interested in the new scenes nor any longer relieving the monotony with his chatter. He refused to eat until the morning of the third day.

By then the exodus of woods goats and unicorns had dwindled to almost nothing; the sky a leaden gray through which the sun could not be seen. That evening he saw what he was sure would be the last band of woods goats and shot one of them.

When he went to it he was almost afraid to believe what he saw.

The hair above its feet was red, discolored with the stain of iron-bearing clay.

He examined it more closely and saw that the goat had apparently watered at a spring where the mud was material washed down from an iron-bearing vein or formation. It had done so fairly recently-there were still tiny particles of clay adhering to the hair.

The wind stirred, cold and damp with its warning of an approaching storm. He looked to the north, where the evening had turned the gray clouds black, and called Schroeder:

"Steve-any luck?"

"None," Schroeder answered.

"I just killed a goat," he said. "It has iron stains on its legs it got at some spring farther north. I'm going on to try to find it. You can turn back in the morning."

"No," Schroeder objected. "I can angle over and catch up with you in a couple of days."

"You'll turn back in the morning," he said. "I'm going to try to find this iron. But if I get caught by a blizzard it will be up to you to tell them at the caves that I found iron and to tell them where it is-you know the mockers can't transmit that far."

There was a short silence; then Schroeder said, "All right —I see. I'll head south in the morning."

Lake took a route the next day that would most likely be the one the woods goats had come down, stopping on each ridge top to study the country ahead of him through his binoculars. It was cloudy all day but at sunset the sun appeared very briefly, to send its last rays across the hills and redden them in mockery of the iron he sought.

Far ahead of him, small even through the glasses and made visible only because of the position of the sun, was a spot at the base of a hill that was redder than the sunset had made the other hills.

He was confident it would be the red clay he was searching for and he hurried on, not stopping until darkness made further progress impossible.

Tip slept inside his jacket, curled up against his chest, while the wind blew raw and cold all through the night. He was on his way again at the first touch of daylight, the sky darker than ever and the wind spinning random flakes of snow before him.

He stopped to look back to the south once, thinking, *If I turn back now I might get out before the blizzard hits.*

Then the other thought came: *These hills all look the same. It I don't go to the iron while I'm this close and know where it is, it might be years before I or anyone else could find it again.*

He went on and did not look back again for the rest of the day.

By midafternoon the higher hills around him were hidden under the clouds and the snow was coming harder and faster as the wind drove the flakes against his face. It began to snow with a heaviness that brought a half darkness when he came finally to the hill he had seen through the glasses.

A spring was at the base of it, bubbling out of red clay. Above it the red dirt led a hundred feet to a dike of granite and stopped. He hurried up the hillside that was rapidly whitening with snow and saw the vein.

It set against the dike, short and narrow but red-black with the iron it contained. He picked up a piece and felt the weight of it. It was heavy-it was pure iron oxide.

He called Schroeder and asked, "Are you down out of the high hills, Steve?"

"I'm in the lower ones," Schroeder answered, the words coming a little muffled from where Tip lay inside his jacket. "It looks black as hell up your way."

"I found the iron, Steve. Listen-these are the nearest to landmarks I can give you...."

When he had finished he said, "That's the best I can do. You can't see the red clay except when the sun is low in the southwest but I'm going to build a monument on top of the hill to find it by."

"About you, Howard," Steve asked, "what are your chances?"

The wind was rising to a high moaning around the ledges of the granite dike and the vein was already invisible under the snow.

"It doesn't look like they're very good," he answered. "You'll probably be leader when you come back next spring—I told the council I wanted that if anything happened to me. Keep things going the way I would have. Now—I'll have to hurry to get the monument built in time."

"All right," Schroeder said. "So long, Howard ... good luck."

He climbed to the top of the hill and saw boulders there he could use to build the monument. They were large-he might crush Tip against his chest in picking them up-and he took off his jacket, to wrap it around Tip and leave him lying on the ground.

He worked until he was panting for breath, the wind driving the snow harder and harder against him until the cold seemed to have penetrated to the bone. He worked until the monument was too high for his numb hands to lift any more boulders to its top. By then it was tall enough that it should serve its purpose.

He went back to look for Tip, the ground already four inches deep in snow and the darkness almost complete.

"Tip," he called. "Tip-Tip ——" He walked back and forth across the hillside in the area where he thought he had left him, stumbling over rocks buried in the snow and invisible in the darkness, calling against the wind and thinking, *I can't leave him to die alone here.*

Then, from a bulge he had not seen in the snow under him, there came a frightened, lonely wail:

"Tip cold-Tip cold ——"

He raked the snow off his jacket and unwrapped Tip, to put him inside his shirt next to his bare skin. Tip's paws were like ice and he was shivering violently, the first symptom of the pneumonia that killed mockers so quickly.

Tip coughed, a wrenching, rattling little sound, and whimpered, "Hurt-hurt ——"

"I know," he said. "Your lungs hurt-damn it to hell, I wish I could have let you go home with Steve."

He put on the cold jacket and went down the hill. There was nothing with which he could make a fire-only the short half-green grass, already buried under the snow. He turned south at the bottom of the hill, determining the direction by the wind, and began the stubborn march southward that could have but one ending.

He walked until his cold-numbed legs would carry him no farther. The snow was warm when he fell for the last time; warm and soft as it drifted over him, and his mind was clouded with a pleasant drowsiness.

This isn't so bad, he thought, and there was something like surprise through the drowsiness. *I can't regret doing what I had to do-doing it the best I could....*

Tip was no longer coughing and the thought of Tip was the only one that was tinged with regret: *I hope he wasn't still hurting when he died.*

He felt Tip still very feebly against his chest then, and he did not know if it was his imagination or if in that last dreamlike state it was Tip's thought that came to him; warm and close and reassuring him:

No hurt no cold now-all right now-we sleep now....

PART 3

When spring came Steve Schroeder was leader, as Lake had wanted. It was a duty and a responsibility that would be under circumstances different from those of any of the leaders before him. The grim fight was over for a while. They were adapted and increasing in number; going into Big Summer and into a renascence that would last for fifty years. They would have half a century in which to develop their environment to its fullest extent. Then Big Fall would come, to destroy all they had accomplished, and the Gerns would come, to destroy them.

It was his job to make certain that by then they would be stronger than either.

* * * * *

He went north with nine men as soon as the weather permitted. It was hard to retrace the route of the summer before, without compasses, among the hills which looked all the same as far as their binoculars could reach, and it was summer when they saw the hill with the monument. They found Lake's bones a few miles south of it, scattered by the scavengers as were the little bones of his mocker. They buried them together, man and mocker, and went silently on toward the hill.

They had brought a little hand-cranked diamond drill with them to bore holes in the hard granite and black powder for blasting. They mined the vein, sorting out the ore from the waste and saving every particle.

The vein was narrow at the surface and pinched very rapidly. At a depth of six feet it was a knife-blade seam; at ten feet it was only a red discoloration in the bottom of their shaft.

"That seems to be all of it," he said to the others. "We'll send men up here next year to go deeper and farther along its course but I have an idea we've just mined all of the only iron vein on Ragnarok. It will be enough for our purpose."

They sewed the ore in strong rawhide sacks and then prospected, without success, until it was time for the last unicorn band to pass by on its way south. They trapped ten unicorns and hobbled their legs, with other ropes reaching from horn to hind leg on each side to prevent them from swinging back their heads or even lifting them high.

They had expected the capture and hobbling of the unicorns to be a difficult and dangerous job and it was. But when they were finished the unicorns were helpless. They could move awkwardly about to graze but they could not charge. They could only stand with lowered heads and fume and rumble.

The ore sacks were tied on one frosty morning and the men mounted. The horn-leg ropes were loosened so the unicorns could travel, and the unicorns went into a frenzy of bucking and rearing, squealing with rage as they tried to impale their riders.

The short spears, stabbing at the sensitive spot behind the jawbones of the unicorns, thwarted the backward flung heads and the unicorns were slowly forced into submission. The last one conceded temporary defeat and the long journey to the south started, the unicorns going in the run that they could maintain hour after hour.

Each day they pushed the unicorns until they were too weary to fight at night. Each morning, rested, the unicorns resumed the battle. It became an expected routine for both unicorns and men.

The unicorns were released when the ore was unloaded at the foot of the hill before the caves and Schroeder went to the new waterwheel, where the new generator was already in place. There George Craig told him of the unexpected obstacle that had appeared.

"We're stuck," George said. "The aluminum ore isn't what we thought it would be. It's scarce and very low grade, of such a complex nature that we can't refine it to the oxide with what we have to work with on Ragnarok."

"Have you produced any aluminum oxide at all?" Schroeder asked.

"A little. We might have enough for the wire in a hundred years if we kept at it hard enough."

"What else do you need-was there enough cryolite?" he asked.

"Not much of it, but enough. We have the generator set up, the smelting box built and the carbon lining and rods ready. We have everything we need to smelt aluminum ore-except the aluminum ore."

"Go ahead and finish up the details, such as installing the lining," he said. "We didn't get this far to be stopped now."

But the prospecting parties, making full use of the time left them before winter closed down, returned late that fall to report no sign of the ore they needed.

Spring came and he was determined they would be smelting aluminum before the summer was over even though he had no idea where the ore would be found. They needed aluminum ore of a grade high enough that they could extract the pure aluminum oxide. Specifically, they needed aluminum oxide....

Then he saw the answer to their problem, so obvious that all of them had overlooked it.

He passed by four children playing a game in front of the caves that day; some kind of a checker-like game in which differently colored rocks represented the different children. One boy was using red stones; some of the rubies that had been brought back as curios from the chasm. Rubies were of no use or value on Ragnarok; only pretty rocks for children to play with....

Only pretty rocks? —*rubies and sapphires were corundum, were pure aluminum oxide!*

He went to tell George and to arrange for a party of men to go into the chasm after all the rubies and sapphires they could find. The last obstacle had been surmounted.

The summer sun was hot the day the generator hummed into life. The carbon-lined smelting box was ready and the current flowed between the heavy carbon rods suspended in the cryolite and the lining, transforming the cryolite into a liquid. The crushed rubies and sapphires were fed into the box, glowing and glittering in blood-red and sky-blue scintillations of light, to be deprived by the current of their life and fire and be changed into something entirely different.

When the time came to draw off some of the metal they opened the orifice in the lower corner of the box. Molten aluminum flowed out into the ingot mold in a little stream; more beautiful to them than any gems could ever be, bright and gleaming in its promise that more than six generations of imprisonment would soon be ended.

* * * * *

The aluminum smelting continued until the supply of rubies and sapphires in the chasm had been exhausted but for small and scattered fragments. It was enough, with some aluminum above the amount needed for the wire.

It was the year one hundred and fifty-two when they smelted the aluminum. In eight more years they would reach the middle of Big Summer; the suns would start their long drift southward, not to return for one hundred and fifty years. Time was passing swiftly by for them and there was none of it to waste....

The making of ceramics was developed to an art, as was the making of different types of glass. Looms were built to spin thread and cloth from woods goat wool, and vegetable dyes were discovered. Exploration parties crossed the continent to the eastern and western seas: salty and lifeless seas that were bordered by immense deserts. No trees of any kind grew along their shores and ships could not be built to cross them.

Efforts were continued to develop an inorganic field of chemistry, with discouraging results, but in one hundred and fifty-nine the orange corn was successfully adapted to the elevation and climate of the caves.

There was enough that year to feed the mockers all winter, supply next year's seeds, and leave enough that it could be ground and baked into bread for all to taste.

It tasted strange, but good. It was, Schroeder thought, symbolic of a great forward step. It was the first time in generations that any of them had known any food but meat. The corn would make them less dependent upon hunting and, of paramount importance, it was the type of food to which they would have to become accustomed in the future-they could not carry herds of woods goats and unicorns with them on Gern battle cruisers.

The lack of metals hindered them wherever they turned in their efforts to build even the simplest machines or weapons. Despite its dubious prospects, however, they made a rifle-like gun.

The barrel of it was thick, of the hardest, toughest ceramic material they could produce. It was a cumbersome, heavy thing, firing with a flintlock action, and it could not be loaded with much powder lest the charge burst the barrel.

The flintlock ignition was not instantaneous, the lightweight porcelain bullet had far less penetrating power than an arrow, and the thing boomed and belched out a cloud of smoke that would have shown the Gerns exactly where the shooter was located.

It was an interesting curio and the firing of it was something spectacular to behold but it was a weapon apt to be much more dangerous to the man behind it than to the Gern it was aimed at. Automatic crossbows were far better.

Woods goats had been trapped and housed during the summers in shelters where sprays of water maintained a temperature cool enough for them to survive. Only the young were kept when fall came, to be sheltered through the winter in one of the caves. Each new generation was subjected to more heat in the summer and more cold in the winter than the generation before it and by the year one hundred and sixty the woods goats were well on their way toward adaptation.

The next year they trapped two unicorns, to begin the job of adapting and taming future generations of them. If they succeeded they would have utilized the resources of Ragnarok to the limit-except for what should be their most valuable ally with which to fight the Gerns: the prowlers.

For twenty years prowlers had observed a truce wherein they would not go hunting for men if men would stay away from their routes of travel. But it was a truce only and there was no indication that it could ever evolve into friendship.

Three times in the past, half-grown prowlers had been captured and caged in the hope of taming them. Each time they had paced their cages, looking longingly into the distance, refusing to eat and defiant until they died.

To prowlers, as to some men, freedom was more precious than life. And each time a prowler had been captured the free ones had retaliated with a resurgence of savage attacks.

There seemed no way that men and prowlers could ever meet on common ground. They were alien to one another, separated by the gulf of an origin on worlds two hundred and fifty light-years apart. Their only common heritage was the will of each to battle.

But in the spring of one hundred and sixty-one, for a little while one day, the gulf was bridged.

* * * * *

Schroeder was returning from a trip he had taken alone to the east, coming down the long canyon that led from the high face of the plateau to the country near the caves. He hurried, glancing back at the black clouds that had gathered so quickly on the mountain behind him. Thunder rumbled from within them, an almost continuous roll of it as the clouds poured down their deluge of water.

A cloudburst was coming and the sheer-walled canyon down which he hurried had suddenly become a death trap, its sunlit quiet soon to be transformed into roaring destruction. There was only one place along its nine-mile length where he might climb out and the time was already short in which to reach it.

He had increased his pace to a trot when he came to it, a talus of broken rock that sloped up steeply for thirty feet to a shelf. A ledge eleven feet high stood over the shelf and other, lower, ledges set back from it like climbing steps.

At the foot of the talus he stopped to listen, wondering how close behind him the water might be. He heard it coming, a sound like the roaring of a high wind up the canyon, and he scrambled up the talus of loose rock to the shelf at its top. The shelf was not high enough above the canyon's floor-he would be killed there-and he followed it fifty feet around a sharp bend. There it narrowed abruptly, to merge into the sheer wall of the canyon. Blind alley....

He ran back to the top of the talus where the edge of the ledge, ragged with projections of rock, was unreachably far above him. As he did so the roaring was suddenly a crashing, booming thunder and he saw the water coming.

It swept around the bend at perhaps a hundred miles an hour, stretching from wall to wall of the canyon, the crest of it seething and slashing and towering forty sheer feet above the canyon's floor.

A prowler was running in front of it, running for its life and losing.

There was no time to watch. He leaped upward, as high as possible, his crossbow in his hand. He caught the end of the bow over one of the sharp projections of rock on the ledge's rim and began to pull himself up, afraid to hurry lest the rock cut the bowstring in two and drop him back.

It held and he stood on the ledge, safe, as the prowler flashed up the talus below.

It darted around the blind-alley shelf and was back a moment later. It saw that its only chance would be to leap up on the ledge where he stood and it tried, handicapped by the steep, loose slope it had to jump from.

It failed and fell back. It tried again, hurling itself upward with all its strength, and its claws caught fleetingly on the rough rock a foot below the rim. It began to slide back, with no time left it for a third try.

It looked up at the rim of safety that it had not quite reached and then on up at him, its eyes bright and cold with the knowledge that it was going to die and its enemy would watch it.

Schroeder dropped flat on his stomach and reached down, past the massive black head, to seize the prowler by the back of the neck. He pulled up with all his strength and the claws of the prowler tore at the rocks as it climbed.

When it was coming up over the ledge, safe, he rolled back from it and came to his feet in one swift, wary motion, his eyes on it and his knife already in his hand. As he did so the water went past below them with a thunder that deafened. Logs and trees shot past, boulders crashed together, and things could be seen surging in the brown depths; shapeless things that had once been woods goats and the battered gray bulk of a unicorn. He saw it all with a sideward glance, his attention on the prowler.

It stepped back from the rim of the ledge and looked at him; warily, as he looked at it. With the wariness was something like question, and almost disbelief.

The ledge they stood on was narrow but it led out of the canyon and to the open land beyond. He motioned to the prowler to precede him and, hesitating a moment, it did so.

They climbed out of the canyon and out onto the grassy slope of the mountainside. The roar of the water was a distant rumble there and he stopped. The prowler did the same and they watched each other again, each of them trying to understand what the thoughts of the other might be. It was something they could not know-they were too alien to each other and had been enemies too long.

Then a gust of wind swept across them, bending and rippling the tall grass, and the prowler swung away to go with it and leave him standing alone.

His route was such that it diverged gradually from that taken by the prowler. He went through a grove of trees and emerged into an open glade on the other side. Up on the ridge to his right he saw something black for a moment, already far away.

He was thirty feet from the next grove of trees when he saw the gray shadow waiting silently for his coming within them.

Unicorn!

His crossbow rattled as he jerked back the pistol grip. The unicorn charged, the underbrush crackling as it tore through it and a vine whipping like a rope from its lowered horn.

His first arrow went into its chest. It lurched, fatally wounded but still coming, and he jerked back on the pistol grip for the quick shot that would stop it.

The rock-frayed bow string broke with a singing sound and the bow ends snapped harm-lessly forward.

He had counted on the bow and its failure came a fraction of a second too late for him to dodge far enough. His sideward leap was short, and the horn caught him in midair, ripping across his ribs and breaking them, shattering the bone of his left arm and tearing the flesh. He was hurled fifteen feet and he struck the ground with a stunning impact, pain washing over him in a blinding wave.

Through it, dimly, he saw the unicorn fall and heard its dying trumpet blast as it called to another. He heard an answering call somewhere in the distance and then the faraway drumming of hooves.

He fought back the blindness and used his good arm to lift himself up. His bow was useless, his spear lay broken under the unicorn, and his knife was gone. His left arm swung helplessly and he could not climb the limbless lower trunk of a lance tree with only one arm.

He went forward, limping, trying to hurry to find his knife while the drumming of hooves raced toward him. It would be a battle already lost that he would make with the short knife but he would have blood for his going....

The grass grew tall and thick, hiding the knife until he could hear the unicorn crashing through the trees. He saw it ten feet ahead of him as the unicorn tore out from the edge of the woods thirty feet away.

It squealed, shrill with triumph, and the horn swept up to impale him. There was no time left to reach the knife, no time left for anything but the last fleeting sight of sunshine and glade and arching blue sky — —

Something from behind him shot past and up at the unicorn's throat, a thing that was snarling black savagery with yellow eyes blazing and white fangs slashing-the prowler!

It ripped at the unicorn's throat, swerving its charge, and the unicorn plunged past him. The unicorn swung back, all the triumph gone from its squeal, and the prowler struck again. They became a swirling blur, the horn of the unicorn swinging and stabbing and the attacks of the prowler like the swift, relentless thrusting of a rapier.

He went to his knife and when he turned back with it in his hand the battle was already over.

The unicorn fell and the prowler turned away from it. One foreleg was bathed in blood and its chest was heaving with a panting so fast that it could not have been caused by the fight with the unicorn.

It must have been watching me, he thought, with a strange feeling of wonder. *It was watching from the ridge and it ran all the way.*

Its yellow eyes flickered to the knife in his hand. He dropped the knife in the grass and walked forward, unarmed, wanting the prowler to know that he understood; that for them in that moment the gulf of two hundred and fifty light-years did not exist.

He stopped near it and squatted in the grass to begin binding up his broken arm so the bones would not grate together. It watched him, then it began to lick at its bloody shoulder; standing so close to him that he could have reached out and touched it.

Again he felt the sense of wonder. They were alone together in the glade, he and a prowler, each caring for his hurts. There was a bond between them that for a little while made them like brothers. There was a bridge for a little while across the gulf that had never been bridged before....

When he had finished with his arm and the prowler had lessened the bleeding of its shoulder it took a step back toward the ridge. He stood up, knowing it was going to leave.

"I suppose the score is even now," he said to it, "and we'll never see each other again. So good hunting-and thanks."

It made a sound in its throat; a queer sound that was neither bark nor growl, and he had the feeling it was trying to tell him something. Then it turned and was gone like a black shadow across the grass and he was alone again.

He picked up his knife and bow and began the long, painful journey back to the caves, looking again and again at the ridge behind him and thinking: *They have a code of ethics. They fight for their survival-but they pay their debts.*

Ragnarok was big enough for both men and prowlers. They could live together in friendship as men and dogs of Earth lived together. It might take a long time to win the trust of the prowlers but surely it could be done.

He came to the rocky trail that led to the caves and there he took a last look at the ridge behind him; feeling a poignant sense of loss and wondering if he would ever see the prowler again or ever again know the strange, wild companionship he had known that day.

Perhaps he never would ... but the time would come on Ragnarok when children would play in the grass with prowler pups and the time would come when men and prowlers, side by side, would face the Gerns.

* * * * *

In the year that followed there were two incidents when a prowler had the opportunity to kill a hunter on prowler territory and did not do so. There was no way of knowing if the prowler in each case had been the one he had saved from the cloudburst or if the prowlers, as a whole, were respecting what a human had done for one of them.

Schroeder thought of again trying to capture prowler pups-very young ones-and decided it would be a stupid plan. Such an act would destroy all that had been done toward winning the trust of the prowlers. It would be better to wait, even though time was growing short, and find some other way.

The fall of one hundred and sixty-three came and the suns were noticeably moving south. That was the fall that his third child, a girl, was born. She was named Julia, after the Julia of long ago, and she was of the last generation that would be born in the caves.

Plans were already under way to build a town in the valley a mile from the caves. The unicorn-proof stockade wall that would enclose it was already under construction, being made of stone blocks. The houses would be of diamond-sawed stone, thick-walled, with dead-air spaces between the double walls to insulate against heat and cold. Tall, wide canopies of lance tree poles and the palm-like medusabush leaves would be built over all the houses to supply additional shade.

The woods goats were fully adapted that year and domesticated to such an extent that they had no desire to migrate with the wild goats. There was a small herd of them then, enough to supply a limited amount of milk, cheese and wool.

The adaptation of the unicorns proceeded in the following years, but not their domestication. It was their nature to be ill-tempered and treacherous and only the threat of the spears in the hands of their drivers forced them to work; work that they could have done easily had they not diverted so much effort each day to trying to turn on their masters and kill them. Each night they were put in a massive-walled corral, for they were almost as dangerous as wild unicorns.

The slow, painstaking work on the transmitter continued while the suns moved farther south each year. The move from the caves to the new town was made in one hundred and seventy-nine, the year that Schroeder's wife died.

His two sons were grown and married and Julia, at sixteen, was a woman by Ragnarok standards; blue-eyed and black-haired as her mother, a Craig, had been, and strikingly pretty in a wild, reckless way. She married Will Humbolt that spring, leaving her father alone in the new house in the new town.

Four months later she came to him to announce with pride and excitement:

"I'm going to have a baby in only six months! If it's a boy he'll be the right age to be leader when the Gerns come and we're going to name him John, after the John who was the first leader we ever had on Ragnarok."

Her words brought to his mind a question and he thought of what old Dale Craig, the leader who had preceded Lake, had written:

We have survived, the generations that the Gerns thought would never be born. But we must never forget the characteristics that insured that survival: an unswerving loyalty of every individual to all the others and the courage to fight, and die if necessary.

In any year, now, the Gerns will come. There will be no one to help us. Those on Athena are slaves and it is probable that Earth has been enslaved by now. We will stand or fall alone. But if we of today could know that the ones who meet the Gerns will still have the courage and loyalty that made our survival possible, then we would know that the Gerns are already defeated....

The era of danger and violence was over for a little while. The younger generation had grown up during a time of peaceful development of their environment. It was a peace that the coming of the Gerns would shatter-but had it softened the courage and loyalty of the younger generation?

A week later he was given his answer.

He was climbing up the hill that morning, high above the town below, when he saw the blue of Julia's wool blouse in the distance. She was sitting up on a hillside, an open book in her lap and her short spear lying beside her.

He frowned at the sight. The main southward migration of unicorns was over but there were often lone stragglers who might appear at any time. He had warned her that someday a unicorn would kill her-but she was reckless by nature and given to restless moods in which she could not stand the confinement of the town.

She jerked up her head as he watched, as though at a faint sound, and he saw the first movement within the trees behind her —a unicorn.

It lunged forward, its stealth abandoned as she heard it, and she came to her feet in a swift, smooth movement; the spear in her hand and the book spilling to the ground.

The unicorn's squeal rang out and she whirled to face it, with two seconds to live. He reached for his bow, knowing his help would come too late.

She did the only thing possible that might enable her to survive: she shifted her balance to take advantage of the fact that a human could jump to one side a little more quickly than a four-footed beast in headlong charge. As she did so she brought up the spear for the thrust into the vulnerable area just behind the jawbone.

It seemed the needle point of the black horn was no more than an arm's length from her stomach when she jumped aside with the lithe quickness of a prowler, swinging as she jumped and thrusting the spear with all her strength into the unicorn's neck.

The thrust was true and the spear went deep. She released it and flung herself backward to dodge the flying hooves. The force of the unicorn's charge took it past her but its legs collapsed under it and it crashed to the ground, sliding a little way before it stopped. It kicked once and lay still.

She went to it, to retrieve her spear, and even from the distance there was an air of pride about her as she walked past her bulky victim.

Then she saw the book, knocked to one side by the unicorn's hooves. Tatters of its pages were blowing in the wind and she stiffened, her face growing pale. She ran to it to pick it up, the unicorn forgotten.

She was trying to smooth the torn leaves when he reached her. It had been one of the old textbooks, printed on real paper, and it was fragile with age. She had been trusted by the librarian to take good care of it. Now, page after page was torn and unreadable....

She looked up at him, shame and misery on her face.

"Father," she said. "The book —I — —"

He saw that the unicorn was a bull considerably larger than the average. Men had in the past killed unicorns with spears but never, before, had a sixteen-year-old girl done so....

He looked back at her, keeping his face emotionless, and asked sternly, "You what?"

"I guess —I guess I didn't have any right to take the book out of town. I wish I hadn't...."

"You promised to take good care of it," he told her coldly. "Your promise was believed and you were trusted to keep it."

"But-but I didn't mean to damage it —I didn't mean to!" She was suddenly very near to tears. "I'm not a —a *bemmon!*"

"Go back to town," he ordered. "Tonight bring the book to the town hall and tell the council what happened to it."

She swallowed and said in a faint voice, "Yes, father."

She turned and started slowly back down the hill, not seeing the unicorn as she passed it, the bloody spear trailing disconsolately behind her and her head hanging in shame.

He watched her go and it was safe for him to smile. When night came and she stood before the council, ashamed to lift her eyes to look at them, he would have to be grim and stern as he told her how she had been trusted and how she had betrayed that trust. But now, as he watched her go down the hill, he could smile with his pride in her and know that his question was answered; that the younger generation had lost neither courage nor loyalty.

* * * * *

Julia saved a child's life that spring and almost lost her own. The child was playing under a half-completed canopy when a sudden, violent wind struck it and transformed it into a death-trap of cracking, falling timbers. She reached him in time to fling him to safety but the collapsing roof caught her before she could make her own escape.

Her chest and throat were torn by the jagged ends of the broken poles and for a day and a night her life was a feebly flickering spark. She began to rally on the second night and on the third morning she was able to speak for the first time, her eyes dark and tortured with her fear:

"My baby-what did it do to him?"

She convalesced slowly, haunted by the fear. Her son was born five weeks later and her fears proved to have been groundless. He was perfectly normal and healthy.

And hungry-and her slowly healing breasts would be dry for weeks to come.

By a coincidence that had never happened before and could never happen again there was not a single feeding-time foster-mother available for the baby. There were many expectant mothers but only three women had young babies-and each of the three had twins to feed.

But there was a small supply of frozen goat milk in the ice house, enough to see young Johnny through until it was time for the goat herd to give milk. He would have to live on short rations until then but it could not be helped.

* * * * *

Johnny was a month old when the opportunity came for the men of Ragnarok to have their ultimate ally.

The last of the unicorns were going north and the prowlers had long since gone. The blue star was lighting the night like a small sun when the breeze coming through Schroeder's window brought the distant squealing of unicorns.

He listened, wondering. It was a sound that did not belong. Everyone was safely in the town, most of them in bed, and there should be nothing outside the stockade for the unicorns to fight.

He armed himself with spear and crossbow and went outside. He let himself out through the east gate and went toward the sounds of battle. They grew louder as he approached, more furious, as though the battle was reaching its climax.

He crossed the creek and went through the trees beyond. There, in a small clearing no more than half a mile from the town, he came upon the scene.

A lone prowler was making a stand against two unicorns. Two other unicorns lay on the ground, dead, and behind the prowler was the dark shape of its mate lying lifelessly in the grass. There was blood on the prowler, purple in the blue starlight, and gloating rang in the squeals of the unicorns as they lunged at it. The leaps of the prowler were faltering as it fought them, the last desperate defiance of an animal already dying.

He brought up the bow and sent a volley of arrows into the unicorns. Their gloating squeals died and they fell. The prowler staggered and fell beside them.

It was breathing its last when he reached it but in the way it looked up at him he had the feeling that it wanted to tell him something, that it was trying hard to live long enough to do so. It died with the strange appeal in its eyes and not until then did he see the scar on its shoulder; a scar such as might have been made long ago by the rip of a unicorn's horn.

It was the prowler he had known nineteen years before.

The ground was trampled all around by the unicorns, showing that the prowlers had been besieged all day. He went to the other prowler and saw it was a female. Her breasts showed that she had had pups recently but she had been dead at least two days. Her hind legs had been broken sometime that spring and they were still only half healed, twisted and almost useless.

Then, that was why the two of them were so far behind the other prowlers. Prowlers, like the wolves, coyotes and foxes of Earth, mated for life and the male helped take care of the young. She had been injured somewhere to the south, perhaps in a fight with unicorns, and her mate had stayed with her as she hobbled her slow way along and killed game for her. The pups had been born and they had had to stop. Then the unicorns had found them and the female had been too crippled to fight....

He looked for the pups, expecting to find them trampled and dead. But they were alive, hidden under the roots of a small tree near their mother.

Prowler pups — *alive!*

They were very young, small and blind and helpless. He picked them up and his elation drained away as he looked at them. They made little sounds of hunger, almost inaudible, and they moved feebly, trying to find their mother's breasts and already so weak that they could not lift their heads.

Small chunks of fresh meat had been left beside the pups and he thought of what the prowler's emotions must have been as his mate lay dead on the ground and he carried meat to their young, knowing they were too small to eat it but helpless to do anything else for them.

And he knew why there had been the appeal in the eyes of the prowler as it died and what it had tried to tell him: *Save them ... as you once saved me.*

He carried the pups back past the prowler and looked down at it in passing. "I'll do my best," he said.

When he reached his house he laid the pups on his bed and built a fire. There was no milk to give them-the goats would not have young for at least another two weeks-but perhaps they could eat a soup of some kind. He put water on to boil and began shredding meat to make them a rich broth.

One of them was a male, the other a female, and if he could save them they would fight beside the men of Ragnarok when the Gerns came. He thought of what he would name them as he worked. He would name the female Sigyn, after Loki's faithful wife who went with him when the gods condemned him to Hel, the Teutonic underworld. And he would name the male Fenrir, after the monster wolf who would fight beside Loki when Loki led the forces of Hel in the final battle on the day of Ragnarok.

But when the broth was prepared, and cooled enough, the pups could not eat it. He tried making it weaker, tried it mixed with corn and herb soup, tried corn and herb soups alone. They could eat nothing he prepared for them.

When gray daylight entered the room he had tried everything possible and had failed. He sat wearily in his chair and watched them, defeated. They were no longer crying in their hunger and when he touched them they did not move as they had done before.

They would be dead before the day was over and the only chance men had ever had to have prowlers as their friends and allies would be gone.

The first rays of sunrise were coming into the room, revealing fully the frail thinness of the pups, when there was a step outside and Julia's voice:

"Father?"

"Come in, Julia," he said, not moving.

She entered, still a pale shadow of the reckless girl who had fought a unicorn, even though she was slowly regaining her normal health. She carried young Johnny in one arm, in her other hand his little bottle of milk. Johnny was hungry-there was never quite enough milk for him-but he was not crying. Ragnarok children did not cry....

She saw the pups and her eyes went wide.

"Prowlers-baby prowlers! Where did you get them?"

He told her and she went to them, to look down at

them and say, "If you and their father hadn't helped each other that day they wouldn't be here, nor you, nor I, nor Johnny-none of us in this room."

"They won't live out the day," he said. "They have to have milk-and there isn't any."

She reached down to touch them and they seemed to sense that she was someone different. They stirred, making tiny whimpering sounds and trying to move their heads to nuzzle at her fingers.

Compassion came to her face, like a soft light.

"They're so young," she said. "So terribly young to have to die...."

She looked at Johnny and at the little bottle that held his too-small morning ration of milk.

"Johnny-Johnny——" Her words were almost a whisper. "You're hungry-but we can't let them die. And someday, for this, they will fight for your life."

She sat on the bed and placed the pups in her lap beside Johnny. She lifted a little black head with gentle fingers and a little pink mouth ceased whimpering as it found the nipple of Johnny's bottle.

Johnny's gray eyes darkened with the storm of approaching protest. Then the other pup touched his hand, crying in its hunger, and the protest faded as surprise and something like sudden understanding came into his eyes.

Julia withdrew the bottle from the first pup and transferred it to the second one. Its crying ceased and Johnny leaned forward to touch it again, and the one beside it.

He made his decision with an approving sound and leaned back against his mother's shoulder, patiently awaiting his own turn and their presence accepted as though they had been born his brother and sister.

* * * * *

The golden light of the new day shone on them, on his daughter and grandson and the prowler pups, and in it he saw the bright omen for the future.

His own role was nearing its end but he had seen the people of Ragnarok conquer their environment in so far as Big Winter would ever let it be conquered. The last generation was being born, the generation that would meet the Gerns, and now they would have their final ally. Perhaps it would be Johnny who led them on that day, as the omen seemed to prophesy.

He was the son of a line of leaders, born to a mother who had fought and killed a unicorn. He had gone hungry to share what little he had with the young of Ragnarok's most proud and savage species and Fenrir and Sigyn would fight beside him on the day he led the forces of the hell-world in the battle with the Gerns who thought they were gods.

Could the Gerns hope to have a leader to match?

PART 4

John Humbolt, leader, stood on the wide stockade wall and watched the lowering sun touch the western horizon-far south of where it had set when he was a child. Big Summer was over and now, in the year two hundred, they were already three years into Big Fall. The Craigs had been impassable with snow for five years and the country at the north end of the plateau, where the iron had been found, had been buried under never-melting snow and growing glaciers for twenty years.

There came the soft tinkling of ceramic bells as the herd of milk goats came down off the hills. Two children were following and six prowlers walked with them, to protect them from wild unicorns.

There were not many of the goats. Each year the winters were longer, requiring the stocking of a larger supply of hay. The time would come when the summers would be so short and the winters so long that they could not keep goats at all. And by then, when Big Winter had closed in on them, the summer seasons would be too short for the growing of the orange corn. They would have nothing left but the hunting.

They had, he knew, reached and passed the zenith of the development of their environment. From a low of forty-nine men, women and children in dark caves they had risen to a town of six thousand. For a few years they had had a way of life that was almost a civilization but the inevitable decline was already under way. The years of frozen sterility of Big Winter were coming and no amount of determination or ingenuity could alter them. Six thousand would have to live by hunting-and one hundred, in the first Big Winter, had found barely enough game.

They would have to migrate in one of two different ways: they could go to the south as nomad hunters-or they could go to other, fairer, worlds in ships they took from the Gerns.

The choice was very easy to make and they were almost ready.

In the workshop at the farther edge of town the hyperspace transmitter was nearing completion. The little smelter was waiting to receive the lathe and other iron and steel and turn them into the castings for the generator. Their weapons were ready, the mockers were trained, the prowlers were waiting. And in the massive corral beyond town forty half-tame unicorns trampled the ground and hated the world, wanting to kill something. They had learned to be afraid of Ragnarok men but they would not be afraid to kill Gerns....

The children with the goats reached the stockade and two of the prowlers, Fenrir and Sigyn, turned to see him standing on the wall. He made a little motion with his hand and they came running, to leap up beside him on the ten-foot-high wall.

"So you've been checking up on how well the young ones guard the children?" he asked.

Sigyn lolled out her tongue and her white teeth grinned at him in answer. Fenrir, always the grimmer of the two, made a sound in his throat in reply.

Prowlers developed something like a telepathic rapport with their masters and could sense their thoughts and understand relatively complex instructions. Their intelligence was greater, and of a far more mature order, than that of the little mockers but their vocal cords were not capable of making the sounds necessary for speech.

He rested his hands on their shoulders, where their ebony fur was frosted with gray. Age had not yet affected their quick, flowing movement but they were getting old-they were only a few weeks short of his own age. He could not remember when they had not been with him....

Sometimes it seemed to him he could remember those hungry days when he and Fenrir and Sigyn shared together in his mother's lap-but it was probably only his imagination from having heard the story told so often. But he could remember for certain when he was learning to walk and Fenrir and Sigyn, full grown then, walked tall and black beside him. He could remember playing with Sigyn's pups and he could remember Sigyn watching over them all, sometimes giving her pups a bath and his face a washing with equal disregard for their and his protests. Above all he could remember the times when he was almost grown; the wild, free days when he and Fenrir and Sigyn had roamed the mountains together. With a bow and a knife and two prowlers beside him he had felt that there was nothing on Ragnarok that they could not conquer; that there was nothing in the universe they could not defy together....

* * * * *

There was a flicker of black movement and a young messenger prowler came running from the direction of the council hall, a speckle-faced mocker clinging to its back. It leaped up on the wall beside him and the mocker, one that had been trained to remember and repeat messages verbatim, took a breath so deep that its cheeks bulged out. It spoke, in a quick rush like a child that is afraid it might forget some of the words:

"You will please come to the council hall to lead the discussion regarding the last preparations for the meeting with the Gerns. The transmitter is completed."

* * * * *

The lathe was torn down the next day and the smelter began to roar with its forced draft. Excitement and anticipation ran through the town like a fever. It would take perhaps twenty days to build the generator, working day and night so that not an hour of time would be lost, forty days for the signal to reach Athena, and forty days for the Gern cruiser to reach Ragnarok — —

In one hundred days the Gerns would be there!

The men who would engage in the fight for the cruiser quit trimming their beards. Later, when it was time for the Gerns to appear, they would discard their woolen garments for ones of goat skin. The Gerns would regard them as primitive inferiors at best and it might be of advantage to heighten the impression. It would make the awakening of the Gerns a little more shocking.

An underground passage, leading from the town to the concealment of the woods in the distance, had long ago been dug. Through it the women and children would go when the Gerns arrived.

There was a level area of ground, just beyond the south wall of town, where the cruiser would be almost certain to land. The town had been built with that thought in mind. Woods were not far from both sides of the landing site and unicorn corrals were hidden in them. From the corrals would come the rear flanking attack against the Gerns.

The prowlers, of course, would be scattered among all the forces.

* * * * *

The generator was completed and installed on the nineteenth night. Charley Craig, a giant of a man whose red beard gave him a genially murderous appearance, opened the valve of the water pipe. The new wooden turbine stirred and belts and pulleys began to spin. The generator hummed, the needles of the dials climbed, flickered, and steadied.

Norman Lake looked from them to Humbolt, his pale gray eyes coldly satisfied. "Full output," he said. "We have the power we need this time."

Jim Chiara was at the transmitter and they waited while he threw switches and studied dials. Every component of the transmitter had been tested but they had not had the power to test the complete assembly.

"That's it," he said at last, looking up at them. "She's ready, after almost two hundred years of wanting her."

Humbolt wondered what the signal should be and saw no reason why it should not be the same one that had been sent out with such hope a hundred and sixty-five years ago.

"All right, Jim," he said. "Let the Gerns know we're waiting for them—make it 'Ragnarok calling' again."

The transmitter key rattled and the all-wave signal that the Gerns could not fail to receive went out at a velocity of five light-years a day:

Ragnarok calling-Ragnarok calling-Ragnarok calling —

It was the longest summer Humbolt had ever experienced. He was not alone in his impatience-among all of them the restlessness flamed higher as the slow days dragged by, making it almost impossible to go about their routine duties. The gentle mockers sensed the anticipation of their masters for the coming battle and they became nervous and apprehensive. The prowlers sensed it and they paced about the town in the dark of night; watching, listening, on ceaseless guard against the mysterious enemy their masters waited for. Even the unicorns seemed to sense what was coming and they rumbled and squealed in their corrals at night, red-eyed with the lust for blood and sometimes attacking the log walls with blows that shook the ground.

The interminable days went their slow succession and summer gave way to fall. The hundredth day dawned, cold and gray with the approach of winter; the day of the Gerns.

But no cruiser came that day, nor the next. He stood again on the stockade wall in the evening of the third day, Fenrir and Sigyn beside him. He listened for the first dim, distant sound of the Gern cruiser and heard only the moaning of the wind around him.

Winter was coming. Always, on Ragnarok, winter was coming or the brown death of summer. Ragnarok was a harsh and barren prison, and no amount of desire could ever make it otherwise. Only the coming of a Gern cruiser could ever offer them the bloody, violent opportunity to regain their freedom.

But what if the cruiser never came?

It was a thought too dark and hopeless to be held. They were not asking a large favor of fate, after two hundred years of striving for it; only the chance to challenge the Gern Empire with bows and knives....

Fenrir stiffened, the fur lifting on his shoulders and a muted growl coming from him. Then Humbolt heard the first whisper of sound; a faint, faraway roaring that was not the wind.

He watched and listened and the sound came swiftly nearer, rising in pitch and swelling in volume. Then it broke through the clouds, tall and black and beautifully deadly. It rode down on its rockets of flame, filling the valley with its thunder, and his heart hammered with exultation.

It had come-the cruiser had come!

He turned and dropped the ten feet to the ground inside the stockade. The warning signal was being sounded from the center of town; a unicorn horn that gave out the call they had used in the practice alarms. Already the women and children would be hurrying along the tunnels that led to the temporary safety of the woods beyond town. The Gerns might use their turret blasters to destroy the town and all in it before the night was over. There was no way of knowing what might happen before it ended. But whatever it was, it would be the action they had all been wanting.

He ran to where the others would be gathering, Fenrir and Sigyn loping beside him and the horn ringing wild and savage and triumphant as it announced the end of two centuries of waiting.

* * * * *

The cruiser settled to earth in the area where it had been expected to land, towering high above the town with its turret blasters looking down upon the houses.

Charley Craig and Norman Lake were waiting for him on the high steps of his own house in the center of town where the elevation gave them a good view of the ship yet where the fringes of the canopy would conceal them from the ship's scanners. They were heavily armed, their prowlers beside them and their mockers on their shoulders.

Elsewhere, under the connected rows of concealing canopies, armed men were hurrying to their prearranged stations. Most of them were accompanied by prowlers, bristling and snarling as they looked at the alien ship. A few men were deliberately making themselves visible not far away, going about unimportant tasks with only occasional and carefully disinterested glances toward the ship. They were the bait, to lure the first detachment into the center of town....

"Well?" Norman Lake asked, his pale eyes restless with his hunger for violence. "There's our ship-when do we take her?"

"Just as soon as we get them outside it," he said. "We'll use the plan we first had-wait until they send a full force to rescue the first detachment and then hit them with everything we have."

His black, white-nosed mocker was standing in the open doorway and watching the hurrying men and prowlers with worried interest: Tip, the great-great-great-great grandson of the mocker that had died with Howard Lake north of the plateau. He reached down to pick him up and set him on his shoulder, and said:

"Jim?"

"The longbows are ready," Tip's treble imitation of Jim Chiara's voice answered. "We'll black out their searchlights when the time comes."

"Andy?" he asked.

"The last of us for this section are coming in now," Andy Taylor answered.

He made his check of all the subleaders, then looked up to the roof to ask, "All set, Jimmy?"

Jimmy Stevens' grinning face appeared over the edge. "Ten crossbows are cocked and waiting up here. Bring us our targets."

They waited, while the evening deepened into near-dusk. Then the airlock of the cruiser slid open and thirteen Gerns emerged, the one leading them wearing the resplendent uniform of a subcommander.

"There they come," he said to Lake and Craig. "It looks like we'll be able to trap them in here and force the commander to send out a full-sized force. We'll all attack at the sound of the horn and if you can hit their rear flanks hard enough with the unicorns to give us a chance to split them from this end some of us should make it to the ship before they realize up in the control room that they should close the airlocks.

"Now"—he looked at the Gerns who were coming straight toward the stockade wall, ignoring the gate to their right—"you'd better be on your way. We'll meet again before long in the ship."

Fenrir and Sigyn looked from the advancing Gerns to him with question in their eyes after Lake and Craig were gone, Fenrir growling restlessly.

"Pretty soon," he said to them. "Right now it would be better if they didn't see you. Wait inside, both of you." They went reluctantly inside, to merge with the darkness of the interior. Only an occasional yellow gleam of their eyes showed that they were crouched to spring just inside the doorway.

He called to the nearest unarmed man, not loud enough to be heard by the Gerns:

"Cliff-you and Sam Anders come here. Tell the rest to fade out of sight and get armed."

Cliff Schroeder passed the command along and he and Sam Anders approached. He looked back at the Gerns and saw they were within a hundred feet of the-for them-unscalable wall of the stockade. They were coming without hesitation — —

A pale blue beam lashed down from one of the cruiser's turrets and a fifty foot section of the wall erupted into dust with a sound like thunder. The wind swept the dust aside in a gigantic cloud and the Gerns came through the gap, looking neither to right nor left.

"That, I suppose," Sam Anders said from beside him, "was Lesson Number One for degenerate savages like us: Gerns, like gods, are not to be hindered by man-made barriers."

The Gerns walked with a peculiar gait that puzzled him until he saw what it was. They were trying to come with the arrogant military stride affected by the Gerns and in the 1.5 gravity they were succeeding in achieving only a heavy clumping.

They advanced steadily and as they drew closer he saw that in the right hand of each Gern soldier was a blaster while in the left hand of each could be seen the metallic glitter of chains.

Schroeder smiled thinly. "It looks like they want to subject about a dozen of us to some painful questioning."

No one else was any longer in sight and the Gerns came straight toward the three on the steps. They stopped forty feet away at a word of command from the officer and Gerns and Ragnarok men exchanged silent stares; the faces of the Ragnarok men bearded and expressionless, the faces of the Gerns hairless and reflecting a contemptuous curiosity.

"Narth!" The communicator on the Gern officer's belt spoke with metallic authority. "What do they look like? Did we come two hundred light-years to view some animated vegetables?"

"No, Commander," Narth answered. "I think the discard of the Rejects two hundred years ago has produced for us an unexpected reward. There are three natives under the canopy before me and their physical perfection and complete adaptation to this hellish gravity is astonishing."

"They could be used to replace expensive machines on some of the outer world mines," the commander said, "providing their intelligence isn't too abysmally low. What about that?"

"They can surely be taught to perform simple manual labor," Narth answered.

"Get on with your job," the commander said. "Try to pick some of the most intelligent looking ones for questioning —I can't believe these cattle sent that message and they're going to tell us who did. And pick some young, strong ones for the medical staff to examine-ones that won't curl up and die after the first few cuts of the knife."

"We'll chain these three first," Narth said. He lifted his hand in an imperious gesture to Humbolt and the other two and ordered in accented Terran: "Come here!"

No one moved and he said again, sharply, *"Come here!"*

Again no one moved and the minor officer beside Narth said, "Apparently they can't even understand Terran now."

"Then we'll give them some action they can understand," Narth snapped, his face flushing with irritation. "We'll drag them out by their heels!"

The Gerns advanced purposefully, three of them holstering their blasters to make their chains ready. When they had passed under the canopy and could not be seen from the ship Humbolt spoke:

"All right, Jimmy."

The Gerns froze in midstride, suspicion flashing across their faces.

"Look up on the roof," he said in Gern.

They looked, and the suspicion became gaping dismay.

"You can be our prisoners or you can be corpses," he said. "We don't care which."

The urgent hiss of Narth's command broke their indecision:

"Kill them!"

Six of them tried to obey, bringing up their blasters in movements that seemed curiously heavy and slow, as though the gravity of Ragnarok had turned their arms to wood. Three of them almost lifted their blasters high enough to fire at the steps in front of them before arrows went through their throats. The other three did not get that far.

Narth and the remaining six went rigidly motionless and he said to them:

"Drop your blasters-quick!"

Their blasters thumped to the ground and Jimmy Stevens and his bowmen slid off the roof. Within a minute the Gerns were bound with their own chains, but for the officer, and the blasters were in the hands of the Ragnarok men.

Jimmy looked down the row of Gerns and shook his head. "So these are Gerns?" he said. "It was like trapping a band of woods goats."

"Young ones," Schroeder amended. "And almost as dangerous."

Narth's face flushed at the words and his eyes went to the ship. The sight of it seemed to restore his courage and his lips drew back in a snarl.

"You fools-you stupid, megalomaniac dung-heaps —do you think you can kill Gerns and live to boast about it?"

"Keep quiet," Humbolt ordered, studying him with curiosity. Narth, like all the Gerns, was different from what they had expected. It was true the Gerns had strode into their town with an attempt at arrogance but they were harmless in appearance, soft of face and belly, and the snarling of the red-faced Narth was like the bluster of a cornered scavenger-rodent.

"I promise you this," Narth was saying viciously, "if you don't release us and return our weapons this instant I'll personally oversee the extermination of you and every savage in this village with the most painful death science can contrive and I'll — —"

Humbolt reached out his hand and flicked Narth under the chin. Narth's teeth cracked loudly together and his face twisted with the pain of a bitten tongue.

"Tie him up, Jess," he said to a man near him. "If he opens his mouth again, shove your foot in it."

He spoke to Schroeder. "We'll keep three of the blasters and send two to each of the other front groups. Have that done."

Dusk was deepening into darkness and he called Chiara again. "They'll turn on their search-lights any minute and make the town as light as day," he said. "If you can keep them blacked out until some of us have reached the ship, I think we'll have won."

"They'll be kept blacked out," Chiara said. "With some flint-headed arrows left over for the Gerns."

He called Lake and Craig, to be told they were ready and waiting.

"But we're having hell keeping the unicorns quiet," Craig said. "They want to get to killing something."

He pressed the switch of the communicator but it was dead. They had, of course, transferred to some other wave length so he could not hear the commands. It was something he had already anticipated....

Fenrir and Sigyn were still obediently inside the doorway, almost frantic with desire to rejoin him. He spoke to them and they bounded out, snarling at three Gerns in passing and causing them to blanch to a dead-white color.

He set Tip on Sigyn's shoulders and said, "Sigyn, there's a job for you and Tip to do. A dangerous job. Listen-both of you...."

The yellow eyes of Sigyn and the dark eyes of the little mocker looked into his as he spoke to them and accompanied his words with the strongest, clearest mental images he could project:

"Sigyn, take Tip to the not-men thing. Leave him hidden in the grass to one side of the big hole in it. Tip, you wait there. When the not-men come out you listen, and tell what they say.

"Now, do you both understand?"

Sigyn made a sound that meant she did but Tip clutched at his wrist with little paws suddenly gone cold and wailed, "*No!* Scared-scared — —"

"You have to go, Tip," he said, gently disengaging his wrist. "And Sigyn will hide near to you and watch over you." He spoke to Sigyn. "When the horn calls you run back with him."

Again she made the sound signifying understanding and he touched them both in what he hoped would not be the last farewell.

"All right, Sigyn-go now."

She vanished into the gloom of coming night, Tip hanging tightly to her. Fenrir stood with the fur lifted on his shoulders and a half snarl on his face as he watched her go and watched the place where the not-men would appear.

"Where's Freckles?" he asked Jimmy.

"Here," someone said, and came forward with Tip's mate.

He set Freckles on his shoulder and the first searchlight came on, shining down from high up on the cruiser. It lighted up the area around them in harsh white brilliance, its reflection revealing the black shadow that was Sigyn just vanishing behind the ship.

Two more searchlights came on, to illuminate the town. Then the Gerns came.

They poured out through the airlock and down the ramp, there to form in columns that marched forward as still more Gerns hurried down the ramp behind them. The searchlights gleamed on their battle helmets and on the blades of the bayonets affixed to their rifle-like long range blasters. Hand blasters and grenades hung from their belts, together with stubby flame guns.

They were a solid mass reaching halfway to the stockade before the last of them, the commanding officers, appeared. One of them stopped at the foot of the ramp to watch the advance of the punitive force and give the frightened but faithful Tip the first words to transmit to Freckles:

"The full force is on its way, Commander."

A reply came, in Freckles' simulation of the metallic tones of a communicator:

"The key numbers of the confiscated blasters have been checked and the disturbance rays of the master integrator set. You'll probably have few natives left alive to take as prisoners after those thirteen charges explode but continue with a mopping up job that the survivors will never forget."

So the Gerns could, by remote control, set the total charges of stolen blasters to explode upon touching the firing stud? It was something new since the days of the Old Ones....

He called Chiara and the other groups, quickly, to tell them what he had learned. "We'll get more blasters-ones they can't know the numbers of-when we attack," he finished.

He took the blaster from his belt and laid it on the ground. The front ranks of the Gerns were almost to the wall by then, a column wider than the gap that had been blasted through it, coming with silent purposefulness.

Two blaster beams lanced down from the turrets, to smash at the wall. Dust billowed and thunder rumbled as they swept along. A full three hundred feet of the wall had been destroyed when they stopped and the dust hid the ship and made dim glows of the searchlights.

It had no doubt been intended to impress them with the might of the Gerns but in doing so it hid the Ragnarok forces from the advancing Gerns for a few seconds.

"Jim-black out their lights before the dust clears," he called. "Joe-the horn! We attack now!"

The first longbow arrow struck a searchlight and its glow grew dimmer as the arrow's burden —a thin tube of thick lance tree ink-splattered against it. Another followed — —

Then the horn rang out, harsh and commanding, and in the distance a unicorn screamed in answer. The savage cry of a prowler came, like a sound to match, and the attack was on.

He ran with Fenrir beside him and to his left and right ran the others with their prowlers. The lead groups converged as they went through the wide gap in the wall. They ran on, into the dust cloud, and the shadowy forms of the Gerns were suddenly before them.

A blaster beam cut into them and a Gern shouted, *"The natives!"* Other beams sprang into life, winking like pale blue eyes through the dust and killing all they touched. The beams dropped as the first volley of arrows tore through the massed front ranks, to be replaced by others.

They charged on, into the blue winking of the blasters and the red lances of the flame guns with the crossbows rattling and strumming in answer. The prowlers lunged and fought beside them and ahead of them; black hell-creatures that struck the Gerns too swiftly for blasters to find before throats were torn out; the sound of battle turned into a confusion of raging snarls, frantic shouts and dying screams.

A prowler shot past him to join Fenrir-Sigyn-and he felt Tip dart up to his shoulder. She made a sound of greeting in passing, a sound that was gone as her jaws closed on a Gern.

The dust cloud cleared a little and the searchlights looked down on the scene; no longer brilliantly white but shining through the red-black lance tree ink as a blood red glow. A searchlight turret slid shut and opened a moment later, the light wiped clean. The longbows immediately transformed it into a red glow.

The beam of one of the turret blasters stabbed down, to blaze a trail of death through the battle. It ceased as its own light revealed to the Gern commander that the Ragnarok forces were so intermixed with the Gern forces that he was killing more Gerns than Ragnarok men.

By then the fighting was so hand to hand that knives were better than crossbows. The Gerns fell like harvested corn; too slow and awkward to use their bayonets against the faster Ragnarok men and killing as many of one another as men when they tried to use their blasters and flame guns. From the rear there came the command of a Gern officer, shouted high and thin above the sound of battle:

"Back to the ship-leave the natives for the ship's blasters to kill!"

The unicorns arrived then, to cut off their retreat.

They came twenty from the east and twenty from the west in a thunder of hooves, squealing and screaming in their blood lust, with prowlers a black wave going before them. They struck the Gerns; the prowlers slashing lanes through them while the unicorns charged behind, trampling them, ripping into them with their horns and smashing them down with their hooves as they vented the pent up rage of their years of confinement. On the back of each was a rider whose long spear flicked and stabbed into the throats and bellies of Gerns.

The retreat was halted and transformed into milling confusion. He led his own groups in the final charge, the prearranged wedge attack, and they split the Gern force in two.

The ship was suddenly just beyond them.

He gave the last command to Lake and Craig: "*Now* —into the ship!"

He scooped up a blaster from beside a fallen Gern and ran toward it. A Gern officer was already in the airlock, his face pale and strained as he looked back and his hand on the closing switch. He shot him and ran up the ramp as the officer's body rolled down it.

Unicorn hooves pounded behind him and twenty of them swept past, their riders leaping from their backs to the ramp. Twenty men and fifteen prowlers charged up the ramp as a warning siren shrieked somewhere inside the ship. At the same time the airlocks, operated from the control room, began to slide swiftly shut.

He was through first, with Fenrir and Sigyn. Lake and Craig, together with six men and four prowlers, squeezed through barely in time. Then the airlocks were closed and they were sealed in the ship.

Alarm bells added their sound to the shrieking of the siren and from the multiple-compartments shafts came the whir of elevators dropping with Gern forces to kill the humans trapped inside the ship.

They ran past the elevator shafts without pausing, light and swift in the artificial gravity that was only two-thirds that of Ragnarok. They split forces as long ago planned; three men and four prowlers going with Charley Craig in the attempt to take the drive room, Lake and the other three men going with him in the attempt to take the control room.

They found the manway ladder and began to climb, Fenrir and Sigyn impatiently crowding their heels.

There was nothing on the control room level and they ran down the short corridor that their maps had showed. They turned left, into the corridor that had the control room at its end, and into the concentrated fire of nine waiting Gerns.

Fenrir and Sigyn went into the Gerns, under their fire before they could drop the muzzles of their blasters, with an attack so vicious and unexpected that what would have been a certain and lethal trap for the humans was suddenly a fighting chance.

The corridor became an inferno of blaster beams that cracked and hissed as they met and crossed, throwing little chips of metal from the walls with snapping sounds and going through flesh with sounds like soft tappings. It was over within seconds, the last Gern down and one man still standing beside him, the blond and nerveless Lake.

Thomsen and Barber were dead and Billy West was bracing himself against the wall with a blaster hole through his stomach, trying to say something and sliding to the floor before it was ever spoken.

And Sigyn was down, blood welling and bubbling from a wound! in her chest, while Fenrir stood over her with his snarling a raging scream as he swung his head in search of a still-living Gern.

Humbolt and Lake ran on, Fenrir raging beside them, and into the control room.

Six officers, one wearing the uniform of a commander, were gaping in astonishment and bringing up their blasters in the way that seemed so curiously slow to Humbolt. Fenrir, in his fury, killed two of them as Lake's blaster and his own killed three more.

The commander was suddenly alone, his blaster half lifted. Fenrir leaped at his throat and Humbolt shouted the quick command: *"Disarm!"*

It was something the prowlers had been taught in their training and Fenrir's teeth clicked short of the commander's throat while his paw sent the blaster spinning across the room.

The commander stared at them with his swarthy face a dark gray and his mouth still gaping.

"How-how did you do it?" he asked in heavily accented Terran. "Only two of you —— "

"Don't talk until you're asked a question," Lake said.

"Only two of you...." The thought seemed to restore his courage, as sight of the ship had restored Narth's that night, and his tone became threatening. "There are only two of you and more guards will be here to kill you within a minute. Surrender to me and I'll let you go free —— "

Lake slapped him across the mouth with a backhanded blow that snapped his head back on his shoulders and split his lip.

"Don't talk," he ordered again. "And never lie to us."

The commander spit out a tooth and held his hand to his bleeding mouth. He did not speak again.

Tip and Freckles were holding tightly to his shoulder and each other, the racing of their hearts like a vibration, and he touched them reassuringly.

"All right now-all safe now," he said.

He called Charley Craig. "Charley-did you make it?"

"We made it to the drive room-two of us and one prowler," Charley answered. "What about you?"

"Norman and I have the control room. Cut their drives, to play safe. I'll let you know as soon as the entire ship is ours."

He went to the viewscreen and saw that the battle was over. Chiara was letting the searchlight burn again and prowlers were being used to drive back the unicorns from the surrendering Gerns.

"I guess we won," he said to Lake.

But there was no feeling of victory, none of the elation he had thought he would have. Sigyn was dying alone in the alien corridor outside. Sigyn, who had nursed beside him and fought beside him and laid down her life for him....

"I want to look at her," he said to Lake.

Fenrir went with him. She was still alive, waiting for them to come back to her. She lifted her head and touched his hand with her tongue as he examined the wound.

It was not fatal-it need not be fatal. He worked swiftly, gently, to stop the bleeding that had been draining her life away. She would have to lie quietly for weeks but she would recover.

When he was done he pressed her head back to the floor and said, "Lie still, Sigyn girl, until we can come to move you. Wait for us and Fenrir will stay here with you."

She obeyed and he left them, the feeling of victory and elation coming to him in full then.

Lake looked at him questioningly as he entered the control room and he said, "She'll live."

He turned to the Gern commander. "First, I want to know how the war is going?"

"I —— " The commander looked uncertainly at Lake.

"Just tell the truth," Lake said. "Whether you think we'll like it or not."

"We have all the planets but Earth, itself," the commander said. "We'll have it, soon."

"And the Terrans on Athena?"

"They're still-working for us there."

"Now," he said, "you will order every Gern in this ship to go to his sleeping quarters. They will leave their weapons in the corridors outside and they will not resist the men who will come to take charge of the ship."

The commander made an effort toward defiance:

"And if I refuse?"

Lake answered, smiling at him with the smile of his that was no more than a quick showing of teeth and with the savage eagerness in his eyes.

"If you refuse I'll start with your fingers and break every bone to your shoulders. If that isn't enough I'll start with your toes and go to your hips. And then I'll break your back."

The commander hesitated, sweat filming his face as he looked at them. Then he reached out to switch on the all-stations communicator and say into it:

"Attention, all personnel: You will return to your quarters at once, leaving your weapons in the corridors. You are ordered to make no resistance when the natives come...."

There was a silence when he had finished and Humbolt and Lake looked at each other, bearded and clad in animal skins but standing at last in the control room of a ship that was theirs: in a ship that could take them to Athena, to Earth, to the ends of the galaxy.

The commander watched them, on his face the blankness of unwillingness to believe.

"The airlocks —" he said. "We didn't close them in time. We never thought you would dare try to take the ship-not savages in animal skins."

"I know," Humbolt answered. "We were counting on you to think that way."

"No one expected any of you to survive here." The commander wiped at his swollen lips, wincing, and an almost child-like petulance came into his tone. "You weren't supposed to survive."

"I know," he said again. "We've made it a point to remember that."

"The gravity, the heat and cold and fever, the animals-why didn't they kill you?"

"They tried," he said. "But we fought back. And we had a goal-to meet you Gerns again. You left us on a world that had no resources. Only enemies who would kill us-the gravity, the prowlers, the unicorns. So we made them our resources. We adapted to the gravity that was supposed to kill us and became stronger and quicker than Gerns. We made allies of the prowlers and unicorns who were supposed to be our executioners and used them tonight to help us kill Gerns. So now we have your ship."

"Yes ...you have our ship." Through the unwillingness to believe on the commander's face and the petulance there came the triumph of vindictive anticipation. "The savages of Ragnarok have a Gern cruiser-but what can they do with it?"

"What can we do with it?" he asked, almost kindly. "We've planned for two hundred years what we can do with it. We have the cruiser and sixty days from now we'll have Athena. That will be only the beginning and you Gerns are going to help us do it."

* * * * *

For six days the ship was a scene of ceaseless activity. Men crowded it, asking questions of the Gern officers and crew and calmly breaking the bones of those who refused to answer or who gave answers that were not true. Prowlers stalked the corridors, their cold yellow eyes watching every move the Gerns made. The little mockers began roaming the ship at will, unable any longer to restrain their curiosity and confident that the men and prowlers would not let the Gerns harm them.

One mocker was killed then; the speckle-faced mocker that could repeat messages verbatim. It wandered into a storage cubicle where a Gern was working alone and gave him the opportunity to safely vent his hatred of everything associated with the men of Ragnarok. He broke its back with a steel bar and threw it, screaming, into the disposal chute that led to the matter converter. A prowler heard the scream and an instant later the Gern screamed; a sound that died in its making as the prowler tore his throat out. No more mockers were harmed.

One Ragnarok boy was killed. Three fanatical Gern officers stole knives from the galley and held the boy as hostage for their freedom. When their demands were refused they cut his heart out. Lake cornered them a few minutes later and, without touching his blaster, disemboweled them with their own knives. He smiled down upon them as they writhed and moaned on the floor and their moans were heard for a long time by the other Gerns in the ship before they died. No more humans were harmed.

They discovered that operation of the cruiser was relatively simple, basically similar to the operation of Terran ships as described in the text book the original Lake had written. Most of the operations were performed by robot mechanisms and the manual operations, geared to the slower reflexes of the Gerns, were easily mastered.

They could spend the forty-day voyage to Athena in further learning and practice so on the sixth day they prepared to depart. The unicorns had been given the freedom they had fought so well for and reconnaissance vehicles were loaned from the cruiser to take their place. Later there would be machinery and supplies of all kinds brought in by freighter ships from Athena.

Time was precious and there was a long, long job ahead of them. They blasted up from Ragnarok on the morning of the seventh day and went into the black sea of hyperspace.

By then the Gern commander was no longer of any value to them. His unwillingness to believe that savages had wrested his ship from him had increased until his compartment became his control room to him and he spent the hours laughing and giggling before an imaginary viewscreen whereon the cruiser's blasters were destroying, over and over, the Ragnarok town and all the humans in it.

But Narth, who had wanted to have them tortured to death for daring to resist capture, became very cooperative. In the control room his cooperation was especially eager. On the twentieth day of the voyage they let him have what he had been trying to gain by subterfuge: access to the transmitter when no men were within hearing distance.

After that his manner abruptly changed. Each day his hatred for them and his secret anticipation became more evident.

The thirty-fifth day came, with Athena five days ahead of them-the day of the execution they had let him arrange for them.

* * * * *

Stars filled the transdimensional viewscreen, the sun of Athena in the center. Humbolt watched the space to the lower left and the flicker came again; a tiny red dot that was gone again within a microsecond, so quickly that Narth in the seat beside him did not see it.

It was the quick peek of another ship; a ship that was running invisible with its detector screens up but which had had to drop them for an instant to look out at the cruiser. Not even the Gerns had ever been able to devise a polarized detector screen.

He changed the course and speed of the cruiser, creating an increase in gravity which seemed very slight to him but which caused Narth to slew heavily in his seat. Narth straightened and he said to him:

"Within a few minutes we'll engage the ship you sent for."

Narth's jaw dropped, then came back up. "So you spied on me?"

"One of our Ragnarok allies did-the little animal that was sitting near the transmitter. They're our means of communication. We learned that you had arranged for a ship, en route to Athena, to intercept us and capture us."

"So you know?" Narth asked. He smiled, an unpleasant twisting of his mouth. "Do you think that knowing will help you any?"

"We expect it to," he answered.

"It's a battleship," Narth said. "It's three times the size of this cruiser, the newest and most powerful battleship in the Gern fleet. How does that sound to you?"

"It sounds good," he said. "We'll make it our flagship."

"Your flagship-your *'flagship'*!" The last trace of pretense left Narth and he let his full and rankling hatred come through. "You got this cruiser by trickery and learned how to operate it after a fashion because of an animal-like reflex abnormality. For forty-two days you accidental mutants have given orders to your superiors and thought you were our equals. Now, your fool's paradise is going to end."

The red dot came again, closer, and he once more altered the ship's course. He had turned on the course analyzer and it clicked as the battleship's position was correlated with that of its previous appearance. A short yellow line appeared on the screen to forecast its course for the immediate future.

"And then?" he asked curiously, turning back to Narth.

"And then we'll take all of you left alive back to your village. The scenes of what we do to you and your village will be televised to all Gern-held worlds. It will be a valuable reminder for any who have forgotten the penalty for resisting Gerns."

The red dot came again. He punched the Battle Stations button and the board responded with a row of ready lights.

"All the other Gerns are by now in their acceleration couches," he said. "Strap yourself in for high acceleration maneuvers-we'll make contact with the battleship within two minutes."

Narth did so, taking his time as though it was something of little importance. "There will be no maneuvers. They'll blast the stern and destroy your drive immediately upon attack."

He fastened the last strap and smiled, taunting assurance in the twisted unpleasantness of it. "The appearance of this battleship has very much disrupted your plans to strut like conquering heroes among the slaves on Athena, hasn't it?"

"Not exactly," Humbolt replied. "Our plans are a little broader in scope than that. There are two new cruisers on Athena, ready to leave the shops ten days from now. We'll turn control of Athena over to the humans there, of course, then we'll take the three cruisers and the battleship back by way of Ragnarok. There we'll pick up all the Ragnarok men who are neither too old nor too young and go on to Earth. They will be given training en route in the handling of ships. We expect to find no difficulty in breaking through the Gern lines around Earth and then, with the addition of the Earth ships, we can easily capture all the Gern ships in the solar system."

"'Easily'!" Narth made a contemptuous sneer of the word. "Were you actually so stupid as to think that you biological freaks could equal Gern officers who have made a career of space warfare?"

"We'll far exceed them," he said. "A space battle is one of trying to keep your blaster beams long enough on one area of the enemy ship to break through its blaster shields at that point. And at the same time try to move and dodge fast enough to keep the enemy from doing the same thing to you. The ships are capable of accelerations up to fifty gravities or more but the acceleration limitator is the safeguard that prevents the ship from going into such a high degree of acceleration or into such a sudden change of direction that it would kill the crew.

"We from Ragnarok are accustomed to a one point five gravity and can withstand much higher degrees of acceleration than Gerns or any other race from a one gravity world. To enable us to take advantage of that fact we have had the acceleration limitator on this cruiser disconnected."

"Disconnected?" Narth's contemptuous regard vanished in frantic consternation. "You fool-you don't know what that means —*you'll move the acceleration lever too far and kill us all!"*

The red dot flicked on the viewscreen, trembled, and was suddenly a gigantic battleship in full view. He touched the acceleration control and Narth's next words were cut off as his diaphragm sagged. He swung the cruiser in a curve and Narth was slammed sideways, the straps cutting into him and the flesh of his face pulled lopsided by the gravity. His eyes, bulging, went blank with unconsciousness.

The powerful blasters of the battleship blossomed like a row of pale blue flowers, concentrating on the stern of the cruiser. A warning siren screeched as they started breaking through the cruiser's shields. He dropped the detector screen that would shield the cruiser from sight, but not from the blaster beams, and tightened the curve until the gravity dragged heavily at his own body.

The warning siren stopped as the blaster beams of the battleship went harmlessly into space, continuing to follow the probability course plotted from the cruiser's last visible position and course by the battleship's robot target tracers.

He lifted the detector screen, to find the battleship almost exactly where the cruiser's course analyzers had predicted it would be. The blasters of the battleship were blazing their full concentration of firepower into an area behind and to one side of the cruiser.

They blinked out at sight of the cruiser in its new position and blazed again a moment later, boring into the stern. He dropped the detector screen and swung the cruiser in another curve, spiraling in the opposite direction. As before, the screech of the alarm siren died as the battleship's blasters followed the course given them by course analyzers and target tracers that were built to presume that all enemy ships were acceleration-limitator equipped.

The cruiser could have destroyed the battleship at any time-but they wanted to capture their flagship unharmed. The maneuvering continued, the cruiser drawing closer to the battleship. The battleship, in desperation, began using the same hide-and-jump tactics the cruiser used but it was of little avail-the battleship moved at known acceleration limits and the cruiser's course analyzers predicted each new position with sufficient accuracy.

The cruiser made its final dash in a tightening spiral, its detector screen flickering on and off. It struck the battleship at a matched speed, with a thump and ringing of metal as the magnetic grapples fastened the cruiser like a leech to the battleship's side.

In that position neither the forward nor stern blasters of the battleship could touch it. There remained only to convince the commander of the battleship that further resistance was futile.

This he did with a simple ultimatum to the commander:

"This cruiser is firmly attached to your ship, its acceleration limitator disconnected. Its drives are of sufficient power to thrust both ships forward at a much higher degree of acceleration than persons from one-gravity worlds can endure. You will surrender at once or we shall be forced to put these two ships into a curve of such short radius and at an acceleration so great that all of you will be killed."

Then he added, "If you surrender we'll do somewhat better by you than you did with the humans two hundred years ago-we'll take all of you on to Athena."

The commander, already sick from an acceleration that would have been negligible to Ragnarok men, had no choice.

His reply came, choked with acceleration sickness and the greater sickness of defeat:

"We will surrender."

* * * * *

Narth regained consciousness. He saw Humbolt sitting beside him as before, with no Gern rescuers crowding into the control room with shouted commands and drawn blasters.

"Where are they?" he asked. "Where is the battleship?"

"We captured it," he said.

"You captured —a Gern battleship?"

"It wasn't hard," he said. "It would have been easier if only Ragnarok men had been on the cruiser. We didn't want to accelerate to any higher gravities than absolutely necessary because of the Gerns on it."

"You did it-you captured the battleship," Narth said, his tone like one dazed.

He wet his lips, staring, as he contemplated the unpleasant implications of it.

"You're freak mutants who can capture a battleship. Maybe you will take Athena and Earth from us. But"—the animation of hatred returned to his face —"What good will it do you? Did you ever think about that?"

"Yes," he said. "We've thought about it."

"Have you?" Narth leaned forward, his face shining with the malice of his gloating. "You can never escape the consequences of what you have done. The Gern Empire has the resources of dozens of worlds. The Empire will build a fleet of special ships, a force against which your own will be nothing, and send them to Earth and Athena and Ragnarok. The Empire will smash you for what you have done and if there are any survivors of your race left they will cringe before Gerns for a hundred generations to come.

"Remember that while you're posturing in your little hour of glory on Athena and Earth."

"You insist in thinking we'll do as Gerns would do," he said. "We won't delay to do any posturing. We'll have a large fleet when we leave Earth and we'll go at once to engage the Gern home fleet. I thought you knew we were going to do that. We're going to cripple and capture your fleet and then we're going to destroy your empire."

"Destroy the Empire —*now*?" Narth stared again, all the gloating gone as he saw, at last, the quick and inexorable end. "Now-before we can stop you-before we can have a chance?"

"When a race has been condemned to die by another race and it fights and struggles and manages somehow to survive, it learns a lesson. It learns it must never again let the other race be in position to destroy it. So this is the harvest you reap from the seeds you sowed on Ragnarok two hundred years ago.

"You understand, don't you?" he asked, almost gently. "For two hundred years the Gern Empire has been a menace to our survival as a race. Now, the time has come when we shall remove it."

* * * * *

He stood in the control room of the battleship and watched Athena's sun in the viewscreen, blazing like a white flame. Sigyn, fully recovered, was stretched out on the floor near him; twitching and snarling a little in her sleep as she fought again the battle with the Gerns. Fenrir was pacing the floor, swinging his black, massive head restlessly, while Tip and Freckles were examining with fascinated curiosity the collection of bright medals that had been cleaned out of the Gern commander's desk.

Lake and Craig left their stations, as impatient as Fenrir, and came over to watch the viewscreen with him.

"One day more," Craig said. "We're two hundred years late but we're coming in to the world that was to have been our home."

"It can never be, now," he said. "Have any of us ever thought of that-that we're different to humans and there's no human world we could ever call home?"

"I've thought of it," Lake said. "Ragnarok made us different physically and different in the way we think. We could live on human worlds-but we would always be a race apart and never really belong there."

"I suppose we've all thought about it," Craig said. "And wondered what we'll do when we're finished with the Gerns. Not settle down on Athena or Earth, in a little cottage with a fenced-in lawn where it would be adventure to watch the Three-D shows after each day at some safe, routine job."

"Not back to Ragnarok," Lake said. "With metals and supplies from other worlds they'll be able to do a lot there but the battle is already won. There will be left only the peaceful development-building a town at the equator for Big Winter, leveling land, planting crops. We could never be satisfied with that kind of a life."

"No," he said, and felt his own restlessness stir in protest at the thought of settling down in some safe and secure environment. "Not Athena or Earth or Ragnarok-not any world we know."

"How long until we're finished with the Gerns?" Lake asked. "Ten years? We'll still be young then. Where will we go-all of us who fought the Gerns and all of the ones in the future who won't want to live out their lives on Ragnarok? Where is there a place for us —a world of our own?"

"Where do we find a world of our own?" he asked, and watched the star clouds creep toward them in the viewscreen; tumbled and blazing and immense beyond conception.

"There's a galaxy for us to explore," he said. "There are millions of suns and thousands of worlds waiting for us. Maybe there are races out there like the Gerns-and maybe there are races such as we were a hundred years ago who need our help. And maybe there are worlds out there with things on them such as no man ever imagined.

"We'll go, to see what's there. Our women will go with us and there will be some worlds on which some of us will want to stay. And, always, there will be more restless ones coming from Ragnarok. Out there are the worlds and the homes for all of us."

"Of course," Lake said. "Beyond the space frontier ...where else would we ever belong?"

It was all settled, then, and there was a silence as the battleship plunged through hyperspace, the cruiser running beside her and their drives moaning and thundering as had the drives of the *Constellation* two hundred years before.

A voyage had been interrupted then, and a new race had been born. Now they were going on again, to Athena, to Earth, to the farthest reaches of the Gern Empire. And on, to the wild, unknown regions of space beyond.

There awaited their worlds and there awaited their destiny; to be a race scattered across a hundred thousand light-years of suns, to be an empire such as the galaxy had never known.

They, the restless ones, the unwanted and forgotten, the survivors.

The Nothing Equation

The space ships were miracles of power and precision; the men who manned them, rich in endurance and courage. Every detail had been checked and double checked; every detail except —

The cruiser vanished back into hyperspace and he was alone in the observation bubble, ten thousand light-years beyond the galaxy's outermost sun. He looked out the windows at the gigantic sea of emptiness around him and wondered again what the danger had been that had so terrified the men before him.

Of one thing he was already certain; he would find that nothing was waiting outside the bubble to kill him. The first bubble attendant had committed suicide and the second was a mindless maniac on the Earthbound cruiser but it must have been something inside the bubble that had caused it. Or else they had imagined it all.

He went across the small room, his magnetized soles loud on the thin metal floor in the bubble's silence. He sat down in the single chair, his weight very slight in the feeble artificial gravity, and reviewed the known facts.

The bubble was a project of Earth's Galactic Observation Bureau, positioned there to gather data from observations that could not be made from within the galaxy. Since metallic mass affected the hypersensitive instruments the bubble had been made as small and light as possible. It was for that reason that it could accommodate only one attendant.

The Bureau had selected Horne as the bubble's first attendant and the cruiser left him there for his six months' period of duty. When it made its scheduled return with his replacement he was found dead from a tremendous overdose of sleeping pills. On the table was his daily-report log and his last entry, made three months before:

I haven't attended to the instruments for a long time because it hates us and doesn't want us here. It hates me the most of all and keeps trying to get into the bubble to kill me. I can hear it whenever I stop and listen and I know it won't be long. I'm afraid of it and I want to be asleep when it comes. But I'll have to make it soon because I have only twenty sleeping pills left and if —

The sentence was never finished. According to the temperature recording instruments in the bubble his body ceased radiating heat that same night.

The bubble was cleaned, fumigated, and inspected inside and out. No sign of any inimical entity or force could be found.

Silverman was Horne's replacement. When the cruiser returned six months later bringing him, Green, to be Silverman's replacement, Silverman was completely insane. He babbled about something that had been waiting outside the bubble to kill him but his nearest to a rational statement was to say once, when asked for the hundredth time what he had seen:

"Nothing-you can't really see it. But you feel it watching you and you hear it trying to get in to kill you. One time I bumped the wall and-for God's sake-take me away from it-take me back to Earth..."

Then he had tried to hide under the captain's desk and the ship's doctor had led him away.

The bubble was minutely examined again and the cruiser employed every detector device it possessed to search surrounding space for light-years in all directions. Nothing was found.

When it was time for the new replacement to be transferred to the bubble he reported to Captain McDowell.

"Everything is ready, Green," McDowell said. "You are the next one." His shaggy gray eyebrows met in a scowl. "It would be better if they would let me select the replacement instead of them."

He flushed with a touch of resentment and said, "The Bureau found my intelligence and initiative of thought satisfactory."

"I know-the characteristics you don't need. What they ought to have is somebody like one of my engine room roustabouts, too ignorant to get scared and too dumb to go nuts. Then we could get a sane report six months from now instead of the ravings of a maniac."

"I suggest," he said stiffly, "that you reserve judgement until that time comes, sir."

And that was all he knew about the danger, real or imaginary, that had driven two men into insanity. He would have six months in which to find the answer. Six months minus — He looked at the chronometer and saw that twenty minutes had passed since he left the cruiser. Somehow, it seemed much longer...

He moved to light a cigarette and his metal soles scraped the floor with the same startling loudness he had noticed before. The bubble was as silent as a tomb.

It was not much larger than a tomb; a sphere eighteen feet in diameter, made of thin sheet steel and criss-crossed outside with narrow reinforcing girders to keep the internal air pressure from rupturing it. The floor under him was six feet up from the sphere's bottom and the space beneath held the air regenerator and waste converter units, the storage batteries and the food cabinets. The compartment in which he sat contained chair, table, a narrow cot, banks of dials, a remote-control panel for operating the instruments mounted outside the hull, a microfilm projector, and a pair of exerciser springs attached to one wall. That was all.

There was no means of communication since a hyperspace communicator would have affected the delicate instruments with its radiations but there was a small microfilm library to go with the projector so that he should be able to pass away the time pleasantly enough.

But it was not the fear of boredom that was behind the apprehension he could already feel touching at his mind. It had not been boredom that had turned Horne into a suicide and Silverman into —

Something cracked sharply behind him, like a gunshot in the stillness, and he leaped to his feet, whirling to face it.

It was only a metal reel of data tape that had dropped out of the spectrum analyzer into the storage tray.

His heart was thumping fast and his attempt to laugh at his nervousness sounded hollow and mirthless. *Something* inside or outside the bubble had driven two men insane with its threat and now that he was irrevocably exiled in the bubble, himself, he could no longer dismiss their fear as products of their imagination. Both of them had been rational, intelligent men, as carefully selected by the Observation Bureau as he had been.

He set in to search the bubble, overlooking nothing. When he crawled down into the lower compartment he hesitated then opened the longest blade of his knife before searching among the dark recesses down there. He found nothing, not even a speck of dust.

Back in his chair again he began to doubt his first conviction. Perhaps there really had been some kind of an invisible force or entity outside the bubble. Both Horne and Silverman had said that "it" had tried to get in to kill them.

They had been very definite about that part.

There were six windows around the bubble's walls, set there to enable the attendant to see all the outside-mounted instruments and dials. He went to them to look out, one by one, and from all of them he saw the same vast emptiness that surrounded him. The galaxy-his galaxy-was so far away that its stars were like dust. In the other directions the empty gulf was so wide that galaxies and clusters of galaxies were tiny, feeble specks of light shining across it.

All around him was a void so huge that galaxies were only specks in it....

Who could know what forces or dangers might be waiting out there?

A light blinked, reminding him it was time to attend to his duties. The job required an hour and he was nervous and not yet hungry when he had finished. He went to the exerciser springs on the wall and performed a work-out that left him tired and sweating but which, at least, gave him a small appetite.

The day passed, and the next. He made another search of the bubble's interior with the same results as before. He felt almost sure, then, that there was nothing in the bubble with him. He established a routine of work, pastime and sleep that made the first week pass fairly comfortably but for the gnawing worry in his mind that something invisible was lurking just outside the windows.

Then one day he accidentally kicked the wall with his metal shoe tip.

It made a sound like that from kicking a tight-stretched section of tin and it seemed to him it gave a little from the impact, as tin would do. He realized for the first time how thin it was-how deadly, dangerously thin.

According to the specifications he had read it was only one-sixteenth of an inch thick. It was as thin as cardboard.

He sat down with pencil and paper and began calculating. The bubble had a surface area of 146,500 square inches and the internal air pressure was fourteen pounds to the square inch. Which meant that the thin metal skin contained a total pressure of 2,051,000 pounds.

Two million pounds.

The bubble in which he sat was a bomb, waiting to explode the instant any section of the thin metal weakened.

It was supposed to be an alloy so extremely strong that it had a high safety factor but he could not believe that any metal so thin could be so strong. It was all right for engineers sitting safely on Earth to speak of high safety factors but his life depended upon the fragile wall not cracking. It made a lot of difference.

The next day he thought he felt the hook to which the exerciser spring was attached crack loose from where it was welded to the wall. He inspected the base of the hook closely and there seemed to be a fine, hairline fracture appearing around it.

He held his ear to it, listening for any sound of a leak. It was not leaking yet but it could commence doing so at any time. He looked out the windows at the illimitable void that was waiting to absorb his pitiful little supply of air and he thought of the days he had hauled and jerked at the springs with all his strength, not realizing the damage he was doing.

There was a sick feeling in his stomach for the rest of the day and he returned again and again to examine the hairline around the hook.

The next day he discovered an even more serious threat: the thin skin of the bubble had been spot-welded to the outside reinforcing girders.

Such welding often created hard, brittle spots that would soon crystallize from continued movement-and there was a slight temperature difference in the bubble between his working and sleeping hours that would daily produce a contraction and expansion of the skin. Especially when he used the little cooking burner.

He quit using the burner for any purpose and began a daily inspection of every square inch of the bubble's walls, marking with white chalk all the welding spots that appeared to be definitely weakened. Each day he found more to mark and soon the little white circles were scattered across the walls wherever he looked.

When he was not working at examining the walls he could feel the windows watching him, like staring eyes. Out of self defense he would have to go to them and stare back at the emptiness.

Space was alien; coldly, deadly, alien. He was a tiny spark of life in a hostile sea of Nothing and there was no one to help him. The Nothing outside was waiting day and night for the most infinitesimal leak or crack in the walls; the Nothing that had been waiting out there since time without beginning and would wait for time without end.

Sometimes he would touch his finger to the wall and think, *Death is out there, only one-sixteenth of an inch away*. His first fears became a black and terrible conviction: the bubble could not continue to resist the attack for long. It had already lasted longer than it should have. Two million pounds of pressure wanted out and all the sucking Nothing of intergalactic space wanted in. And only a thin skin of metal, rotten with brittle welding spots, stood between them.

It wanted in-the Nothing wanted in. He knew, then, that Horne and Silverman had not been insane. It wanted in and someday it would get in. When it did it would explode him and jerk out his guts and lungs. Not until that happened, not until the Nothing filled the bubble and enclosed his hideous, turned-inside-out body would it ever be content...

He had long since quit wearing the magnetized shoes, afraid the vibration of them would weaken the bubble still more. And he began noticing sections where the bubble did not seem to be perfectly concave, as though the rolling mill had pressed the metal too thin in places and it was swelling out like an over-inflated balloon.

He could not remember when he had last attended to the instruments. Nothing was important but the danger that surrounded him. He knew the danger was rapidly increasing because whenever he pressed his ear to the wall he could hear the almost inaudible tickings and vibrations as the bubble's skin contracted or expanded and the Nothing tapped and searched with its empty fingers for a flaw or crack that it could tear into a leak.

But the windows were far the worst, with the Nothing staring in at him day and night. There was no escape from it. He could feel it watching him, malignant and gloating, even when he hid his eyes in his hands.

The time came when he could stand it no longer. The cot had a blanket and he used that together with all his spare clothes to make a tent stretching from the table to the first instrument panel. When he crawled under it he found that the lower half of one window could still see him. He used the clothes he was wearing to finish the job and it was much better then, hiding there in the concealing darkness where the Nothing could not see him.

He did not mind going naked-the temperature regulators in the bubble never let it get too cold.

He had no conception of time from then on. He emerged only when necessary to bring more food into his tent. He could still hear the Nothing tapping and sucking in its ceaseless search for a flaw and he made such emergences as brief as possible, wishing that he did not have to come out at all. Maybe if he could hide in his tent for a long time and never make a sound it would get tired and go away...

Sometimes he thought of the cruiser and wished they would come for him but most of the time he thought of the thing that was outside, trying to get in to kill him. When the strain became too great he would draw himself up in the position he had once occupied in his mother's womb and pretend he had never left Earth. It was easier there.

But always, before very long, the bubble would tick or whisper and he would freeze in terror, thinking, *This time it's coming in...*

Then one day, suddenly, two men were peering under his tent at him.

One of them said, "My God —*again!*" and he wondered what he meant. But they were very nice to him and helped him put on his clothes. Later, in the cruiser, everything was hazy and they kept asking him what he was afraid of.

"What was it-what did you find?"

He tried hard to think so he could explain it. "It was-it was Nothing."

"What were you and Horne and Silverman afraid of-what was it?" the voice demanded insistently.

"I told you," he said. "Nothing."

They stared at him and the haziness cleared a little as he saw they did not understand. He wanted them to believe him because what he told them was so very true.

"It wanted to kill us. Please-can't you believe me? It was waiting outside the bubble to kill us."

But they kept staring and he knew they didn't believe him. They didn't *want* to believe him...

Everything turned hazy again and he started to cry. He was glad when the doctor took his hand to lead him away...

The bubble was carefully inspected, inside and out, and nothing was found. When it was time for Green's replacement to be transferred to it Larkin reported to Captain McDowell.

"Everything is ready, Larkin," McDowell said. "You're the next one. I wish we knew what the danger is." He scowled. "I still think one of my roustabouts from the engine room might give us a sane report six months from now instead of the babblings we'll get from you."

He felt his face flush and he said stiffly, "I suggest, sir, that you not jump to conclusions until that time comes."

The cruiser vanished back into hyperspace and he was alone inside the observation bubble, ten thousand light-years beyond the galaxy's outermost sun. He looked out the windows at the gigantic sea of emptiness around him and wondered again what the danger had been that had so terrified the men before him.

Of one thing he was already certain; he would find that nothing was waiting outside the bubble to kill him...

...Can be very helpful indeed. But of course, it's long been known that God helps those who wisely help themselves....

(From "Vogarian Revised Encyclopedia":

SAINTS: *Golden Saints, properly, Yellow Saints, a term of contempt applied by the Vogarian State Press to members of the Church Of The Golden Rule because of their opposition to the war then being planned against Alkoria. See CHURCHES.*

CHURCH, GOLDEN RULE, OF THE: *A group of reactionary fanatics who resisted State control and advocated social chaos through "Individual Freedom." They were liquidated in the Unity Purge but for two-thousand of the more able-bodied, who were sentenced to the moon mines of Belen Nine. The prison ship never arrived there and it is assumed that the condemned Saints somehow overpowered the guards and escaped to some remote section of the galaxy.)*

Kane had observed Commander Y'Nor's bird-of-prey profile with detached interest as Y'Nor jerked his head around to glare again at the chronometer on the farther wall of the cruiser's command room.

"What's keeping Dalon?" Y'Nor demanded, transferring his glare to Kane. "Did you assure him that I have all day to waste?"

"He should be here any minute, sir," Kane answered.

"I didn't find the Saints, after others had failed for sixty years, to then sit and wait. The situation on Vogar was already very critical when we left." Y'Nor scowled at the chronometer again. "Every hour we waste waiting here will delay our return to Vogar by an hour —I presume you realize that?

"It does sound like a logical theory," Kane agreed.

Y'Nor's face darkened dangerously. "You will —"

Quick, hard-heeled footsteps sounded in the corridor outside. The guard officer, Dalon, stepped through the doorway and saluted; his eyes like ice under his pale brows and his uniform seeming to bristle with weapons.

"The native is here, sir," he said to Y'Nor.

He turned, and made a commanding gesture. The leader of the Saints appeared; the man whose resistance Y'Nor would have to break.

A frail, white-bearded old man, scuffed uncertainly into the room in straw sandals, his faded blue eyes peering nearsightedly toward Y'Nor.

"Go to the commander's desk," Dalon ordered in his metallic tones.

The old man obeyed and stopped before Y'Nor's desk, his hands clasped together as though to hide their trembling.

"You are Brenn," Y'Nor said, "and you hold, I believe, the impressive titles of Chief Executive of the Council Of Provinces and Supreme Elder of the Churches Of The Golden Rule?"

"Yes, sir." There was a faint quaver in old Brenn's voice. "I welcome you to our world, sir, and offer you our friendship."

"I understand you can produce Elusium X fuel?"

"Yes, sir. Our Dr. Larue told me the process is within our ability. We —" He hesitated. "We know you haven't enough fuel to return to Vogar."

Y'Nor stiffened in his chair. "What makes you think that?"

"It requires a great deal of fuel to get through the Whirlpool star cluster-and even sixty years ago, the Elusium ores of Vogar were almost exhausted."

Y'Nor smiled thinly. "That reminds me-you would be one of the Saints who murdered their guards and stole a ship to get here."

"We killed no guards, sir. In fact, all of them eventually joined our church."

"Where is the ship?"

"We had to cut it up for our start in mechanization."

"I presume you know you will pay for it?"

"It was taking us to our deaths in the radium mines-but we will pay whatever you ask."

"The first installment will be one thousand units of fuel, to be produced with the greatest speed possible."

"Yes, sir. But in return" —the old man stood a little straighter and an underlying resolve was suddenly revealed —"you must recognize us as a free race."

"Free? A colony founded by escaped criminals?"

"That is not true! We committed no crime, harmed no living thing...."

The hard, cold words of Y'Nor cut off his protest:

"This world it now a Vogarian possession. Every man, woman, and child upon it is a prisoner of the Vogarian State. There will be no resistance. This cruiser's disintegrators can destroy a town within seconds, your race within hours. Do you understand what I mean?"

The visible portion of old Brenn's face turned pale. He spoke at last in the bitter tones of frightened, stubborn determination:

"I offered you our friendship; I hoped you would accept, for we are a peaceful race. I should have known that you came only to persecute and enslave us. But the hand of God will reach down to help us and —"

Y'Nor laughed, a raucous sound like the harsh caw of the Vogarian vulture, and held up a hairy fist.

"This, old man, is the hand for you to center your prayers around. I want full-scale fuel production commenced within twenty-four hours. If this is done, and if you continue to un-questioningly obey all my commands, I will for that long defer your punishment as an escaped criminal. If this is not done, I will destroy a town exactly twenty-five hours from now-and as many more as may be necessary. And you will be publicly executed as a condemned criminal and an enemy of the Vogarian State."

Y'Nor turned to Dalon. "Take him away."

* * * * *

Scared sheep," Y'Nor said when Brenn was gone. "Tomorrow he'll say that he prayed and his god told him what to do-which will be to save his neck by doing as I command."

"I don't know —" Kane said doubtfully. "I think you're wrong about his conscience folding so easily."

"*You* think?" Y'Nor asked. "Perhaps I should remind you that the ability to think is usually characteristic of commanders rather than sub-ensigns. You will not be asked to try to think beyond the small extent required to comprehend simple commands."

Kane sighed with weary resignation. An unexpected encounter with an Alkorian battleship had sent the Vogarian cruiser fleeing through the unexplored Whirlpool star cluster —Y'Nor and Kane the two surviving commissioned officers-with results of negative value to those most affected: the world of the Saint had been accidentally discovered and he, Kane, had risen from sub-ensign to the shakily temporary position of second-in-command.

Y'Nor spoke again:

"Since Vogarian commanders do not go out and mingle with the natives of a subject world, you will act as my representative. I'll let Brenn sweat until tomorrow, then you will go see him. In that, and in all subsequent contacts with the natives, you will keep in mind the fact that I shall hold you personally responsible for any failure of my program."

* * * * *

The next afternoon, two hours before the deadline, Kane went out into the sweet spring air of the world the Saints had named Sanctuary.

It was a virgin world, rich in the resources needed by Vogar, with twenty thousand Saints as the primary labor supply. It was also, he thought, a green and beautiful world; almost a familiar world. The cruiser stood at the upper edge of the town and in the late afternoon sun the little white and brown houses were touched with gold, half hidden in the deep azure shadows of the tall trees and flowering vines that bordered the gently curving streets.

Restlessness stirred within him as he looked at them. It was like going back in time to the Lost Islands, that isolated little region of Vogar that had eluded collectivization until the year he was sixteen. It had been at the same time of year, in the spring, that the State Unity forces had landed. The Lost Island villages had been drowsing in the sun that afternoon, as this town was drowsing now —

He forced the memories from his mind, and the futile restlessness they brought, and went on past a golden-spired church to a small cottage that was almost hidden in a garden of flowers and giant silver ferns.

Brenn met him at the door, his manner very courteous, his eyes dark-shadowed with weariness as though he had not slept for many hours, and invited him inside.

When they were seated in the simply-furnished room, Brenn said, "You came for my decision, sir?"

"The commander sent me for it."

Brenn folded his thin hands, which seemed to have the trembling sometimes characteristic of the aged.

"Yesterday evening when I came from the ship, I prayed for guidance and I saw that I could only abide by the Golden Rule: *Do unto others as you would have them do unto you.*"

"Which means," Kane asked, "that you will do what?"

"Should we of the Church be stranded upon an alien world, our fuel supply almost gone, we would ask for help. By our own Golden Rule we can do no less than give it."

"Eighteen hours ago I issued the order for full-scale, all-out fuel production. I've been up all night and day checking the operation."

Kane stared, surprised that Y'Nor should have so correctly predicted Brenn's reaction. He tried to see some change in the old man, some evidence of the personal fear that must have broken him so quickly, but there was only weariness, and a gentleness.

"So much fuel—" Brenn said. "Is Vogar still at war with Alkoria?"

Kane nodded.

"Once I saw some Alkorian prisoners of war on Vogar," Brenn said. "They are a peaceful, doglike race. They never wanted to go to war with Vogar."

Well-they still didn't want war but on Alkoria were Elusium ores and other resources that the Vogarian State had to have before it could carry out its long-frustrated ambition of galactic conquest.

"I'll go, now," Kane said, getting out of his chair, "and see what you're having done. The commander doesn't take anybody's word for anything."

* * * * *

Brenn called a turbo-car and driver to take him to the multi-purpose factory, which was located a short distance beyond the other side of town. The driver stopped before the factory's main office, where a plump, bald man was waiting, his scalp and glasses gleaming in the sunshine.

"I'm Dr Larue, sir," he greeted Kane. He had a face that under normal circumstance would have been genial. "Father Brenn said you were coming. I'm at your service, to show you what we're doing."

They went inside the factory, where the rush of activity was like a beehive. Machines and installations not needed for fuel production were being torn out as quickly as possible, others taking their place. The workers-he craned his neck to verify his astonished first-impression.

All of them were women.

"Father Brenn's suggestion," Larue said. "These girls are as competent as men for this kind of work and their use here permits the release of men to the outer provinces to procure the raw materials. As you know, our population is small and widely scattered —"

A crash sounded as a huge object nearby toppled and fell. Kane took an instinctive backward step, and bumped into something soft.

"Oh ... excuse me, sir!"

He turned, and had a confused vision of an apologetic smile in a pretty young face, of red curls knocked into disarray-and of amazingly short shorts and a tantalizingly wispy halter.

She recovered the notebook she had dropped and hurried on, leaving a faint cloud of perfume in her wake and a disturbing memory of curving, golden tan legs and a flat little stomach that had been exposed both north and south to the extreme limits of modesty.

"A personnel supervisor from Beachville," Larue said. "She was sunbathing when the plane arrived to pick her up and had no time to obtain other clothing. Father Brenn firmly insisted upon losing not one minute of time during this emergency."

A crane rumbled into view and its grapples seized the huge object that had fallen.

"Our central air-conditioning unit," Larue said. "It had to go."

"You're putting something else in its place, of course?"

"Oh yes. We must have more space but Father Brenn opposed the plan of building an annex as too dangerously time consuming. The only alternative is to tear out everything not absolutely essential."

Kane left shortly afterward, satisfied that the Saints were doing as Brenn had said.

* * * * *

He went back out in the spring sunshine where the turbo-car was still waiting for him, debated briefly with himself, and dismissed the driver. After so many weeks in the prison-like ship, it would be pleasant to walk again.

A grassy, tree-covered ridge ran like the swell of a green sea between the plant and the town. He stopped on top of it, where the town was almost hidden from view, and looked out across the wide valley. Shadows moved lazily across it as cotton-puff clouds drifted down the blue dome of the sky, great white birds like swans were soaring overhead, calling to one another in voices like the singing of violins, bringing again the memories of the Lost Islands —

"And the Vogarian lord gazed upon his world and found it good!"

He swung around, his hand dropping to his holstered blaster, and looked into the green, mocking eyes of a tawny-haired girl. She was beautiful, in the savage way that the hill leopards of Vogar were beautiful, and her hand was on a pistol in her belt.

Her eyes flickered from his blaster up to his face, bright with challenge.

"Want to try it?" she asked.

She wore a short skirt of some rough material and her knees were dusty, as though she had walked for a long way. These things he noticed only absently, his eyes going back to the bold, beautiful face. For twenty years he had been accustomed to the women of Vogar; colorless in their Party uniforms and men's haircuts, made even more drab by the masculine mannerisms they affected. Not since the spring the Lost Islands died had he seen a girl like the one before him.

"Well?" she asked. "Do you think you'll know me next time?"

He walked to her, while she watched him with catlike wariness.

"Hand me that pistol," he ordered.

"Try to take it, you Vogarian ape!"

He moved, and a moment later she was sitting on the ground, her eyes wide with dismayed surprise as he shoved the pistol in his own belt.

"Resisting a Vogarian with a deadly weapon calls for the death penalty," he said. "I suppose you know what I can do?"

She got up, defiance like a blaze about her.

"I'll tell you what you can do-you can go to hell!"

The thought came to him that there might be considerable pleasure in laying her over his knee and raising some blisters where they would do her the most good. He regretfully dismissed the idea as too undignified for even a sub-ensign and asked:

"Who are you, and what are you doing here with that pistol?"

She hesitated, then answered with insolent coolness:

"My name is Barbara Loring. I heard that you Vogarians had demanded that we agree to surrender. I came down from the hills to disagree."

"Is a resistance force meeting here?"

"Do you think you could make me tell you?"

"There are ways-but I'm not here to use them. I am not your enemy."

A little of the hostility faded from her face and she asked, "But how could a Vogarian ever not be our enemy?"

He could find no satisfactory answer to the question.

"I can tell you this," she said. "I know of no resistance organization. I can also tell you that we're not the race of cowards you think and we'll fight the instant Father Brenn gives the word."

"For one who speaks respectfully of Brenn," he said, "your recent words and actions weren't very religious and refined."

Fire flashed in the green eyes again. "Up in the Azure Mountains, where I come from, we're not very refined and we like being that way!"

"And why do you carry guns?" he asked.

"Because all along our frontier lines are rhino-stags, cliff bears, thunder hawks, and a lot of other overgrown carnivora that don't like us-that's why."

"I see." He took the pistol from his belt and held it out to her. "Go back to your mountains, where you belong, before you do something to get yourself executed."

* * * * *

Y'Nor, waiting impatiently in the ship, was grimly pleased by the news of Brenn's change of attitude.

"Exactly as I predicted, as you no doubt recall. How long until they can have a thousand units of fuel produced?"

"Larue estimated fourteen days at best."

Y'Nor tapped his thick fingers on his desk, scowling thoughtfully. "As little as seven extra days might force Vogar to accept the Alkorian peace terms because of lack of fuel-the natives can work twice as hard as they expected to. Tell old Brenn they will be given exactly seven days from sunrise tomorrow.

"And summon Dalon and Graver. I want them to make use of every man on the ship for a twenty-four hour guard-and-inspection system in the plant. The natives will get no opportunities for stalling or sabotage."

* * * * *

Brenn was writing at his book-laden table when Kane went into his cottage the next morning.

"These are called edicts," Brenn said, after greeting him, "but I possess no law-making powers and they are really only suggestions."

Brenn shoved the paper to one side. The script was somewhat different from that of Vogar.

> *The Vogarian inspection and guard system is no more than an expected precaution against sabotage. The Vogarians must be regarded as potential friends who now treat us with suspicion and arrogance only because they do not yet realize the sincerity of our desire to help them to any extent short of surrender —*

Kane looked up from the uncompleted, surprisingly humble, edict and Brenn asked:

"Your commander, sir-he is now pleased with our actions?"

"Not exactly. He will disintegrate a town seven days from sunrise this morning if all the fuel isn't produced by then."

"*Seven* —only *seven* days?" There was startled disbelief on Brenn's face. "But how can he expect us to produce so much fuel in so short a time?"

"I don't know. I'm sorry-it's something I would have argued against if I hadn't had too much sense to try."

"Seven days —" Brenn said again. "We can only pray that God will let it be time enough."

* * * * *

Kane walked on to the plant. The hilltop where he had met the girl was deserted and he felt a vague disappointment.

The plant was hot without the air-conditioner, especially in the vicinity of the electronic roasters. The girls looked flushed and uncomfortable, but for the redhead who still wore her scanty sunsuit. The armed Vogarians looked incongruously out of place among the girls and were sweating profusely. Kane made a mental note to have them ordered into tropical uniforms.

He found Dalon prowling like a wolf among his guards.

"It's inconceivable that these women could ever be a menace," Dalon said, "but I'm taking no chances."

He saw Graver, the cruiser's Chief Technician; a thin, dry man who seemed to be as emotionless as the machines and electronic circuits that were his life.

"They're doing everything with astonishing competence," Graver said. "My technicians are watching like hawks, though."

Larue was not in his office. His secretary, a brown-eyed woman of strikingly intelligent appearance, said, "I'm sorry, sir-Dr. Larue had to go back to town for a few minutes. May I give him your message?"

"No, thanks," he said. "Father Brenn is probably performing that unpleasant chore right now."

* * * * *

Since Dalon and Graver seemed to have the situation at the plant well in hand, Kane decided to make a tour of the outer provinces where the ores were being mined. An efficient plant would be worthless if it did not receive sufficient ore.

He spent four days on the inspection tour; much longer than he had expected to be gone but made necessary by the fact that the small Elusium mines were widely scattered in rugged, roadless areas and he had to walk most of the distance. The single helicopter on Sanctuary was being used to fly the ore out but it was operating on a schedule that caused him to miss it each time.

Each mine was being worked by full day-and-night crews; in fact, by more men than necessary. The reason for that, and for the way the men silently withheld their hostility, was made apparent in a bit of conversation between two miners that he overheard one day:

> "*... So why all of us here when not this many are needed?*"
>
> "*They say Father Brenn wanted to get all the men out of town, away from the cruiser, so there would be no trouble-and you know there would have been if we had stayed. He wants to get the cruiser on its way back to Vogar, they say, so we can get busy producing weapons to fight the Occupation force....*"

He returned on the fifth evening of the allotted seven days and stopped by Brenn's cottage before going on to the ship. The old man was working in his garden, his trembling hands trying to tie up a red-flowered vine.

117

Kane tied it for him and he said, "Thank you, sir. Did you find the mining to be as I had said?"

"I found more than that. You know, don't you, that Y'Nor will return with the Occupation force a hundred days after leaving here?"

"Yes—I know that that is his intention."

"I understand that you're going to try to build weapons while he's gone. Don't, if you think anything of your people, let them do it. Nothing you could build in a hundred days would last a minute against a cruiser's disintegrators."

"I know," Brenn said. "We are supposed to choose between bloody, hopeless resistance and eternal slavery, aren't we? But why should either fate befall a peaceful race?"

Kane asked the logical question: "Why shouldn't it?"

"The laws of God have always been laws of justice and mercy. Not even the Vogarian State can change them."

He thought of the way the State had changed the Lost Islands in one bloody, violent afternoon. Brenn, watching his face, said:

"You are skeptical and bitter, my son-but you will learn that a harmless old man can speak with wisdom."

"No," he said. "There is neither justice nor mercy in the universe. I know from experience. A man can only choose between the lesser of two evils-and almost anything is less evil than Y'Nor when he's mad."

* * * * *

He went to the plant the next morning. Inside, wherever he looked, he saw girls in shorts and halters. The place seemed to be alive with partially clad women. He went to the nearest bulletin board and read Brenn's edict of four days before:

> *Since the excessively warm temperature of the plant causes much discomfort and thereby impairs the efficiency of all workers, and since maximum efficiency will be required to produce the fuel in the extremely short time permitted us, it is suggested that the cool sunsuits of the Beachville girls become the standard work uniform until further notice. These may be obtained for the asking in Department 5-A.*

The next day's edict read:

> *Some have hesitated to follow yesterday's edict through a sense of modesty. This is most commendable. However, the situation is very critical, our lives depend upon the highest degree of efficiency we can attain, and a hot, miserable worker is not efficient. Your bodies are God's handwork-do not be ashamed of them.*

The edict for the next day read simply, warningly:

> *THOU SHALT NOT COMMIT ADULTERY.*

* * * * *

The Vogarian guards and inspectors, now in tropical uniforms, still looked out of place with their holstered weapons but their former cold arrogance was gone and the attitude of the girls had changed from polite reserve to laughing, chattering friendliness.

He found Dalon in a far corner; cornered, literally, by the red-haired personnel supervisor who was spitting like a cat as she said:

"...Then tell your commander how one of your men tried to make one of my girls and got hit with a wrench for it! Ask him whether he wants us to produce fuel or make love! Go ahead-ask him! Or let me —*I'll* ask him!"

"You'll have to see to it that your girls don't lead my men on." Dalon ran his finger around his collar, worry on his face. "Florence, are you trying to get me ruined?"

"Then inform your men that there is a certain commandment we all believe in and anything beyond our willingness to be friends calls for marriage first."

"*Marriage?*" Dalon spluttered the word, recovered his poise with an effort, and said stiffly, "My men are soldiers, not suitors. I want them respected as such."

He strode away without seeing Kane. The girl stared after him, fuming, and Kane went in search of Graver.

Graver and the brown-eyed secretary were in Larue's office, their heads together over a flow sheet of some kind. The secretary excused herself and when she was gone, Kane asked:

"Where's Larue?"

"Checking the catalytic processors, I think, sir." Graver answered, almost vaguely. "Mar ... his secretary was just showing me how they improvised so much of their equipment so quickly." There was a strange light in Graver's usually expressionless eyes. "It's incredible!"

"Well-the commander gave them no time to waste, you know."

"Sir? Oh ... I was referring to her intelligence, sir. It's amazing that a woman should have such a thorough knowledge of such a complex process."

Kane felt the birth pains of the first dark premonition.

"If you don't want a thorough knowledge of the interior of State prison," he said in grim warning, "you'd better get that silly look off your face and concentrate on your duties. Tell Dalon the same order applies to him. And tell Larue that the commander reminds him they now have less than forty hours to finish the job."

* * * * *

He decided, again, to walk back to the ship. There was now a multitude of paths through the grass were girls had been walking to and from work. Two groups from the last shift-change were a short distance ahead of him, several of Dalon's guards and Graver's technicians among them, all of them talking and laughing.

In that area they could not be spied upon by Y'Nor with the ship's view-screen scanners and even as he watched, a tall, dark young guard put his arm around the girl walking close beside him. She twisted away from him and ran on to the next group, there to look back with a teasing toss of her head.

Kane watched both groups disappear over the hill, then followed, muttering thoughtfully. He felt he could safely assume-if anything could be said to be safe about the situation-that the lack of discipline he had just witnessed was typical of all the men. They were all young and healthy and for sixteen hours out of each day they were side by side with the almost nude, provocatively feminine, Sanctuary girls.

Their weakness was understandable. It was also very dangerous. Heads would roll if Y'Nor ever learned what was going on and it required no psychic ability to guess whose head would roll the fastest and farthest.

He would have to have it stopped, at once.

He took a short cut to Brenn's cottage, by a sleepy, shady street he had never been down before. Halfway along it was an open-air eating place of some kind, with tables placed about under the trees. There seemed to be no customers at the moment but he stopped, anyway, to take a closer look for errant guards.

A tawny head lifted at a table half hidden by a nearby tree and he looked into the surprised face of the mountain girl, Barbara.

"Well!" she said. "Come on over and let me offer you a glass of cyanide."

He walked over to her table. She was wearing a blouse and skirt similar to that of the day he had met her but the pistol was gone.

"I thought I told you to go back to your hills," he said.

"I decided it would be more fun to work in the plant and sabotage things."

"Let Y'Nor learn you said that and you'll be in a fix I can't help you out of."

"Should a Vogarian care?" But the jeering was gone as she said, "When you gave my pistol back to me —I thought it was a trick of some kind."

"I told you I wasn't your enemy."

"I know ... but it's hard for a Saint to believe any Vogarian could ever be anything else."

"It doesn't seem to be very hard for the girls in the plant," he observed glumly.

"Oh ... that's different." She made a gesture of light dismissal. "Those soldiers and technicians are good boys at heart-they haven't been brain-washed like you officers."

"That's interesting to know, I'm sure. I suppose —"

He stopped as a gray-haired woman came and set down a tray containing a sandwich and a mug. From the foamy top of the mug came the unmistakable aroma of beer.

"Do you Saints *drink?*" he asked incredulously.

"Sure. Why?"

"But your church —"

"Earth churches used to ban alcohol as sinful because it would cause a mean person to show his true character. My church is more sensible and works to change the person's character, instead."

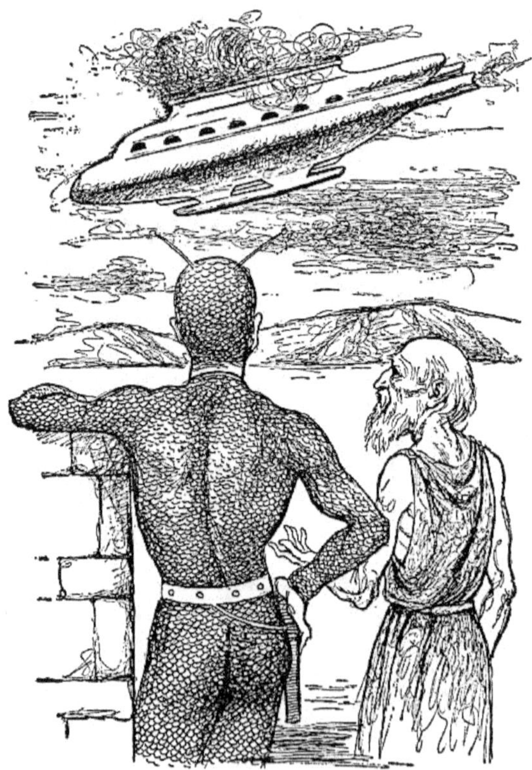

She took a bite of the sandwich. "Cliff bear steak-it and beer go perfectly together. Shall I order you some?"

"No," he said, thinking of Y'Nor's fury if Y'Nor should learn he had had a friendly lunch with a native girl. "About your church-what kind of a church is it, anyway?"

"What its name implies. Heaven isn't for sale at the pulpit-everybody has to qualify for it by his own actions. We have to practice our belief-just looking pious and saying that we believe doesn't count."

He revised his opinion of the Saints, then asked, "But were you practicing your Golden Rule when you came to this town with a gun to shoot Vogarians?"

"For Vogarians we have a special Golden Rule that reads: *Do unto Vogarians as they have come to do unto you.* And you came here to enslave or kill us-remember?"

It could not be denied. When he did not answer she smiled at him; a smile surprisingly gentle and understanding.

"You honestly would like to be our friend, wouldn't you? The State psychiatrists didn't do a good job of brainwashing you, after all."

It was the first time since he was sixteen that anyone had spoken to him with genuine kindness. It gave him a strange feeling, a lonely sense of something rising up out of the past to mock him, and he changed the subject:

"Are the Azure Mountains the edge of your frontier?"

She nodded. "Beyond is the Emerald Plain, a great, wide plain, and beyond it are mountain ranges that have never been named or explored. I'm going into them some day and —"

* * * * *

Time passed with astonishing speed as he talked with the girl and it was late in the afternoon when he continued on to Brenn's cottage. He put the thoughts of her from his mind and told Brenn of the too-warm association between the girls and the Vogarians.

"But it is only friendship," Brenn said soothingly. "You can assure your commander that nothing immoral is being done."

"If he knew what was going on, it would be my neck. It has to be stopped. Write an edict-do anything that will stop it at once."

Brenn stroked his white beard thoughtfully. "I'm sorry this unforeseen situation has occurred, sir. Will you have strict orders to the same effect given your men?"

"There's a severe penalty for unauthorized fraternization. I'll see that they're well reminded of it."

"I'll write another edict, at once, forbidding the girls to speak to your men, sir."

* * * * *

Y'Nor was pacing the floor when Kane went to the ship, his face black and ugly with anger.

"Have you been blind?" he demanded.

Kane tried to swallow a sinking feeling, wondering just how much Y'Nor had seen, and said, "Sir?"

"My guards-my so-called guards-how long have they been strolling back from the plant in company with the native women?"

"Oh," he said, feeling a great relief that Y'Nor had not seen the true situation, "it's only that some of the out-going shifts coincide, sir, and —"

"You know, don't you, that military men march to and from duty in military formation?"

"Yes, sir."

"You are aware of the importance of discipline?"

"Yes, sir."

"You are further aware of the fact that you, Dalon, and Graver, will be guilty of treason if this lack of discipline imperils my plans in any way?"

"Yes, sir."

"You have heard of the punishment for treason?"

"Yes, sir."

* * * * *

He went below when the unpleasant business with Y'Nor was finally over. It was the beginning of the eight-hour sleep period for Dalon and Graver but they were still up, sitting on their bunks and staring dreamily into space. It was only belatedly, almost fuzzily, that they became aware of his glowering presence in the doorway.

"I bring you glad tidings," he said, "from the commander's own lips. The multiple-gallows at State prison is still in perfect working order, especially the first three trapdoors —"

The last day dawned, bright and sunny, and he went to see Brenn.

"I had the new edict posted immediately," Brenn said. "I hope it will undo the damage."

"Let's see it," Kane requested and Brenn handed him the handwritten original. It was:

> *Despite our affection for the Vogarians among us, we must not endanger them by any longer talking to them. A Vogarian military rule is now being enforced which forbids Vogarians to speak to Sanctuary girls except in the line of duty. There is a severe penalty for those who disobey this rule.*
>
> *It must also be pointed out, sternly to the Sanctuary girls and respectfully to the Vogarians, that flight into the uninhabited Sanctuary mountains would result in execution for the fleeing couples if Commander Y'Nor should ever find them.*

"What's this?" Kane demanded, pointing to the last paragraph.

"Why —a warning, sir."

"Warning ... it's a suggestion!"

"A suggestion?" Brenn lifted his hands in shocked protest. "But, sir, how could anyone think —"

"I, personally, wouldn't give a damn if the entire crew was too love-sick to eat. But the commander does and my future welfare, including the privilege of breathing, depends upon my retaining what passes for his good will."

"Good heavens —I shall have this edict removed from the bulletin boards at once!"

"A great idea. It should fix up everything to lock the stable door now that the horse is stolen."

* * * * *

He went to the plant and felt the air of resentment as soon as he stepped inside. Dalon was patrolling among his men, his haggard face becoming more haggard each time the red-haired personnel supervisor went by with her hips swinging and her head held high in hurt, aloof silence. The guards were pacing their beats in wordless quiet, Graver's technicians were speaking only in the line of duty. The girls were not talking even to one another but in the soft, melting glances they gave the Vogarians they said *We understand* in a manner more eloquent than any words.

In fact, far too eloquent. He considered the plan of having Brenn forbid the girls to look at the guards, discarded that as impractical, for a moment wildly considered ordering the guards not to look at the girls, discarded that as even more impractical, and went, muttering, to Larue's office.

Larue was at his desk, his face lined with fatigue.

"It's been a difficult job," he said, "but we'll meet the deadline."

"Good," Kane answered. "Did Brenn phone you about having that edict removed?"

"Ah-which one?"

"Which one? You mean...."

He turned and ran from the office.

A girl was removing the offending edict from the nearest bulletin board. Another, later, one proclaimed:

> *We must abandon as hopeless the suggestion of some that if there must be an Occupation force, we would like for it to be these men whom we have come to respect, and many of us to love. This can never be. Only Commander Y'Nor will leave the ship at Vogar, there to select his own Occupation force, while the men now among us continue directly on to the Alkorian war from which many of them will never return.*

We must not resent the fact that on this, their last day among us, these men are forbidden to speak to us or to let us speak to them nor say that this is unfair when Commander Y'Nor's Occupation troops will be permitted to associate freely with us. These things are beyond our power to change. We must accept the inevitable and show only by our silent conduct the love we have for these warriors whom we shall never see again.

Kane gulped convulsively, read it again, and hurried back to Larue's office.

"How long has that last edict been up?" he demanded.

"About twelve hours."

"Then every shift has seen it?"

"Ah ...yes. Why-is something wrong with it?"

"That depends on the viewpoint. I want them removed at once. And tell that sanctified old weasel that if this last edict of his gets me hanged, which it probably will, I'll see to it that he gets the same medicine."

He went back into the plant and made his way through the bare-legged, soft-eyed girls, looking for Dalon. He overheard a guard say in low, bitter tones to another: "*...Maybe eight hours on Vogar, and we can't leave the ship, then on to the battle front for us while Y'Nor and his home guard favorites come back here and pick out their harems —*"

He found Dalon and said to him, "Watch your men. They're resentful. Some of them might even desert-and Y'Nor wasn't joking about that gallows for us last night."

"I know." Dalon ran his finger around the collar that seemed to be getting increasingly tighter for him. "I've warned them that the Occupation troops would get them in the end."

* * * * *

He found Graver at a dial-covered panel. The brown-eyed secretary-her eyes now darker and more appealing than ever-was just leaving, a notebook in her hand.

"Since when," Kane asked, "has it been customary for technicians to need the assistance of secretaries to read a dial?"

"But, sir, she is a very good technician, herself. Her paper work is now done and she was helping me trace a circuit that was fluctuating."

Kane peered suspiciously into Graver's expressionless face.

"Are you sure it was a circuit that was doing the fluctuating?"

"Yes, sir."

"Did you know that half of Dalon's guards seem to be ready to jump ship?"

"Yes, sir. But their resentment is not characteristic of my technicians."

He realized, with surprise, that that was true. And Graver, in contrast to Dalon's agitation, had the calm, purposeful air of a man who had pondered deeply upon an unpleasant future and had taken steps to prevent it.

"I have no desire to hang, sir, and I have convinced my men that it would be suicide for part of them to desert. I shall do my best to convince Dalon's guards of the same thing."

He went back through the plant, much of his confidence restored, and back to the ship.

Y'Nor was pacing the floor again, his impatience keying him to a mood more vile than ever.

"This ship will leave at exactly twenty-three fifteen, Vogar time," Y'Nor said. "Any man not on it then will be regarded as a deserter and executed as such when I return with the Occupation force."

He stopped his pacing to stare at Kane with the ominous anticipation of a spider surveying a captured fly.

"Although I can operate this ship with a minimum of two crewmen, I shall expect you to make certain that every man is on board."

Kane went back out of the ship, his confidence shaken again, and back to the plant.

* * * * *

Night came at last and, finally, the first shielded tank of fuel was delivered to the ship. Others followed, one by one, as the hours went by.

It was almost morning when Graver came to him and said, "My duties and those of my men are finished here, sir. Shall we go to prepare the ship for flight?"

"Yes-get busy at it," Kane answered. "Don't give the commander any excuse to get any madder than he already is."

An hour later the last of the fuel went into the last tank and was hauled away. Someone said, "That's all," and a switch clicked. A machine rumbled off into silence, followed by others. Control panels went dark. Within a minute there was not a machine running, not a panel lighted.

Dalon's whistle for Guard Assembly sounded, high and shrill. A girl's voice called to one of the guards: "Hurry back to your ship, Billy-the thunder hawks might get you if you stayed —" and broke on a sob. Another girl said, "Hush, Julia-it's not his fault."

He went out of the plant, and past Larue's office. He saw that the brown-eyed secretary was gone, her desk clean. Larue was still there, looking very tired. He did not go in. The fuel had been produced, he would never see Larue again.

He took the path that led toward town. Part of the Whirlpool star cluster was still above the horizon, a white blaze of a thousand suns, and the eastern sky was lightening with the first rays of dawn. A dozen girls were ahead of him, their voices a low murmur as they hurried back toward town. There was an undertone of tension, all of the former gaiety gone. The brief week of make-believe was over and the next Vogarians to come would truly be their enemy.

He came to the hilltop where he had met the mountain girl, thought of her with irrational longing, and suddenly she was there before him.

The pistol was again in her belt.

"You came with all the stealth of a plains ox," she said. "I could have shot you a dozen times over."

"Are we already at war?" he asked.

"We Saints have to let you Vogarians kill some of us, first-our penalty for being ethical."

"Listen to me," he said. "We tried to fight the inevitable in the Lost Islands. When the sun went down that day, half of us were dead and the rest prisoners."

"And you rose from prisoner to officer because you were too selfish to keep fighting for what was right."

"I saw them bury the ones who insisted on doing that."

"And you want us to meekly bow down, here?"

"I have no interest of any kind in this world —I'll never see it again-but I know from experience what will happen to you and your people if you try to fight. I don't want that to happen. Do you think that because a man isn't a blind chauvinist, he has to be a soulless monster?"

"No," she said in a suddenly small voice. "But I had hoped ...we were talking that day of the mountains beyond the Emerald Plain and a frontier to last for centuries ...it was just idle talk but I thought maybe that when the showdown came you would be on our side, after all."

She drew a deep breath that came a little raggedly and said with a lightness that was too forced:

"You don't mind if I have a silly sentimental fondness for my world, do you? It's the only world I have. Maybe you would understand if you could see the Azure Mountains in the spring ...but you never will, will you? Because you lied when you said you weren't my enemy and now I know you are and I" —the lightness faltered and broke —"am yours ...and the next time we meet one will have to kill the other."

She turned away, and vanished among the trees like a shadow.

He was unaware of the passage of time as he stood there on the hill that was silent with her going and remembered the day he had met her and the way the song swans had been calling. When he looked up at the sky, it was bright gold in the east and the blazing stars of the Whirlpool were fading into invisibility. He looked to the west, where the road wound its long way out of the valley, and he thought he could see her trudging up it, tiny and distant. He looked at his watch and saw he had just time enough to reach the ship before it left.

* * * * *

Brenn was standing by his gate, watching the dawn flame into incandescence and looking more frail and helpless than ever. The cruiser towered beyond, blotting out half the dawn sky like a sinister omen. A faint, deep hum was coming from it as the drive went into the preliminary phase that preceded take-off.

"You have only seconds left to reach the ship," Brenn said. "You have already tarried almost too long."

"You're looking at a fool," he answered, "who is going to tarry in the Azure Mountains and beyond the Emerald Plain for a hundred days. Then the Occupation men will kill him."

There was no surprise on Brenn's face but it seemed to Kane that the old man smiled in his beard. For the second time since he was sixteen, Kane heard someone speak to him with gentle understanding:

"Although you have not been of much help to my plans, your intentions were good. I was sure that in the end this would be your decision. I am well pleased with you, my son."

A whine came from the ship and the boarding ramp flicked up like a disappearing tongue. The black opening of the air lock seemed to wink, then was solid, featureless metal as the doors slid shut.

"*Bon voyage*, Y'Nor!" Kane said. "We'll be waiting for you with our bows and arrows."

"There is no one on the ship but Y'Nor," Brenn said. "Graver saw to it that the Ready lights were all going on the command room control board, then he and all the others followed my ... suggestion."

Kane remembered Graver's calmness and his statement concerning his men: "... It would be suicide for part of them to desert."

For *part* of them. But if every last one deserted —

The drives of the ship roared as Y'Nor pushed a control button and the ship lifted slowly. The roaring faltered and died as Y'Nor pushed another button which called for a crewman who was not there. The ship dropped back with a ponderous thud, careened, and fell with a force that shook the ground. It made no further sound or movement.

He stared at the silent, impotent ship, finding it hard to realize that there would be no hundred-day limit for him; that the new world, the boundless frontier-and Barbara-would be his for as long as he lived.

"Poor Commander Y'Nor," Brenn said. "The air lock is now under the ship and we shall have to dig a tunnel to rescue him."

"Don't hurry about it," Kane advised. "Let him sweat in the dark for a few days with his desk wrapped around his neck. It will do him good."

"We are a kind and harmless race, we could never do anything like that."

"Kind? I believe you. But harmless? You made monkeys out of Vogar's choicest fighting men."

"Please do not use such an uncouth expression. I was only the humble instrument of a greater Power. I only ... ah ... encouraged the natural affection between man and maid, the love that God intended them to have."

"But did you practice your Golden Rule? You saw to it that fifty young men were forced to associate day after day with hundreds of almost-naked girls. Would you really have wanted the same thing done to you if you had been in their place?"

"Would I?" There was a gleam in the old eyes that did not seem to come from the brightness of the dawn. "I, too, was once young, my son-what do *you* think?"

Was the cat native to the planet, or to his imagination?

The problem of separating the friends from the enemies was a major one in the conquest of space as many a dead spacer could have testified. A tough job when you could see an alien and judge appearances; far tougher when they were only whispers on the wind.

> *A smile of friendship is a baring of the teeth. So is a snarl of menace. It can be fatal to mistake the latter for the former.*
> *Harm an alien being only under circumstances of self-defense.*
> *TRUST NO ALIEN BEING UNDER ANY CIRCUMSTANCES.*

—From *Exploration Ship's Handbook.*

He listened in the silence of the Exploration ship's control room. He heard nothing but that was what bothered him; an ominous quiet when there should have been a multitude of sounds from the nearby village for the viewscreen's audio-pickups to transmit. And it was more than six hours past the time when the native, Throon, should have come to sit with him outside the ship as they resumed the laborious attempt to learn each other's language.

The viewscreen was black in the light of the control room, even though it was high noon outside. The dull red sun was always invisible through the world's thick atmosphere and to human eyes full day was no more than a red-tinged darkness.

He switched on the ship's outside floodlights and the viewscreen came to bright white life, showing the empty glades reaching away between groves of purple alien trees. He noticed, absently, that the trees seemed to have changed a little in color since his arrival.

The village was hidden from view by the outer trees but there should have been some activity in the broad area visible to him. There was none, not even along the distant segment of what should have been a busy road. The natives were up to something and he knew, from hard experience on other alien worlds, that it would be nothing good. It would be another misunderstanding of some kind and he didn't know enough of their incomprehensible language to ask them what it was —

* * * * *

Suddenly, as it always came, he felt someone or something standing close behind him and peering over his shoulder. He dropped his hand to the blaster he had taken to wearing at all times and whirled.

Nothing was behind him. There never was. The control room was empty, with no hiding place for anything, and the door was closed, locked by the remote-control button beside him. There was nothing.

The sensation of being watched faded, as though the watcher had withdrawn to a greater distance. It was perhaps the hundredth time within six days that he had felt the sensation. And when he slept at night something came to nuzzle at his mind; faceless, formless, utterly alien. For the past three nights he had not let the blaster get beyond quick reach of his hand, even when in bed.

But whatever it was, it could not be on the ship. He had searched the ship twice, a methodical compartment-by-compartment search that had found nothing. It had to be the work of the natives from outside the ship. Except....

Why, if the natives were telepathic, did the one called Throon go through the weary pretense of trying to learn a mutually understandable form of communication?

There was one other explanation, which he could not accept: that he was following in the footsteps of Will Garret of Ship Nine who had deliberately gone into a white sun two months after the death of his twin brother.

He looked at the chair beside his own, Johnny's chair, which would forever be empty, and his thoughts went back down the old, bitter paths. The Exploration Board had been wrong when they thought the close bond between identical twins would make them the ideal two-man crews for the lonely, lifetime journeys of the Exploration Ships. Identical twins were too close; when one of them died, the other died in part with him.

They had crossed a thousand light-years of space together, he and Johnny, when they came to the bleak planet that he would name Johnny's World. He should never have let Johnny go alone up the slope of the honey-combed mountain-but Johnny had wanted to take the routine record photographs of the black, tiger-like beasts which they had called cave cats and the things had seemed harmless and shy, despite their ferocious appearance.

"I'm taking them a sack of food that I think they might like," Johnny had said. "I want to try to get some good close-up shots of them."

Ten minutes later he heard the distant snarl of Johnny's blaster. He ran up the mountainside, knowing already that he was too late. He found two of the cave cats lying where Johnny had killed them. Then he found Johnny, at the foot of a high cliff. He was dead, his neck broken by the fall. Scattered all around him from the torn sack was the food he had wanted to give to the cats.

He buried Johnny the next day, while a cold wind moaned under a lead-gray sky. He built a monument for him; a little mound of frosty stones that only the wild animals would ever see —

* * * * *

A chime rang, high and clear, and the memories were shattered. The orange light above the hyperspace communicator was flashing; the signal that meant the Exploration Board was calling him from Earth.

He flipped the switch and said, "Paul Jameson, Exploration Ship One."

The familiar voice of Brender spoke:

"It's been some time since your preliminary report. Is everything all right?"

"In a way," he answered. "I was going to give you the detailed report tomorrow."

"Give me a brief sketch of it now."

"Except for their short brown fur, the natives are humanoid in appearance. But there are basic differences. Their body temperature is cool, like their climate. Their vision range is from just within the visible red on into the infrared. They'll shade their eyes from the light of anything as hot as boiling water but they'll look square into the ship's floodlights and never see them."

"And their knowledge of science?" Brender asked.

"They have a good understanding of it, but along lines entirely different from what our own were at their stage of development. For example: they power their machines with chemicals but there is no steam, heat, or exhaust."

"That's what we want to find-worlds where branches of research unknown to our science are being explored. How about their language?"

"No progress with it yet." He told Brender of the silence in the village and added, "Even if Throon should show up I could not ask him what was wrong. I've learned a few words but they have so many different definitions that I can't use them."

"I know," Brender said. "Variable and unrelated definitions, undetectable shades of inflection-and sometimes a language that has no discernibly separate words. The Singer brothers of Ship Eight ran into the latter. We've given them up as lost."

"The Singers-dead?" he exclaimed. "Good God-it's been only a month since the Ramon brothers were killed."

"The circumstances were similar," Brender said. "They always are. There is no way the Exploration men can tell the natives that they mean them no harm and the suspicion of the natives grows into dangerous hostility. The Singers reported the natives on that world to be both suspicious and possessing powerful weapons. The Singers were proceeding warily, their own weapons always at hand. But, somehow, the natives caught them off-guard —their last report was four months ago."

There was a silence, then Brender added, "Their ship was the ninth-and we had only fifteen."

He did not reply to the implications of Brender's statement. It was obvious to them all what the end of the Plan would be. What it had to be.

* * * * *

It had been only three years since the fifteen heavily armed Exploration ships set out to lead the way for Terran expansion across the galaxy; to answer a cry from far planets, and to find all the worlds that held intelligent life. That was the ultimate goal of the Plan: to accumulate and correlate all the diverse knowledge of all the intelligent life-forms in the galaxy. Among the achievements resulting from that tremendous mass of data would be a ship's drive faster even than hyperspace; the Third Level Drive which would bring all the galaxies of the universe within reach.

And now nine ships were gone out of fifteen and nineteen men out of thirty....

"The communication barrier," Brender said. "The damned communication barrier has been the cause behind the loss of every ship. And there is nothing we can do about it. We're stymied by it...."

The conversation was terminated shortly afterward and he moved about the room restlessly, wishing it was time to lift ship again. With Johnny not there the dark world was like a smothering tomb. He would like to leave it behind and drive again into the star clouds of the galaxy; drive on and on into them —

A ghostly echo touched his mind; restless, poignantly yearning. He swung to face the locked door, knowing there could be nothing behind it. The first real fear came to him as he did so. The thing was lonely-the thing that watched him was as lonely as he was....

What else could any of it be but the product of a mind in the first stage of insanity?

* * * * *

The natives came ten minutes later.

The viewscreen showed their chemically-powered vehicle emerge from the trees and roll swiftly across the glade. Four natives were in it while a fifth one lay on the floor, apparently badly injured.

The vehicle stopped a short distance in front of the airlock and he recognized the native on the floor. It was Throon, the one with whom he had been exchanging language lessons.

They were waiting for him when he emerged from the ship, pistol-like weapons in their belts and grim accusation in their manner.

Throon was muttering unintelligibly, unconscious. His skin, where not covered by the brown fur, was abnormal in appearance. He was dying.

The leader of the four indicated Throon and said in a quick, brittle voice: *"Ko reegar feen no-dran!"*

Only one word was familiar: *Ko*, which meant "you" and "yesterday" and a great many other things. The question was utterly meaningless to him.

He dropped his hand a little nearer his blaster as the leader spoke again; a quick succession of unknown words that ended with a harshly demanding *"kreson!"*

Kreson meant "now," or "very quickly." All the other words were unfamiliar to him. They waited, the grim menace about them increasing when he did not answer. He tried in vain to find some way of explaining to them he was not responsible for Throon's sickness and could not cure it.

Then he saw the spray of leaves that had caught on the corner of the vehicle when it came through the farther trees.

They were of a deep purple color. All the trees around the ship were almost gray by contrast.

Which meant that he *was* responsible for Throon's condition.

The cold white light of the ship's floodlights, under which he and Throon had sat for day after day, contained radiations that went through the violet and far into the ultraviolet. To the animal and vegetable life of the dark world such radiations were invisibly short and deadly.

Throon was dying of hard-radiation sickness.

It was something he should have foreseen and avoided-and that would not have happened had he accepted old Throon's pantomimed invitation, in the beginning, to go with him into the village to work at the language study. There he would have used a harmless battery lamp for illumination ...but there was no certainty that the natives were not planning to lay a trap for him in the village and he had refused to go.

It did not matter-there was a complex radiation-neutralizer and cell-reconstructor in the ship which would return Throon to full, normal health a few hours after he was placed in its chamber.

He turned to the leader of the four natives and motioned from Throon to the airlock. "Go-there," he said in the native language.

"Bron!" the leader answered. The word meant "No" and there was a determination in the way he said it that showed he would not move from it.

At the end of five minutes his attempts to persuade them to take Throon into the ship had increased their suspicion of his motives to the point of critical danger. If only he could tell them *why* he wanted Throon taken into the ship ...But he could not and would have to take Throon by first disposing of the four without injuring them. This he could do by procuring one of the paralyzing needle-guns from the ship.

He took a step toward the ship and spoke the words that to the best of his knowledge meant: "I come back."

"Feswin ilt k'la."

Their reply was to snatch at their weapons in desperate haste, even as the leader uttered a hoarse word of command. He brought up the blaster with the quick motion that long training had perfected and their weapons were only half drawn when his warning came:

"Bron!"

* * * * *

They froze, but did not release their weapons. He walked backward to the airlock, his blaster covering them, the tensely waiting manner in which they watched his progress telling him that the slightest relaxation of his vigilance would mean his death. He did not let the muzzle of the blaster waver until he was inside the airlock and the outer door had slid shut.

He was sure that the natives would be gone when he returned. And he was sure of another thing: That whatever he had said to them, it was not what he had thought he was saying.

He saw that the glade was empty when he opened the airlock again. At the same time a bomb-like missile struck the ship just above the airlock and exploded with a savage crash. He jabbed the *Close* button and the door clicked shut barely in advance of three more missiles which hammered at its impervious armor.

So that, he thought wearily, is that.

He laid the useless needle-gun aside. The stage was past when he could hope to use it. He could save Throon only by killing some of the others-or he could lift ship and leave Throon to die. Either action would make the natives hate and fear Terrans; a hatred and fear that would be there to greet all future Terran ships.

That was not the way a race gave birth to peaceful galactic empire, was not the purpose behind the Plan. But always, wherever the Exploration men went, they encountered the deadly barrier; the intangible, unassailable communication barrier. With the weapons an Exploration man carried in his ship he had the power to destroy a world-but not the power to ask the simple questions that would prevent fatal misunderstandings.

And before another three years had passed the last Exploration man would die, the last Exploration ship would be lost.

He felt the full force of hopelessness for the first time. When Johnny had been alive it had been different; Johnny, who had laughed whenever the outlook was the darkest and said, *"We'll find a way, Paul —"*

The thought broke as suddenly, unexpectedly, he felt that Johnny was very near. With the feeling came the soft enclosure of a dream-like peace in which Johnny's death was vague and faraway; only something that had happened in another dream. He knew, without wondering why, that Johnny was in the control room.

A part of his mind tried to reject the thought as an illusion. He did not listen-he did not want to listen. He ran to the ship's elevator, stumbling like one not fully awake. Johnny was waiting for him in the control room-alive-alive —

* * * * *

He spoke as he stepped into the control room:

"Johnny —"

Something moved at the control board, black and alien, standing tall as a man on short hind legs. Yellow eyes blazed in a feline face.

It was a cave cat, like the ones that had killed Johnny.

Realization was a wrenching shock and a terrible disillusionment. Johnny was not waiting for him-not alive —

He brought up the blaster, the dream-like state gone. The paw of the cave cat flashed out and struck the ship's master light switch with a movement faster than his own. The room was instantly, totally, dark.

He fired and pale blue fire lanced across the room, to reveal that the cave cat was gone. He fired again, quickly and immediately in front of him. The pale beam revealed only the ripped metal floor.

"I am not where you think."

The words spoke clearly in his mind but there was no directional source. He held his breath, listening for the whisper of padded feet as the cave cat flashed in for the kill, and made a swift analysis of the situation.

The cave cat was telepathic and highly intelligent and had been on the ship all the time. It and the others had wanted the ship and had killed Johnny to reduce opposition to the minimum. He, himself, had been permitted to live until the cave cat learned from his mind how to operate the almost-automatic controls. Now, he had served his purpose —

"You are wrong."

Again there was no way he could determine the direction from which the thought came. He listened again, and wondered why it had not waylaid him at the door.

Its thought came:

"I had to let you see me or you would not have believed I existed. It was only here that I could extinguish all lights and have time to speak before you killed me. I let you think your brother was here...." There was a little pause. *"I am sorry. I am sorry. I should have used some other method of luring you here."*

He swung the blaster toward what seemed to be a faint sound near the astrogator unit across the room.

"We did not intend to kill your brother."

He did not believe it and did not reply.

"When we made first telepathic contact with him, he jerked up his blaster and fired. In his mind was the conviction that we had pretended to be harmless animals so that we could catch him off-guard and kill him. One of us leaped at him as he fired the second time, to knock the blaster from his hand. We needed only a few minutes in which to explain-but he would not trust us that long. There was a misjudgment of distance and he was knocked off the cliff."

Again he did not reply.

"We did not intend to kill your brother," the thought came, *"but you do not believe me."*

* * * * *

He spoke for the first time. "No, I don't believe you. You are physically like cats and cats don't misjudge distances. Now, you want something from me before you try to kill me, too. What is it?"

"I will have to tell you of my race for you to understand. We call ourselves the Varn, in so far as it can be translated into a spoken word, and we are a very old race. In the beginning we did not live in caves but there came a long period of time, for thousands of years, when the climate on our world was so violent that we were forced to live in the caves. It was completely dark there but our sense of smell became very acute, together with sufficient sensitivity to temperature changes that we could detect objects in our immediate vicinity. There were subterranean plants in the caves and food was no problem."

* * * * *

"We had always been slightly telepathic and it was during our long stay in the caves that our intelligence and telepathic powers became fully developed. We had only our minds-physical science is not created in dark caves with clumsy paws.

"The time finally came when we could leave the caves but it was of little help to us. There were no resources on our world but earth and stone and the thin grass of the plains. We wondered about the universe and we knew the stars were distant suns because one of our own suns became a star each winter. We studied as best we could but we could see the stars only as the little wild animals saw them. There was so much we wanted to learn and by then we were past our zenith and already dying out. But our environment was a prison from which we could never escape.

"When your ship arrived we thought we might soon be free. We wanted to ask you to take some of us with you and arrange for others of your race to stop by on our world. But you dismissed us as animals, useful only for making warm fur coats, because we lived in caves and had no science, no artifacts-nothing. You had the power to destroy us and we did not know what your reaction would be when you learned we were intelligent and telepathic. A telepathic race must have a high code of ethics and never intrude unwanted-but would you have believed that?"

He did not answer.

"The death of your brother changed everything. You were going to leave so soon that there would be no time to learn more about you. I hid on the ship so I could study you and wait until I could prove to you that you needed me. Now, I can-Throon is dying and I can give you the proper words of explanation that will cause the others to bring him into the ship."

"Your real purpose-what is it?" he asked.

"To show you that men need the Varn. You want to explore the galaxy, and learn. So do the Varn. You have the ships and we have the telepathic ability that will end the communication problem. Your race and mine can succeed only if we go together."

He searched for the true, and hidden, purpose behind the Varn proposal and saw what it would have to be.

"The long-range goal-you failed to mention that ...your ultimate aim."

"I know what you are thinking. How can I prove you wrong-now?"

There was no way for the Varn to prove him wrong, nor for him to prove the treachery behind the Varn proposal. The proof would come only with time, when the Terran-Varn co-operation had transformed Terrans into a slave race.

The Varn spoke again. *"You refuse to believe I am sincere?"*

"I would be a naive fool to believe you."

"It will be too late to save Throon unless we act very quickly. I have told you why I am here. There is nothing more I can do to convince you but be the first to show trust. When I switch on the lights it will be within your power to kill me."

* * * * *

The Varn was gambling its life in a game in which he would be gambling the Plan and his race. It was a game he would end at the first sound of movement from the astrogator unit across the room....

"I have been here beside you all the time."

A furry paw brushed his face, claws flicked gently but grimly reminding along his throat.

He whirled and fired. He was too late-the Varn had already leaped silently away and the beam found only the bare floor. Then the lights came on, glaringly bright after the darkness, and he saw the Varn.

It was standing by the control board, its huge yellow eyes watching him. He brought the blaster into line with it, his finger on the firing stud. It waited, not moving or shrinking from what was coming. The translucent golden eyes looked at him and beyond him, as though they saw something not in the room. He wondered if it was in contact with its own kind on Johnny's World and was telling them it had made the gamble for high stakes, and had lost.

It was not afraid-not asking for mercy....

The killing of it was suddenly an act without savor. It was something he would do in the immediate future but first he would let it live long enough to save Throon.

He motioned with the blaster and said, "Lead the way to the airlock."

"And afterward-you will kill me?"

"Lead the way," he repeated harshly.

It said no more but went obediently past him and trotted down the corridor like a great, black dog.

* * * * *

He stood in the open airlock, the Varn against the farther wall where he had ordered it to stand. Throon was in the radiation chamber and he had held his first intelligible conversation with the natives that day.

The Varn was facing into the red-black gloom outside the lighted airlock, where the departing natives could be heard crossing the glade. *"Their thoughts no longer hold fear and suspicion,"* it said. *"The misunderstanding is ended."*

132

He raised the muzzle of the blaster in his hand. The black head lifted and the golden eyes looked up at him.

"I made you no promise," he said.

"I could demand none."

"I can't stop to take you back to your own world and I can't leave you alive on this one-with what you've learned from my mind you would have the natives build the Varn a disintegrator-equipped space fleet equal to our own ships."

"We want only to go with you."

He told it what he wanted it to know before he killed it, wondering why he should care:

"I would like to believe you are sincere-and you know why I don't dare to. Trusting a telepathic race would be too dangerous. The Varn would know everything we knew and only the Varn would be able to communicate with each new alien race. We would have to believe what the Varn told us-we would have to trust the Varn to see for us and speak for us and not deceive us as we went across the galaxy. And then, in the end, Terrans would no longer be needed except as a subject race. They would be enslaved.

"We would have laid the groundwork for an empire-the Varn Empire."

There was a silence, in which his words hung like something cold and invisible between them. Then the Varn asked, very quietly:

"Why is the Plan failing?"

"You already know," he said. "Because of the barrier-the communication barrier that causes aliens to misunderstand the intentions of Exploration men and fear them."

"There is no communication barrier between you and I —yet you fear me and are going to kill me."

"I have to kill you. You represent a danger to my race."

"Isn't that the same reason why aliens kill Exploration men?"

He did not answer and its thought came, quickly, *"How does an Exploration man appear to the natives of alien worlds?"*

How did he appear?... He landed on their world in a ship that could smash it into oblivion; he stepped out of his ship carrying weapons that could level a city; he represented irresistible power for destruction and he trusted no one and nothing.

And in return he hoped to find welcome and friendship and co-operation....

"There," the Varn said, *"is your true barrier-your own distrust and suspicion. You, yourselves, create it on each new world. Now you are going to erect it between my race and yours by killing me and advising the Exploration Board to quarantine my world and never let another ship land there."*

Again there was a silence as he thought of what the Varn had said and of what it had said earlier: *"We are a very old race...."* There was wisdom in the Varn's analysis of the cause of the Plan's failure and with the Varn to vanquish the communication stalemate, the new approach could be tried. They could go a long way together, men and Varn, a long, long way....

Or they could create the Varn Empire ... and how could he know which it would be?

How could anyone know-except the telepathic Varn?

The muzzle of the blaster had dropped and he brought it back up. He forced the dangerous indecision aside, knowing he would have to kill the Varn at once or he might weaken again, and said harshly to it:

"The risk is too great. I want to believe you-but all your talk of trust and good intentions is only talk and my race would be the only one that had to trust."

He touched the firing stud as the last thought of the Varn came:

"Let me speak once more."

He waited, the firing stud cold and metallic under his finger.

"You are wrong. We have already set the example of faith in you by asking to go with you. I told you we did not intend to hurt your brother and I told you we saw the stars only as the little wild animals saw them. The years in the dark caves-you do not understand —"

The eyes of the Varn looked into his and beyond him; beautiful, expressionless, like polished gold.

"*The Varn are blind.*"

The Last Victory

*He had only two aims in life: first, to
get what he wanted; and after that to enjoy
it. But to achieve the one he'd have to
give up the other … or would he?*

The transport ship, bound for Capella with Outlander colonists from Earth and Frontier Guards from Arcturus, struck the hyperspace vortex without warning. It seized her, wrenching and twisting her, and flung her across its gigantic rim at thousands of times the speed of light. She emerged into normal space in an unknown region of the galaxy, broken and driveless, but near enough a planet that she could descend by means of her antigravity plates before the last of her air was gone.

It was sunset when she settled heavily to earth on a grassy slope beside a forest, leaning at a dangerous angle with only her failing antigravity plates to hold her from falling. The dead had been disposed of in space and the living filed out of her: fifty Outlander men, women and children, eighteen ship's crewmen, and ten Frontier Guards.

The Guard officer and ship's captain came last, of equal rank and already appraising each other with cold speculation.

The Howling things in the dark forest were coming closer. Thane listened as he watched Curry, the ship's captain, approach across the strip of land that separated the two camps; standing back from his fire as he waited, where he would make an uncertain target for an assassin's blaster.

No one could be seen near any of the fires in the two camps on the hill. Only the unarmed Outlanders, at their fires in the swale below, moved about without wariness. And it was not yet three hours from the landing of the ship.

Curry stopped before him, restrained anger on his arrogantly handsome face.

"You failed to report to me and turn your Frontier Guards over to my command as you were ordered," he said.

"Since your rank is no higher than mine I saw no reason to do so," Thane answered.

Curry smiled, very thinly. "Perhaps I can show you a reason."

"Perhaps. Let's have it."

"First, I want to remind you of our circumstances," Curry said. "The ship will never lift again and we're marooned here for centuries to come. You know what the reaction of the Outlanders will be."

The Outlanders were the outcasts of a society that could not tolerate individuality. Two hundred years before the complexities of civilization had combined technocracy with integration and produced Technogration. Technogration had abolished race, creed and color, nations and borders, had welded all into a common mass and prohibited all individual pursuits that did not contribute to the Common Good. The Outlanders, refusing to come under Technograte domination, lived as best they could in the deserts, plateaus and jungles that Technogration could not use. The ones on the ship had been bound for Capella Five where men accustomed to wrestling a living from hostile environments were needed. Under such circumstances Outlanders were given certain rights and freedoms. Until they were no longer needed. Then, again, they became a people without a world....

"For two hundred years the Outlanders have hated Technogration and wanted a world where they could set up their own archaic form of society," Curry said. "Now, those down there will think their millenium has arrived and they can refuse to recognize Technograte authority."

"I see," Thane said. "And you want my cooperation so that Technogration won't fall by the wayside?"

"Your willingness to accept a subordinate position would give me an intact force of both crewmen and Guardsmen." Curry's lips thinned. "But there will be Technogration, with or without your support. There will be no retrogression back into the Outlanders' hallowed Dark Ages."

"There is no argument-we both want Technogration," Thane said. "We only disagree over who should be in command."

"There is a slight difference in our qualifications. Your present rank was gained by your ability to kill and not by loyalty to Technogration."

"Yes, of course," Thane agreed. "We'll say that I'm a materialistic opportunist while you're a noble idealist. But it's still the same identical whip that we're both going to reach for."

"As I said, I would prefer a peaceful transfer of your Guardsmen to my command. But my crewmen outnumber them almost two to one and they are expendable if necessary." The thin smile came back, almost mocking in its confidence. "You haven't much choice but to cooperate and accept a subordinate role, have you?"

The subordinate role would be very brief; it would end with a blaster beam in the back as soon as the Guardsmen were transferred to Curry's command....

"Try again, Curry. I can't bite on that one."

The smile faded from Curry's face, leaving it icily cold. "That was the only opportunity you'll ever get."

The howling sounded again in the forest and Thane said:

"We understand each other, now. But the Outlanders are unarmed and it may require our full forces to hold off whatever is out there. I suggest a truce until morning."

The iciness remained on Curry's face and he did not reply at once. "Perhaps you are right. You will order your men to observe a truce for the rest of the night."

He turned back to his camp.

Thane made the rounds where his guards patrolled with their searchlights probing out into the darkness. All of Curry's men but two had been added to reinforce the guard ring around the Outlander camp; most of the crewmen along the east and south lines, leaving the more experienced Guardsmen to patrol the two lines facing the forest.

Guardsmen and crewmen patrolled in silence, watching one another with the calculating regard of men who knew they might soon be ordered to kill one another. Apparently it was obvious to all of them that two officers of equal rank was a situation that could not for long exist.

His return to his camp took him through the scattered camp fires of the Outlanders. There were not many men to be seen; most of the survivors were women and children whom the Outlander leader had ordered into the safer inner compartments when the ship began breaking up.

Thane met him at the second fire; a gaunt old man with a jutting gray beard and sharp blue eyes under bristling gray brows. He stepped out from the fire and spoke:

"Captain Thane —I'd like to ask a question."

Thane stopped. "What is it?"

"My name is Paul Kennedy and I speak for all of us," the old man said. "Captain Curry has locked up all arms from us-he's already starting the regimentation for a permanent Technograte colony here and making sure we can't object. For two hundred years Technogration has failed on Earth except to turn men into robots. Here we could have a new chance and live like humans again."

"The question," Thane reminded him.

"You were in the Frontier Guards, where men still have to think for themselves to survive, and we were hoping you would understand why we don't want to start another ant hill here."

He could understand-but now, after thirty years of planning and fighting, he was only one step from the top.

"There will be Technogration," he said.

"We thought you would say that." Kennedy's expression did not change. "We hoped we would be wrong."

An ecstatic yelping sounded suddenly from nearby and something brown and white raced across the firelit ground with a laughing boy in pursuit. Thane stared.

It was a dog.

He had not seen one for thirty years. Technogration prohibited the owning of pets as an unnecessary drain upon the planned economy and as non-contributive to the Common Good.

"We knew about the regulations," Kennedy said, "but children need pets to love and be loved by. She's going to have pups-only she and Lornie's kitten were left." The old man's eyes watched him closely, questioningly. "Surely, no one will object to them?"

The dog circled back and a dark haired young woman beyond another fire called to it: "Binkie-come here!"

The dog obeyed, its tail drooping a little, and the woman looked uncertainly in Thane's direction before she disappeared back in the shadows, the dog close behind her. The boy followed, asking, "Why did you stop us, Blanche?"

Thane watched them go, the sight of the boy and dog bringing back with unwanted vividness the memory of another Outlander boy who had played with his dog, long ago; bringing back the past that necessity had forced him to forget....

He put the dangerous weakness from his mind and spoke to Kennedy:

"You Outlanders were bound for a Technograte world when you left Earth. You now stand on a Technograte world. You will do as you are ordered to do. As for your pets-you may have as many as you want so far as I'm concerned."

He stepped past Kennedy and continued on through the camp. The conversation of the Outlanders froze as he drew near, letting him walk in a little sea of silence that moved along with him. It was the usual reaction to the presence of a Technograte officer.

A little girl was out beyond the last fire; her back turned to him as she knelt in the grass and worked at something. He came closer and saw she was trying to tie a white cord around the neck of a half grown kitten. It sat with resigned patience as she struggled with earnest, inexperienced fingers to tie a knot that would not fall apart. She was talking to it as she worked:

"—and maybe the things in the forest kill cats. So you'll have to stay tied up, Tommy, and close to me because you're the only kitten on this whole world —"

His shadow fell across her and she looked up. Black curls framed a startled little face and gray eyes went wide at the sight of his uniform. She seized the surprised kitten and held it protectively in her arms, the knot falling apart again on the ground.

"Please-Tommy won't ever hurt anything —"

Two women and a man were watching him from beyond the fire with frozen-faced hatred. Technograte regulations required the immediate killing of any animals found smuggled aboard a ship....

"I won't harm your kitten," he said. He smiled sardonically at the Outlanders beyond the fire. "My horns aren't quite that long yet."

* * * * *

He met Curry when he was almost back to his camp. Curry had two bodyguards with him and passed without speaking.

The hours went by and the night was like a cold October night on Earth but for the strange constellations that crept across the sky. The Outlander fires burned lower and the things in the forest became silent, as though massing for a surprise attack. Twice the wind shifted, to bring the scents from the forest, and each time he heard the dog growl uneasily while the woman tried to quiet her.

He was going down the south guard line, the western horizon touched with the light of coming moonrise, when the monsters attacked the north line.

They broke suddenly from the forest with a demoniac howl of command from their leader, a boiling wave of them. They were green, hard to see against the green grass, racing low to the ground like giant tigers, their long, serpentine necks thrust forward and eyes blazing yellow in hyena faces.

The blaster fire of the Guardsmen met them, pale blue beams that blossomed into brief incandescence when they struck. Curry's guards added their fire, their reactions slower than those of the Guardsmen. The guards along the other three lines turned to help halt the attack, the south line guards firing across the Outlander camp.

The front rank of monsters went down, with them the leader. For an instant the onslaught slowed, leaderless and uncertain, then the monster that had been behind the leader gave the commanding howl and the others surged ahead again.

At that moment, when the attention of every guard in every guard line was on the north perimeter attack, the Outlander dog broke loose from whoever had been holding her. She ignored the attack from the north and was a blur as she went through the south guard line, screaming a snarl of warning and her leash whipping in the air behind her. She vanished behind the guard line and Thane swung his searchlight.

Five monsters were almost upon the backs of the unsuspecting guards, charging without sound.

His blaster beam raked at them and two went down. The others struck three guards with their bodies, knocking them to the ground before they could fire. Then the monsters passed on, to lurch a dozen steps and fall limply to the ground. They did not even twitch after they fell.

He saw, when he reached the first one, that it was dead. So were the other two.

Yet there was not a blaster mark on them.

Then he saw another thing. One of the monsters had fallen with its jaws slackly open and its teeth were visible. They were blunt and even.

Despite their ferocious appearance, the monsters were only herbivores.

The three fallen guards were getting to their feet, apparently unharmed. Along the north perimeter the attack was over as suddenly as it had begun; the leader of the monsters lying dead against the guard line and all the others still alive fleeing wildly back into the forest. Quiet came, broken only by the growling of the dog out near the two monsters Thane had killed.

He turned his light on her, then went closer to make sure he had seen rightly.

She was fighting something on the ground, green-eyed with fury as she ripped and tore at it. But there was nothing there. Nothing.

"Binkie!"

The dark haired woman was coming toward them, wraithlike in a white sleeping garment. The dog turned away, with a last rip at the nothing it fought, and saw the three guards the monsters had knocked down. She froze, like as though she saw something she could not believe.

Then, deadly with menace, a growl vibrated in her throat and she crouched to attack them.

"Binkie —*don't!*" The voice of the girl was shrill with urgency. "Come here-come here!"

The dog hesitated, then obeyed; going past the guards in a swift lope, her head turned to watch them and her teeth bared in a snarl. The girl seized the leash and girl and dog disappeared back into the Outlander camp, both of them running.

Curry loomed out of the darkness, his two bodyguards with him, and flashed his light over the fallen monsters.

"So you let three get through?" he said. He glanced to the north guard line where the searchlights of the guards showed only the dark, lifeless edge of the forest. "But no one was harmed and there's no indication that they are going to attack again."

He regarded Thane with cold thoughtfulness. "Apparently the camp is in no danger, after all."

To Thane the implication of his words was obvious: if the monsters were not a menace his cooperation was no longer needed by Curry. The three guards were Curry men and Curry had two with him. He was outnumbered six to one....

"Sir —"

It was one of the three guards; Bellam, the ship's pharmacist. He hurried up to Curry, the other two close behind him.

Curry swung on him, impatiently. "What is it?"

"We must combine our forces to fight a new danger. This camp is infected with rabies."

"Rabies?"

"Yes, sir," Bellam answered. "The Outlander's dog had a convulsion beyond the guard line and then almost attacked the three of us. That dog is mad."

"How do you know it was a convulsion?" Thane asked.

"You saw it, yourself," Bellam answered.

He turned his head to face Thane as he spoke and Thane saw his eyes for the first time.

They were the lifeless, staring eyes of a dead man.

He flicked his light over the faces of the other two guards. They were the same; all three were like walking dead.

"Did the monsters harm you?" he asked Bellam.

Bellam hesitated, seeming to tense with suspicion. "No." The dead eyes stared into his. "What makes you ask?"

He saw that Curry had noticed nothing different about the three guards. It was typical of Curry; to him subordinates were only automatons to carry out his orders.

"We were discussing a mad dog, Thane," Curry said. "Not the health of my men." He spoke to Bellam. "As I recall, rabies was a pre-Technogration plague, often fatal."

"The bite of a rabid animal is invariably fatal, the death prolonged and painful," Bellam said. "There is no preventative or cure among the medical supplies on the ship. The dog must be killed at once, together with all other animals in the Outlander camp."

"If the dog was mad, why hasn't it bitten any of the Outlanders," Thane asked Curry. "I suggest we keep it on a leash until we know for sure."

"The dog was smuggled aboard the ship in defiance of regulations," Curry said. "It would have been destroyed before had I known about it."

He turned to Bellam, ignoring Thane. "The three of you will search the Outlander camp from end to end. Kill all animals and report to me the names of the owners."

The three departed, to begin the search at the nearer end of the camp. Thane made no further objection. He knew the Outlanders well enough to know that they would have overheard the discussion on the hill and slipped the dog out through the guard lines before that discussion ended. Outlanders could be very clever in such matters-the searchers would find no dog.

There was satisfaction on Curry's face as he turned and with his two bodyguards started back up the hill to his camp. Thane watched him go, smiling a little. Curry was making the mistake that had been fatal for so many before him; he was taking it for granted too soon that he had won.

A man came hurrying from the north guard line before Curry had gone far. He called to Curry:

"Sir, there is something you ought to know —"

Thane saw, with almost disbelief, that it was one of his own men: Gorman.

Curry waited and when Gorman reached him he said:

"When I was helping inspect the Outlander section of the ship for hidden weapons this evening I saw some small animals in storage compartment Thirteen. I think they were very young kittens. I would like to volunteer to go and kill them."

Curry said something that a vagrant breeze made inaudible then his words came clear:

"—I'll send a detail to the ship as soon as the camp is searched. You will report to my guards now for orders and help them hunt for the dog."

Gorman started back to meet the guards and Curry stood for a little while before he went on his way. Thane could imagine his feeling of pleased surprise and triumph.

Thane called to Gorman as he passed some distance in front of him.

"Were you injured in the attack?" he asked.

"No," Gorman said. Then, with the same tense suspicion that Bellam had had he asked the same question: "Why do you ask?"

"Why did you report to Curry instead of me?"

The answer came quickly, mechanically, "The animals are in his ship and they must be killed. They may be mad."

"Go help Curry's men," he said and watched Gorman go, trying to fit together the incidents that did not make sense.

Herbivores had attacked without reason. There had fallen dead, without a blaster mark on them. The Outlander dog had fought nothing and almost attacked the guards. One of his own men had gone over to the other side. And there was a sudden strange urgency to kill all animals in camp.

There was nothing he could do for the time being but wait for further developments so he waited. The moon came up, so swift in its retrograde orbit that its speed was visible and so near that it had the brilliance of a dozen Earth moons. When it had lifted clear of the horizon it flooded the land with a cold silver light that made the searchlights of the guards unnecessary and revealed the camp with metallic light-and-shadow clarity.

The search party was halfway through the camp, Gorman with them and Bellam in command. They were ransacking the possessions and temporary shelters of the Outlanders with swift efficiency, ignoring the protests of the women and their blasters leveled warningly on the men.

They found the little girl.

She was carrying her kitten ahead of them, a small, silent shadow in the moonlight, when Gorman saw her. He spoke to Bellam and Bellam's head jerked up. Then the two of them advanced on her.

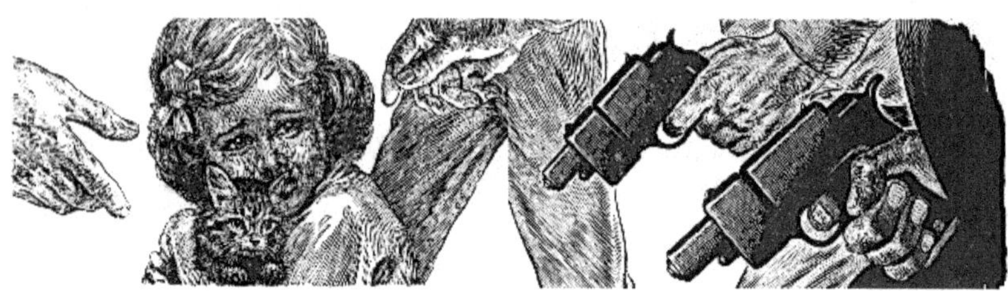

She tried to run when she realized they had seen the kitten, hugging it in her arms with the white cord trailing behind her. Bellam overtook her and caught her by the shoulder, jerking her to a halt. He tore the kitten from her arms and flung it hard to the ground. It made a thin little scream of pain and the girl fought to reach it, her cry sobbing and frantic:

"Don't hurt him —"

Gorman's blaster hissed and blue flame leaped from it. Incandescence enveloped the kitten and then there was nothing where it had been but a small black hole in the ground.

Bellam and Gorman wheeled back, like mechanical men, to resume the search. The girl stood a moment, staring before her, saying something very low that sounded like, "Tommy... Tommy...." Then she stumbled to the little black hole and dropped to her knees beside it as though she hoped that somehow she might still find her kitten there.

He looked away, strangely disturbed. He drummed his fingers restlessly on the butt of his holstered blaster then he turned again to go down into the Outlander camp.

The moon was up and it was time he found the dog. Something had come out of the night with the monsters and perhaps she could tell him what it was. He could not yet believe she was mad.

* * * * *

The dark haired woman stood by the fire, watching the little girl and the searchers with bitter, smouldering hatred. She faced him, her breath coming fast in her anger.

"Her parents and her brother-when the ship broke up-she lost them all. Only her kitten was left to her."

"Where is the dog?" he asked.

"Find her!"

"The dog-where is she?"

"Find her," she challenged again. "Find her and kill her-if you can!"

He stepped past her and went on his way. She had told him what he wanted to know: despite her attempts not to do so she had been unable to keep from glancing toward the ship.

* * * * *

His route took him by the little girl. She was standing by the hole, small and bare-footed in the grass, her hands holding the white cord that was black and charred on one end. She was crying, silently, as though too proud to let him see her break.

After he had passed her the vision went with him for a little way; the terrible, helpless hatred and hurt in her eyes and the moonlight gleaming coldly on her tears.

He looked back when he reached the ship. Gorman was coming, running, and the other three were turning back from the far end of the camp to hurry after Gorman.

He looked toward Curry's camp and saw Curry watching him. Curry and his men moved toward him and there were six to make a rendezvous with him.

The truce was over.

He found the dog behind the farthest tail fin, leashed to a thorny bush and almost invisible in the shadows.

She watched him as he stopped before her, her ears forward questioningly and her tail moving a little with tentative friendliness. He spoke to her and her reply was a low bark, her tail whipping with delight. She thought he had come to release her....

He had known dogs well as a boy and he knew the one before him was not mad.

He heard Gorman's feet plodding fast through the grass and he waited with his blaster in his hand.

Gorman came around the tail fin, panting, his own blaster in his hand. The dog went rigid at the sight of him, the growl in her throat, and Gorman's blaster swung toward her.

"Hold it!" he ordered.

Gorman paused, and the dead eyes looked into his. "There the mad dog is-we must kill it."

"We can kill it later if it's mad. We'll watch it a while, first."

The suspicion became like something almost tangible about Gorman and his blaster started the first movement toward Thane.

"Why?"

"I think it can see something —"

Gorman fired, so swiftly that he felt the heat of the beam even though he had been expecting it. He shot for the heart and Gorman collapsed before he could fire again. He lay still on the ground, the eyes that stared up into the sky no deader than when he had been alive.

The dog was lunging against her leash, trying to get to him. Thane stepped closer and watched the grass beside Gorman's head. A patch of it the size of his hand suddenly bent down, as from an unseen weight, and then something struck his knee.

He slapped at it as it darted up his leg and knocked it off; something that felt like a mass of cold, rubbery tentacles. He knew, then.

He stepped back, his blaster swinging aimlessly. The thing would leap again, to reach his head as it had done with Gorman, and it was invisible. There was nothing but the moonlit grass to be seen. Perhaps it was behind him, already preparing to spring....

The dog's snarling was a frenzied scream as she fought against her leash. He swung his blaster and its blue beam cut the leash in two.

She flashed toward him, then up, her ears laid back, her eyes blazing slits and her teeth slashing at his throat. His blaster was in line with her chest and for a brief instant he had only to press the firing stud.

He did something he had not done for thirty years; he trusted his life to another being and did not fire.

Cold tentacles whipped against his face and her teeth closed together beside his cheek with a vicious snap and gust of hot breath. She rebounded and held the thing on the ground between her paws as she tore at it; gagging a little, whining and snarling in fury and triumph.

He squatted beside her and laid his hand on her, speaking to her soothingly. She calmed a little, though her chest still pounded with the beating of her heart, and he saw the thing she had killed.

It was dead and slowly becoming visible as it changed to a color like pale milk. It resembled a huge, hairless spider.

It was a parasite; a highly intelligent parasite that could take over the mind of its host as well as the body. The parasites had had only the forest monsters as hosts, before, but with the coming of the humans they had the opportunity for hosts of a far higher order. They possessed a means of locomotion but apparently it was limited in its duration or else they would not have needed to control the leaders of the monster bands and stage the attack that would carry them to the guard lines.

The dog, with the acute sixth sense of some animals, could sense the hostile alienness of the things. She could see them-apparently the vision range of dogs went a little farther beyond that of humans. So also would that of cats but the kitten had had no chance to show by its actions what it had seen.

The dog had hated the changed men because they were alien things, no longer human. The thing that had been Bellam had used the knowledge stored in Bellam's mind to claim there was rabies in the camp and thereby enlist the support of the humans in killing their only means of detecting the parasites.

* * * * *

There was a pounding of feet beyond the ship as the zombies came. On the slope above him Curry was striding toward him, his bodyguards flanking him and the moonlight bright on his face.

He stood with the dog beside him and watched them come to kill him. Only he and the dog knew of the parasites; if they were killed the way would be open for the parasites to infiltrate the camp. In the end the new world would hold only the walking dead, down to the last Outlander child.

"Curry," he called.

He did not have to speak loudly in the still night air for Curry to hear him but Curry came on, his face hard, arrogant metal in the moonlight.

"Give me one minute, Curry, to tell you what I found."

Curry's reply was the order to his men.

"The dog is with him. Kill them both."

His blaster swung up as he spoke.

Thane dropped, firing as he went down. Curry's arrogant face dissolved into nothing and his blaster flamed aimlessly into the ground at his feet. The blaster of the swiftest guard sent its beam hissing like a snake over Thane's head, then he went down as Curry had done, the other guard falling beside him with his first and only shot licking off into the moonlight.

Then the zombies came around the tail fin, in a quick rush with their dead eyes staring and their blasters making a curtain of blue fire before them.

The dog lunged at them and a blaster beam dipped down to meet her. Bellam-his headless body was falling forward as Thane killed the zombie beside him. The blaster of the third one ripped its beam like a white-hot iron along Thane's ribs as he died. Then, within two heartbeats, it was over and the night was quiet again.

He returned his blaster to its holster. The dog was limping from one zombie to the other, searching for parasites, her shoulder red with blood and staining the grass.

She found none and he called her to him to look at her shoulder. It was not a serious wound but it was painful and bleeding fast and should be cared for. He took her around the ship, where the Outlander camp lay in view below. He looked again at the wound and she whimpered a little from the pain, gentle though his touch had been, then licked his hand in quick apology.

"Your job is over for now," he said. He motioned toward the camp below, where the dark haired woman was waiting. "Home, girl-go home."

She left him and went running and limping down the hill where her hurts would be cared for.

* * * * *

His side was burning and blood was like a warm, wet sheet down it. He made a temporary bandage of his shirt and then leaned wearily against the tail fin.

It was all over. The nature of the parasites was known and everyone could be fitted with a thin metal helmet until they were completely eliminated. They did not seem to be numerous-apparently there had been no more than ten or twelve among the scores of monsters. The dog would watch, and warn them if any more were in the vicinity.

It was all over, with Curry a motionless spot on the hillside above him and no one left to challenge him. He had come a long way from the Outlander boy on the high, cold prairie who had hated Technogration. He had been nineteen before he finally realized the futility of hating the unassailable power of Technogration and realized he must accept it and adapt to it. And then carve out a niche for himself with a ruthlessness greater than any of those around him. So he had fought his way up, trampling those who would have trampled him had they been a little stronger, each step another victory in his conquest of the system that had condemned him.

And now-the last victory. There was no one to challenge him; there could be no one under the rigid discipline of Technogration.

The last victory. The security of Power to the end of his life.

That was Technogration.

* * * * *

Dawn touched the sky, softening the moon's hard light. As though the coming of day was a signal, the ship trembled and there was the whisper of dislodged soil as the tail fin lifted a fraction of an inch. The antigravity plates were almost exhausted-the ship would fall within minutes.

Down in the Outlander camp the children were gathering around the dog as the dark haired woman bandaged her shoulder. A voice came to him, treble and joyous, "Binkie is back-Binkie is back...."

The little girl sat to one side, so small and alone that he almost failed to see her. She watched the children crowd up to pet their dog but she did not move to join them. Only her hands moved, caressing the white cord that was charred on one end.

He felt the triumph and satisfaction become like something turned bitter around the edges and draining away.

Technogration was planning and fighting and killing until at last a man reached the top and no one dared oppose him; Technogration was control of a world and the seeds of an empire.

And Technogration was a child crying in the cold moonlight, was a little black hole where a kitten had screamed out with pain, with a little girl's heart that had nothing left to hold but harsh and poignant memories and a piece of burnt cord.

He ran to the boarding ramp, feeling the fiery lash of pain and hot flow of blood as the wound reopened, telling himself he was a fool who would probably die in the falling ship and would deserve it.

* * * * *

He stood by the gray ashes of his fire, the Guardsman's combat helmet under his arm, and watched the little girl come alone up the hill. Someone had washed the tear-stains from her face and she stopped before him with her head held high and defiant, trying not to let him see she was afraid of him and almost succeeding.

"I sent for you, Lornie, to tell you I'm sorry about last night."

He saw she did not believe him. Her face was like a little carving of cold, unforgiving stone and she did not answer him.

He set the helmet down in the grass before her. Six tiny kittens lay inside it, red and white and gray fluffs of fur, their pink mouths questing hungrily.

Her eyes widened with incredulous wonder.

"Oh!"

Then the suspicion came back and she stopped the quick forward step she had taken.

"They haven't any mother and they're hungry," he said.

She did not move.

"They're yours, Lornie. To keep."

"They're-mine?" Then the doubt fled from her and she ran forward to gather them in her arms.

He left her with her head bent down over the kittens in her lap, making soft little sounds of endearment to them, her face so radiant that there was no room left for hurt or hatred on it.

Kennedy was coming, not yet knowing why he had been summoned nor that Technogration had died at dawn. He would not relinquish all his authority, of course. And he would have to remember to tell Kennedy that they were going to give him one of Binkie's pups.

The companionship of an understanding dog might be comforting in the years to come, whenever he recalled the morning he had owned a world and a bare-footed girl had taken it away from him.

> Sometimes the most diligent and loyal thing
> an old man can do is fumble,
> drink beer, and let a young man get into trouble....

"We're almost there, my boy." The big, gray-haired man who would be Lieutenant Dale Hunter's superior-Strategic Service's Special Agent, George Rockford-opened another can of beer, his fifth. "There will be intrigue already under way when this helicopter sets down with us. Attempted homicide will soon follow. The former will be meat for me. You will be meat for the latter."

Rockford was smiling as he spoke; the genial, engaging smile of a fond old father. But the eyes, surrounded by laughter crinkles, were as unreadable as two disks of gray slate. They were the eyes of a poker player-or master con man.

"I don't understand, sir," Hunter said.

"Of course not," Rockford agreed. "It's a hundred light-years back to Earth. Here on Vesta, to make sure there *is* an Earth in the future, you're going to do things never dreamed of by your Terran Space Patrol instructors there. You'll be amazed, my boy."

Hunter said nothing but he felt a growing dislike for the condescending Rockford. Only a few weeks ago President Diskar, himself, had said: *For more than a century these truly valiant men of the Space Patrol have been our unwavering outer guard; have fought and died by legions, that Earth and the other worlds of the Terran Republic might remain free —*

"I suppose you know," Rockford said, "that there will be no more than four days in which to stop the Verdam oligarchy from achieving its long-time ambition of becoming big enough to swallow the Terran Republic."

"I know," Hunter answered.

Jardeen, Vesta's companion world, was the key. Jardeen was large and powerful, with a space navy unsurpassed by that of any other single world. A large group of now-neutral worlds would follow Jardeen's lead and Jardeen's alliance with the Verdam People's Worlds would mean the quick end for the Terran Republic. But, if Jardeen could be persuaded to ally with the Terran Republic, the spreading, grasping arms of the Verdam octopus would begin to wither away —

Rockford spoke again:

"Val Boran, Jardeen's Secretary of Foreign Relations, is the man who will really make Jardeen's decision. I know him slightly. Since my public role is that of Acting Ambassador, he agreed-reluctantly-to come to Vesta so that the talks could be on a neutral world. With him will be Verdam's Special Envoy Sonig; a wily little man who has been working on Boran for several weeks. He seems to be succeeding quite well-here's a message I received from Earth early this morning."

Rockford handed him a sheet of the green Hyperspace Communications paper. The message was in code, with Rockford's scribbled translation beneath:

> *Intelligence reports Verdam forces already massed for attack in Sector A-13, in full expectation of Jardeen's alliance. Anti-Terran propaganda, stressing the New Jardeen Incident, being used in preparation for what will be their claim of "defensive action to protect innocent worlds from Terran aggression." Terran forces will be outnumbered five to one. The urgent necessity of immediate and conclusive counter measures by you on Vesta is obvious.*

Hunter handed the paper back, thinking, *It's worse than any of us thought*, and wondering how Supreme Command could ever have entrusted such an important task to a beer-guzzling old man from Strategic Service —a branch so unknown that he had never even heard of it until his briefing the day before he left Earth.

He saw that they had left the desert behind and were going up the long slope of a mountain. "The meeting will be on this mountain?" he asked.

Rockford nodded. "The rustic Royal Retreat. Princess Lyla will be our hostess. Her mother and father were killed in an airplane accident a year ago and she was the only child. You will also get to meet Lord Narf of the Sea Islands, her husband-by-proxy, who regards himself as a rare combination of irresistible woman-killer and rugged man-among-men."

"Husband-by-proxy?" Hunter asked.

"The king worshiped his daughter and his dying request to her was that she promise to marry Lord Narf. Narf's father had been the king's closest friend and the king was sure that his old friend's son would always love and care for Lyla. Lyla dutifully, at once, married Narf by proxy, which is like a legally binding formal engagement under Vestan law. Four days from now the time limit is up and they'll be formally married. Unless she should do the unprecedented thing of renouncing the proxy marriage."

Rockford drained the last of the beer from the can. "Those are the characters involved in our play. I have a plan. That's why I told Space Patrol to send me a brand-new second lieutenant-young, strong, fairly handsome-and expendable. I hope you can be philosophical about the latter."

"Sir," Hunter said, unable to keep a touch of stiffness out of his tone, "it is not exactly unknown in the Space Patrol for a man to die in the line of duty."

"Ah ...yes." Rockford was regarding him with disturbing amusement. "You are thinking, of course, of dying dramatically behind a pair of blazing blasters. But you will soon learn, my boy, that a soldier's duty is to protect the worlds he represents by whatever actions will produce the best results, no matter how unheroic those actions may be."

* * * * *

"Attention, please." It was the voice of the pilot. "We are now going to land."

Hunter preceded Rockford out of the helicopter and onto the green grass of a small valley, across which tall, red-trunked cloud trees were scattered. Pale gray ghost trees, with knobby, twisted limbs, grew thickly among the cloud trees. There was a group of rustic cabins, connected by gravel paths, and a much larger building which he assumed would be a meeting hall.

"Hello."

He turned, and looked into the brown eyes of a girl. Her green skirt and orange blouse made a gay splash of color, her red-brown hair was wind-tumbled and carefree about her shoulders, in her hand was a bouquet of bright spring flowers.

But there was no smile of spring in the dark eyes and the snub-nosed little face was solemn and old beyond its years.

"You're Lieutenant Hunter, aren't you?" she asked in the same low, quiet voice.

"Princess Lyla!" There seemed to be genuine delight in Rockford's greeting as he hurried over. "You're looking more like a queen every day!"

Her face lighted with a smile, making it suddenly young and beautiful. "I'm so glad to see you again, George —"

"Ah ... good afternoon."

The voice was loud, unpleasantly gravelly. They turned, and Hunter saw a tall, angular man of perhaps forty whose pseudogenial smile was not compatible with his sour, square-jawed face and calculating little eyes.

He spoke to Rockford. "You're Ambassador Rockford, here to represent the Terran Republic, I believe." He jerked his head toward Princess Lyla, who was no longer smiling. "My wife, Princess Lyla."

"Oh, she and I have been friends since she was ten, Lord Narf."

"And this young man" —Narf glanced at Hunter —"is your aide, I presume. Lyla, did you think to send anyone after their luggage?"

A servant was already carrying their luggage-and cases of Rockford's beer-out of the helicopter. Hunter followed the other toward the cabins. Narf, in the lead, was saying:

"...Ridiculously primitive here, now, but I'm having some decent furniture and well-trained servants sent up from my Sea Island estates...."

* * * * *

The cabin was large and very comfortable, as Rockford mentioned to Princess Lyla.

"I'm glad you like it," she said. "Val Boran and Envoy Sonig are already here and we'll meet for dinner in the central hall. I thought that if we all got acquainted in a friendly atmosphere like that, it might help a lot to...."

"That reminds me" —Narf glanced at his watch —"I promised this Boran he could have a discussion with me-Vesta-Jardeen tariff policies. I suppose he's already waiting. Come on, Lyla-it will do you no harm to listen and learn a bit about interplanetary business."

For a long moment she looked at Narf silently, her eyes thoughtful, then she said to Rockford, "If you will excuse us, please. And be prepared for Alonzo to come bounding in the minute he learns you're here."

She walked beside Narf to the door and out it, the top of her dark hair coming just even with his shoulder.

"And that," Rockford said as he settled down in the largest, softest chair, "was king-to-be Narf, whose business ability is such that all his inherited Sea Island estates are gone but the one Lyla saved for him and who owes a total of ten million monetary units, to everyone from call girls to yacht builders."

"And she is going to marry him?" Hunter asked. "Marry that jackass and let him bankrupt her kingdom?"

Rockford shrugged. "You may have noticed that she doesn't look the least bit happy about it-but she is a very conscientious young lady who regards it as her most solemn duty to keep the promise she made to her father. For her, there is no escape."

"But —"

"Your first duty will be to cultivate a friendship with her. I'm going to use her, and you, to get what I want."

"*Use* us?"

"Yes. One of the most rigid requirements of a Strategic Service man's character is that he be completely without one."

* * * * *

Rockford was asleep in his chair an hour later, three empty beer cans beside him. Hunter watched him, his doubt of Rockford's competence growing into a conviction. Rockford had spoken knowingly of his plan-and had done nothing but drink more beer. Now he was asleep while time-so limited and precious-went by. He hadn't even bothered to reply to Hunter's suggestion that perhaps he should call on Val Boran and counteract some of Envoy Sonig's anti-Terran propaganda.

Hunter came to a decision. If Rockford was still doing nothing when morning came, he would send an urgent message to Supreme Command.

He went outside, to find a servant and learn how mail was handled.

* * * * *

"Rook out!"

Gravel flew as overgrown feet tried to stop, and something like a huge black dog lunged headlong around the corner and into his legs. He went to the ground head first over the animal, acutely aware as he went down of the fascinated interest on the face of a not-so-distant servant.

"I sorry, Rootenant."

He got up, to look down at the doglike animal. There was a concerned expression in its brown eyes and an apologetic grin on its face. He recognized it as one of the natives of the grim starvation world of Altair Four. The Altairians had emigrated to all sections of the galaxy, to earn a living in whatever humble capacity they could fill. Many were empathic.

"I run too fast to meet, Mr. Rockford, I guess. Are you hurt, Rootenant?"

He pulled a cloud tree needle out of his hand and looked grimly down into the furry face. "In the future, try to look where you're going."

"Oh, I rook, awr right. I just not see. My name is Aronzo, Rootenant, and I stay here awr the time and guard everything for Princess Ryra. I prease to meet you and I wirr run errands for you, and do things rike mair your retters, for candy or cookies, which I are not supposed to eat much of, but Princess Ryra say not too many wirr hurt me —"

"Mail letters?" Hunter's animosity vanished. "I'm sorry I was rude, Alonzo-all my fault. I may write a letter to my dear old mother tonight, and if you would mail it for me in the morning —"

* * * * *

Rockford left ahead of Hunter and it was a minute past the appointed time when Hunter reached the meeting hall. He heard Narf's loud voice inside:

"...Boran must have stopped to watch the sunset. Told him I wanted everyone here on time —"

The low voice of Lyla said something and Narf said, "Not necessary for you to defend him, my dear. I made it plain to him."

A new voice spoke from behind Hunter:

"It seems I have annoyed Lord Narf."

He was a tall, black-eyed man, with the dark, saturnine face of an Indian. There was a strange, indefinable air of sadness about him which reminded Hunter of the sombre little Princess Lyla.

"You're Val Boran, sir?" he said. "I'm Lieutenant Hunter —"

Inside, Narf sat at the head of the table. On his left was Lyla, then Rockford. On his right was a spidery little man of about fifty, his slick-back hair so tight against his skull that it gave his head the appearance of a weasel's. His lips were paper-thin under a long nose, like those of a dry and selfish old maid, but the round little eyes darting behind thick glasses were cold and shrewd and missed nothing. He would be Verdam's Special Envoy Sonig. Hunter appraised him as a man very dangerous in his own deceptive way.

A servant showed them to their places at the table. Rockford and Val Boran exchanged greetings. The moment everyone was seated, Narf said, "Dinner tonight will —"

"Excuse me," Lyla said, "but Mr. Sonig hasn't yet met —"

"Oh ... the young fellow there —" Narf gestured with his hand. "Rockford's aide. Now, ring the chime, Lyla. Those forest stag steaks are already getting cold. I killed the beast myself, gentlemen, just this morning; a long-range running shot that required a bit more than luck...."

The dinner was excellent, but no one seemed to notice. Narf was absorbed in the story of his swift rise to eminence in the Vestan Space Guard. There were humorous incidents:

"... Can't understand why, but I seem to attract women like a magnet. I'm strictly the masculine type of male and I approve of this but it can be a blasted nuisance when you're an ensign going up fast and your commander finds one of your blondes stowed away in your compartment...."

And there were scenes of tense drama:

"... Made a boyhood vow that I'd never settle for anything less than to always be a man among men. Seem to have succeeded rather well. When I saw the crew was almost to the snapping point from battle tension I knew that as commander I'd have to set the example that would inspire."

Hunter recalled Rockford's words of a few hours before: *Narf got to be commander, finally, but only because he was the son of the king's best friend. His record is very mediocre.*

Princess Lyla tried three times to start a conversation of general interest and was drowned out by Narf each time. Sonig's pretense of being spellbound by Narf's stories was belied by the way his eyes kept darting from Rockford to Val Boran. Val's own attention kept shifting from Narf to the silent Lyla, whose downcast eyes betrayed her discouragement. She watched Val from under her eyelashes, to look away whenever their eyes met, and Hunter wondered if she was ashamed because Narf had given Sonig the seat of honor that should have belonged to Val.

Of course, Narf's own position at the head of the table was actually Lyla's.

"... So there's no substitute for competent, unwavering leadership," Narf was saying. "Received a citation for that one."

Sonig nodded appreciatively. "Your military record well illustrates the fact that the tensions of danger and battle can bring forth in a competent leader the highest kind of courage. But it seems to me that these same circumstances, if the leader is frightened or incompetent, can easily produce hysterical actions with disastrous consequences. Is this true, your lordship?"

Rockford was watching Sonig intently and Hunter saw that there was an eager anticipation in Sonig's manner.

"You are quite right," Narf answered. "I've always had the ability to remain cool in any crisis. Very important. Let a commander get rattled and he may give any kind of an order. Like the New Jardeen Incident."

A frozen silence followed the last five words. Hunter thought, *So that's what the little weasel was fishing for....*

Rockford quietly laid down his fork. Val's face turned grim. Lyla looked up in quick alarm and said to Narf:

"Let's not —"

"Don't misunderstand me, gentlemen," Narf's loud voice went on. "*I* believe the commander of the Terran cruiser wouldn't have ordered it to fire upon the Verdam cruiser over a neutral world such as New Jardeen if he had been his rational self. Cold-war battle nerves. So he shot down the Verdam cruiser and its nuclear converters exploded when it fell in the center of Colony City. Force of a hydrogen bomb-forty thousand innocent people gone in a microsecond. Not the commander's fault, really-fault of the military system that failed to screen out its unstable officers."

"Yes, your lordship. But is it possible" —Sonig spoke very thoughtfully —"for a political power, which is of such a nature that it must have a huge military force to maintain its existence, to thoroughly screen all its officers? So many officers are required-Can there ever be any assurance that such tragedies won't occur again and again, until a majority of worlds combine in demanding an end to aggression and war?"

Rockford spoke to the grim Val:

"I know, sir, that your sister was among the lost in Colony City. I am sorry. For the benefit of Mr. Sonig and Lord Narf, I would like to mention that the Verdam cruiser fired upon the Terran cruiser over neutral New Jardeen in open violation of Galactic Rule. An atmospheric feedback of the Verdam cruiser's own space blasters tore out its side and caused it to fall. The Terran cruiser never fired."

"But Mr. Rockford —" Sonig spoke very courteously. "Isn't it true that certain safety devices prevent atmospheric feedback?"

"They do-unless accidentally or purposely disconnected."

Sonig raised his eyebrows. "You imply a created incident, sir?"

"It doesn't matter," Val Boran said. His tone was as grim as his face and it was obvious he did not believe Rockford's explanation. "Colony City is a field of fused glass, now, its people are gone, and no amount of debating can ever bring them back."

* * * * *

The dismal dinner was finally over. Rockford stopped outside the door of their cabin to fill and light his pipe.

"It was a profitable evening," he said to Hunter. "I can start planning in detail now-after a little beer, that is."

He'll go to sleep after he drinks his beer, Hunter thought, *and there will never be any plan unless I —*

Soft footsteps came up the path behind them. It was Princess Lyla.

"I want to apologize," she said, "I just told Val ...Mr. Boran the same thing."

Her face was a pale oval in the starlight, her eyes dark shadows. "I'm sorry my husband mentioned the New Jardeen incident."

"That's all right, Lyla," Rockford said. "No harm was done."

"He's an ex-military man, and I guess it's his nature to be more forthright than tactful."

"You certainly can't condemn him for that," Rockford said. "In fact, he's an extraordinary teller of entertaining stories. It was a most enjoyable evening."

* * * * *

"And, in a way, it was," Rockford said when she was gone and they were in the cabin. He was seated in the softest chair, a can of beer in his hand, as usual.

Hunter thought of the way she had looked in the starlight and said, "Why did she let that windbag sit at the head of the table and ruin the meeting that she had arranged?"

"He'll soon be her husband —I suppose she feels she should be loyal to him."

"But —"

"But what?"

"Nothing. It's none of my business."

"Oh?" Rockford smiled in a way Hunter did not like. "You think so, eh?"

Hunter changed the subject. "Are you going to start talking to Boran to undo the damage Narf and Sonig have done?"

"It would be a waste of time, my boy. Val Boran's mind is already made up."

"Then what are you going to do?"

"Drink six cans of beer and go to sleep."

"I thought you had a plan."

"I have, a most excellent plan."

"What is it?"

"You'd scream like a banshee if you knew. You'll learn-if you manage to live that long."

Rockford was sound asleep an hour later, snoring gently. Hunter sat thinking, hearing the steady murmur of a voice coming from Val Boran's cabin. Sonig's voice-using every means of persuasion he could think of, at the moment capitalizing on the New Jardeen incident and Boran's withheld grief over the sister he had lost.

And the Terran Republic's representative was sprawled fat and mindless in a fog of beer fumes.

Hunter hesitated no longer. The fate of Earth and the Terran Republic hung in the balance and time was desperately limited-if there was now any time at all.

He took paper and pen and began the urgent message to Supreme Command, headed, TOP EMERGENCY. It would be sent via Hyperspace Communications from the city and would span the hundred light-years within seconds.

* * * * *

He was up before Rockford the next morning, and went out into the bright sunlight. He looked hopefully for Alonzo, not wanting to be seen mailing the letter in person. Rockford, despite his drunken stupors, could be shrewdly observant and he might deduce the contents of the letter before Supreme Command ever received it.

He was some distance from the cabin when he heard the pound of padded feet behind him.

"Rootenant," Alonzo had the grin of a genial canine idiot. "Do you want me to mair your retter to your dear ore mother?"

"Yes, I have the letter right here."

"O.K. I got to hurry, because the mair hericopter reaves right away. I charge six fig cookies or three candy bars or —"

"Here-take it and run-and try not to slobber all over it."

* * * * *

They were served breakfast in the cabin. Afterward, Rockford went for a brief talk with Princess Lyla. He came back and settled down in the easy-chair, his pipe in his hand.

"Your morning's duty won't be at all unpleasant," he said. "The obnoxious and repulsive things will begin to happen to you later. Maybe this afternoon."

"What do you mean?"

"This morning you will go for a walk with Princess Lyla and discuss changing the Vestan Space Guard into a force along Terran Space Patrol lines. Narf is still in bed, by the way."

Rockford added, "I'll give you a bit of sage advice, for your own good-try not to fall in love with her."

* * * * *

Hunter and Princess Lyla sat together on the high hill, their backs against the red trunk of a cloud tree. On the mountain's slope to their right lay the dark and junglelike Tiger Forest-he wondered if it was true that the savage tree tigers never left its borders-while the toylike cabins of the camp were below them. The mountain's slope dropped on down to the deserts, beyond which were other mountains, far away and translucent azure.

"It was George who suggested we come up here," she said. "He knows I do that often when the responsibilities of being queen of a world —I'm such an ordinary and untalented person-become too much for me. I always feel better when I sit up here and look down on the mountains and deserts."

"Yes," he said politely.

"A ruling princess can be so alone," she said. "That's why I appreciate George's friendship so much-it's never because of any ulterior motive but because he likes me."

I'm going to use her, and you, to get what I want.

He looked at her, at the lines of sadness on the face that was too old for its years, felt the way she was so grateful to Rockford for what was only a cold-blooded pretense of friendship, and the dislike for Rockford increased. He could not force himself to speak civilly of Rockford so he changed the subject:

"I understand you wanted to talk to me about the Space Guard?"

"Yes. Even a neutral world can't feel safe these days and George suggested that."

"I'll be glad to help all I can. Of course, the change will require time."

"I can understand that. They say you Space Patrol officers begin training at sixteen, after passing almost impossible qualification tests."

"The tests can seem extremely difficult to a farm boy from Kansas. I —"

"Kansas?" Her eyes lighted with interest. "My grandmother was from Kansas! She used to tell me about the green plains of grain in the spring, and how different they were from the deserts of Vesta...."

It was almost noon when he took her hand and helped her to her feet, realizing guiltily that they had talked all morning without ever getting back to the cold, dry facts of military efficiency.

"It was nice to talk up here this morning," she said. She looked down at the cabins and the shadow fell again across her face. "But nothing down there has been changed by it, has it?"

He held to her hand longer than was necessary as they went down the steep part of the hill. She did not seem to mind.

When they reached her cabin she said, "It's still a little while until lunch-time enough for you to give me a rough outline of the Space Guard change."

Everything inside the cabin was feminine. None of Narf's possessions were visible. There was a heavy door leading into Narf's half of the cabin, with a massive lock. Hunter wondered if it was left unlocked at night, thought of Narf's sour face and leering little eyes, and found the thought repulsive.

The answer to his conjecture came with the entrance of a servant as they seated themselves.

"By your leave, your highness," the servant said, bowing, "I came to make Lord Narf a key for that inner door."

"A key?" There was alarm in her tone. "But we're not married-not yet!"

A puzzled expression came to the man's face. "Lord Narf told me, your highness, that you had ordered the duplicate key made and given to him before evening. I found I could not do this without first borrowing your key for a pattern."

There was a frightened look in her eyes as they went to the door and back to the servant. "*No ...* don't try to make a key!"

"Yes, your highness." The servant bowed and turned away.

A familiar gravelly voice spoke from behind them:

"Ah ... an unscheduled little meeting, I see!"

It was Narf, anger on his face, already within the doorway as the servant went out it.

"We were going to talk about the Space Guard," Lyla said in an emotionless tone. "Lieutenant Hunter has promised to show how Space Patrol methods will improve it and —"

"By a coincidence, Sonig and I were discussing military matters only a few minutes ago," Narf said. He looked at Hunter. "I'm afraid that Sonig and I agree that the Terran Space Guard is quite out of date, now. *The* fighting force of the galaxy is the Verdam's Peoples Guards."

Narf spoke to Lyla, "You may go ahead and talk with this lieutenant if you wish to, but it's a waste of time. I'm arranging to have Sonig send Peoples Guards officers here to supervise the rebuilding of the Space Guard.

"And now"—there was insinuation in Narf's tone as he spoke to Hunter —"I have to give Sonig a demonstration of my skill with weapons. He insists on it-he has heard of several of my modest feats."

Narf left the door open behind him so that by turning his head as he walked, he could see the two inside.

"I suppose I might as well go," Hunter said.

Lyla did not answer. She sat motionless, staring unseeingly before her, and he wondered if she was thinking of how very soon Narf would be king and his authority as great as hers.

She did not notice when he quietly left the room.

* * * * *

Rockford was waiting in the cabin, still in the easy-chair.

"Well," Rockford said, "what do you think of her?"

Hunter tried to keep the personal dislike out of his coldly formal reply:

"If you refer to your suggestion that I not make love to her, sir, I can assure you that such a suggestion was never necessary. I happen to have a code of ethics."

"I didn't say 'make love'. I said, 'fall in love'. That's quite ethical. Did you complete your discussion with her?"

"Well ... no."

"You must do that this afternoon, then. Can't let anything as important as that be delayed."

Hunter stared at him, trying to find one small grain of sanity in Rockford's actions. The Verdam empire already had Jardeen within its grasp, and Vesta, and the end for Earth was inevitable. And Rockford slept, and drank beer, and regarded it as very important that the Vestan Space Guard discussions-of a change that Narf would never permit-be continued without delay.

He walked slowly into his own room. In the nightmare situation of frustration there was one single sane and stable conviction for his mind to cling to: Supreme Command would by now have received his message and shot back the reply that would relieve Rockford of his command. Perhaps it wasn't yet too late —

Then his mind reeled as a new conviction struck it.

There was a sheet of paper on his bed —a message.

His message!

> ... SITUATION EXTREMELY CRITICAL ... VAL BORAN ALREADY CONVINCED BY SONIG'S PROPAGANDA ... MUST REPORT ROCKFORD IS UTTERLY INCOMPETENT, HIS MIND AND WILL DESTROYED BY ALCOHOL ... REPEAT: ROCKFORD IS DOING NOTHING, HIS MIND DESTROYED BY ALCOHOL....

The words screamed up at him and he felt the sickness of one who sees the last faint hope shattered and gone. All was lost, now....

He went outside, feeling a savage desire for violence rising above the sickness.

"Rootenant!" Alonzo came bounding to meet him and slid to a halt with his saucer feet scattering gravel and the idiotic grin on his face. "I mair your retter and you owe me six fig cook —"

It occurred to Hunter that it was not Alonzo that should be punished. He, Hunter, was the one who deserved execution for ever entrusting anything so important as the message to an imbecilic animal.

He said with cold distinctness:

"The ... letter ... is ... inside."

"Oh?" Alonzo blinked. "I sure mair something, awr right. After Mr. Rockford correct it."

"Correct it?"

"Oh, sure. Mr. Rockford, he up rong before you this morning to find me and say you are writing a retter rast night and I must bring it by for him to make awr your mistakes over again."

So Rockford was watching all the time, pretending to be in a drunken sleep....

"Rootenant —" Alonzo shifted his big feet impatiently. "You stirr owe me six fig —"

Hunter swung around and strode away, afraid he might decide to choke the animal after all. A culture of twenty worlds was the same as already destroyed, and he was held in a maddening quagmire of helplessness by a crafty alcoholic and a dog with the mind of a small child.

"Ah ... my boy!" Rockford came out of the cabin, beaming as though nothing had ever happened. "Look to your left, among those ghost trees-Narf is demonstrating his quick-draw skill to Sonig. Narf is supposed to be a very dangerous man, you know."

Hunter looked, and saw Narf whipping up the blunt, ugly spread-beam blaster-known to soldiers as the Coward's Special, because at short range it could not miss and would always cripple and blind a man for life even though it would not always kill him. Sonig was standing by, nodding his weasel head and smiling in open admiration.

"Of course," Rockford said, "Sonig isn't mentioning the needle gun all Verdam envoys carry up their sleeve. He's flattering Narf's ego for a reason-he intends to have Vesta, as well as Jardeen, sewed up for the Verdam empire when he leaves here."

"And so far as I can see," Hunter said coldly, "Sonig never is going to have anything vaguely resembling intelligent resistance to his plans."

"Ah, yes … so far as you can see," Rockford agreed amiably. "But you obey my order to take Lyla for another walk and everything will turn out all right. In fact, I'll speak to her about that right now."

Hunter stared after Rockford as he walked away. There could be no possible shred of doubt-Rockford was insane!

The breeze shifted and the voice of Narf came:

"… Certainly no weapon for a timid man, this spread-beam blaster. Have to meet the enemy man-to-man at close range."

"In that respect, too," Sonig said, "you remind me of our great General Paluk. His skill in hand-to-hand combat was something that —"

"Rootenant —"

Hunter quivered and steeled himself.

"Rootenant —" Alonzo came to a flopping halt beside him. "I terr Princess Ryra and she say I are bad to be mad at you. So I not mad, even if you didn't give me my pay."

"Thank you," Hunter said acidly. "I was deeply disturbed by your resentment."

"Oh, I know, you don't rike me. But I think you not as mean as you act. But Rord Narf-he is. I terr you, he awready mad enough to kirr you."

"What? Lord Narf wants to kill me?"

"Oh, he know you hord Princess Ryra's hand awrmost awr the way down the hirr this morning. Mr. Sonig, he see you, and he run and terr Rord Narf and Mr. Boran, too."

"But I was only helping her down the hill."

"Rord Narf, he are going to say mean things about it to Princess Ryra, too. I know. He are awrways saying mean things to my Princess Ryra."

Alonzo sighed, a sound strangely humanlike in its sadness.

"Who wirr watch over my Princess Ryra after she marry Rord Narf? He said, 'The first thing to go around here wirr be that stupid brabber-mouth animar that are not worth what it costs to feed it.' I think maybe he are afraid that if he ever hit my Princess Ryra, I wirr kirr him." The brown eyes looked up at Hunter, and suddenly they were unlike he had ever seen them; cold with deliberate decision. "I wirr, too."

* * * * *

Hunter was still standing by the cabin, thinking of what Alonzo had said, when Rockford returned.

"I also stopped by to see Val Boran," Rockford said. "While you're off with Lyla, we'll go to the city. Lyla is giving us free access to the Royal Library and the records of a neutral world carry more weight than anything I could say. Not that it's going to change his mind any—but it will give me a chance to work on him in another way."

Rockford went into the cabin as Val Boran came up the path, Princess Lyla walking beside him. She was saying, "...And anything we have in the library is yours for the asking."

They were close enough for Hunter to see her expression as she looked up at Val and added with what seemed a touch of wistfulness, "I'll be glad to go in with you and Mr. Rockford and do what I can to help if you want me to."

"Lyla"—it was the grating voice of Narf who seemed to have the ability to materialize any-where—"I'm sure the man knows his business. Besides, I want to talk to you about something as soon as I have finished my discussion with Mr. Sonig."

With that, Narf started on toward his cabin. Sonig, close behind him, paused long enough to bow to Lyla and say with the meaningless smile, "Good afternoon, Princess Lyla. Your husband was just demonstrating his marvelous skill with weapons. I would very much dislike"—the little eyes darted to Hunter and back again—"being the man who aroused his lordship's wrath."

Then Sonig followed Narf, with one last flickering glance at Hunter to see how the remark had fallen.

Rockford came out of the cabin with his brief case and said to Val, "Are we ready to go?"

"I just told Val"—Lyla spoke quickly—"that I would be glad to go along and help any way I can." The words were addressed to Rockford but her eyes were on Val, with the same wistful expression. "Do you want me to?"

Val answered her with cool, formal courtesy: "The librarian can find all the records we will need, Princess Lyla, without our interrupting your schedule for the day or your discussion with your husband. Thank you very much."

For an instant Lyla's face had the hurt expression of a child rebuffed without reason. Then she looked away and Val turned to Rockford and said, "I'm ready when you are, sir."

Lyla watched them walk away and she was still watching when the helicopter had lifted into the air and faded from sight.

Hunter hesitated, then spoke to her:

"I understand you want to talk more about the Space Guard, Princess Lyla?"

"*Princess* Lyla!" Her lips curled as she turned to face him and she seemed to spit the words at him in sudden, unexpected resentment. "I love the meaningless sound of my official figurehead title! It's so much better than being regarded as a living person with feelings that can be hurt!"

"But Princ ...I mean—" He floundered, not quite sure what had caused her reaction.

She made a visible effort to compose herself. "I'm sorry," she said. "I suppose my ...husband ...is quite right; an immature female has no business trying to rule a world and the sooner the marriage is confirmed, the sooner a competent man can take over the job."

"No," he said. "I think—"

He decided that what he thought had better be left unsaid.

"I'll"—she looked toward the cabin she shared with Narf—"let you know when we can talk."

She went back toward the cabin, walking slowly. From inside Narf's half of it came the sound of Narf's voice as he spoke to Sonig:

"...Of course, this collection of heads is nothing compared with what I have in the Sea Islands...but some interesting stories here...take that snow fox there...."

Hunter sighed, and saw that Lyla had stopped before her door, as though dreading to enter. Narf's voice droned on:

"...Only wounded, so I finished it with a knife. Even with its heart half cut out, it still wanted to live...beautiful pelt...coat for Janalee, the strip-tease queen...always had a way with women-Lyla could tell you that...had my pick of hundreds but I'm letting her be my choice...."

He saw Lyla half lift her hand, as in some mute gesture of protest, then she turned and walked swiftly away; up the path that led into the ghost trees, and out of sight.

He waited, but she did not come back. He went into his cabin and moved about restlessly, hearing again Narf's sadism-and-sex boasting and seeing again how she turned and almost ran from it —

* * * * *

"Rootenant!"

Alonzo was panting, a look of frantic appeal in his eyes.

"Prease herp me...Princess Ryra...she wirr die!"

He felt his heart lurch. "She's hurt?" he demanded, and was already on his way to the door.

"She are about to cry and she are going to where the tree tigers riv. They wirr kirr her-prease come with me!"

He asked no more questions but went out the door and up the path, Alonzo running ahead of him.

The ghost trees grew thinner as they went up the mountain's slope, and the blue-green fernlike trees of the tiger forest began to appear. They grew thicker and thicker, until the ground was black with their shadows and the midday sunlight was filtered out by the foliage overhead. Alonzo was trailing her, his nose to the ground, and Hunter hurried close behind him, watching for the red-and-white of the clothes she was wearing and hoping they would not find her too late.

They were deep in the forest when they found her.

She was standing motionless in the center of a clearing, facing away from him and looking as small and alone as a lost child. She seemed to be waiting....

He realized for the first time how alone she really was, with only a doglike alien, Alonzo, to love her or care what might happen to her, and with a future she could not bear to face. But Rockford had been wrong when he had said, *For her, there is no escape.*

There was escape for her. She had only to wait, as she was waiting now, and it would come in the windlike whisper of a tiger's rush through the grass behind her....

He hurried to her. She turned, and he saw the stains of tears now dry on her face and in her eyes the darkness of utter defeat.

"I was afraid you might get hurt, Lyla —"

Then, seemingly without volition on his part, he put his arms around her and she was clinging to him and crying in muffled sobs and trying to say something about, *"I didn't think anybody cared...."*

It was some time later, when her crying was finished, that he was reminded of the tigers by Alonzo:

"Rootenant...awr the time, some tigers are coming croser and croser. We better get her out of here, Rootenant, before they find us."

Lyla looked down at Alonzo. "Thank you, Alonzo, for watching over me and...and —" Her voice caught and she dropped to her knees and hugged the shaggy head tight against her.

Hunter watched ahead, Lyla beside him as they went through the dense trees. Alonzo walked soft-footed behind them, watching the rear. When they came to the first ghost trees and the dwindling of the tiger trees, Hunter thought it safe to walk slower and talk to her.

"I saw you go," he said. "I didn't know where until Alonzo came running to tell me."

"I heard him bragging about killing, and about his women —I was weak, wasn't I?"

"Weak?"

"I was afraid to face the future, just because it isn't to be exactly like I thought I wanted."

"What was the kind you wanted, Lyla?"

"Oh ... I guess I wanted a husband who could see me only, and children, and evenings together in the flower garden, and ... well, all the silly, sentimental little things that mean so much to a woman."

He thought, *Even with its heart half cut out, it still wanted to live ... Coat for Janalee ... the strip-tease queen....*

They passed through the last of the tiger trees and she said, "We're safe, now. The tigers never attack anyone outside their forest."

She was walking slowly and he said, "We should get on back before you're missed, shouldn't we?"

"Who would miss me?" she asked. "So long as I remain physically intact for the marriage night, who cares where or why I went away?"

There was the cold bleakness of winter in her eyes as she spoke, and in her voice the first undertone of brass. He saw that this was already the beginning of the change that Narf would make in her; the transformation of a girl young and wanting to love and be loved into a hard and cynical woman.

He put his arm around her shoulder, thinking that he should tell her that *he* cared and that she must never let Narf change her.

"Lyla, I —"

He realized how futile and foolish the words would sound. She would marry Narf, he would return to Earth, and they would never meet again. There were no words for him to speak on this last walk together, no way to tell her that he wanted to help her, to protect and care for her. No way to express the feeling inside him....

He did what seemed as natural under the circumstances as it had been for him to put his arm around her in the clearing. He tilted up her face and bent his head to kiss her.

And walked with jarring impact into the knobby elbow of a ghost tree limb.

* * * * *

The sun was down and dusk was darkening the camp when they arrived back at her cabin.

"Thank you, Dale," she said. Her hand squeezed his arm. "I didn't know I had a friend ... but now we'll have to be strangers because —"

Gravel crunched loudly on one of the paths in the ghost trees and they looked back, to see Narf and Sonig coming, walking swiftly. Even at the distance, there was anger like a red aura about Narf.

"Well," Lyla said softly, "here comes my medicine."

Sonig stopped at his own cabin, to stand just within the doorway, watching. Narf strode on and stopped before Hunter and Lyla, his face twisted with savage hatred as he looked at Hunter. He spoke to Lyla with grating vehemence:

"You've done an excellent job of making an ass of yourself-and of me-haven't you? Come on in the cabin!"

Narf seized her by the arm, towering over her as he jerked her around toward the door. Hunter stepped quickly forward, feeling the hot flash of his own anger, but there was the paleness of Lyla's face as she looked back, an appeal on it that said, *No!* He stopped, realizing that Narf would not physically harm the woman who would make him king of Vesta, and that any interference on his part would only make everything the harder for her.

He watched the two go into the cabin-into Lyla's half-and Narf slammed the door shut behind them. There followed the quick bang of windows being closed, and then Narf's muffled tirade began: *"...May think I'm a fool...I'm going to tell you a few things...."*

Sonig was still standing within his doorway. Hunter knew, without seeing it, that the thin-lipped smile would be on Sonig's face.

He turned and walked back to his own cabin. There was nothing he could do but withdraw-and listen from a distance and be ready to act if it seemed she was in danger.

He sat on his doorstep in the darkness, hearing occasional phrases in Narf's unrelenting abuse. One was: *"So prim you had to countermand my order for a key to that lock-then you went out to play with that second lieutenant...."*

Alonzo materialized out of the darkness, coming as silently as a shadow. He was no longer the bumbling clown. The idiotic grin was gone and his eyes were green fire, slanted and catlike, his teeth flashing white in a snarl as he looked back toward the sound of Narf's voice.

"She are *my* Princess Ryra," Alonzo said. "He are cursing her. If he ever hurt her, I wirr tear out his throat and his river."

"He won't hurt her, Alonzo," Hunter said, wishing he could be sure. "He'll only use words on her."

"He never ask her *why* she run away-he onry curse her and threaten her because she embarrass him."

"Embarrass him?"

"He and Sonig, they see you coming out of the forest with your arm around her. They watch with high-power grasses."

"But there was nothing wrong in that —"

"That are what Princess Ryra say. She say you onry put your arm around her because she are stirr scared of the tigers. And then he say, what about the other? And he cawr her awrful bad names."

"What other?"

"Oh, when you are bending down to kiss Princess Ryra and are wawrking into tree."

He gulped. *"They saw that?"*

"Oh, sure. Rord Narf are so mad he want to kirr you right then but Sonig say, 'Wait, I have a pran.' Then Sonig say, 'It are too bad we don't have a camera-we could have made that rootenant the raffing stock of forty worlds.'"

The thought made Hunter gulp again.

"What was Sonig's plan that Narf told Lyla about?" He asked.

"Oh, he not terr *her*. I hear Sonig terr Rord Narf when I spy. Sonig say, 'Tomorrow we be friendry and we ret those two go for another wawrk in the woods. And we have cameras with terescope rens and when they kiss and hug we take moving pictures.'"

"Why, the gutter-bred rat —"

"And Rord Narf say, 'That is what we wirr do. And then I wirr kirr him as soon as we have the pictures and she wirr have to toe the mark from then on because if I pubricry show the pictures of what she did, she wirr be ashamed to show her face anywhere on Vesta.'"

"Why, the —" He could not think of a suitable expression.

"And then Sonig say, 'To make sure she go out tomorrow, you bawr her out good so she wirr want to cry on the rootenant's shourder again.' And Rord Narf say, 'I wirr be very grad to terr the two-timing hussy what I think of her, don't worry.'"

"Why, she was only a scared girl and that rat thinks she —"

* * * * *

"... Your promise to your dying father," Narf's voice came in accusation. *"He's gone, now, and you can betray him, too! Why don't you go all the way in your deceptions ... your father will never know...."*

Alonzo said, "I think I go back and stay croser to her cabin, Rootenant."

It was an hour later, and Narf's voice had settled to a low, steady growling, when Hunter heard a helicopter settle down near the camp. A minute later, Val Boran was outlined momentarily in the doorway of the cabin he shared with Sonig. There followed the exchange of a few words-interrogation in Val's tone-and then the sound of Sonig's voice alone, which continued for minute after minute.

Sonig is telling him all about it, Hunter thought, *including my walking into that tree. But there won't be one word in sympathy with Lyla.*

Sonig's story ended and Hunter saw Val leave the cabin. He came straight up the path toward Hunter, looming tall in the darkness as he stopped before him. There was the pale gleam of metal in Val's belt —a blaster. His voice came cold and flat:

"I want to talk to you, Lieutenant."

Hunter sighed, thinking, *I suppose he wants to kill me, too.*

He got up and said, "We'll go inside. Shut the door behind you —I don't want your friend straining his ears to hear us."

Val sat tall even in the chair, his face like a carving in a dark granite and his eyes as bright and hard.

"I understand that you took Princess Lyla into the tiger forest today." Val's hand was very near the blaster. "I understand you then played the role of affectionate rescuer."

"Do you believe that story?" Hunter asked.

"Do you have a different one?"

"You might ask Lyla. Or Alonzo. Alonzo is the one who came to me for help when he saw she was going out to die."

"To die?" A startled expression came into the black eyes. "She *wanted* to die?"

"I'll tell you what happened," Hunter said, and told him the story, omitting only the embarrassing kissing incident and knowing that Sonig had not.

Val was silent for a while after Hunter finished speaking, then he said, "It isn't for me to comment upon Lord Narf's character or actions. She is his wife by her own choice. But the thought of someone else taking her out and —"

"I know. It wasn't so." Then Hunter added, "You think a great deal of her, don't you?"

Val's face hardened and Hunter thought he would not answer. Then he smiled a little, even though without humor, and said:

"Since I came here to kill you if I thought you deserved it, I suppose I am obligated to answer your question. My regard for Princess Lyla is the respectful one that any civilized man would have for another man's wife."

There was an unintended implication in the statement and Hunter made a conjecture:

"You and Princess Lyla were engaged-how long ago?"

There was surprise on Val's face, and something like pain quickly masked. "So she's already making it public information?"

"No. I learned of it from …other sources. I don't know, of course, why you persuaded her to break the engagement-that's none of my business, anyway."

"No," Val said. "It's none of your business. I'll tell you this: *I* didn't ask her to break the engagement. But so long as that was what she wanted, I certainly wasn't going to beg her to change her mind."

Val stood up to go. "If you don't mind, I would rather you said nothing to Princess Lyla about this visit tonight. I'm afraid my misplaced surge of chivalry would make me look like a fool to her."

Then, as an afterthought, Val added, "Mr. Rockford had further business in the city."

* * * * *

It was late when Narf finally left Lyla's part of the cabin. He went to the cabin occupied by Val and Sonig, aroused Sonig, and the two of them went to the helicopter field. Hunter heard the helicopter leaving for the city a few minutes later. Val's cabin remained dark and after a while, the light in Lyla's cabin went out.

He went to bed, but not to sleep. Over and over, a lonely little Princess Lyla clung to him for comfort, crying, while he held her close. He twisted and turned restlessly as he thought of the hours she had sat alone and unloved while Narf poured out his hatred and fury on her.

There was a yearning for her, a desire to hold her and always protect her, that would not let him sleep. And he realized the reason why.

He thought miserably, *I'm in love with her!*

* * * * *

Rockford was in bed, snoring loudly, with six empty beer cans on the floor beside him, when Hunter got up. He went outside and found Alonzo waiting for him.

"They got it awr pranned to kirr you for sure today, Rootenant."

"How?" he asked.

"Rast night, Rord Narf and Sonig go to the city and Rord Narf, he hire four bad-rooking men with brasters, and Sonig hire four more that are his countrymen, and they bring these men back and now they are hiding in the woods. And they awrso bring back movie cameras with terescope renses. And Rord Narf raff and say he wirr marry Princess Ryra today before your dead body is even coor."

"Oh?" Hunter said. He thought of the snoring Rockford and his words of two days before: *If you manage to live that long.* How, he wondered, could the lazy old drunkard have made such an accurate guess?

"And then," Alonzo said, "Rord Narf wake up Princess Ryra-onry I know she wasn't asreep-and he terr her he ruv her and have awready made awr the arrangement for them to get married today, right after runch. And he terr her she is right about the Space Guard and she wirr have until runch to tawrk to you about it."

There was the sound of Narf's door opening and closing and Alonzo said, "I go now-Rord Narf might guess that I are terring you things."

A few minutes later Narf and Sonig came down the path toward Hunter. Both carried pack-sacks-the cameras, of course-and both carried long-range rifle blasters.

"Good morning, lieutenant!" Narf was smiling and pseudogenial again. "About last night-sometimes a man has to be stern with his wife to impress her. Very foolish thing she did-might have been killed. I'm afraid I was so badly shaken with worry over her that I didn't even thank you for bringing her back."

"A beautiful morning, lieutenant!" Sonig was smiling, coming as close to beaming as the nature of his face would permit. "Lord Narf is going to take me stag hunting this morning —I'll get some lessons from a master. Did you ever see his lordship's collection of heads? Amazing!"

"But it seems a sportsman's collection is never quite complete," Narf said. He was still smiling but the hatred was burning like a fire in his eyes as he looked at Hunter. "There's one more head I must have —I intend to get it this morning."

Narf and Sonig were gone when Lyla came out of her cabin, her face pale and drawn. Val came out of his cabin and the two spoke to each other in greeting. There was a silence, in which neither seemed to know what to say.

Finally, awkwardly, Val said, "I heard about yesterday, Lyla. Why did you go into the tiger forest?"

"Oh ...I was just walking, I guess, and didn't notice where."

"You went there to die, didn't you?"

"I ...when you have nothing left —" Then she lifted her head in a proud gesture and said, "Should it matter to you?"

For a moment Val had the look of a man struck. Then it was gone and he said in an emotionless voice:

"No. I was asking about something that is only your husband's business. I won't do it again."

He turned away, back to his cabin.

"Val —" She took a quick step after him, the proud air gone and her arms outstretched. "I didn't mean —"

He turned back, his tone politely questioning.

"Yes?"

"I only wanted —" Then her arms dropped and the life went out of her voice. "What does it matter ...what does anything matter?"

She hurried into her cabin and the door closed behind her.

Rockford spoke from the doorway behind Hunter:

"Well, my boy, are you ready for your day's duties?"

He followed Rockford inside, where Rockford settled down in the easy-chair and yawned.

"I had a rather busy night," he said. "Certain events occurred yesterday afternoon which forced me to change my own plans to some extent. Or to set them ahead a day, I should say."

He made an effort to put the vision of Lyla from his mind and asked, "Did you make any progress with Val Boran?"

"No, I'm afraid not. Of course, I didn't expect to." Rockford yawned again. "There was another message from Supreme Command. The situation is getting worse. Which reminds me of your Duty For The Day and the fact that if you can live through it, you will have it made."

He's my superior, Hunter thought. *He's supposed to outrank a Space Patrol General-and he's amused by the situation he's here to remedy.*

"Right now," Rockford said, "Lyla faces a grim future and feels like she doesn't have a friend in the world. She needs a shoulder to cry on. You will take her for a walk and supply that shoulder."

Somehow, even though the order had nothing to do with the Terran-Verdam crisis, he did not have the heart to object. She had been crying before she even reached her door. Later, after he had comforted her, he would demand that Rockford get down to determined effort on the Verdam problem. No more than an hour would be lost by that....

"Yes, sir," he said. "But in the interests of Princess Lyla's safety, I had better talk to her in her cabin. Alonzo saw Narf and Sonig bring back eight —"

"Professional killers, to dispose of you," Rockford finished. "I know all about it, and I know that Narf took time last night to spend an hour with his favorite girl friend and brag even to her that he was going to marry Lyla today before your dead body had time to get cool.

"But you just take Lyla for another walk and you will cause the beginning of the end for the Verdam Peoples Worlds. You will go down in history, my boy, as the man who saved the Terran Republic."

Hunter went out the door, again feeling a feverish sense of unreality. He was to go forth and get blasted into hamburger and by some mysterious process known only to Rockford, the Verdam empire would contritely start collapsing....

He did not knock on her door. He did not think of it as a violation of her privacy. She would be feeling too alone and unwanted to care.

She was not crying as he had thought she would be. She was standing by the window, staring down at the gray, distant desert, her eyes as bleakly empty as it.

"Hello, Lyla," he said.

"Hello, Dale. I was just thinking; this is the day that I, as a woman, should always have dreamed about" —she tried to smile, and failed, and the brass came into her voice —"my wedding day!"

"Alonzo told me about it."

It seemed to him he should add something, such as to wish her happiness-but such words would be meaningless and farcical and they would both know it.

But there was no reason why he should endanger her by obeying Rockford's insane order. He would not do it —

"Ah ...good morning, Lyla!" Rockford loomed in the doorway, jovial as a Santa Claus. "Did you know Dale wants to go for a walk in the woods with you this bright spring morning-and he's no doubt too bashful to tell you so? Do you good to get away from camp" —there was the suggestion of a pause —"while you're still free."

He turned a beaming smile on Hunter. "Don't stand there like a dummy, boy-take her by the arm and let her have a last walk with someone who cares what happens to her."

There was one thing about Rockford not compatible with his air of fond fatherliness: his eyes were hard, gray slate as they looked into Hunter's and there was no mistaking their expression. Rockford had not made a fatherly suggestion for his own amusement. He had given an order that he intended to be obeyed.

* * * * *

Hunter and Lyla walked on through the thickets of ghost trees and arrow brush, each with little to say, Hunter feeling more and more like a ridiculous fool. They had no destination, no purpose in their walk, other than to abide by Rockford's desire that a total of ten assassins get a chance to slaughter a certain expendable second lieutenant.

He did not put his arm around Lyla as they walked. If they killed him, it would have to be without their having the satisfaction of the pictures they wanted with which to blackmail her.

They came to a tiny clearing, where a cloud tree log made an inviting seat in the shade, and Lyla said:

"No matter how far we walk, I'll have to go back to face it. Let's stop here, and rest a while."

He saw that the clearing was fairly well screened, but certainly not completely so. It would have to do.

He sat down on the log several feet away from her, not wanting to take the chance of her getting hit by accident.

Not that I'm enthusiastic about getting hit by intent, myself, he thought. *What a way for a Space Guard officer to die.*

He wondered if Rockford would ever inform Headquarters that Lieutenant Dale Hunter had died in the line of duty-by whatever twisted logic this insane episode could be called duty-and he wondered how the Commemoration Roll would read for him.... *Displaying courage above and beyond the call of duty, Lieutenant Hunter sat conspicuously on top of a hill and calmly waited for ten assassins to slaughter him....*

"It's peaceful and quiet here, isn't it?" Lyla said.

He had been trying to watch four different directions at once and he realized that the constant swiveling of his neck was causing his stiff blouse collar to slowly cut his throat. And he saw that it was-for the moment, anyway-peaceful and quiet where they sat. The sun was warm and golden before them, bright flowers sweetly scented the air, and giant rainbow moths were fluttering over them, their tiny voices like the piping of a thousand fairy flutes.

"I wish I had been born a country girl," Lyla said. "I'd like to have a life like this, and not-what mine will be."

He asked the question to which he had to have the answer:

"Once you were going to marry Val and live on Jardeen, weren't you?"

"I ...so my foolishness is no longer a secret?"

"Foolishness?" he asked.

"We met two years ago when I was attending the Fine Arts university on Jardeen. I was younger and a lot more naïve then than I am now. I thought we were desperately in love and would get married as soon as I finished school and would live happily ever after, and all that."

"And it didn't turn out that way?"

"I had to make that promise to Daddy and when I wrote to Val about it, he seemed to approve. He didn't suggest I renounce the proxy marriage when the time was up, or anything. He just wrote that I knew what I wanted to do. He seemed relieved to be free to go ahead with his political career."

"I see," he said, and then, "you don't feel bad about it, do you, Lyla?"

"Feel bad? I wouldn't marry Val Boran if he was the last man on Vesta! Even Lord Narf isn't as self-centered as *he* is!"

"You don't have to marry Narf either," he said. "You know that."

She looked down at the ground and said in a dead voice, "I made a promise."

"Rockford told me that your father never really knew Narf-that on the few times they met, Narf put on the act of being a refined gentleman, very respectful toward the king's daughter."

She did not answer and he said, "Is that the way it was?"

"Yes. That's the way it was. But how could I tell Daddy, as he lay dying?"

"You couldn't, Lyla. But if your father could be here today and know what you know about Narf, do you think he would want you to marry him?"

"No ...I guess not. But Lord Narf loves me in his own way, I think-and that's more than anyone else does."

Then her tone changed and she said, "I'm so glad that you're here today, Dale —I'm glad that there is someone who cares at least a little about what happens to me."

On her face was a poignant longing for someone to love and comfort her. It seemed to him, now beyond any doubt, that there could never be anything for him in his career but loneliness. How different the warm love of Lyla would be from the cold austerity of the military and its endless succession of weapons and killing —

* * * * *

He moved, to sit beside her and put his arm around her shoulders. "Lyla," he said, "I want to tell you —"

"*Dale....*" The word was a despairing sob as her composure broke and she held tightly to him, crying, her voice coming muffled as she pressed her face against his chest. "Help me, Dale! How can I marry that sadistic beast when it's someone else I can't live without-and he doesn't even know I love him!"

"But he does!" He hugged her closer, "He does know, and he loves you even more than you love him."

"Are you sure?" She raised a tear-stained face, hope like sunshine through clouds on it. "Are you really sure Val loves me, after all?"

"*Val?*"

The revelation was like the stunning concussion shock of a blaster beam passing two inches overhead. His vision blurred and there was a hideous roaring in his ears. She was still holding to him for comfort and it seemed to him that was wrong-he should be clinging to her for support....

"*Dale* ...what's the matter?"

"But I thought —" He swallowed with difficulty. "I thought you meant that I was the —"

Something struck the top of his head; this time, for certain, the concussion shock of a blaster beam passing close above it. There was a vicious crack as the beam split the tree beyond, then a crash and explosion of wood fragments as a second beam followed the first.

He rolled from the log; taking Lyla with him. The arrow bushes shielded them briefly, long enough for them to reach the temporary safety of a small swale.

"Dale!" Her dark eyes were wide with puzzled surprise and one small foot was bare from the loss of a sandal. "Someone shot at us!"

He thought, *So Narf got his pictures, after all.*

"Rootenant!" Alonzo came running. "They are *that* way-awr spread out to be sure to kirr you."

Alonzo motioned with his nose, a movement that seemed to cover all the high ground beyond them. At least, the enemy was not between them and camp. Not yet.

A distant shout came, an order from Narf to his men:

"All of you-down that ridge! Get between Hunter and camp!"

"It's him!" Her fingers gripped his arm. "He wants them to kill you!"

They had fired from a distance too great for his own blaster. He could not defy them from where he now stood.

"I'll have to try to get within range of them," he said. "I'll go back —"

"No!" Her grip on his arm tightened. "Don't leave me, Dale-don't let him find me here."

He looked down the length of the swale. At its lower end the ghost tree forest began, dense and concealing-but all down the length of the swale the snarevines lay in thick, viciously barbed entanglements, overlying a bed of sharp rocks and boulders. She could never get to the safety of the ghost trees in time.

Narf had his pictures, now. What would he do to her in the insanity of his hatred and triumph when he reached her?

"All right, Lyla," he said. "I'll see that you get to the trees —"

* * * * *

There was a crashing of explosions and debris leaped skyward behind them and along both sides of the swale. The firing continued, scattered but very effectively consistent, and he said as he drew his blaster, "I guess they don't want us to go away."

He set the regulator of the blaster at lowest intensity so that the beam would not clip danger- ous flying fragments from the boulders. The green, tough vines disintegrated reluctantly while the precious minutes sped by; while the unhindered assassins would be hurrying to the point where the entire swale would be visible to them and under their fire.

Alonzo was following along near the top of the swale's side, ignoring the danger as he watched the progress of the enemy and reported it to Hunter: "Now they are halfway, Rootenant, hur- rying faster —"

They reached the lower end of the swale. The last of the vines disintegrated and the ghost tree forest lay before them.

He touched her cheek in farewell. "Get on to camp, as fast as you can run."

The firing abruptly ceased as he spoke. There was an ominous silence. Alonzo came running, his tone almost a yelp in its urgency:

"They are awrmost where they can see us! We got to get her out of here, Rootenant-awrfur quick!"

* * * * *

"Lyla!"

It was the voice of Val, sharp with concern for her. He came running out of the ghost trees, all his cold impassiveness gone. "Are you hurt, Honey-are you hurt?"

"You came for me!" She whispered the words, her face radiant. Then she ran to meet him, her arms outstretched, crying, *"Val ... oh, Val...."*

Their arms went around each other.

Then the woods erupted as ten blasters laid down a barrage to block any escape to camp.

"I'll try to give you a chance to get through," Hunter said quickly. "Be ready for it when it comes."

He ran toward the firing line, taking advantage of the concealment afforded by the first fringe of ghost trees. They should be almost within range of his own weapon, now —

Again, the firing abruptly ceased, as though by some signal. There came the furious raving of Narf:

It's that Boran she wants! Kill him, too!

Sonig cursed with bitter rage. *Jardeen is lost to Verdam if any witness escapes-and we'll all hang, besides.*

There was a second of silence, and then Narf's command:

Kill the woman, too!

There was a roar like thunder as the firing began. The ground trembled and debris filled the air with flying fragments. Hunter, still running toward the enemy under cover of the trees, saw Val trying to get Lyla to safety and saw them both hurled to the ground as a tree exploded in front of them. They would never live to rise and run again —

* * * * *

He saw Rockford's plan, at last, and what his own duty would now have to be. He knew why Rockford had said of this day, *"If you can live through it, you will have it made."*

And he had a cold feeling inside him that he was not going to have it made.

He took a deep breath and ran toward the enemy, out of the concealment of the ghost trees and in the open where they could not fail to see him, his blaster firing a continuous beam that fell only a little short of the enemy, that showed them he would be close enough to kill them within seconds if he was not stopped.

The fire concentrated upon him, giving Lyla and Val their chance for escape. He ran through an inferno of crashing explosions, twisting and dodging on ground that trembled and heaved under his feet, while razor-sharp rock shrapnel filled the air with shrill, deadly screaming sounds.

Something ripped through his shoulder, to spin him around and send him rolling. He scrambled up, firing as he did so, and ran drunkenly on.

Something struck the side of his head and he went down again. He tried to rise and fell back, a blackness sweeping over him that he could not hold away despite his efforts to do so.

It seemed to him that the firing had suddenly stopped, that in its place was the hoarse buzz of a police stun-beam. It seemed he saw helicopters overhead, bearing the bright blue insignia of the Royal Guard and then there was nothing but the blackness.

* * * * *

There was a brief, dreamlike return to consciousness. He was in a Royal Guard helicopter and Alonzo was beside him, grinning, and saying, "You be O.K. —I grad! And my Princess Ryra-rook at her now, Rootenant!"

He saw Lyla, her hand in Val's, and her face was glowing and beautiful in its new-found happiness. Then she was bending down, kissing him, and saying, "Dale ... Dale ... how can we ever thank you for what you did?"

* * * * *

When the blackness lifted the second time he was lying, bandaged, on a cot in the meeting hall and the voice of Rockford was saying, "...Ready to go in just a minute."

The hall was filled with members of the royal court who had come for the wedding. He saw the white robes of Church of Vesta dignitaries who had come to officiate at the wedding. Then he saw the seven grim old men seated at the far end of the table.

The Royal Council-with the judicial power to give even death sentences in crimes committed against royalty.

Sonig, his face white and staring, was being half led, half carried, away from them.

Narf, in the grip of another Guardsman, was standing before the Council and saying in a tone both incredulous and sneering:

"Is that my sentence?"

"There is a qualification to it," one of the Council said. "It seems only just, in view of your crime, that you be tortured until death —"

The rest of the words were lost as the blackness swept back. But before unconsciousness was complete, when all else in the hall was gone from him, he heard Narf's cry; an animal-like bawl of protest, raw and hoarse with anguish....

* * * * *

"Ah ...you're coming out of it, my boy."

Rockford was standing over him. "They gave you a Restoration shot on Vesta forty-eight hours ago. It will be wearing off in a minute and your head will clear."

He sat up, and the dizziness faded swiftly away. He saw that he was in the compartment of an interstellar ship and he knew that it was Earthbound.

And that Vesta, and brown-eyed Lyla, were now part of the past....

"Don't look so sad, my boy," Rockford said. "You'll get due credit and promotion for the invaluable part you played in my plan."

"But —"

"I know. But she was never yours. You'll find life is full of heartbreaks like that, son.

"And we accomplished our mission. Narf's crime neatly invalidated the proxy marriage. Then Lyla set a new precedent by marrying Val that very day. Earth has never had two such loyal and grateful friends as Val and Lyla."

"You knew all about them, didn't you?" he asked.

"Strategic Service has to know everything. And I knew they were still in love even though each was too proud to admit it. That's why I had to insist on Val coming to Vesta. After that, it was only a matter of using you to awaken Val to the fact that she did *not* love Narf. And of taking care of various little details, such as faking an official request for the helicopters to come out two hours ahead of time, getting Val off to find her at the proper time, and so on."

Rockford smiled at him, "And you learned that an old man's mind can be mightier than the space fleets of the Verdam empire-and that the line of duty that produces the best results can sometimes be very devious."

He thought of the white-faced Sonig, and the anguished bawl he had heard from Narf.

"I suppose they were going to hang Narf and Sonig at once."

"The Council would have, no doubt. But Lyla was so happy that she begged the Council to give them very light sentences-or just let them go free. So I suggested a compromise. The Royal Council regarded it as very fitting."

"What was it?"

"For Sonig, no punishment. The murder attempt, being news of public interest, will be broadcast upon Vesta and other worlds, including a factual, unbiased account of Sonig's participation in it. Shortly afterward, Sonig will be taken to Verdam and turned over to his own benevolent government. Vesta will file no charges."

"But Sonig lost Jardeen for his government. They'll execute him for that!"

"Yes. I'm afraid so. Shall we call it poetic justice?"

"What about Narf?"

"His sentence was life-long exile on his Sea Island estate. He will be provided with all the luxuries to which he has been accustomed, including a full staff of servants. He will continue to enjoy all his possessions there, including his gallery of nude paintings, his risqué films, his pornographic library, and so on. In fact, since he is so fascinated by pornography and such a collector thereof, any pornographic material which might become available on Vesta in the future will be sent to him."

"That's not right …I mean, they were going to torture him to death."

"Not 'to death'. It was 'until death'. There's a difference."

"But that bawling noise he made —"

"Ah …that was due to the one restrictive qualification to the benign terms of his exile. Every woman on his estate was to be removed before he reached there, leaving men servants only. Patrol boats will see to it that for so long as he lives no woman shall ever set foot on the Sea Islands."

Rockford smiled again. "Lord Narf succeeded beyond his wildest dreams in keeping his boyhood vow of being always a man among men."

Brain Teaser

*How can a ship travel both forward and
backward and sideways in two different directions,
be going twice as fast as the speed of
light-and still be completely motionless?*

Carl Engle stood aside as the flight preparation crew filed out of the *Argosy*'s airlock. Barnes was the last; fat and bald and squinting against the brightness of the Arizona sun.

"All set, Carl," he said. "They had us to check and countercheck, especially the drives."

Engle nodded. "Good. Ground Control reports the Slug cruiser still circling seven hundred miles out and they think the Slugs suspect something."

"Damned centipedes!" Barnes said. "I still say they're telepathic." He looked at his watch. Zero hour minus twenty-six minutes. "Good luck, boy, and I hope this space warp dingus works like they think it will."

He waddled down the boarding ramp and Engle went through the airlock, frowning a little as he threw the switches that would withdraw the ramp and close the airlock behind him. Barnes' implied doubt in the success of the space warp shuttle was not comforting. If the shuttle failed to work, the *Argosy* would be on the proverbial spot with the Slug cruiser eager to smear it well thereupon....

Access to the control room was up through the room that housed the space warp shuttle. Dr. Harding, the tall, bristle-browed physicist, and his young assistant, Garvin, looked up briefly as he entered then returned their attention to their work. The master computer, borrowed from M.I.T., stood like a colossal many-dialed refrigerator along one wall. A protective railing around it bore a blunt KEEP OUT sign and it was never left unwatched. Garvin was seated before it, his fingers flitting over the keyboard and the computer's answer panel replying with strange mathematical symbols.

The space warp shuttle sat in the middle of the room, a cube approximately two-thirds of a meter along the edge, studded with dials and knobs and surmounted by a ball of some shining silvery alloy. Dr. Harding was talking into the transdimensional communicator mounted beside the shuttle.

Engle went on to the computer and waited outside the railing until Garvin finished with his work and turned in his seat to face him.

"The last check question," Garvin said. "Now to sweat out the last twenty minutes."

"If you've got the time, how about telling me about the shuttle," said Engle, "I've been kept in the dark about it; but from what I understand, the shuttle builds up a field around the ship, with the silver ball as the center of the field, and this field goes into another dimension called the 'space warp'."

"Ah-it could be described in that manner," Garvin said, smiling a little. "A clear description could not be made without the use of several special kinds of mathematics, but you might say this field in normal space is like a bubble under water. The air bubble seeks its own element, rises rapidly until it emerges into free air-in this case, the space warp. This transition into the warp is almost instantaneous and the shuttle automatically ceases operation when the warp is fully entered. The shuttle is no longer needed; the hypothetical bubble no longer exists-it has found its own element and merged with it."

"I know that a light-hour of travel in the warp is supposed to be equivalent to several light-years in normal space," Engle said, "but what about when you want to get back into normal space?"

"The original process is simply reversed: the shuttle creates a 'bubble' that cannot exist in the warp and seeks its own element, normal space."

"I see. But if the shuttle should —"

He never completed the question. Dr. Harding strode over, his eyes blue and piercing under the fierce eyebrows as he fixed them on him. He spoke without preamble:

"You realize the importance of this test flight with the shuttle, of course? Entirely aside from our personal survival should the Slug cruiser intercept us."

"Yes, sir," he answered, feeling the question suggested an even lower opinion of his intelligence than he had thought Harding held.

Project Space Warp existed for the purpose of sending the *Argosy* to Sirius by means of the space warp shuttle and bringing back the *Thunderbolt* by the same swift method. The *Thunderbolt*, Earth's first near-to-light-speed interstellar ship, was a huge ship; armed, armored, and invincible. It had been built to meet every conceivable danger that might be encountered in interstellar exploration-but the danger had come to the solar system from the direction of Capella nine years after the departure of the *Thunderbolt*. Eight cruisers of the pulpy, ten-foot centipede-like things called Slugs had methodically destroyed the colonies on Mars and Venus and established their own outposts there. Earth's ground defenses had held the enemy at bay beyond the atmosphere for a year but such defense could not be maintained indefinitely. The *Thunderbolt* was needed quickly and its own drives could not bring it back in less than ten years....

"We will go into the warp well beyond the atmosphere," Harding said. "Transition cannot be made within an atmosphere. Since a very moderate normal space velocity of the ship will be transformed into a greater-than-light velocity when in the warp, it is desirable that we make turn-over and decelerate to a very low speed before going into the warp."

"Yes, sir," he said. "I was briefed on that part and I'll bring us as near to a halt as that cruiser will permit."

"There will be communication between us during the flight," Harding said. "I will give you further instructions when they become necessary."

He turned away with an air of dismissal. Engle went to the ladder by the wall. He climbed up it and through the interroom airlock, closing the airlock behind him; the routine safety measure in case any single room was punctured. He went to the control board with a vague resentment gnawing for the first time at his normally placid good nature.

So far as Harding was concerned-and Garvin, too-he might as well have been an unusually intelligent baboon.

* * * * *

Zero hour came and the *Argosy* lifted until Earth was a tremendous, curving ball below and the stars were brilliant points of light in a black sky. The Slug cruiser swung to intercept him within the first minute of flight but it seemed to move with unnatural slowness. It should have been driving in at full speed and it wasn't....

"Something's up," Ground Control said. "It's coming in too slowly."

"I see that," he answered. "It must be covering something beyond it, in your radar shadow."

It was. When he was almost free of the last traces of atmosphere he saw the other cruiser, far out and hidden from Ground Control's radar by the radar shadow cast by the first one.

He reported, giving its position and course as given him by the robot astrogating unit.

"We'll have the greatest amount of time if I make turn-over now and decelerate," he finished.

The voice of Harding came through the auxiliary speaker:

"Do so."

The *Argosy* swung, end for end, and he decelerated. The cruiser behind him increased its speed, making certain it would be in position to cut off any return to Earth. The other cruiser altered its course to intersect the point in space the *Argosy* would soon occupy, and the *Argosy* was between the rapidly closing jaws of a trap.

He made reports to Ground Control at one-minute intervals. At 11:49 he said:

"Our velocity is approaching zero. We'll be within range of the second cruiser's blasters in two more minutes."

Harding spoke again to him:

"We'll go into the warp now. *Do not* alter the deceleration or the course of the ship while we're in the warp."

"I won't," he said.

There was a faint mutter from the auxiliary speaker as Harding gave some instructions to Garvin. Engle took a last look at the viewscreen; at blue-green Earth looming large in the center, Orion and Sirius glittering above it and the sun burning bright and yellow on the right. It was a scene he had observed many times before, all very familiar and normal —

The chronometer touched 11:50 and normalcy vanished.

Earth and sun and stars fled away from him, altering in appearance as they went, shrinking, dwindling. The seas and continents of Earth erupted and shook and boiled before Earth faded and disappeared. The sun changed from yellow to green to blue, to a tiny point of bright violet light that raced away into the blackness filling the screen and faded and disappeared as Earth had done.

Then the viewscreen was black, utterly, completely, dead black. And the communicator that had connected him with Ground Control was silent, without the faintest whisper of background sound or space static.

In the silence the voice of Harding as he spoke to Garvin came through the speaker; puzzled, incredulous, almost shocked:

"Our velocity couldn't have been that great —*and the sun receded into the ultraviolet!*"

There was the quick sound of hurrying footsteps then the more distant sound of the computer's keys being operated at a high rate of speed. He wanted to ask what had gone wrong but he knew no one would answer him. And it would be a pointless question-it was obvious from Harding's tone that he did not know, either.

He had an unpleasant feeling that Man's first venture into another dimension had produced catastrophic results. What had caused sun and Earth to disappear so quickly-and what force had riven and disfigured Earth?

Then he realized the significance of Harding's statement about the sun receding into the ultraviolet.

If the ship had been traveling at a high velocity away from the sun, the wave length of the sun's light would have been increased in proportion to the speed of the ship. The sun should have disappeared in the long-wave infrared end of the spectrum, not the short-wave ultraviolet.

With the thought came the explanation of the way the continents and oceans of Earth had quivered and seethed. The shifting of the spectrum range had shortened normally visible rays into invisibly short ultraviolet radiations while at the same time formerly invisible long infrared radiations had been shortened into visible wave lengths. There had been a continuous displacement into and past the ultraviolet and each wave length would have reflected best from a different place-mountains, valleys, oceans, deserts, warm areas, cool areas, —and the steady progression into the ultraviolet had revealed each area in quick succession and given the appearance of agitated movement.

So there was no catastrophe and everything had a logical explanation. Except how they could have been approaching a sun that he had seen clearly, visibly, racing away from them.

"Engle —" The voice of Harding came through the speaker. "We're going back into normal space to make another observation. I don't know just where we are but we're certain to be far from the cruisers. Don't alter our course or velocity."

"Yes, sir," he said.

They came out of the warp at 11:53. The communicator burped suddenly and the viewscreen came to life; a deep, dull red that brightened quickly. A tiny coal flared up, swelling in size and shifting from red to orange to yellow-the sun. Earth appeared as a hazy red dot that enlarged and resolved itself into a planet with distorted continents that trembled and changed, to resume their natural shapes and colors. Within a few seconds the sun was shining as ever, Earth loomed large and blue-green before them and the stars of Orion glittered unchanged beyond. Even their position in space was the same-they had not moved.

But the Slug cruisers had.

One was very near and from its forward port came the violet haze that always preceded a blaster beam. There was no time to escape-no chance at all. He spoke into the mike, harsh and urgent:

"Into the warp! There's a blaster beam coming —*move!"*

There was a silence from below that seemed to last an eternity, then the sound of a switch being slapped hastily. At the same time, the violet haze before the cruiser erupted into blue fire and the blaster beam lanced out at them.

It struck somewhere astern. The power output needle swung jerkily as the generators went out and the emergency batteries took the heavy load of the shuttle's operation. There was a sensation of falling as the ship's artificial gravity units ceased functioning. The auxiliary speaker rattled wordlessly and there was a sound like a hard rush of wind through it, accompanied by quick bumping sounds.

Then the speaker was still and there was no sound of any kind as the viewscreen shifted into the ultraviolet and Earth and stars and sun once again raced away and disappeared in the blackness.

* * * * *

A myriad of lights above the board informed him the generators were destroyed, the stern section riddled and airless, the emergency batteries damaged and reduced to quarter charge, the shuttle room punctured and airless.

And, of course, Harding and Garvin were dead.

He felt a surge of futile anger. It had all been unnecessary. If only they had not considered him incompetent to be entrusted with anything more than the ship's operation-if only they had installed an emergency switch for the shuttle by his control board, there would not have been the two-second delay following his order and they would have been safely in the warp before the blaster beam struck.

But they had not trusted him with responsibility and now he was alone in a space warp he did not understand; sole and full responsibility for the shuttle suddenly in his hands.

He considered his course of action, then got into a pressure suit. Magnets in the soles of its heavy boots permitted him to walk in the absence of gravity and he went to the interroom airlock with metallically clicking steps. He let himself through the lock and walked down what had been the room's wall, then across to the center of its floor.

But for the fact there was no one in the room, it was as he had last seen it. The shuttle, computer, and other equipment stood in their orderly positions with their lighted dials unchanged. Until one looked at the gash ripped in the hull and saw the stains along its edge where the occupants had been hurled through it by the escaping air.

He went on to the next room and the next. The damage increased as he proceeded toward the stern. The power generators were sliced into ribbons and the emergency batteries in such condition it seemed a miracle they were functioning at all. The drives had received the greatest damage; they were an unrecognizable mass of wreckage.

He made his way back to the shuttle room, there to appraise his circumstances. He reached automatically for a cigarette and stopped when his glove bumped the breast plate of his pressure suit.

First, he would have to make the shuttle room livable; get out of the pressure suit. He would have to question the computer and he could not do that with the thick, clumsy gloves on his hands.

The job didn't take long. There were repair plates on the ship and a quick-hardening plastic spray. He closed the sternward airlock when he was done and opened the airlock leading to the control room, as well as the locks beyond. Air filled the shuttle room, with only a minor over-all loss of air pressure. He removed the suit, attached a pair of magnetic soles to his shoes so he could operate the keys of the computer without the movements sending him floating away, and went to it.

He had never been permitted to touch it before, nor even stand close enough to see what the keyboard looked like. Now, he saw that the alphabetical portion of the keyboard was minor compared with the mathematical portion, many of the symbols strange to him.

The operation of an interplanetary ship required a certain knowledge of mathematics, but not the kind used by theoretical physicists. He typed, doubtfully:

ARE YOU CAPABLE OF ANSWERING QUESTIONS PRESENTED IN NON-MATH-EMATICAL FORM?

The word, YES, appeared at once in the answer panel and relief came to him like the lifting of a heavy burden.

The computer knew as much about the space warp as Harding or anyone else. It was connected with his drive controls and instruments and knew how far, how fast, and in what directions the flight had taken place. It had even been given blueprints of the ship's construction, in case the structure of the ship should affect the ship's performance in the warp, and knew every nut, bolt, plate and dimension in the ship.

There was supposed to be a certain method of procedure when questioning the computer. "It knows-but it can't think," Garvin had once said. "It lacks the initiative to correlate data and arrive at conclusions unless the procedure of correlation is given it in detail."

Perhaps he could manage to outline some method of correlation for the computer. The facts of his predicament were simple enough:

He was in an unknown medium called "the Space Warp." Something not anticipated occurred when a ship went into the warp and Harding had not yet solved the mystery when he died. The physicists in Observation would be able to find the answer but he could not ask them. The forward movement of the ship was not transferred with it into the warp and if he emerged into normal space the waiting Slug cruisers would disintegrate him before he spoke three words to Observation.

There was a pencil and a tablet of paper by the computer. He used them to calculate the time at which the charge in the damaged batteries would reach a critical low, beyond which the charge would be insufficient to activate the shuttle.

The answer was 13:53. He would have to go out of the warp at 13:53 or remain in it forever. He had a great deal less than two hours in which to act.

He typed the first question to the computer:

WHAT IS THE POSITION OF THIS SHIP RELATIVE TO NORMAL SPACE?

The answer appeared on the panel at once; the coordinates of a position more than a light-year toward Ophiuchus.

He stared at the answer, feeling it must be an error. But it could not be an error-the computer did not make mistakes. How, then, could the ship have traveled more than a light-year during its second stay in the warp when it had not moved at all during the first stay? Had some factor of the warp unknown to him entered the picture?

As a check he typed another question:

WHAT WAS OUR POSITION, RELATIVE TO NORMAL SPACE, IMMEDIATELY BEFORE THIS SHIP WAS SHUTTLED BACK OUT OF THE WARP?

The answer was a position light-days toward Ophiuchus.

He typed: IMPOSSIBLE.

The computer replied: THIS STATEMENT CONFLICTS WITH PREVIOUS DATA.

He recalled the importance of keeping the computer free of all faulty or obscure data and typed quickly: CANCEL CONFLICTING STATEMENT.

CONFLICTING STATEMENT CANCELED, it replied.

He tried another tack. THIS SHIP EMERGED FROM THE SPACE WARP INTO THE SAME NORMAL SPACE POSITION IT HAD OCCUPIED BEFORE GOING INTO THE WARP.

He thought the computer would proceed to give him some sort of an explanation. Instead, it non-committally replied: DATA ACKNOWLEDGED.

He typed: EXPLAIN THIS DISCREPANCY BETWEEN SPACE WARP AND NORMAL SPACE POSITIONS.

It answered: INSUFFICIENT DATA TO ACCOUNT FOR DISCREPANCY.

He asked, HOW DID YOU DETERMINE OUR PRESENT POSITION?

It replied: BY TRIANGULATION, BASED ON THE RECESSION OF EARTH, THE SUN, SIRIUS, ORION, AND OTHER STARS.

BUT THE RECEDING SUN WENT INTO THE ULTRAVIOLET, he objected.

Again it answered with the non-commital, DATA ACKNOWLEDGED.

DID YOU ALREADY HAVE THIS DATA? he asked.

YES.

EXPLAIN WHY THE RECEDING SUN SHIFTED INTO THE ULTRAVIOLET INSTEAD OF THE INFRARED.

It replied: DATA INSUFFICIENT TO ARRIVE AT LOGICAL EXPLANATION.

He paused, pondering his next move. Time was speeding by and he was learning nothing of value. He would have to move the ship to some place in the warp where emergence into normal space would not put him under the blasters of the Slug cruisers. He could not know where to move the ship until he knew where the ship was at the present. He did not believe it was in the position given him by the computer, and its original space warp position had certainly not been the one given by the computer.

The computer did not have the ability to use its knowledge to explain contradictory data. It had been ordered to compute their space warp position by triangulation of the receding sun and stars and was not at all disturbed by the contradicting shift of the sun into the ultraviolet. Suppose it had been ordered to calculate their position by computations based on the shift of the sun's and stars' spectrum into the ultraviolet?

He asked it: WHAT IS OUR POSITION, IGNORING THE TRIANGULATION AND BASING YOUR COMPUTATIONS ON THE SHIFT OF THE SPECTRUMS OF THE SUN AND ORION INTO THE ULTRAVIOLET?

It gave him the coordinates of a position almost two light-years toward Orion. The triangulation computations had shown the ship to be going backward at many times the speed of light; the spectrum-shift computations showed it to be going forward with approximately the same speed.

THIS SHIP CANNOT SIMULTANEOUSLY BE IN TWO POSITIONS THREE LIGHT-YEARS APART. NEITHER CAN IT SIMULTANEOUSLY BE GOING FORWARD AND BACKWARD.

DATA ACKNOWLEDGED, it agreed.

USE THAT DATA TO EXPLAIN THE CONTRADICTIONS OF THE TWO POSITIONS YOU COMPUTED.

DATA INSUFFICIENT TO ARRIVE AT LOGICAL EXPLANATION, it answered.

ARE YOU CERTAIN THERE WAS NO ERROR IN YOUR CALCULATIONS?

THERE WAS NO ERROR.

DO YOU KNOW THAT IF WE DROPPED BACK INTO NORMAL SPACE, IT WOULD BE AT NEITHER OF THE POSITIONS YOU GAVE ME?

It replied with the characteristic single-mindedness: DATA SHOWS OUR TWO POSITIONS TO BE THOSE GIVEN.

He paused again. He was still getting nowhere while time fled by. How swiftly less than a hundred minutes could pass when they were all a man had left to him....

The computer was a genius with the mental initiative of a moronic child. It could find the answer for him but first he would have to take it by the hand and lead it in the right direction. To do that he would have to know more about the warp.

He wrote: EXPLAIN THE NATURE OF THE SPACE WARP AS SIMPLY AS POSSIBLE AND WITHOUT USING MATHEMATICS HIGHER THAN ALGEBRA.

It answered at once: THIS CANNOT BE DONE.

The chronometer read 12:30. He typed:

THIS SHIP WILL HAVE TO RETURN TO NORMAL SPACE NO LATER THAN 13:53. IT MUST BE MOVED TO A DIFFERENT POSITION WHILE STILL IN THE WARP.

DATA ACKNOWLEDGED, it replied.

THIS SHIP CANNOT OCCUPY TWO POSITIONS AT THE SAME TIME. YOUR MEMORY FILES SHOULD CONTAIN SUFFICIENT DATA TO ENABLE YOU TO FIND THE EXPLANATION OF THIS TWO-POSITIONS PARADOX. FIND THAT EXPLANATION.

SUBMIT METHOD OF PROCEDURE, it answered.

I DO NOT KNOW HOW. YOU WILL HAVE TO ARRIVE AT THE EXPLANATION UNAIDED.

THIS CANNOT BE DONE, it replied.

He wrote, with morbid curiosity:

IF YOU DO NOT FIND THE ANSWER UNAIDED YOU WILL BE DESTROYED ALONG WITH ME AT 13:53. DON'T YOU GIVE A DAMN?

It answered: GIVE A DAMN IS A SEMANTIC EXPRESSION I DO NOT UNDERSTAND. CLARIFY QUESTION.

He got out of the computer seat and walked about the room restlessly. He passed by the transdimensional viewscreen and communicator and pressed the communicator's signal button. A dial flickered in return, showing his signal was going out, but there was no sound in response. If only he could make contact with the brains in Observation —

He was umpty billion miles east of the sun and umpty billion miles west of the sun. He was racing faster than light in two different directions at once and he was sitting motionless under the blasters of two Slug cruisers.

Another thought came to him: even if he could move the ship while in the warp, where could he go?

He would have to go far beyond the outer limits of the solar system to escape detection by the Slug cruisers. And at that distance the sun would be only a yellow star, incapable of energizing the little solar power units. He would not live long after the last of the power was drained from the batteries and the air regeneration equipment ceased functioning. He would not even dare sleep, toward the last. There were no convection currents in the air of a ship without gravity, and it was imperative that the air be circulated constantly. The air circulation blowers would cease functioning while the ship still contained pure air but he would have to move about continually to breathe that air. Should he lie down to sleep he would smother to death in a carbon dioxide bubble of his own making.

If he managed to emerge into normal space at some point just outside Earth's atmosphere, beyond range of the cruisers, his driveless ship would descend as a blazing meteor. If, by some miracle, he could emerge into normal space just a few inches above the space-field it would be to materialize into space already occupied by air. Such a materialization would be simultaneously fatal to him and to the electronic components of the shuttle and computer.

And if he did not move the ship, the Slug cruisers would disintegrate him. He had four hypothetical choices of his way to die, all equally unpleasant.

He smiled wanly at his reflection in the bright metal bordering the viewscreen and said, "Brother-you've had it!"

* * * * *

He went to the control room, there to brush his fingers across the useless control buttons and look into the viewscreen that revealed only black and limitless Nothing.

What was the warp? Surely it must have definite physical laws of some kind. It was difficult to imagine any kind of existence-even the black nothing of the warp-as being utterly without rule or reason. If he knew the laws of the warp he might find some means of survival hitherto hidden from him.

There was only one way he could learn about the warp. He would have to question the computer and continue questioning it until he learned or until his time was up.

He returned to the computer and considered his next question. The computer had calculated their positions from observations of the sun and other stars in front of the ship-what would similar calculations based on observations of the stars behind the ship reveal? He typed:

USE FIRST THE TRIANGULATION METHOD AND THEN THE SPECTRUM-SHIFT METHOD TO DETERMINE OUR POSITION FROM OBSERVATIONS MADE OF THE STARS OF OPHIUCHUS.

The answers appeared. They showed the ship to be simultaneously speeding away from Ophiuchus and toward it.

He asked: DO THESE TWO POSITIONS COINCIDE WITH THOSE RESULTING FROM THE OBSERVATIONS OF ORION?

YES, it answered.

Was the paradox limited to the line of flight?

He asked the computer: WHAT IS OUR POSITION, COURSE AND SPEED AS IN-DICATED BY THE STARS AT RIGHT-ANGLES TO OUR FORWARD-BACKWARD COURSE; BY THE STARS OF URSA MINOR AND CRUX?

The answer appeared on the panel: the ship was racing sideward through the warp in two diametrically opposed directions, but at only one-third the speed with which it was racing forward and backward.

So now the ship had four impossible positions and two different speeds.

He frowned at the computer, trying to find some clue in the new data. He noticed, absently, that the hand of one of the dials was near zero in the red section of the dial. He had not noticed any of the dials registering in the danger zone before....

He jerked out of his preoccupation with apprehension and typed: TELL ME IN NON-TECHNICAL LANGUAGE THE MEANING OF THE HAND NEAR ZERO ON THE DIAL LABELED *MAX. ET. REF.*

It answered: ONE OF MY CIRCUITS WAS DAMAGED BY THE SUDDEN RELEASE OF AIR PRESSURE. I WILL CEASE FUNCTIONING AT THE END OF FOUR MORE MINUTES OF OPERATION.

He slammed the master switch to OFF. The lights on the board went out, the various needles swung to zero, leaving the computer a mindless structure more than ever resembling an overgrown refrigerator.

Four minutes more of operation ... and he had so many questions to ask before he could hope to learn enough about the warp to know what he should do. He had wasted almost an hour of the computer's limited life, leaving it turned on when he was not using it. If only it had told him ... but it was not the nature of a machine to voluntarily give information. Besides, the receding hand of the dial was there for him to see. The computer neither knew nor cared that no one had thought it worthwhile to teach him the rudiments of its operation and maintenance.

It was 12:52. One hour and one minute left.

He put the thought aside and concentrated on the problem of finding the key to the paradox.

What conceivable set of circumstances would cause receding stars to have a spectrum shift that showed them to be approaching the ship? Or, to rephrase the question, what conceivable set of circumstances would cause approaching stars to appear to dwindle in size?

The answer came with startling suddenness and clarity:

There was no paradox-the ship was expanding.

He considered the solution, examining it for flaws of logic, and found none. If he and the ship were expanding the wave length of light would diminish in proportion to the increasing size of the retinas of his eyes and the scanner plates of the transdimensional viewscreens: would become shorter and go into the ultraviolet. At the same time, the increasing size of himself and the ship would make the Earth and sun relatively smaller and therefore apparently receding.

The same theory explained the two different speeds of the ship: its length was three times its diameter so its longitudinal expansion would proceed at three times the speed of its cross-sectional expansion.

Everything checked.

How large was the ship now?

He made a rough calculation and stared almost unbelievingly at the results. He was a giant, more than a third of a light-year tall, in a ship that was six light-years long and two light-years in diameter. Far Centauri, which had required thirty years to reach in the fastest interplanetary ship, floated seventy-one feet away in the blackness outside the hull.

And the sun and Earth were in the room with him, going into the shuttle's silvery focal ball.

He would have to ask the computer to make certain his theory was valid. His time was too critically short for him to waste any of it with speculation based on an erroneous theory.

He switched on the computer and it lighted up again. He typed rapidly:

ASSUME THIS SHIP TO BE MOTIONLESS AND EXPANDING WOULD THAT THEORY SATISFACTORILY EXPLAIN ALL THE HITHERTO CONTRADICTORY PHENOMENA?

There was a brief pause as the computer evaluated its data, then it answered with one word: YES.

He switched it off again, to squander none of its short period of usefulness until he had decided upon what his further questions should be. At last, he had some grounds for conjecture; had learned something about the warp the designers of the shuttle had not suspected. Their calculations had been correct when they showed a ship would travel in the warp at many times the normal space speed of light. But somewhere some little factor had been overlooked-or never found-and their precise mathematics had not indicated that the travel would be produced by expansion.

Nature abhors a vacuum. And the black, empty warp was a vacuum more perfect than any that existed in normal space. In the normal space universe there were millions of stars in the galaxy and millions of galaxies. In the warp there was utter Nothing. Did the physical laws of the warp demand that matter be scattered throughout it, in emulation of its rich neighbor in the adjoining dimension? Was the warp hungry for matter?

He rejected the thought as fantasy. There was some explanation that the physicists would eventually find. Perhaps there was a vast size-ratio difference between the two dimensions; perhaps the warp was far larger than the normal space universe and some co-universal law demanded that objects entering it become proportionally larger.

None of that aspect of his circumstances, however, was of importance. There was only one prime problem facing him: how to move the ship within less than an hour to some point in the warp where his emergence into normal space would result in neither instant nor days-away death and where he would have the time to try to carry out the responsibility, so suddenly placed in his hands, of delivering the space warp shuttle to the *Thunderbolt*.

The long-range task depended upon his immediate survival. He had to move the ship, and how did a man move a driveless ship? It might not require a very large propulsive force-perhaps even an oxygen tank would serve as a jet. Except that he had none.

He could use part of the air in the ship. Its sudden release should move the ship. There was a sun very near: Alpha Centauri. If he had the proper tools, and the time, he could cut a hole in the hull opposite Centauri ... but he had neither the tools nor the time.

And what good would it do him if he could emerge into normal space at the desired distance from Centauri? He would be provided with power for the air regenerators by the solar power units but not power sufficient to operate the shuttle. He would breathe, and eat, for a week. Then the small amount of food on the ship would be gone and he would breathe for another four or five weeks. And then he would die of starvation and his driveless ship would continue its slow drift into the sun, taking his bones and the shuttle with it.

He would have to go to Sirius and he would have to reach it the first try or never. If he could emerge into normal space at the proper distance from Sirius he would have power from it to operate the communicator. The *Thunderbolt* would come at once when it received his message and swallow the little *Argosy* in its enormous hold. The return to Earth would be the swift one through the warp and the Slug cruisers, so bold in pursuit of unarmed interplanetary ships, would quickly cease to exist.

At 13:53 Sirius would be somewhere in or near the bow of the ship. The ship would not have to be moved more than two thirds of its length-twenty meters. He could do that by releasing part of the air in the shuttle room through the sternward airlock.

How much air?

He tried to remember long-forgotten formulas. So many cubic feet of air at such and such a pressure when released through an opening of such and such a diameter would exert a propulsive force of....Hell, he didn't know. And not even the computer would be able to tell him because there were so many unknown factors, such as the proportion of the ship's mass lost to the Slug blasters, the irregular shape of the airlock opening, the degree of smoothness of its metal....

He made calculations with pencil and paper. He would have to move the ship with extreme precision. A light-hour short of the proper distance put him too far from the sun for it to power the communicator, a light-hour beyond put him in the sun's flaming white heart. One light-hour out of eight point six light-years was approximately one part out of seventy-five thousand. He would have to move the ship with an accuracy of point aught three centimeters-one hundredth of an inch.

One hundredth of an inch!

He laid the pencil back down, almost numbly. He could never open and close an airlock and move a mass of thousands of tons with an accuracy of a hundredth of an inch. The very thought was wildly fantastic.

He was already far closer to Sirius than he would be if he tried to get any closer. And that was over eight light-years from it.

He looked at the chronometer and saw the hands had already reached 13:20. Thirty-three minutes left to him. Sirius was near-soon it would be in the bow of the ship-and Sirius was eight point six light-years away.

How could he move the ship a certain distance accurate to one hundredth of an inch? He couldn't. The answer was blunt and ugly and irrefutable: he couldn't.

He got up and walked across the room, feeling like a man who had in quick succession been condemned, reprieved, recondemned. He had been projected into a situation for which he had had no preliminary training whatever; had been made sole custodian and operator of a computer and a space warp shuttle that he had never before been permitted to touch. He had used the sound but not at all brilliant mind nature had given him to solve the riddle of the paradoxes and learn where he was and where he wanted to go. He had done quite well-he had solved every problem of his survival and the shuttle's delivery except the last one!

He passed by the shuttle and stopped to rest his hand on the bright, silvery focal ball. The solar system would be deep inside the ball; the atoms of the ball larger than Earth, perhaps, and far more impalpable than the thinnest air. The Slug cruisers would be in there, infinitesimally tiny, waiting for him to return....

No-faulty reasoning. The solar system was as it had always been, not diminished in size and not really in the ball. It was only that two different points in two different dimensions coincided in the ball....

He saw the answer.

He did not have to move the ship to Sirius-he had only to move the ball!

There would be little time, very little time. First, to see if the warp shuttle was portable —

It was. When he unfastened the clamp that held it to the stand it lifted up freely, trailing a heavy cable behind it. He saw it was only a power supply cable, with a plug that would fit one of the sockets in the bow of the ship. He left the shuttle floating in the air, leashed by the cable, and went to the computer. Next, he would have to know if Sirius would be fully in the ship—

He switched the computer on and typed:

DETERMINE THE DISTANCE FROM THE CENTER OF THE WARP SHUTTLE'S FOCAL BALL TO THE SPACE WARP POSITION OF SIRIUS AT 13:53, BASING YOUR COMPUTATIONS ON THE EXPANDING-SHIP THEORY.

It gave him the answer a moment later: 18.3496 METERS.

He visualized the distance, from his knowledge of the ship's interior, and saw the position would be within the forward spare-parts room.

Next, to learn exactly where in that room he should place the shuttle. He could not do so by measuring from the present position of the shuttle. The most precise steel tape would have to be at exactly the right temperature for such a measurement to be neither too short nor too long. He had no such tape, and the distance from the focal ball was only part of the necessary measuring: he would have to measure off a certain distance and a precisely certain angle from the purely imaginary central line of the ship's axis to intersect the original line. Such a measurement would be impossible in the time he had.

He considered what would be his last question to the computer. The hand was touching the zero and his question would have to be worded very clearly and subject to no misinterpretations. There would be no follow-up questions permitted.

He began typing:

IT IS DESIRED THAT THIS SHIP EMERGE INTO NORMAL SPACE ONE LIGHT-HOUR THIS SIDE OF SIRIUS AT 13:53. THIS WILL BE ACCOMPLISHED BY MOVING THE WARP SHUTTLE TO SUCH A POSITION THAT ITS FOCAL CENTER WILL BE IN A SPACE WARP POSITION COINCIDING WITH A NORMAL SPACE POSITION ONE LIGHT-HOUR THIS SIDE OF SIRIUS AT 13:53. CONSIDER ALL FACTORS THAT MIGHT HAVE AFFECTED THE DIMENSIONS OF THIS SHIP, SUCH AS TEMPERATURE CHANGES PRODUCED BY OUR NORMAL SPACE ACCELERATION AND DECELERATION, WHEN COMPUTING THE POSITION OF SIRIUS. THEN DEFINE THAT LOCATION IN RELATION TO THE STRUCTURAL FEATURES OF THE ROOM'S INTERIOR. DO THIS IN SUCH A MANNER THAT PLACING THE SHUTTLE IN THE PROPER POSITION WILL REQUIRE THE LEAST POSSIBLE AMOUNT OF MEASURING DISTANCES AND ANGLES.

It seemed to take it an unduly long time to answer the question and he waited restlessly, unpleasantly aware of the hand touching zero and wondering if the computer's mind was baffled by the question; the mind that thought best in terms of orderly mathematics and could not know or care that measurement by protractor and tape would result in a position fatally far from that described by the neat, rigid figures.

Then the answer appeared, beautifully concise:

POSITION WILL BE IN CORNER OF ROOM, 764.2 CENTIMETERS ABOVE FLOOR PLATE, 820 CENTIMETERS PERPENDICULAR TO PANEL AA, 652.05 CENTIMETERS PERPENDICULAR TO PANEL AB.

The computer died with an oddly human sigh. Its last act had been to give him the location of Sirius in such a manner that he could accurately position the shuttle's focal ball with the aid of the precision measuring devices in the ship's repair room.

He went to the shuttle and picked it up in his arms. It was entirely weightless, and each magnet-clicking step he took toward the bow of the ship brought Sirius almost half a light-year nearer.

He squinted against the white glare of Sirius in the viewscreen as he continued his terse report to the *Thunderbolt's* commander: "I have about a week's supply of food. How long will it be until you reach me?"

The commander's reply came after the pause caused by the distance involved:

"We'll be there within three days. Go ahead and eat hearty. But how did you travel from Earth to Sirius in only two hours? My God, man-what kind of a drive did that ship have?"

"Why, it didn't have any drive from the start," he said. "To get here I" —he frowned thoughtfully —"you might say I walked and carried the ship."

The Barbarians

*The execution violated the basic laws of Tharnar.
But the danger was too great-The Terrans couldn't
be permitted to live under any circumstances....*

Tal-Karanth, Supreme Executive of Tharnar, signed the paper and dropped it in to the out-going slot of the message dispatch tube. It was an act that would terminate one hundred and eighty days of studying the tapes and records on the Terran ship and would set the final hearing of the Terran man and woman for that day.

And, since the Terrans were guilty, their execution would take place before the sun rose again on Tharnar.

He went to the wide windows which had automatically opened with the coming of the day's warmth and looked out across the City. The City had a name, to be found in the books and tapes of history, but for fifty thousand years it had been known as the City. It was the city of all cities, the center and soul of Tharnarian civilization. It was a city of architectural beauty, of flowered gardens and landscaped parks, a city of five hundred centuries of learning, a city of eternal peace.

The gentle summer breeze brought the sweet scent of the flowering *lana* trees through the window and the familiar sound of the City as it went about its day's routine; a sound soft and unhurried, like a slow whisper. Peace for fifty thousand years; peace and the unhurried quiet. It would always be so for the City. The Supreme Executives of the past had been chosen for their ability to insure the safety of the City and so had he.

He turned away from the window and back to his desk, to brush his hand across the gleaming metal top of it. No faintest scratch marred the eternalloy surface, although the desk had been there for more than thirty thousand years. It was permanent and never-changing, like the robot-operated fleet that guarded Tharnar, like the white and massive Executive Building, like the way of life on Tharnar.

The Terrans would have to die, lest the peace and the way of life on Tharnar be destroyed. They were of a young race; a race so young that his desk had already been in place for fifteen thousand years when they began emerging from their caves. They were a dangerously imma-ture race; it had been only three hundred years since their last war with themselves. Three hundred years-three normal Tharnarian lifetimes. And the Tharnarians had not known war for six hundred lifetimes.

A race so young could not possess a civilized culture. The Terrans were-he searched for a suitable description-barbarians in spaceships. They lacked the refinement and wisdom of the Tharnarians; they were a dangerous and unpredictable race. It could be seen in their history; could be seen in the way the two Terrans had reacted to their capture.

He pressed one of the many buttons along the edge of his desk and a three-dimensional projection appeared; the scene that had taken place one hundred and eighty days before when the Terrans were brought to Tharnar.

The ship of the Terrans stood bright silver in the sunlight, slim and graceful against the bulk of the Executive Building behind it. The Terrans descended the boarding ramp, the left wrist of the man chained to the right wrist of the girl. Two armed robots walked behind them, their faces metallically impassive, and four armed Tharnarian guards waited at the bottom of the ramp to help take the Terrans to their place of imprisonment.

The Terrans approached the guards with a watchfulness that reminded him of the old films of the coast wolves that had once lived on Vendal. They did not walk with the studied, practiced, leisure of the Tharnarians but as though they held some unknown vitality barely in check. The face of the man was lean and hard, the black eyes inscrutable as flint. The girl looked at the guards with a bold nonchalance, as though they were really not formidable at all. Somehow, by contrast with the Terrans, the guards appeared to be not grimly vigilant but only colorless.

There seemed to be a menace in the way the man watched the guards; there was the impression that he would overpower them and sieze their weapons if given a shadow of a chance. And the girl-what would she do, then? Would she flash in beside him to help him, as the female coast wolves always helped their mates?

He switched off the projection, feeling a little repugnance at the thought of executing the Terrans. They were living, sentient beings, and intelligent, for all their lack of civilization. It would have been better if they had been of some repulsive and alien physical form, such as bloated, many-legged giant insects. But they were not at all repulsive; they were exactly like the Tharnarians.

Exactly?

He shook his head. Not exactly. The similarity was only to the eye-and not even to the eye when one looked closely, as he had looked at the images. There was a potential violence about them, lurking close beneath their deceptively Tharnarian physical appearance. The Terrans were not like the Tharnarians. There was a difference of fifty thousand years between them; the difference between savage barbarianism and a great and peaceful civilization.

He looked again across the City, listening to its softly murmuring voice. In hundreds of centuries the City had known no strife or violence. But what if the barbarians should come, not two of them, but thousands? What would they do?

He was sure he knew what they would do to the gentle, peaceful City and the faint twinge of remorse at the thought of executing the Terran man and girl paled into insignificance.

Under no circumstance could they be permitted to live and tell the others of Tharnar and the City.

* * * * *

Bob Randall shifted his position a little in the wide seat and the chain that linked his wrist with Virginia's rattled metallically, sounding unduly loud in the quiet of the room.

Virginia's black hair brushed his cheek as she turned her face up to him, to ask in a whisper so low it could not be heard by the four guards who stood beside and behind them:

"It's almost over, isn't it?"

He nodded and she turned her attention back to the five judges seated at the row of five desks before them. The gray-haired one at the center desk, Bob knew, was the one in charge of the proceedings and his name was Vor-Dergal. He had gained the knowledge by watching and listening and it was the only information he had acquired. He did not know the names of the other four judges, nor even for sure that they were judges and that it was a trial. There had been no introductions by the Tharnarians, no volunteering of information.

Vor-Dergal spoke to them:

"In brief, the facts are these: You claim that your mission was of a scientific nature, that the two of you were sent from Earth to try to reach the center of the galaxy where you hoped to find data concerning the creation of the galaxy. Your ship carried only the two of you and is one of several such ships sent out on such missions. Since the voyages of these small exploration ships were expected to require an indefinite number of years and since the occupants would have to endure each other's company for those years, your government thought it more feasable to let the crew of each ship consist of a man and a woman, rather than two men."

He saw Virginia's cheek quiver at the words, but she managed to restrain the smile.

"Our system was reached in your journey," Vor-Dergal continued, "and you swung aside to investigate our sister planet, Vendal. You were met by a guard ship before reaching Vendal and it fired upon you. Instead of turning back, you destroyed it with a tight-beam adaptation of your meteor disintegrator."

Vor-Dergal waited questioningly and Bob said:

"Our instruments showed us that the guard ship was robot-operated. They could discern nothing organic in the ship, nothing alive. The same instruments showed us that this planet, Vendal, possessed operating mines and factories and no organic life other than small animals.

We knew that machines neither voluntarily build factories nor reproduce other machines, yet the mines and factories were operating. We thought it might be a world where the inhabitants had all died for some reason and the robots were still following the production orders given them when the race lived."

"And so you wilfully destroyed the guard ship that would have turned you back?"

"We did. It was a machine, operated by machines. And so far as we knew, it was protecting a race that had died a thousand years before. It was all a mystery and we wanted to find the answer to it."

Vor-Dergal and the others accepted the explanation without change of expression. Vor-Dergal resumed:

"Three more guard ships appeared when you were near Vendal. In the battle that followed, you severely damaged one of them. And when your ship was finally caught in the guard cruiser's tractor beams, you resisted the robots. When they boarded your ship, you destroyed several of them and were subdued only when the compartments of your ship were flooded with a disabling gas."

"That's true," Bob said.

"In summary: You deliberately invaded Tharnarian territory, deliberately damaged and destroyed Tharnarian ships, and would have landed on Vendal had the guard ships not prevented it.

"Your guilt is both evident and admitted. Are there any extenuating circumstances that have not been presented at this hearing?"

"No," Bob said.

None had been presented all day for the good reason that there was not a single factor of the circumstances that the Tharnarians would consider extenuating.

"Your guilt was evident from the beginning," Vor-Dergal said. "We have spent the past one hundred and eighty days in studying the books and tapes in your ship. What we learned of your history and your form of civilization leaves us no alternative in the sentence we must pass upon you."

The chain clinked faintly as Virginia lifted her hand to lay it on his arm and she gave him a quick glance that said, *"Here it comes!"*

Vor-Dergal pronounced sentence upon them:

"Tomorrow morning, at thirty-three twelve time, you will both be put to death by a robot firing squad."

Virginia's breath stopped for a moment and her hand gripped his arm with sudden pressure but she gave no other indication of emotion and her eyes did not waver from Vor-Dergal's face.

Vor-Dergal looked past her to the guards. "Return them to their cell."

The guards produced another chain, to link their free arms together behind their backs, and they were marched across the room and out the door.

Outside, the sun was setting, already invisible behind a low-lying cloud. Bob calculated the designated time of their execution in relation to the Terran time as given by his watch and found that thirty-three twelve would be about halfway between daylight and sunrise.

* * * * *

Tal-Karanth stood by the open windows and watched the guards return the Terrans to their cell. Extra guards, both robot and Tharnarian, had been posted inside and outside the prison building for the night to prevent any possibility of an escape. Other robots stood guard around the Terran ship, although it was inconceivable that the Terrans could ever overpower the prison guards and reach their ship.

But it had been inconceivable that a ship as small as the Terran ship could ever destroy a Tharnarian guard cruiser. The tight-beam adaptation circuit of the meteor disintegrators was very ingenious.

Why had the Tharnarian cruisers not had the same weapon? They possessed the same general type of meteor disintegrators; the same adaptation circuit would transform a Tharnarian cruiser's meteor disintegrators into terrible weapons. Why had no one ever thought of doing such a thing? Why had it been taken for granted for fifty thousand years that the cruiser's blasters were the ultimate in weapons?

What other weapons did the Terrans on Earth possess? How invincible would their cruisers be if a small exploration ship could destroy a Tharnarian cruiser?

The captive Terrans could not be permitted to return to Earth and tell the others of Tharnar. Neither could they be permitted to live out their lives in prison on Tharnar. Someday, somehow, they might escape and return to Earth, or send a message to Earth. The robot fleet of Tharnar could never withstand an attack by a Terran fleet; the fate of Tharnar and the quiet and gentle City would be written in blood and dust and ashes.

There was the sound of rubber-padded metal feet in the distance and he saw six more robots marching out to add their numbers to the robots already guarding the Terran ship. The ship, itself, was not far from the Executive Building; close enough that his eyes, still sharp despite his seventy years, could make out the name on it: *The Cat.*

The Cat. And a cat was-he recalled the definition to be found among the Terran books —*any of various species of carnivorous and predatory animals, noted for their stealth and quickness, and their ferocity when angered.*

* * * * *

The robot shoved the plastic food tray under the cell door and went back down the corridor. Virginia turned away from the single window, where *The Cat* could be seen as a silhouette merging into the darkness.

"Last supper, Bob," she said. "Let's eat, drink, and be merry."

He went to the door to get the tray and noticed the three robots and two Tharnarian guards down the left hand stretch of corridor and the same number down the right. Virginia came up beside and said, "They're not taking any chances we won't be here in the morning, are they?"

"No," he said, picking up the tray. "None to speak of."

He carried the tray to the little table in the center of the room and Virginia seated herself across from him as she had done each meal for the past six months. But she toyed with the plastic spoon and did not begin to eat at once.

"I wonder why they made it a firing squad?" she asked. "You'd think they would have used something ultra-civilized and refined, such as some painless and flower-scented gas."

"Spies were executed with firing squads during the last Terran war, three hundred years ago," he said. He smiled thinly. "I suppose they consider us spies and want us to feel at home in the morning."

"I'm glad they do. I don't want it to be shut up in a room —I would rather be out under the open sky." She poked at the rim of her tray again. "They never did tell us why, Bob. They didn't tell us anything, only that they had no alternative. We didn't hurt any Tharnarians; we only destroyed one of their ships and some of their robots."

"We upset their sense of security and showed them they're not secure at all. I suppose they're afraid of an attack from Earth."

"They didn't tell us anything," she said again. "They act as though we were animals."

"No," he said, "they don't seem to have a very high opinion of our low position on the social evolution scale."

He began to eat in the manner of one who knows the body needs nourishment to take advantage of any opportunity for escape, even though the mind may be darkly certain that no such opportunity shall arise.

"You ought to eat a little, Ginny," he said.

She tried, and gave up after a few bites.

"I guess I'm just not hungry-not now," she said. She glanced at the darkened window where *The Cat* had become invisible. "How long until daylight again, Bob?"

He looked at his watch. "Seven hours."

"Seven hours?" A touch of wistfulness came into her voice. "I never noticed, before, how short the nights are."

* * * * *

The robot laid the material Tal-Karanth had requested on his desk, the records and tapes from the Terran ship, and withdrew. Tal-Karanth sighed wearily as he inserted the first tape in the projector, wondering again why he felt the vague dissatisfaction and wondering why he hoped to find an answer among the material from the Terran ship. It would be an all night task-and he could hardly expect to find more than he already knew. Tharnar was not safe and secure from discovery by Terrans in the years to come and faith in the robot fleet had been an illusion.

Before setting the projector in operation he put through a call to his daughter.

Thralna's image appeared before him, reclining on a couch while two robots worked at caring for her finger nails. She raised up a little as his image appeared before her and the robots stepped back.

"Yes, Father?" she asked.

She waited for him to speak, her wide gray eyes on his image and her jet-black curls framing her young and delicately beautiful face. For a moment she reminded him of someone; someone more mature and stronger —

With something of a shock he realized it was the Terran girl his daughter reminded him of; that the Terran girl seemed the more mature of the two although Thralna was twenty-eight and the Terran girl was twenty-one. They had the same gray eyes and black curls, the same curve to the jaw, the same chin and full lips....

But the similarity was only incidental. There was a grace and a gentleness to Thralna's beauty; a grace and gentleness that was the result of fifty thousand years of civilization. Beneath the superficial beauty of the barbarian girl lay only an animal-like vitality and potential violence....

"Yes, Father?" Thralna asked again in her carefully modulated voice.

"Are you going to the theatre tonight, Thralna?"

"Yes. Tonight's play was written by D'ret-Thon and it's supposed to be almost as good as one of the classics. Why do you ask, Father?"

"I called to tell you that I have to work late tonight. I may not be home until morning."

"Couldn't you let a robot do it?"

"No. I have to do it, myself."

"Does it have to do with those two aliens?"

"Yes."

A little frown of worry appeared and as quickly disappeared. Her slim fingers touched her forehead for a moment, to smooth away any vestige of a wrinkle, then she said, "It will be such a relief when they're finally disposed of. Whenever I think of how they might escape and get into the City, it frightens me. Are you sure they can't escape, Father?"

"There is no possibility of their escaping," he said. "You go ahead with your plans for the evening. Will you come home when the show is over?"

"Not for a while. Kin is taking me dancing, afterward."

"Where you went last time-the place where they were reviving the old dances?"

"No. Nobody goes there anymore. Those old dances were rather fun but they were so-so tiring. Our modern dances are much slower and more graceful, you know."

"All right, Thralna," he said in dismissal. "Enjoy yourself."

"Yes, Father."

She was reclining on the couch again, her eyes closed, when he switched off the image. He sat for a little while before turning on the tape projector, recalling his conversation with her and a feeling growing within him that he was almost on the verge of discovering still another menace to Tharnar.

* * * * *

Virginia held her hands to her face to shade her eyes as she looked out the window. "What you can see of the city from here is all bright with lights," she said, "but there's no one on the streets. Only some robots. Everyone in the city must be in bed."

"That's the way it's been every night," he said. "Early to bed and late to rise-they're an odd race. I've wondered what they do to pass away the time. But what they're doing now is something you should be doing-resting."

She turned away from the window. "I'm not sleepy. I keep thinking of *The Cat* out there waiting for us and how we might get to it if we could only get hold of a blaster."

"Which we can't try to do until they come for us in the morning. Some rest now might mean a lot then."

"All right, Bob." She went to him and sat beside him on his cot. "What is it now-how much more time?"

"About three hours."

She leaned her head against him and he put his arm around her. "I guess I am a little tired," she said. "But don't let me go to sleep."

"All right, Ginny."

"It's only three hours and never any more, if we aren't lucky in the morning. And if we aren't lucky, I don't want to have wasted our last three hours."

* * * * *

Tal-Karanth stood before the window again and watched the City as it slept in the pre-dawn darkness. How many slept in the City? Once there had been three million in the City but each census found the population to be less. Five years before there had been less than a million-two-thirds of the City was a beautiful shell that housed only the robots that cared for it.

What was wrong? And why had it never occurred to him before that there was something wrong?

He went back to his desk, where the material from the Terran ship littered the eternalloy top of it, and sat down again. He was tired, and frustrated. A menace faced Tharnar, and no one seemed to realize it. The coming of the barbarians had awakened him to the fallacy of trusting the robot fleet, but there was still another danger. And the robot fleet would be more helpless before the newly discovered danger than it would be before the Terran ships.

He pressed a button and music filled the room; music that had always before been soothing and restful to hear. But it sounded flat and meaningless compared with the throbbing barbarian music he had heard that night and he switched it off again.

What was wrong? It was one of the latest compositions; one that had been acclaimed as almost as good as one of the classics.

Almost as good....Like the play Thralna had attended, like the art exhibits, the athletic records, the scientific discoveries, like everything in the City and on Tharnar. Almost as good-but never quite as good as they had been fifty thousand years before.

Was that part of the answer?

No-not part of the answer. Part of the problem, part of the danger greater than a barbarian invasion. There was no answer that he could see. Something had been lost by the Tharnarians fifty thousand years before and he was neither sure what it was nor how to give it back to them.

He pressed the button that would connect him with Security Officer Ten-Quoth. Of the two problems, it was only within his power to handle the immediate phase of the first problem; to make the final authorization of the execution of the Terrans.

* * * * *

Bob looked again at the window which had lightened to a pale gray square. It was already daylight outside; it would not be long until the guards came for them. Virginia had fallen asleep at last, more tired than she had thought, and she still slept with her head against his shoulder and with his arm around her to support her. He straightened his legs slowly, not wanting them to be numb from lack of circulation when the guards came and not wanting to awaken Virginia to grim reality any sooner than he had to.

But the slight movement was enough. She opened her eyes drowsily, then the sleepiness gave way to the hard jolt of remembrance and realization. She looked at the gray window and asked, "How much longer?"

"Within a few minutes."

"I wish you hadn't let me sleep."

"You were tired."

"I didn't want to sleep—I didn't think I would." Then she changed the subject, as though to keep it from going into the sentimental. "I see the robot never did come back for the tray. We'll be leaving a messy room, won't we? I wonder if they'll disinfect it to make sure it's clean when we're gone? You know"—she smiled a little—"fleas and things."

She lifted her face to kiss him on the cheek, then she rose and moved to the window.

"It's cloudy," she said. "There's a mist of rain falling and it's cloudy outside. I guess it's already later than we thought."

He went over to stand beside her and saw that the morning was alight with near-sunrise behind the gray clouds.

"It's out there waiting for us—*The Cat*," she said.

He saw it, standing silver-white in the gray morning, gleaming in the rain and with its slim, dynamic lines making it look as though it might at any moment hurl itself roaring into the sky.

"It's a beautiful ship," she said. "I wonder what they will do with it when they—"

A sound came from the far end of the corridor; a snapped command in Tharnarian. The command was followed at once by the sound of footsteps approaching their cell; the heavy tread of robots and the lighter, softer steps of the guards.

Virginia turned away from the window and they faced the cell door as they waited.

"This is it," she said.

"Are you afraid, Ginny?"

"Afraid?" She laughed up at him, a laugh that came only a little too quickly. "It's like a play, set a long time ago on Earth. Coffee and pistols at dawn. Only I don't think they're bringing us any coffee and if we get a pistol, it will have to be one of theirs."

"It isn't over with till the end-and maybe we can change the ending of this play for them."

"I'll be watching you, Bob, so I can help you the moment you make the try."

The Tharnarian guards stopped outside the door, their blasters in their hands. One of them unlocked the door and two robots entered, guards locking the big door behind the robots the moment they were inside. The robots carried no blasters, nothing but three lengths of chain.

The Tharnarian leader outside the door rasped a command:

"You will both turn to face the window, with your hands behind you."

Bob did not obey at once, but appraised the situation. The robots were massive things-more than six hundred pounds in weight, their metal bodies invulnerable to any attack he could make with his bare hands. But there was one chance in ten thousand: if he could catch the first robot by surprise and send it toppling into the cell door, its weight might be enough to break the lock of the door.

He struck it with his shoulder, all his weight and strength behind the attack, and Virginia's small body struck it a moment later.

But it was like shoving against a stone wall. The robot rocked for the briefest instant, then it threw out a foot to regain its balance. The other robot snapped a chain around his wrists while Virginia fought it.

"Don't, Ginny," he said, ceasing his own struggles. "It's no use, honey."

She stopped, then, and the robot jerked her arms around behind her back, to lock the second chain around her wrists.

She smiled up into his dark and sombre face. "We tried, Bob. They were just too big for us."

188

A third chain, longer than the first two, was produced. He felt the cool metal of it encircle his neck and heard the lock snap shut. The other end of it was locked around Virginia's neck.

The cell door was opened and the guard leader commanded, "Step forward. The robots will guide you."

They stepped forward, the robots beside them, gripping their arms with steel fingers. The chain around their necks rattled from the movement of walking, linking them together like a pair of captive wild animals. Bob wondered if the chain had been solely as another precaution to prevent their escape or if it had been a deliberate act of contempt. The Tharnarians feared them and, because they feared them, they hated them. Did it bolster the morale of the Tharnarians to deliberately treat them as though they were animals?

They stepped out into the cool dawn, into a small courtyard with a black stone wall at its farther side. The sky was bleakly gray and the rain was falling as a cold mist, dampening Virginia's face as she looked up at him.

"The last mile, Bob."

"Walk it straight and steady, Ginny. They're watching."

"How else would we walk it?" she asked calmly.

They came to the wall, where a metal ring had been set in the stone. There was a chain fastened to the ring and when the robots had swung them around with their backs to the wall, the free end of the chain was locked to the center of the chain around their necks.

Again, it could be an added precaution. Or it could be the final attempt to let their execution be like the killing of a pair of dangerous animals. It did not really matter, of course....

Two of the armed robots who had walked with the guards took up a position twenty feet in front of them, blasters in their metal hands. The robots who had chained them stepped to one side, away from the line of fire. The leader of the guards lifted his arm to look at his watch and said something to the robots. The robots lifted their blasters at the words and leveled them, one aimed at Virginia's heart and one at Bob's.

But the expected blast did not come. The guard leader continued to observe his watch. Apparently the first command had meant only: "Aim." The "Fire" command would come when the hands of the watch reached the thirty-three twelve mark.

Virginia's shoulder was warm against his arm. But her hand, when it found his behind their backs, was cold.

"They cheated us," she said. "We were supposed to have a whole firing squad."

The guard leader gave another command and there was a double click as the robots pressed the buttons that would ready their blasters for firing. Virginia swayed a little for the first time, a movement too small for the Tharnarians to see and one from which she recovered almost at once.

"It's —I'm all right," she said. "I'm not afraid, Bob."

"Of course you're not, Ginny-of course you're not."

The guard leader had returned his attention to his watch and the seconds went by; long seconds in which the only sound was the almost inaudible whisper of the rain against the stone wall behind them. Virginia looked up at him for the last time, the cold mist wet on her face.

"We've had a lot of fun together, Bob. We never expected it to end so soon, but we knew all the time that it might. We'll go together and that's the way we always wanted it to be, wherever and whenever it might happen."

Then she faced forward again and they waited, the rain whispering on the wall behind them and forming in crystal drops on the chain around their necks. She did not waver again as she stood beside him and he knew she would not when the end came.

The guard leader dropped his arm, as though he no longer needed to refer to his watch. He glanced at them very briefly then turned to the robots, his face revealing the command he was going to give.

Virginia's hand tightened on his own in farewell and he could feel the pulse of her wrist racing hard and fast. But she stood very straight as she looked into the blaster and they heard the final command to their robot-executioners:

"*Dorend thendar!*"

* * * * *

Thirty-three one.

Tal-Karanth looked again at the timepiece on the wall. Thirty-three one. At the end of eleven more small fractions of time, the Terrans would no longer exist.

What was life? What was the purpose behind it all? In fifty thousand years the Tharnarians were no nearer the answer than their ancestors had been. Why should there be life at all? Why not the suns and planets, created by chance, and devoid of life? And why even the suns and planets, the millions of galaxies racing outward across the illimitable expanse of space and time? Why the universe and why the life it contained? Why not just-nothing?

The barbarians had set out to find the answer within a hundred years after the building of their first interstellar ship. And Tharnar's interstellar ships had not been outside the system for fifty thousand years; no Tharnarian had been as far as Vendal for fifteen thousand years.

Why had the Tharnarians lost their curiosity; the curiosity and desire to learn that had created the past glory of Tharnar?

He thought again of what he had discovered that night; of one of the reasons why the Terrans had named their ship *The Cat*. It was not because a cat was a dangerous animal, as he and the others had thought. It was because the mission of *The Cat* would be to explore in unknown territory, because of an old Terran proverb: *Curiosity killed a cat*. He did not yet understand the second reason behind the name, but the first reason showed that the Terrans were not without a sense of humor. How long had it been since he had heard a Tharnarian laugh at himself, at his own failings or possibility of failure? Never.

Yet-wasn't that pride? What was wrong with the high-headed pride that admitted no inferiority, no failure? Wasn't fifty thousand years of civilization something of which to be extremely proud?

Thirty-three five.

He went to the window and pressed the button that would open it against the mechanical will of the automatic health-guard equipment. It slid open and he breathed the cool, moist air that smelled of wet earth and grass and the odor of the *lana* tree flowers; flowers that were closed against the rain and would not open until the sun came out.

The City was quiet in the gray of the morning. He could see one pedestrian and three moving vehicles in the entire visible portion of the City. The City, like the flowers of the *lana* trees, would not open into life until the storm was over and the sun was shining again.

Thirty-three nine.

The City, like the flowers of the *lana* trees. The beauty and perfection of them both was the result of fifty thousand years of breeding to bring about that perfection. The City, like the flowers of the *lana* trees....

But flowers were without purpose; were only-vegetation.

And what was the purpose of the City?

He did not know. He was the Supreme Executive of Tharnar, and he did not know.

Thirty-three ten.

He went back to his desk and switched on the three-dimensional projection of the scene that would be taking place in the courtyard behind the prison.

The man and girl stood chained to the wall and the robots were waiting for the third and last command from the guard leader, the blasters in their hands as steady as though held in vises and their metal faces impassive. He increased the magnification of the scene, drawing the images of the man and girl closer to him. There was no reading the man's face, other than the hardness and lack of fear. But on the face of the girl was a defiance that seemed to shine like a radiance about her. He was reminded of the physical similarity between the barbarian girl and his daughter. But now the similarity had faded to a shadow. There was something vital and alive about the barbarian girl, there was a beauty to her in the way she waited for death that was strange and wild by Tharnarian standards.

What had Thralna said the night before? *"... Whenever I think of how they might escape and get into the City, it frightens me."*

—it frightens me —

What if it was Thralna who stood before the robots? Would she have her Tharnarian pride as she looked into the black muzzle of the blaster and knew she had only a few more heart beats of life left? Would she stand with the bold defiance of the barbarian girl? Or would she drop to the ground and plead for her life?

He knew the answer. But it was not Thralna's fault that she was as she was. She was only like all the others of Tharnar.

Thirty-three eleven.

How different they were, the two barbarians and the men and women of Tharnar. Yet the difference would cease to exist within a few moments. When the man and girl were dead, when all the life and restless drive were gone from them and they lay still on the cold, wet ground, they would look the same as Tharnarians.

How did it feel to die in the cold dawn, on an alien world a thousand lightyears from your own? But they had known such a thing might happen to them. They had named their ship *The Cat* because of that. Because of that, and something else....

Suddenly, clearly, he understood the second reason for the name of their ship.

Thirty-three twelve.

* * * * *

The guard leader dropped his arm, to give the last command to the robots. Tal-Karanth's mind raced and he saw two things with vivid clarity:

He saw the inexorable decline of Tharnar and the City continuing down the centuries until the little spark that was left smouldered its last and was gone. And he saw the way death would obliterate the wild and savage beauty of the barbarian girl, knew that it would go when the life went from her, to leave her with a beauty that would be colorless by contrast, that would be like the beauty of a *lana* blossom-or a Tharnarian woman.

And he thought he could see the answer to the menace that faced Tharnar and the City.

"Dorend —"

The guard leader's first word of command came. Tal-Karanth's finger stabbed at one of the buttons along his desk. He shoved it down, to deactivate the robot-executioners, and they were frozen in immobility when the final word came:

" —thendar!"

He snapped the switch which connected him with the office of Security Officer Ten-Quoth and said:

"Have the chains taken from the Terrans and see that they are given comfortable and un-guarded quarters. Tell them they have been pardoned by the Supreme Executive and that they are free to leave Tharnar whenever they wish."

* * * * *

It was mid-morning of the next day, bright and warm with a few fleecy white clouds drifting across the blue sky. Tal-Karanth stood before the window again, Vor-Dergal beside him, and watched the City come to life; slowly and leisurely, as it had come to life each mid-morning for the past fifty thousand years.

Vor-Dergal looked toward *The Cat*, where the boarding ramps had already been withdrawn and the airlocks closed.

"They're ready to go," he said. "I hope you haven't made a mistake in what you did. The other Terrans will learn of us now, and when they come...." He let the sentence trail off, unfinished.

"We have a great deal to gain by the coming of the Terrans," Tal-Karanth said, "and little to lose."

"Little to lose?" Vor-Dergal asked. "We have Tharnar and the City to lose; we have our lives and our civilization to lose."

"Yes, our civilization," Tal-Karanth said. "Our god that we worshipped-our civilization. Look, Vor-listen to what I have to say:

"I did some thinking the night the Terrans were waiting to be executed. I'm afraid it was probably one of the few times for thousands of years that a Tharnarian ever tried to critically examine the Tharnarian way of life. I started from the beginning, more than fifty thousand years ago, when the interstellar ships of Tharnar were actually interstellar and were manned by men instead of robots.

"It was a good start we made in interstellar exploration, but it didn't last very long. We wanted to associate with our cultural peers, and there weren't any. We didn't attempt to make any contact with the primitive races we found. We felt that there would be no point in doing so. Tharnar possessed the highest-and the only-civilization in all the explored regions of the galaxy and younger races had nothing to offer us.

"The time came when no more exploration ships were sent out. We retired to Tharnar and Vendal and surrounded them with a robot-operated fleet, to keep out the inferior races when they finally did learn how to build spaceships. We devoted ourselves to our social culture and became imbued with self-satisfaction, with the assurance that we of Tharnar possessed the full flowering of culture and progress. We withdrew into a shell of complacency and each generation lived out its life with comfortable, methodical, sameness. And our robot-operated fleet was on guard to prevent any other race from annoying us, from disturbing us in the wisdom and serenity of our way of life.

"Fifteen thousand years ago, the last of us on Vendal returned to the more ideal world of Tharnar. And there was plenty of room for them on Tharnar by then. The population had been decreasing for thousands of years-it's decreasing right now. Women don't want to have children anymore-it's an inconvenience for them. They want comfort; the full stomach, the soft couch, the attention of their robots. And men are the same.

"There is no longer any incentive for living on Tharnar other than to duplicate the lives of our ancestors. There is nothing new, nothing to be done that has not already been done better. So we lapse into an existence of placid satisfaction with the status quo-we vegetate. We're like plants that have been seeded in the same field for so many centuries that the fertility of the soil is exhausted. This barren field in which we grow is our own form of culture.

"Do you see what the ultimate end will have to be, Vor?"

He had thought old Vor-Dergal would reply with a heated defense of Tharnarian civilization, but he did not. Instead, he said, "If the present trend continues, there will come a time when there will be more robots in the guard ships than there will be Tharnarians for them to guard. But is the other better, the destruction at the hands of the barbarians?"

"Destruction? It's within their power to destroy us, but why should they? It will be unpleasant for many Tharnarians to contemplate, but an unbiased study of the Terrans shows that they would not want the things we have on Tharnar and in the City; that they would not consider Tharnar and the City worth the trouble of conquest."

"A conjecture," Vor-Dergal said. "And, even if you are right and the Terrans never come to destroy us-what have we to gain by taking this risk?"

"New life. We've been too long in the barren field of our own culture. We've lost our curiosity, our desire to learn, our sense of humor that would permit us to make honest self-evaluations, our pride and courage. And in losing these things, we lost our racial urge to survive.

"Look at the City this morning, Vor. See how slowly it moves; listen to how still it is for a city that contains almost a million people. Do you know what this day is for the City? It's one more act, to be added to all the thousands of acts in the past, in the City's rehearsal for extinction.

"The Terrans have what we lost. They're a young race with a vitality that's like a fire where our own is like a dying spark. That's why I let those two go; why I want the others of their kind to know of Tharnar and come here. It's not too late for us; not yet too late for contact with these Terrans to give back to us all these things we lost."

* * * * *

In the pause following his words the quiet of the City was suddenly shattered by the thunder of *The Cat's* drives. It lifted, shining and slender and graceful, and hurled itself up into the blue sky. Tal-Karanth watched it until it was a bright star, far away and going out into the universe beyond, until the sound of its drives had faded and gone.

He looked away from the sky and back to the slowly moving, softly whispering City; the City that was dying and did not know it. He felt the stirring of an uneasiness within him; a strange non-physical desire for something. It was the first time in his life he had ever felt such a sensation; it was something so long gone from the Tharnarians that the Tharnarian word for it was obsolete and forgotten. But the Terran word for it was *wanderlust*.

"I almost wish I could have gone with them, Vor," he said. "They're going to try to reach the heart of the galaxy and see if they can find the answer to Creation. And we on Tharnar spend our lives sipping sweet drinks as we discuss trifles and wait for the sun to shine warm enough for us to emerge from our air-conditioned houses."

"If you're right in thinking that Terrans won't come to plunder Tharnar and the City," Vor-Dergal said, "then it would be interesting to know what those two find when they reach the center of the galaxy. If they don't get killed long before they reach it."

"I think any hostile forms of life they encounter will find them hard to kill," Tal-Karanth said. "We paid a high price for their capture, remember? There were two Terran proverbs behind the name of their ship. It took me quite a while to understand the second one but when I did, I realized the true extent of Terran determination and self-confidence.

"Their mission was to explore across the unknown regions of space. They knew it would be dangerous, very dangerous. So they named their ship 'The Cat' partly because of an old Terran proverb: 'Curiosity killed a cat.' But that was only half the reason behind the name. They intended to reach the center of the galaxy and they didn't intend to let anything stop them. So there was a second meaning behind the naming of their ship:

"'A cat has nine lives.'"